Omens of Wolves and Witches

Clan of Shadows #2

C.D. Britt

Phoenyx Publishing, LLC

Cover by Hannah Sternjakob

Interior art by Marialuna Grassi

Map from Inkarnate

Developmental editing by Enchanted Author Co.

Copy/Line editing and Proofreading by Katie Bucklein and Nikki Fixtion

ISBN (paperback): 979-8-9918574-7-5

ISBN (eBook): 979-8-9918574-6-8

To the women finding their voice... let's rage.

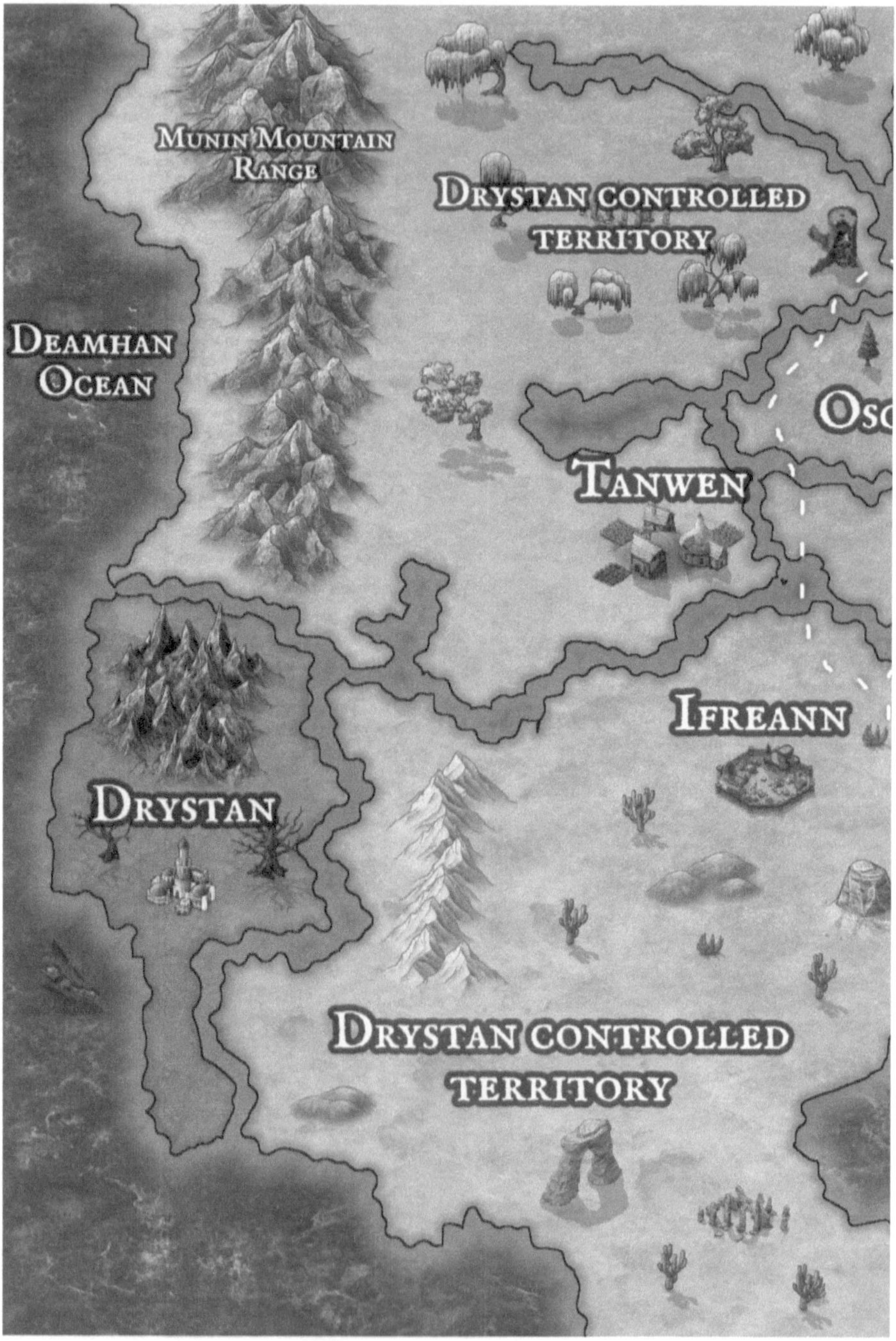

MUNIN MOUNTAIN RANGE
DRYSTAN CONTROLLED TERRITORY
DEAMHAN OCEAN
TANWEN
OSC
IFREANN
DRYSTAN
DRYSTAN CONTROLLED TERRITORY

DEARIL MOUNTAIN RANGE
CETHIN
BEIRA SEA
ARTAIR CHANNEL
GAR
ARTHMAEL
BRONAGH OCEAN
TREW
DOVER
GULF OF MERROW

Contents

Listen to the very music that inspired *Omens of Wolves and Witches* while you read!

Playlist:

Rest in Peace by Dorothy

Village Song by Paris Paloma

Help Yourself by Bryde

Run On by Jamie Bower & King Sugar

The Pines by Roses and Revolutions

Which Witch by Florence + the Machine

Sophia <144> (Feat. Nicole Perretti) by Meg Myers

Power Over Me by Dermot Kennedy

Daylight by David Kushner

Sound off the Sirens by Sam Tinnesz

Afraid by The Neighbourhood

Nothing You Can Take From Me by Rachel Zegler and The Covey Band

Killer Inside of Me by Willyecho

Down by Simon & Trella

Lapse by Black Math

You're Not Welcome by Naethan Apollo

Wolves of the Revolution by The Arcadian Wild

Avalanche by Steelfeather

Between Wind and Water by Hael

Yeti by Paris Paloma and Old Sea Bridge

Skeletons by Pop Evil

Shadow Warriors by Philipp Beesen

Skin and Bones by David Kushner

Seven Nation Army by Power-Haus and Duomo

Voices by Hidden Citizens and Vanessa Campagna

Running with the Wolves by AURORA

War of Hearts by Ruelle

Trigger by Chinchilla

Take Over by Hidden Citizens and Ruelle

Big Bad Wolf by Roses & Revolutions

Lovely (with Khalid) by Billie Eilish

The Line by Twenty One Pilots & Arcane

Trust Issues by Emei

The Wolf by PHILDEL

Savages by Kerli

Wolf by Boy Epic

Look What You Made Me Do by Kurt Hugo Schneider and Kirsten
Collins

Don't Give Up by Ursine Vulpine and Annaca

King of Disappointment by Echos

Fix You by Tommee Profitt, Stanaj, and Staarz

Just A Girl by Florence + The Machine

Good Girls by Josie Edwards

Cruel World by Tommee Profitt and Sam Tinnesz

Glow in the Dark by Vian Izak and Ekaterina Shelehova

Where We Rise by Neoni

Dangerous by Rivals

It's Just Beginning by X V I

Chapter 1

Bryn hadn't slept much since the night her throat was torn open, and the wind slicing through the ruins of Tanwen promised she wouldn't start now.

Firelight illuminated the skeletal remains of the stone buildings around their camp, shadows twisting and writhing as if the dead themselves were watching. Her fingers traced the raised, angry scar on her neck, its tightness a palpable reminder of her brush with mortality.

Declan handed her a steaming bowl of stew, and she dropped her hand to grab it, savoring the warmth as she watched the flames dance. Their whispered heat spread throughout the campsite, now that the desert was growing colder with the setting sun.

On the open sands, a fire was a perilous beacon, attracting Rovers bent on murder and theft, a threat underscored by the mangled bodies they'd come across on their journey to Tanwen.

The desert bore witness to the demise of many caravans; their rough camps destroyed by Rovers, their wounded left for the scavengers. Yet, while the fire posed a danger, hypothermia was an equally significant threat.

Unlike the almost constant sticky, desert heat of Ifreann, Tanwen's evenings brought a sharp, chilling wind.

Around the camp, Bryn and her friends sat, mirroring each other with downcast eyes and slumped shoulders; the silence heavy. It was like this every night since they'd been on the road, staring off into the distance, quiet and pensive. The first night, her mind had raced, trying to decipher whether their silence was strategic or a sign of lingering shock. For her, it had been both.

Justin stood abruptly, breaking the tense atmosphere, before putting his empty bowl near the large, dented black pot Declan stored in his magically expansive bag containing all their belongings. As Justin walked to the truck, he picked up Travis's old rifle, checking it over before jumping onto the hood and seating himself on top to keep a vigilant watch overnight.

He was visibly just as worn as the rest of them, his hand moving through his golden-blond hair before he settled his elbows on his knees. His hair was longer now, facial hair on the cusp of becoming a beard, and shadows darkened the skin under his crystal-blue eyes.

In Ifreann, he was always impeccably groomed—a sharp contrast to the unshaven, disheveled man taking first watch on the truck. A far cry from the pillar of justice she remembered walking the streets of Ifreann.

A hiccup pulled Bryn's focus from Justin to Sage. The midwife's glassy hazel eyes reflected the faint, flickering light of the fire as she stared into it, a lost look etched on her face. Though Sage held a bowl, she had yet to put the spoon to her lips. With an expression of torment, Bryn's cousin Jace whispered plea after plea for her to eat as he wiped away her tears with the pads of his thumbs.

Bryn couldn't say she blamed her. This, Tanwen, had been Sage's birthplace, and even though they knew the wraiths had come through, to see the destruction in person...

A sudden tingle ran down Bryn's spine, announcing the magic of Danu before she appeared.

Danu materialized first, her form shimmering into view between Bryn and the others, then Callum, the druid who helped to tether her to the mortal plane with his own magic, arrived.

"Hello, my children," Danu gave a frail smile as she took in their ragtag group. Bryn heard the sharp squeak of metal followed by the crunch of footsteps in the sand, and she knew Justin was coming back.

"Why do I get the feeling you're not here to tuck us in and say goodnight?" Kessler asked, his green eyes moving to Declan, who had frozen still as a statue, whiskey eyes narrowed on Danu with his spoon halfway to his mouth.

The smile on Danu's elderly face faltered, and Bryn's stomach twisted with a sickening feeling. Her gaze moved over the group, all of them now looking at Danu with a mix of suspicion and confusion on their faces. All but Caden, whose eyes always seemed to be staring off into another world these days.

"You were right in your decision to search for Bryn's mother and her people. You will find allies there, and dear Bryn"—Danu turned to her, placing her gnarled fingers together as if in prayer—"you will need all the allies you can get if you hope to defeat the king."

"Oh, boy," Justin muttered as he seated himself next to Kessler on a weathered stone, running his hand through his unkempt hair. "Looks like she's 'bout to spring another doozy on us."

Bryn tilted her head and narrowed her eyes at Danu, the prickling sensation of anxiety at Danu's words making her skin crawl. "You say that as if you will not be joining us on this little jaunt across the ruined lands."

Callum stepped forward, his voice firm: "She will not." Bryn's gaze, burning like the Ifreann sun at high noon, snapped toward him as he continued: "Danu is far too weak to stay in the mortal realm any longer and must move to the Otherworld lest her power cease to exist altogether."

Bryn opened her mouth to speak, but Declan beat her to it. "You forced this on us, and now you abandon us when we need you most?"

She was used to Declan's temper, something she'd lived with in Ifreann, but his posture was menacing as he drew closer to Danu. It was nothing like she'd seen before; his reaction less fury and fire, and more controlled burn. It felt off, but then they'd never been in this situation before. Who was she to judge since she was hardly herself anymore either?

Callum's sudden movement between Declan and Danu made the air thrum with palpable energy, the scent of ozone sharp in the air, a stark warning against further provocation. Hopefully, Declan knew better than to test the ancient druid's resolve.

Even the Morrigan, as battle-hardened as she may be, might not emerge from that conflict unscathed.

"We are supposed to travel on, and somehow know what to do without you?" Bryn bit back the harsh words gathering on her tongue before she unleashed them on the already visibly weakened goddess. She clenched her jaw, trying to ignore the riled druid while focusing on Danu; frustration rising to the surface as her nails bit into her palms.

While Bryn understood that Danu was weakening, her power only as strong as the dying earth, they also had no way of knowing where to go and what to do after they found Bryn's mother.

The Tuatha Dé Danann were lost at sea, and now the captain was abandoning the ship.

"Of course, it is as you have done in all your immortal lives. Never have you truly needed my guidance before." Danu's milky blue eyes met Bryn's. "You and Dagda have always been the ones to lead the Tuatha Dé Danann."

Her stomach knotted, her mouth too dry to respond to Danu, as if she even could when her mind reeled. When had Bryn ever been a leader? Her time in Ifreann was spent avoiding attention, a stark contrast to stepping into the spotlight to lead.

Terrified was too small a word to describe her feelings on leadership, yet Danu looked at her with so much confidence, Bryn could almost pretend she was worthy of it.

With a gentle, mothering touch, Danu took Bryn's hand in hers. "You know the way, Bryn, even if you think you don't." She gave Bryn's hand a gentle squeeze, the papery skin over Danu's knuckles tightening, revealing a network of blue veins. "Trust your instincts and the Morrigan. I can see you keep her repressed, but at some point, you will need her fully. The sooner you open yourself to her, the better."

"She's dying," Sage said, her voice thick with unshed tears after hours of weeping. Bryn turned to look at Sage, meeting her hazel eyes. "Keeping her here would only make us lose her faster."

Jace nodded at her words as he tucked Sage against him. "If she is in the Otherworld"—his eyes flickered to Bryn's before he carefully substituted the term Bryn used for the realm—"Faerie, then she will not be lost forever."

Bryn could see that the mother goddess was thinner, paler, and fading fast compared to when she first met her in Ifreann. It was obvious Danu had very little time left.

But did she want to lead the group? Not really. Justin felt more like the reasonable choice of leader, yet Danu knew more than any of them, and she chose Declan and Bryn just as she had hundreds of years ago.

Danu offered a sympathetic squeeze to Bryn's hand, her lips curving in a soft, regretful expression. "Trust yourself, and those who follow you will come to trust you as well."

Bryn released a shaky laugh, trying to ignore the sting of tears at the back of her eyes when Danu's hand slipped away.

The air shimmered with a soft, ethereal glow as Danu, with a tenderness that broke through the hold Bryn had on her tears, tucked a strand of Bryn's auburn curls behind her ear.

"I must go, but I will be with you in the spirit of nature along your journey." With a wink, Danu stepped back. "I have all the faith in you, my children."

The mist swirled around her, obscuring her and Callum's forms, and leaving Bryn in the silence of the desert and her thoughts.

She'd only just come into her powers as the Morrigan, and now she was to be the leader. A leader with little in the way of direction. There were no maps of the post-Collapse world, and it was anyone's guess what the maelstrom of storms and world-ending events had done to change the landscape should they even find a map from before.

Biting her lip, she took in her friends, all of them standing next to her, without questioning Danu's judgment. They had faith in her, and while it felt unearned on her part, it would feel worse to let them down.

They had traveled beside her to fight a king who sent his demons into towns to murder innocent people that did not comply with his wishes.

The very innocents who stood where she did now, making their last stand before being cut down for not bending a knee.

Someone had to step between the darkness and the light.

She squared her shoulders, her resolve hardened by the memory of those who survived against all odds after the Collapse only to be killed by a king no one wanted.

"You've got to be gods-damn kidding me!" Declan yelled, cutting into her thoughts, before jumping up to pace next to the fire. "She brings this shit to our doorstep and bails?"

Bryn balled her fists at her sides as Declan lost himself to his temper. His anger only further fueled her anxiety about the new task and her responsibility to lead them all to Cethin without Danu.

"She was weakening, and we all knew it." But Bryn's words did nothing to assuage the large man's anger.

Whimpering gently, Finian, Justin's ever-loyal hound, settled next to Justin with his canine eyes locked on Declan, assessing the larger man.

"Yes, then set us on an impossible road only to abandon us. Fantastic!" Declan grabbed his bag, which was lying next to the small line of rocks they'd been sitting on, before walking off to the bed of the truck, where two sleeping bags were set up.

It was all too much. The overwhelming pressure and Declan's childish behavior ignited a fierce fire within Bryn, a feeling she'd always suppressed in Ifreann.

"Declan!" Bryn snapped, pointing at the ground in front of her. "We're the leaders! You cannot walk off when it gets hard! Get back over here so we can discuss what comes next."

Her ex-lover turned, the rage simmering dangerously in his whiskey-colored eyes as he stomped back toward her. Justin jumped up, Finian bristling at his side, but both man and animal held back, watching from her periphery.

Declan now stood over her, his breath fanning her face with each angry huff. "She left us. There is no way we can lead anything when we have zero fucking idea what we're even doing."

Tilting her chin up, she glared at him. "Then we figure it out. We didn't fight in Ifreann only to give up now."

As he leaned in closer, strands of his long, unbound red hair feathered her face. She knew he wanted her to back down, but she also wasn't the same lost lamb she'd been before the Morrigan.

"Face it, *Phantom Queen*," Declan sneered, and Bryn just barely kept her hands from shoving him back. "We're goners and the longer this goes on, we will rot with every other person who thought they could win." When he waved his hand out toward the town turned graveyard, Sage gasped. Bryn snarled in anger at Declan for being so willing to give up and to throw it in their faces.

One last try. That was all Bryn was willing to give him. Her loyalty was stretched far too thin.

"You are either going to lead beside me, or you will get the hell out of my way."

Declan's eyes blazed at her words, his jaw tightening until the sound of his grinding teeth was all she could hear.

"Then be my guest. You lead and I will follow, but I won't die in a pointless battle that some goddess sent us on only to abandon us in the very beginning." With those parting words, he spun, stalking past the truck as Bryn and Justin watched him disappear into the darkness.

Justin nodded to her before he took off after Declan. To do what, Bryn couldn't imagine, but he was the only one who had been able to calm Declan's rages back home. A pulse of anger not her own thrummed through her, the Morrigan, and Bryn shuddered, pushing the deity to the back of her mind as much as she could. Something she'd done almost daily since Ifreann. It was in her weaker moments or when distracted that the Morrigan tried to wrest control.

All the adrenaline from the argument left her in one big burst, and she fell back onto the stone she'd been sitting on before Danu's arrival. A sense of being watched had her turning to find Caden's dark brown eyes locked on her for a long, uncomfortable moment before he made his way back to the truck where he would remain until they left.

Bryn knew they needed to reach civilization soon to help him heal his arm as well as his soul. To shatter the wall of silence and isolation he'd built around himself, a shell of quiet misery. She missed Caden's infectious smile and his quick wit, never failing to lighten the mood with a joke.

Now, he barely acknowledged them at all anymore. He was a ghost of his former self.

To top it all off, they had a king straight from the Fomorian hellscape ruling over their land with a giant target on her and her friends' backs. Most of the people Bryn had grown up with were dead because that very king used his wraiths, or soul-eating monsters known as Sluaghs, to attack Ifreann.

All because Danu gave a bunch of twentysomethings a stone that brought back the powers of the Tuatha Dé Danann and told them they were reborn gods.

"We have to kill him." Jace broke the heavy silence of the camp and Bryn's tumultuous thoughts. Surprising her, she had to reroute her thoughts to realize he meant the king and not Declan. Though with the way Declan was acting, Bryn wouldn't immediately say no to taking him down a peg.

The rhythmic clinking of spoons against ceramic bowls ceased as those remaining turned their attention to him. Jace held each person's gaze one by one until his eyes came to rest on Bryn's. "The king has to die."

"How do you suppose we get through his wraiths? Look around. It hardly looks like we could hold our own." Kessler shook his head, flinching when his words pulled a quiet sob from Sage. He quickly murmured an apology before focusing back on his food.

"I knew they attacked Tanwen." Her watery voice choked off anything Bryn might have said, and she tuned into Sage's words as if they were gospel. "But this was savagery. This was beyond anything I could ever fathom ... they butchered my people."

At Sage's words, Jace's blue eyes met Bryn's, but Bryn saw the image of his mother dying in the sand, a death she had caused in her own act of savagery. Her own aunt, who had abused her so viciously in her youth after her father had passed but was still Jace's mother, dead at Bryn's hand.

Swallowing past the guilt, Bryn nodded. "Then that's what we do. We travel to Cethin, state our case, get an army and invade Drystan while the king is still sending his wraiths out hunting for us." She made it sound so easy, but they all knew the truth. "We can do this. We just need to figure it out, one step at a time."

"Your mama got an army we're unaware of?" Kessler lifted an eyebrow as he brought a spoonful of stew to his mouth. She knew he was trying to lighten the mood *and* satiate his curiosity, but it only riled her. More so from her own insecurity about how to pull it all off, especially when Declan was acting like a child. She pushed back her wild curls and straightened her spine.

"Callum said they haven't fallen to King Bres yet, so they have to have numbers. Numbers we wield as a weapon against him. We'll kill the bastard before he even sees it coming." She didn't add *somehow* aloud, but was sure everyone there was thinking the same as her. It all felt too impossible.

Everyone went quiet as Kessler returned to his meal, and Finian loped off after Justin. Eventually, Sage rubbed her eyes and stood, whispering a goodnight to Bryn before she moved to the truck where a bedroll waited for her.

Jace stood to follow, stopping by Bryn to squeeze her shoulder, his scent heavy with the wood smoke of the fire. It was supposed to reassure her, but the truth of their situation was far too heavy a burden.

The path to Cethin was a complete mystery, which would force her to devise a strategy fueled by gut feelings and hazy recollections from her life as the Morrigan before the Collapse.

They may have memories coming to the surface every day of their godly lives, but no one in their group had found their footing. Not enough to navigate the world and their powers without the mother goddess.

The very earth where the source of their powers resided had been destroyed, which made pulling energy from it difficult, if not downright disastrous.

They needed to learn what they were truly capable of. They needed to train in those powers in order to master them, which meant practicing skills that were incredibly rusty from centuries of disuse.

It was almost hysterical that they were the only hope for humanity.

Chapter 2

B ryn jolted awake, unsure of what had woken her. Not that it was hard to do so when she was a fitful sleeper to begin with, always listening for her aunt's footsteps on the worn wooden floorboards leading to her room back home. But since her soul merged with the goddess of everything that goes bump in the night, she rarely slept more than a few hours.

Now she had to worry about the supernatural, wraiths and King Bres, as well as fellow humans, the Rovers. Having her throat cut once was enough, but a band of Rovers stumbling across their camp would guarantee it happening again.

She could live through it, but a human like Caden could not, and he'd been through enough as it was.

It had taken her longer than she would have liked to fall asleep with the heavy feeling of specters and ghosts of those who had once lived on this soil looking over the living as they slept. She could almost feel their gazes, and the question of their intent—whether to safeguard or to harm—weighed heavily on her mind.

Sitting up from her leather and fur bedroll, she scanned their surroundings for anything out of the ordinary. All was quiet now around the dying campfire, stillness filling the ruins as her friends slept. Justin and Kessler had to be somewhere nearby in the darkness, keeping a watchful eye out since it was their shift to guard the group.

Kian huffed out a curl of misty breath before curling back into a ball next to her roll. Perhaps Kian's return from watch had been what woke her.

Every night, he would return to the fire after checking around their camp, falling quickly to sleep. Never in his human form, which she missed more and more, even though in Ifreann she had thought him her adversary, an assassin sent to kill her. That was before memories returned to them, and he could no longer hide his behavior and actions behind the veil of being the enemy as he had before.

Knowing she wouldn't find sleep again soon, she stood, brushing off the red sand that still managed to make it inside her bedroll. A small growl left Kian. One eye opened before he shook his head, closing it and falling back into rhythmic breathing. It was his way of telling her to go back to sleep, but she was far too awake now.

Stepping out of the camp circle around the fire, Bryn looked out into the inky darkness of the world around them. There was no moon for them to see by tonight, so she didn't dare venture too far from the only light they had.

Past one of the small, broken stone walls, Caden stood with his back to the group. Her feet were carrying her toward him before her brain caught up with her actions. His dark brown hair was unbound and matted, the wisps of hair free to move in the night breeze whispering across his face as he focused on some faraway place. Only ruins and sand lay before him, and it was far too dark to see anything since they were on the edge of the firelight. She couldn't imagine what he was so focused on outside of his own mind.

He cradled his handless stump, and she wondered if it would be better to head the other way and avoid disturbing him. Caden had made it clear on more than one occasion that he wanted to be left alone to ruminate.

"Did you see him?" Caden's watery voice broke the silence before he turned his red-rimmed eyes from hours of crying on her. Guilt ate at her when she realized none of them had seen Caden shed those tears. "When he died. Did you see him?"

Bryn swallowed the lump forming in her throat, but couldn't quell the shiver that racked through her at the thought of Travis's last moments. It haunted her, seeing her friend bleeding and dying in the sand without any hope of survival. His words of forgiveness in Faerie were agonizingly persistent, replaying incessantly in her thoughts as the guilt she couldn't save him ate away at her.

"Did you?" His voice deepened as he stepped toward her, his pain palpable in the air between them as it contorted his beautiful face.

"I did. He … he said he would watch over us. That he thought of you … at the end." The words felt too small for the pain etching such harsh lines on Caden's face.

He turned toward her, his lip curled and fists clenched at his sides.

"You let him die!" He snapped, his voice loud enough to make a small animal scavenging about nearby scurry off.

Bryn stepped back as Caden squared off with her, his chest bumping into hers. His nostrils flared as his deep voice cut through her panic. "You could have saved him. You could have kept me from losing my … my best friend!"

"I couldn't—"

A low, menacing growl interrupted Bryn, making the hairs on the back of her neck stand on end.

Kian prowled toward Caden, head down and hackles raised. Black lips pulled back from razor-sharp teeth.

"Oh, fuck you, too. You think I give half a shit if you tear me apart?" Caden let out an unhinged laugh. "Do it!" Throwing his arms out to the sides, the wrapping around his bound wrist, where his hand should have been, was coming undone. Just as Caden was. "Kill me!"

"Whoa!" Justin was suddenly there between them, pushing Caden back as Finian barked at their feet, jumping around. "Hold up. I am not sure what could have happened this early in the damn mornin', but that's enough. Take a breather."

Yanking himself from where Justin had a hold of his shirt, Caden sneered at Bryn before he stormed off toward the truck. Her eyes burned as she watched Caden's shoulders slump before he yanked the door of the truck open and slipped in.

His words hit the very nerve screaming at her in the darkest part of the night that she could have saved Travis. If she had taken action with her visions, known she possessed the ability to foresee events instead of not believing in herself, she could have saved lives.

"Now, wanna tell me what happened?" Justin's eyes did not hold condemnation like she would expect, but concern. "He hasn't said a word until today."

Finian whined as he nosed at her hand, her fingers moving along Finian's head and down into the fur at his neck. Kian huffed from her other side, but she ignored him. It was all too much for her to wrap her head around this late, or early, as Justin said.

Swallowing down the burn of emotions, Bryn wiped her tears away with her sleeve before she answered.

"He asked about Travis. Wanted to know why I couldn't—wouldn't save him."

"Ah." Justin crossed his arms, shaking his head before holding her stare. "Couldn't have saved him, Brynnie. You know this."

Logically, yes, she did. But logic wasn't what had a chokehold on her. How many people had died in Ifreann because she refused to push herself, to acknowledge the truth right before her? It was a mistake she wouldn't make twice.

Bryn now understood her visions weren't a symptom of mental illness, but rather the divine power of a goddess. With new clarity, she promised herself she would use these prophetic glimpses to plan strategically.

A hand on her elbow pulled her from the spiral of negative emotions she was heading down. Justin gave her a light squeeze, a silent question. Was she okay? No, she wasn't, but she nodded to him anyway as she wrapped her arms around her stomach.

The crunch of Justin's boots on rocks and broken stones echoed in the quiet morning hours as he walked back to where he kept watch. Shaking out her arms, she made to follow, her eyes catching on Declan, who stood leaning against the hood of the truck, roused by Caden's shouts.

His eyes held all the condemnation that Justin's didn't.

Straightening her shoulders, she marched past Declan into camp, but as she passed him, she realized it wasn't her that Declan was staring at with such irritation.

It was Kian who nipped at Declan from where he followed Bryn, earning a curse.

Had Bryn been in a better mood, she might have laughed at the act, but exhaustion overwhelmed her on every level, as it usually did since they escaped Ifreann.

Settling onto her bedroll, she lay back, worrying that sleep wouldn't take her but hoping for the best anyway. Kian curled up next to her, his large, warm body giving her far more heat than the fire.

Something in the way Kian acted toward Declan made her think of Caden's anger at her. With her breathing slowing and the rhythmic breaths of Kian against her, she worked through her rampant thoughts.

As she dropped off to dreamland, a large clue deep inside her soul said she was missing an obvious connection. She just wasn't sure exactly what that was.

Chapter 3

The start of a new day meant they were leaving Tanwen. A relief since the remnants of the town were painful for all of them, and most especially Sage, a child of Tanwen. It was best that they moved on and didn't linger. To head east and hope to find some proper places to rest along the way.

East, where her mother's people lived, and possibly allies against the danger the king posed to them. Bryn hoped that since Cethin had held back the king's wraiths, they would align with her to defeat the king once and for all.

Relief at that potential outcome suffused Bryn's bones as she stretched out her sore muscles, joints popping, from another night of sleeping on the hard ground. Her skin, still feeling the burn from days of travel in the desert sun, calmed with the sharp coolness of the morning air. Making a fist with her fingers before shaking them out, Bryn took a deep breath and walked until she found Sage standing before an enormous structure, just as broken as the rest, but still majestic even in its decay.

Bryn could almost see it as it once had been.

Though broken and crumbling, the white slate of the large marble pillars and stairs still revealed the sparkling marble veins. The stained-glass windows, with their shattered blues, greens, and purples, were a ghostly echo of their former glory, hinting at once vibrant scenes of nature, a world untouched by time.

"It was a library." Sage's voice broke the silence as Bryn stopped next to her. "The largest building in our town, aside from the greenhouse. Everyone met here for town meetings, weddings, or anytime there was something to celebrate or discuss ... it was the cornerstone of our entire community." Sage waited a beat before she continued. "The day before we left, my cousin was married here. White desert blooms decorated the entire entrance. I stole one. It's in one of my books where I preserved it. I can still imagine my cousin and her husband dancing along to the beat of the drums and strumming of the guitars. Now..."

A tear fell along Sage's cheek, down to her jaw, and Bryn pushed back her aversion to touch. She knew she wouldn't have a vision of death by comforting her friend, but old habits died hard. Tapping her ear three times, she calmed enough to pull Sage into a hug.

Bryn tried to focus on comforting her friend, but her heart pounded in her chest at the proximity of another person. It was progress, though, and proof that Bryn was healing inner wounds. There was still the urge to pull away, or bite into her cheek to distract herself from the mental pain, but she had more control over it. She was okay, Sage was safe, and for once, her nervous system listened, letting her return to a functional state from the immediate panic that had taken place.

Running her hand up and down Sage's back, Bryn imagined a tiny Sage, her small hand clasped in her parents', the scent of old books filling the air as they walked into the library. Warm light filled the windows, painting the room in hues of bright green, blue, and red as people of all ages gathered, a flurry of activity and chatter. The sound of their laughter and voices filled the entryway.

With a gasp, Sage pulled away from Bryn, her cheeks stained with fresh tears, her eyes wide with ones unshed. "How ... how did you do that?"

"Do what?" Confused, Bryn narrowed her eyes, the silence amplifying her uncertainty as she stepped back from Sage, her arms crossing defensively over her chest.

"I..." Sage looked to the library and back again. "I felt you in my head, you pulled a memory ... it was weird, like you could see through my eyes. My parents walking into the building with me—"

"That was your memory? I thought I was just imagining it." Bryn felt her breath hitching in her throat, a cold sweat breaking out on her skin at the thought of invading her friend's personal space. "I am so sorry. I have no idea how I did that." Bryn stumbled away, but Sage took her hand in hers, pulling her back.

"It's okay! It's okay, but this is a new power and one that could help us tremendously." Bryn disliked the thoughtful, almost calculating expression in Sage's eyes. "What if you could help us each pull the memories we need for this battle to the forefront of our minds? That way, we don't have to wait for triggers to spark them."

Bryn's stomach churned with unease. "I'm not sure how comfortable I feel digging around in your mind, Sage. How the hell am I supposed to help you do that anyway, since I'm not sure how I did it just now?"

Bryn heard a familiar voice whisper into her mind: *"Because it takes both of us to do so."* Cyerra, her crow familiar, who had been missing for days while they traveled the dusty roads, suddenly reappeared on a stone wall near Bryn, her black iridescent feathers gleaming in the sunlight. A dark rainbow of colors as the light moved over her small body. The single, pristine white feather on her chest, a stark contrast to her otherwise black plumage, distinguished her from any crow Bryn had ever read about. *"That is a part of my power I share with you."*

"Where have you been?" Bryn narrowed her eyes at the crow. Cyerra's beady eyes, like chips of obsidian, glinted in the sunlight as she flew and landed on a crumbling column. Some of the aged stone cracked under her talons as Cyerra found a sturdy place to settle herself. Sage's words, however, cut through the bright scene, bringing Bryn back to their urgent discussion.

"Is that the same crow?" Sage asked, tilting her head and giving Bryn a momentary reprieve from their conversation.

"Yes." Bryn huffed in annoyance, the sound sharp and frustrated as Cyerra's unwavering, unapologetic gaze burned into her. "Apparently, with her, I'm capable of digging around in people's heads. An additional power no one has bothered to remind me I'm capable of."

"Where would the fun be if I told you everything right away?"

Bryn stepped toward the bird, fingers clenched, before Sage pulled her back with a laugh. "Fantastic! Now we can move on and find a safe place to try out your power!"

Taking a deep breath and releasing it, Bryn focused back on Sage.

"Sage, I don't know enough about this power to dig through people's minds. Not to mention how uncomfortable that would be for everyone—" Sadness washed over Sage's expression at Bryn's words, extinguishing the brief glimpse of her inquisitive former self.

With a sigh, Bryn ran her hands over her face before letting them drop to her sides. "Fine, I can try with everyone's consent."

Sage nodded, but her prior spark of excitement had already been extinguished. She gazed again at the remnants of her childhood home before giving Bryn a small, brittle smile full of profound sadness. "Let's leave this place."

With a nod to Sage, they trudged through the red sand toward the truck, the rusty metal gleaming under the harsh sun, a beacon of random colors from the spare parts Kessler had picked up over the years. Only Kessler's magic could keep such an aging machine, a relic from life before the Collapse, running.

"Ready?" Kessler approached from the front of the truck, broken bits of stone and sand crunching under his boots, and met them at the tailgate where Sage stood, eyes closed, taking deep breaths.

"East until nightfall, then we regroup and see... where my instinct sends us next." Bryn looked at Kessler. "We good to go that far today?"

Kessler nodded, giving her a small salute. "Yes, ma'am!" Before turning toward the driver's side of the old, rusted truck.

Pulling down the tailgate, the metal groaned, showering Bryn's boots with flakes of orange and red rust. She wiped her hands on her linen skirt, the rough fabric scratching against her skin, before hopping into the truck bed and offering her hand to Sage to help her up. With quiet resolve, Sage squeezed her hand, and together they settled into the bed, the tattered blue tarp—shredded in places by the relentless wind—billowing slightly above them.

Cyerra had returned to her flight above them before letting out a caw and swirling down to land on the edge of the truck bed near where Bryn sat.

"Fresh tracks ahead. Be wary."

"What kind of tracks?" Bryn asked, concern biting at her about what could be out there. A trading caravan? Rovers?

"Horses. I didn't realize at first since I've never been around so much nothing and it's hard for me to focus on details in miles and miles of beige nonsense." As she moved closer to Bryn, the beat of her wings punctuated her words *"If you could hurry it up and make it to your mother's village so I can stretch my legs, it would be the least you can do for putting me through this torturous and repetitive nonsense."*

Bryn's lips tilted before she called out to the rest of them. "Cyerra caught horse prints on the sands, so we need to be vigilant."

"And fast."

Bryn raised an eyebrow but didn't repeat the words, earning a painful peck at her ear from Cyerra before she took flight again. Bryn hissed from the painful peck as Justin called for everyone's attention.

"You heard Bryn, keep your eyes open. Didn't sleep last night, too bad, you're not sleeping now. We can rest when we're safe. Let's roll out." Justin slapped Kessler on the back as he moved to the tailgate.

Everyone quickly and quietly found their seats. Justin and Jace settled in the back with Bryn and Sage, while Bryn stared out at the desert city. Its crumbled structures, a knife of pale beige against the intense blue sky, and the silence broken only by the occasional creak of the vehicle as the truck slowly moved forward.

It was so bizarre to think of the Collapse as an event that was just as much a product of magic as it was of human neglect. Having learned the truth of it all had altered so much of what she knew of their history.

Soon, the buildings blurred into a dizzying spin of color and motion until only the endless expanse of red sand remained. Not long after, the earth's hue reverted to its usual beige as Kian and Finian ran alongside the speeding truck, the wind whipping through their fur. A black speck in the distance soared alongside them, Cyerra coasting on the warm, dry desert breeze.

Feeling someone watching Bryn, she turned to look into Caden's eyes. His glare burned into her with damnation for all her perceived transgressions from the front seat as he watched her through the dusty back window. Unable to hold his stare, she looked away before she lost her composure.

Bryn wasn't sure what hurt more: that he blamed her for everything, or that the mirthful, humorous, and laid-back bartender she'd considered a friend had died with Travis back on the blood-soaked sand of Ifreann.

Chapter 4

Bryn noticed the tracks Cyerra mentioned as soon as they left Tanwen, and she wondered if whoever had made them had been nearby the whole time. It didn't help that the desert was a blur of cacti and random tumbleweeds, a monotonous play that made it difficult to stay vigilant against any Rovers moving about looking for their next victim.

Her eyes dry from staring at the sandy landscape for so long, she looked to where Jace rested against the truck. He had his arm around Sage, whose head drooped in her struggle to stay awake, and ran a knuckle along her cheek. Bryn wished she had that kind of love and tenderness with someone. Where even at her most vulnerable, she could trust them to be delicate and caring.

The reminder of Kian's last look toward her in the battle of Ifreann fluttered through her mind, and out of habit, she ran her hand over the scar on her throat. Jace caught the movement before he raised an eyebrow, concerned. She dropped her hand while giving him a reassuring smile and looked back out over the sands to keep watch.

The sun fell lower and lower in the sky; the truck slowed before picking up speed again, a sign that Kessler was wavering himself and needed a break. Justin sat at the tailgate, rifle resting on the edge, scanning the landscape. Bryn wondered if the familiar weight of responsibility over their small group settled over him as it did her. He seemed to embrace his new role as protector of a few, a far cry from his days as sheriff when he had a whole town to mete out justice.

A flash of light in the distance had Justin moving the rifle with the fluidity of someone well-trained with firearms, his body going perfectly still as he looked through the makeshift scope. He snapped his head in the direction of Kessler, yelling out something, but it was hard to hear over the wind.

Justin scrambled toward the cab of the truck as the vehicle veered violently to the right. Bryn slammed into the side of the truck bed, Justin on top of her, throwing his hands out at the last minute so he didn't crush her.

"Rovers!" Justin yelled into her ear before pushing away and grabbing the open window, pulling himself to the cab to yell the same thing to Kessler.

Bryn sat up, dizziness making her stomach turn as she pushed her hand into her hair. The jarring bounce of the truck added to her disorientation, but she knew immediately that the wet warmth at the base of her skull was blood. Stars swam in her vision, but she saw Sage flat in the truck bed, motioning to Bryn to get down with a shaky hand.

A heavy thud echoed off the side of the truck as it listed precariously, followed by a string of frustrated curses from Kessler in the cab as he wrestled with the steering wheel. Another loud thud sounded, joined by two more in quick succession, the sound increasing in volume each time.

"Rovers!"

The word finally penetrated Bryn's addled brain. She scurried to the floor beside the bed where Jace and Sage took cover. Jace grabbed Bryn's shoulder, moving her hair aside as they tried to stay flat, a difficult feat, while the truck swerved from side to side. "It's healing already," he muttered, shoving her head down as a rifle appeared through the back window, firing a deafening crack that worsened her splitting headache.

Justin had moved back to the tailgate in the chaos, his rifle up, the recoil the only way she knew he was shooting since her hearing was going in and out. Crawling and ignoring Jace's hissed curse, Bryn took a spot next to Justin as he reloaded.

In the distance, black shapes grew larger, the ominous forms of men on horseback, gaining on the truck, firearms in their hands. They continued to come at the vehicle from all sides before one made contact with a tire. The loud pop served as the only warning before the truck jolted violently, Justin losing his balance and falling back into Bryn, knocking the breath out of her lungs.

Almost tilting to the side completely, the truck came to a halt, falling back onto all four tires, their entire group going with it. Tumbling onto her hands and knees, Justin over her, she barely heard him yell to take cover before someone tore open the tailgate and grabbed her ankle, pulling her out before she could comprehend what was happening.

Only angry screams filled the air as someone shoved Bryn to the ground, putting a knee on her back.

Sage and Jace were next to her, but she could hear the scuffling of Justin fighting before someone fired a shot and the fight stopped.

"Justin!" Bryn yelled, trying to get up. Her body revolted against her, her stomach churning as she panicked.

Justin's face was suddenly next to hers, his expression pinched in pain, but he tried to smile as a Rover held him down, another patting him over, checking to see what he had on him.

"Grazed me..." he murmured, sand going into his mouth as he spoke, but she wasn't an idiot. There was pain in his crystal-blue eyes.

Bryn felt the sharp tug of someone's hand in her hair, lifting her brutally as they did the same to Jace, Sage, and Justin. Bryn's eyes darted around desperately, seeking an escape, but all she could see were the Rovers pressed in on all sides—black rags, black paint, and skull-like white faces—a suffocating cage of certain death. Not one spot for any of them to flee without a bullet in the back.

Turning her head to the side, she could see Declan, Caden, and Kessler lined up behind them before a fist slammed into her mouth. Blood flooded it as she tasted the tang of iron on her tongue.

"Don't move," a hard voice rasped from behind her.

Several of the men grabbed ropes, pulling them tight as they walked toward Bryn and her group.

A calm settled over Bryn, her breath evening out as she watched them. She was no longer human, and she needed to remember that. Her tattoos lit up, a vibration from the ink beneath her skin thrumming through her. Boosting the magic in her veins.

As the Rover approached, she reacted, her hand snatching the rope in a swift motion. With a powerful spin, she moved behind him; the rope tightening around his throat with suffocating pressure.

Chaos erupted.

With a grunt, Jace shoved a Rover away from Sage as she called a geyser of sand from the earth, the impact of the sandstorm-force assault shaking the ground. Declan roared as he grabbed two men and, with unbelievable strength, slammed them into each other, knocking both men unconscious with a sickening crunch.

Justin had two guns in hand, most likely weapons from the two bodies at his feet, as he leaned against the back of the truck, his left pant leg soaked with blood. Every bullet hit its mark. Every bullet a kill shot.

Bryn yanked on the rope until the man was unconscious before she dropped him, grabbing a knife sheathed at the belt around his waist.

Feeling someone behind her, Bryn spun right as a flash of silver took down a man with a gun, one that was aimed at the back of her head. Kian tore into the man as Finian was quick to take down another Rover who moved in too close to Justin.

Bryn ran at a man closing in on Caden, ducking down as bullets rained against the truck. Her knife found its way into the Rover's side, right into his heart as she dropped him, shoving Caden into the truck and slamming the door behind him.

There was no way out of this. They could fight, die, and come back, but that left Caden vulnerable. Far too vulnerable, and they needed to end this before someone managed to get him.

A gun went off next to her, Bryn ducking to avoid being shot. Her eyes widened at the sight of the bullet mere inches from her face, hovering in the air before it erupted into a flash of fire.

The gunman who shot at her now lay on the sand with a crooked neck. Kessler stood over him, his hands up, sweat beading on his upper lip and brow. "Just in time, huh?" he gave a small smirk before someone clubbed him with a weapon, taking his focus from her.

Bryn threw her knife, watching it sink into the Rover's throat before Kessler took another hit.

"Stop!" someone yelled and all the Rovers went silent, their eyes on Bryn and her group as they waited. A taller man, his rags not nearly as worn as the rest of his Rovers, stepped forward. "What kind of magic is this?"

Breathing heavily, Bryn looked at Declan, his face covered in blood splatter, but he said nothing.

Bryn's rage was palpable as she seethed at the leader, spitting out, "You messed with the wrong fucking people," each word laced with venomous anger as she held his dark gaze. "We are the Tuatha Dé Danann."

"The who?" The leader tilted his head, another Rover walking to join him, but was halted by the leader holding his hand up. "It doesn't matter." He waved his hand before dropping it to his side. "Just give us what you have and we will leave you be."

Bryn looked around. Countless Rovers lay bleeding and dying, begging for help or a swift death.

"Not sure you have the upper hand here," Kessler said before Bryn could speak. "Maybe you should head on out."

The leader walked toward Bryn, his gait smooth, not a scratch on him as he stopped before her, his eyes piercing her as she ground her molars together to keep herself from losing her tongue to her rage. "Perhaps you should do I as I ask before your friend gets hurt." He nodded to something behind her.

Turning, Bryn's vision went red as a Rover walked around the front of the truck, a gun in hand pointed at Caden's temple. Whipping back around to the leader, she stepped up into the man's face. "Call him off!"

"Give us your goods, and I will."

Bryn knew they had no intention of letting Caden live. Never had a group survived a Rover attack as far as she knew. Working through possible actions, the man holding the gun on Caden suddenly howled in pain.

A collective gasp arose as everyone watched the man's arm, grotesquely twisting as the bone snapped, the gun clattering to the ground. With a sickening pop and wrench, his leg twisted, the kneecaps facing the wrong direction before the Rover fainted.

Jace walked past them as he eyed the remaining Rovers, his gaze stopping on the leader. "Get back on your horses and leave us." Jace positioned himself between Caden and the others, arms loose at his sides, fingers flexing, feet apart, his muscles tense.

Bryn raised an eyebrow at Jace before she turned to the leader. "Unless you want to teach your men how to walk again, I suggest you take his advice."

The leader gazed impassively at the mangled Rover, his expression un-readable, before shifting his attention back to Bryn. Before anyone else could react, a sharp knife lodged itself deep into her chest, grating against her rib bone. He twisted the weapon and something inside Bryn snapped, her tattoos lighting up a bright blue, her hand reaching up to the leader of the Rovers and her nails stabbing into the sides of his face as his eyes went wide, bleeding.

A guttural snarl tore from her as the man thrashed, his body convulsing before a sphere of light erupted from his lips, his form then slumping lifelessly to the bloodied sand beneath him.

With an ear bleeding piercing scream, Bryn ripped the knife out, tossing it to the side before crushing the orb in her fist. It burst, facets of light falling to the ground like dying embers.

Fear in their eyes, the Rovers ran as fast as they could to their horses, the sound of their boots on the ground a rhythmic beat before they took off, leaving their dead behind.

With heavy breaths, Bryn followed them, her blood turning to ice in her veins as the Morrigan continued to puppet her body.

Teeth bit gently into her hand, tugging her back, and she spun to face the silver wolf.

Kian.

Bryn fell to her knees, her mind becoming her own once again as Kian nuzzled up to her.

What had she done? No, not her. The Morrigan.

The primal urge to finish the men off was strong, and as much as Bryn tried to push the Morrigan back down, she was not willing. Bryn was right to fear how powerful she was. It was more obvious than ever that the Morrigan had the upper hand and could take over whenever she felt like it.

Always there, just beneath the surface, a danger to all those around her.

The Morrigan escaped her chains in Ifreann and there was no putting her back now.

"Now that we have a moment, anyone want to help me dig a bullet out?" Justin slowly slid down the truck, and everyone moved into action, Bryn watching but keeping her distance.

Jace was the first to Justin, tearing his pant leg open.

"It healed over already. I'll need to cut you back open. Declan? Can you help Justin into the back of the truck where my bag is?"

Bryn watched Declan pick Justin up as if he were feather light and not a man probably closing in on two hundred pounds. Jace was quick to follow into the bed of the truck, already in doctor mode.

It was only after all the chaos had settled, people milling about as Sage and Jace worked to get the bullet out of Justin's leg, that Bryn realized she was shaking. Her body felt weak and sluggish as she walked to the truck, leaning against it. Exhaustion rode heavily on her and she struggled to stay awake.

"We used too much power. If we are gods of nature"—Kessler waved to the barren desert—"we were pulling on our own reserves. We will have to camp sooner to recover."

Bryn dropped to the ground, leaning her head against the side of the truck. She was too tired, too scared, to argue, but Sage wasn't.

"Here?" Sage asked, looking around at the blood-soaked sand, her expression pinched. "What about the Rovers returning or predators?"

Rubbing the back of his neck, Kessler looked out across the dunes. Bryn watched as Declan walked up to him, the men whispering before nodding.

"We move down wind, camp between dunes for the night. Have more than two on watch," Bryn said aloud, the Morrigan pushing the words even through her clenched teeth toward the end when she fought back.

No one argued with her, which was a relief since she was too tired to stand her ground.

The sound of people moving about lulled Bryn as she closed her eyes, her mind going back to the orb in her fist, over and over again. Her mind tried to understand what she had done without asking the Morrigan for a memory or explanation.

The deity was smug, an uncomfortable contrast to Bryn's own feelings of confusion and fear.

"Come on," Kessler was helping Bryn to stand, and she realized she must have dozed off since the sun was dipping below the horizon. The group was moving from the truck, past another dune where they were making camp on the low end, Kian and Jace at the top keeping an eye out.

Justin slept on a bedroll while his leg healed from the impromptu procedure.

Bryn crawled to her sleeping mat, the others who were able, doing the same.

Curling up on her mat between Kessler and Sage, none of them willing to have a fire that could lead the Rovers back to them, they tried to sleep close together for warmth. Kian nosed his way between Kessler and Bryn in his wolf form, settling next to her, pushing her arm over him and laying his head on her hip.

A tear slipped down her cheek as she worked through her new reality of sharing space with someone so primal. Of working through her new role as leader while fighting her own mind.

They'd survived a Rover attack but Bryn was sure if there was such a thing as luck, they were running out, and fast.

If they ever had any luck at all.

Chapter 5

Over a week had passed since they left Tanwen, the days were lost to monotony and the slow pace of their trek was evident in the straggling group: Caden, his greasy, dark brown blood-matted hair plastered to his face from his lack of concern for hygiene, lagged behind. Justin's annoyance was palpable as he struggled to keep pace with the group while trying to assist Caden. Both men looked ready to pummel each other.

The weather did not help. Bryn had thought the heat of Ifreann was hell, but trekking the desert without cover was another game altogether. It did not take much to see the frustration in the group while they slowly plodded along, stripping off clothing as they grew too warm from the desert sun during the day before bundling back up again as their sweat dried at night, freezing against their skin. The cold more and more biting as they moved further east and Bryn knew they needed to move faster before the ice and snow met them. Something they were not prepared to deal with at all.

With the truck, they would have made far better time, but no one said anything about that.

Kessler was quiet, more than usual for the blacksmith, since they'd had to leave the truck behind. Aware of the truck's importance to him—years of labor and what carried them in their escape from Ifreann—she knew that despite his skills with metal, the flat tires with no spares available rendered it unusable.

The tension rose each day as they walked, every small movement or sound turning into a fight. They just walked, slept, argued, and ate. Bryn hoped that once they made it to a town that had amenities, they might be relaxed enough to work through what had happened.

"We should make—"

Justin interrupted Jace. "No, we need to move our butts and get to civilization as soon as possible. Being out in the open like this is not—"

"Oh, would you shut up!" Declan yelled, his voice raspy from disuse. "What are we rushing off to? Another town ready to be murdered by wraiths? More innocents we bring nothing but dark omens to with our mere presence?" Declan spun, looking at each member of the group. "Don't you get it yet? We're screwed, and this is all pointless!"

"Declan..." Bryn warned, seeing that he was unraveling thread by thread and they needed him to be strong. Bryn needed it, too. She wasn't sure she could lead the group herself. Declan stared at her, a grim set to his jaw, before hoisting his heavy pack higher on his shoulder and dismissing her with his back as he walked away. Turning back to the group, ignoring Declan, she steeled her nerves.

"We need to keep going. Cethin can't be far now and once there, we can rest and regroup ... hopefully with more people. We are so close now, we just have to keep going before the freezing season fully hits."

Her words were met with averted eyes and furrowed brows. They were getting far too close to losing hope and Declan was not helping. They were all unraveling from the stress.

"Let's go," she said with an air of authority she didn't feel. Perhaps now would have been a good time for the Morrigan's assertive dominance, but Bryn could only feel her essence, not her presence right now.

Bryn pushed her pack higher on her shoulder and started walking again, hoping they would follow. There was nothing more to say out in the open desert with the memories trailing them like the ghosts of their past failures.

Another blast of wind and sand, stinging her eyes and whipping at her clothes, forced Bryn to re-tighten her scarf as something dark green on the horizon caught her eye as she stood atop a large sand dune.

"What is that?" Sage asked from behind her, grabbing Bryn's elbow to steady herself. As if Sage knew what it was but couldn't believe it.

"It's a gods-damned tree!" Declan yelled, whooping. "That means we gotta be close!" With those words, he took off. Justin, Jace, and Kessler jogging to catch up as Kian and Finian ran ahead, their slick dark forms a blur along the landscape.

Bryn squinted, unsure how Declan knew that, but the men were moving fast, their lethargy a memory as they found their second wind.

Caden walked past Bryn, his expression still vacant even in the excitement of it all as he murmured, "Let's go see a tree."

With a reassuring squeeze on Bryn's arm, Sage urged them forward; the women followed the men toward the massive tree, its branches reaching like arthritic fingers. As they gained ground, they could see more and more trees in the distance. As if a forest were slowly working to encroach on the desert, a battle of nature.

The desert sun beat down on their faces as they walked from tree to tree. Along the way, the trees grew from struggling saplings to voluminous, strong trees, their roots firmly planted in the earth. The yielding sand transitioned to packed earth, the forest's scent—cedar and damp soil—becoming increasingly distinct. No more dry desert air and sand abrading their skin.

A dividing line between the world they knew, the desert full of death, pushed up against life itself. A dense forest spread out before them the further they moved in toward the sporadic growth of vegetation.

"It's unbelievable…" Sage whispered, so lost in her astonishment she tripped over a rock. Bryn caught her by the arm before she hit the ground, and Sage's laugh broke the silent awe of the group and had Bryn's heart feeling lighter than it had in weeks, maybe months.

Was this Cethin? Had they finally made it?

"I can feel the pull of nature deep in my soul," Sage whispered and Bryn furrowed her brows. She could feel nature, but it was like a ripple along the surface of the water. Like Bryn could tap into it but wasn't able to submerse herself in it.

"I can feel the life cycles of the forest. The trees are giving new life to the seedlings growing between them. I can feel the roots of the ones here and the ones gone before," Sage whispered in awe. Bryn smiled, but was sure it didn't meet her eyes, and instead of saying anything, she moved her attention to the forest before them.

Trees for as far as the eye could see, hills of them, so tall that clouds slipped between the tops of them. Green. So much green and the smell was fresh, like her lungs were opened more than ever now that they were no longer inhaling particles of sand. Birds and wildlife echoed through the forest, the floor alive with plant life.

It was Faerie on Earth, and Bryn couldn't feel the connection that Sage had described. Instead, she could feel the bones of the past beneath the soil and something deeper within. The small pulses of light she could see in her mind's eye beckoned her to come further into the forest.

Sage dropped to the ground next to Bryn, laughing, as she pushed her hands into the mossy undergrowth and the lush grass grew, flowers budding and blooming in seconds instead of days.

"We need to stay together! Who knows what's out here!" Justin yelled from somewhere ahead of Bryn.

Sage ignored him as sobs and laughter mixed with the cacophony of birds singing from the trees. The flora around Sage had grown higher, moving toward her like sentient beings.

"How is this here when the rest of the world is dying?" Kessler mumbled from somewhere nearby, breaking the magic of the moment.

"Damn good question," Justin responded, and all went quiet when Kian's hackles rose and Finian snarled, sensing something coming their way just as Bryn did.

The men moved back toward Sage and Bryn, the group gathering together to face the new threat.

Bryn closed her eyes and homed in on the fragments of light in the depths of the forest making their way toward them as the birds in the trees fell silent.

The group cautiously advanced, Kian and Finian, their powerful muscles rippling beneath their fur, peeled away from the main body, leading the way, their keen senses already alerted to a danger the others hadn't yet seen.

The sound of twigs snapping had Sage jumping up and rejoining the group. Bryn, Kessler, Declan, and Caden moved forward where Justin grabbed Finian's collar, holding the hound back. Kian continued forward, his silver ear twitching, his lips pulled back, showing dangerously sharp teeth.

"Duck," Cyerra ordered in her mind right as a high-pitched whistle whooshed past Bryn's ear, making her jump and spin around. An arrow punctured the ground at Jace's feet.

"Stop!" Justin yelled, his voice cracking with frustration, throwing one hand up, his other remaining firmly on the pistol at his waist.

As if shot from a cannon, Kian was a blur, a flash of silver disappearing into the dense forest. Bryn reacted instantly, moving to follow him, but Declan's firm grasp on her arm halted her pursuit.

"He's capable of dying now." Bryn tried to pull her arm back, but Declan tightened his hold and shook his head.

"The demon will be fine. Stay with us."

Before Bryn could snap back at Declan, a deep, gravelly voice, like the rumble of distant thunder, cut through the air. "Well, what do we have here?"

Bryn roughly tore her arm away from Declan's grasp, but instead of fleeing, she remained rooted to the spot, bracing herself as a colossal man, easily twice Bryn's size, crashed through the undergrowth, snapping branches echoing through the trees in his wake. Dark red hair, the same shade as his chest-length beard, threaded through with silver that was a testament to his age. His massive frame made his gait a lumbering waddle as he pushed through the dense undergrowth to stand before them.

Cyerra dove low and landed on Bryn's shoulder, her talons digging into her linen shirt, making Bryn wince. *"Be wary."*

"Was it the arrow shot at me that made you think we should be cautious?" Bryn said as Cyerra's gaze, sharp with an uncanny intelligence, swept over the men.

"You've a lot of nerve running up on our home, stranger." His voice, harsh and resonant, echoed like a guitar string vibrating in the air. Bryn chafed at the sound but controlled her reaction to avoid further insult.

Biting her lip, she fought to keep silent and assess the threat before she made a move that would definitely end with an arrow in her body. Cyerra's tiny, daggered claws bit deeper into her skin at his approach.

Unfortunately, Declan had no such qualms. "Well, shoot first and ask questions later. Seems to work well for you, huh?"

The immense man, a mountain of flesh and red hair, narrowed his bushy brows at Declan before his jaw dropped open. All signs of worry left his face as he forcefully pushed past Bryn and Sage, the force of his movement nearly knocking them down. Justin pulled his pistol, but three men emerged from the forest, their crossbows trained on him, the sharp click of cocking mechanisms filling the air.

"Eoin?" the giant man roared, pulling Declan into a bone-crushing hug. Never did she think Declan would be the *smaller* man.

Several more men came out of the trees with arrows nocked but not lifted or aimed at anyone in particular. She supposed that should be a reassurance, but it did not feel like it. It felt more like she stood before a coiled snake, ready to strike.

Kian was nowhere to be seen, Finian was sitting next to where Justin stood, his eyes and ears on high alert, catching everything going on around them.

"Name is Declan," Declan responded as he untethered himself from the man. "Not Eoin."

"You look just like my brother ... unless ... wait, Declan you say?" he whispered, his hands faltering as he moved toward Declan again. Perhaps reaching for another hug, but Declan moved even further back, his face pinched with irritation. "My brother's son! You've returned, my boy!"

Without warning, Declan was back in the man's arms as he slapped Declan's back hard enough to make Bryn flinch. That would have broken something in her had he done that to her, but Declan only raised his eyebrows at Bryn and their group. His entire life, Declan had thought the mayor of Ifreann, Aaron Rafferty, was his father until he found out he was adopted.

Bryn couldn't imagine finding out her father, the man who raised her, was not her actual parent.

But there was something far too unsettling about Declan's "uncle" being the one to show up first to greet them. She couldn't tell if the man was telling the truth about Declan's parentage or not.

Releasing Declan after another awkward hug, the man grinned at him. Slapping Declan's shoulders just as hard as he had his back, he turned to the men who waited by the trees, their arrows still ready.

"Eoin's boy is back!" he roared, the sound echoing through the still morning air as he pulled Declan into a painful-looking headlock and half-dragged, half-carried him toward the shadowy depths of the woods. The men with arrows exchanged glances, but their lack of failed to perturb the man claiming to be Declan's uncle.

Declan twisted from his grip, but the man grabbed his hand, raising it in the air as he faced the people who waited on his orders. "The heir of Osgar is back!"

"Osgar? This isn't Cethin?" Bryn said before she could stop herself, breaking the cheer of the men around her at the man claiming to be Declan's uncle's words. With a smug look, he turned and gazed at her.

"That's quite a bit further, little miss, but thank all the gods you were wrong since we have our boy back!"

That statement ignited shouts from the men, all of whom lowered their weapons, and it reminded Bryn of howling wolves. Yet it did not comfort her in the way the howls of the wolves in Faerie did. This felt wrong, even corrupt somehow.

Not one man gave her group, aside from Declan, a welcome smile. Instead, they held their cold, emotionless eyes on them as if they were a threat.

"*I do not trust them,*" Cyerra said into her mind.

Bryn didn't either; the man claiming to be his uncle held his gaze on Cyerra a moment too long, just as Arioch had before Ifreann's catastrophic downfall, making her heart pound with a terrifying sense of déjà vu.

As much as Bryn wanted to cower away, the Morrigan made her hold the man's gaze when his eyes drifted from Cyerra to her. Her hands trembled and her heart pounded as the Morrigan made a stand using her body.

A soft snort of amusement escaped him as he turned, waving them to follow, the Morrigan releasing her hold on Bryn at last.

Unsettled with the Morrigan closer to the surface than she'd been since the Rover attack, Bryn followed the men into the forest, hoping she wasn't leading her group into an ambush.

Being a leader was not for the faint of heart.

Deeper into the forest they went, Bryn bringing up the rear of the group as Declan walked between his uncle and another man whose presence radiated authority. The rest of his uncle's men made a circle around Declan, effectively cutting him off from the people he'd traveled with.

There was a statement being made here.

"This seems ... odd," Kessler whispered as he slowed to walk beside Bryn. "Something is really botherin' me here, and it's not just having to leave my truck behind."

A smile tugged at Bryn's mouth at the odd attachment the man had to the hunk of metal. Before she could respond, Justin was at her other side, his gun drawn but aimed at the ground.

"I feel the same way." Justin kept his eyes trained more on the unknown men before him than on the surroundings as he had their entire journey.

It was obvious who he found to be more of a threat. "I'm not sure if it's just a feeling, like something is actually wrong, or just being around new people after living in an isolated place where strangers were a threat."

That was a good point, and Bryn could see from Kessler's expression that he felt the same way.

"We should give them the benefit of the doubt then," Kessler agreed, but as he spoke, something in Bryn knew trusting them completely would come back and bite them in the ass.

"We have no idea who these people are and if his uncle is who he says he is. We stay in pairs, no one alone at any point, and—"

Bryn's words froze in her throat as the group halted their march, a hush falling over them as the sounds of their collective movement faded when the men who had encircled Declan and his uncle split apart. With an almost smug look, Declan's uncle swaggered to where Bryn stood with Justin and Kessler, bypassing Sage and Jace. Bryn looked to Declan's uncle's entourage, their faces grim, as if a momentous decision had happened in the five minutes they had been walking.

"We have places along the forest edge where our hunters stay. You may find a night's rest before you continue on your adventure, whatever that may be!" Looking over his shoulder at the grim faces of his men, he cut a smile to them before returning his focus to Bryn. "Then you will join us in an evening feast."

A flash of furious outrage replaced the grim expressions on his men's faces before settling into impassive stoicism; their eyes, however, still burned with barely contained anger. They did not seem to agree with their leader about what should be done with the strangers, but they didn't push back against his decision. How much power did this man have over the community they were about to walk into?

Not giving them a chance to speak or ask questions, Declan's supposed uncle turned away, throwing his arm around Declan's shoulders as he marched them forward through the darkening forest.

A man with pale, sallow skin that had been left behind turned toward Bryn as Declan and the rest of the new group kept on. The sickly looking man stared at them longer than was comfortable before lowering his bow, his visage bringing back the screams and the stench of death left by the wraiths. Yet, he was mortal since the usual vibrant hum of power in her veins, a sensation like a thousand tiny sparks, remained dormant, unlike when the wraiths were near.

"This way," the guard rasped, the crossbow held loosely but menacingly at his side. The air hung heavy with an unspoken threat. Bryn shivered, a cold sweat prickling her skin as she wondered if their hosts would treat them as guests or prisoners.

If her group hadn't needed the rest, she'd have walked them away from Osgar.

"Now I'm extremely uncomfortable," Kessler whispered, his arm brushing hers as they walked back to the forest's edge, following the guard. "Am I wrong in feeling like we're purposefully being separated from Declan?"

"No, you're not." Bryn felt a prickling unease, a sense of foreboding different from the chilling dread that had preceded the wraiths' attack.

Not a death omen, but nothing good, either.

Chapter 6

The small, cramped hunting cabins offered only a rusted, metal-framed bed, the air heavy with the musty odor of damp wood and mildew, a smell that clung to the back of the throat. A lumpy mattress, stained and faded beyond recognition, lay on the rickety frame, its thinness a testament to years of use.

Their sole amenity was a single outhouse, with its peeling paint and the stench of stale urine and feces hanging in the air. It was enough to make Bryn want to run back to Tanwen before she even stepped inside.

Settling onto the rough-hewn front porch of her small cabin, more of a shack really, Bryn folded her arms on the railing, the splintery wood digging into her elbows, and tried to calm the building dread within herself.

A flap of wings overhead reminded Bryn that Cyerra had taken off to spy for her. Her hope that Cyerra had something tangible about the man proclaiming Declan his nephew rose up within Bryn, only to be cut down by Cyerra almost immediately.

"I flew over to catch something from the odd one, thinking he is Declan's kin, but they are shut away in their little wooden fortresses reminiscing about nonsense even Declan wouldn't remember."

Of course they were. "Thank you, Cyerra, for trying." Bryn ran her hands over her face, up into her hair and, with a tug, ground herself by biting into her cheek to cull the worsening anxiety. She hated that she still had to use pain as a center for herself, and it would need to stop being a crutch at some point. No longer was she the weak little girl in Ifreann but being traumatized by abuse and death her whole life wasn't something that would heal in a month. A thought she kept repeating to herself every day.

"Darling, you've finally found somewhere the sun won't reduce me to ash. I appreciate that," a familiar and incredibly missed voice spoke up. Bryn turned toward the woman, tears stinging her eyes at the sight of Niamh emerging from the trees. Stopping, Niamh held her arms out wide, giving Bryn a chance to make the choice herself on whether she could handle the touch, and Bryn let the tears slip free. Moving quickly, Bryn let herself be enveloped in a hug from the woman who had been her anchor and stand in mother for Bryn as a child and young woman. The familiar perfume that was all Niamh, cinnamon, oak, and apple, centered Bryn for the first time since they'd left Ifreann.

Bryn loved her just as much as she always had, even after it came to light that she was also a vampire.

"I've missed you," Bryn whispered into Niamh's black silken tresses before she pulled back.

"Darling, I've been around this whole time, watching from the shadows while traveling in the veil." Pulling at one of Bryn's curls, Niamh let out a low laugh. "Time to find the baths around here, my girl. This will not do."

With a grimace, Bryn waved to the small, smelly outhouse. "That's our only bathroom and I doubt there's a shower."

The curl of Niamh's lip told her everything the woman thought about that without saying a word.

"Then," Niamh pulled Bryn's arm through hers. "We shall find our little water witch and get ourselves a nice bath before we face those so obviously *generous* people. One must feel the absolute best when dealing with the worst."

Without waiting for Bryn's answer, Niamh hauled her by her arm away from the cabin and pulled her down a worn path. The obviously bent foliage and well-worn path whispered of something beyond the dense vines and trees. A subtle change in the light and sounds hinted at a hidden place. Sage met them halfway, her eyes alight. "Come on! I found something amazing!"

Niamh winked at Bryn. "See?"

Walking behind Sage, the dense trees opened to reveal a waterfall and small pool that rendered Bryn speechless. Crystal clear water roared over the fall, streaming down into a tiny lake. Pebbles made up the lake bed, and small fish moved about through the pristine water.

"I've never seen so much water in one place..." Bryn whispered, stepping forward, as Niamh dropped her arm. Turning to look back at her friend, Niamh waved her on.

"I will bathe tonight, since I'd prefer not to pollute the water with my ashes." Niamh pointed to the sun above the foliage with a small chuckle before looking Bryn over. "I will bring you some clothes and leave them for you here at the edge. That outfit should have been burned the moment you left Ifreann." Before Niamh turned, her smile grew sad, her eyes growing distant. "It used to be like this all over the world."

Bryn waited, wanting to make sure Niamh would be okay, but Niamh shook herself before clapping her hands together. "Well, darling, get washed up. I'll find you something with less road dust and blood."

"Catch!" Sage called out from where she stood nearby, tossing a small beige item at Bryn. Bryn caught it and turned over the brown package to see what was written on the paper. Soap! For the first time in weeks. "I asked nicely for a bar of soap, though I think the guard gave it to me for his own comfort since we smell something awful. I'll give you some privacy and head back later." Sage winked before twirling away from her as she made her way back through the trees.

She had a feeling Sage needed privacy because she wouldn't be bathing alone. Bryn cringed, not wanting that mental picture of her cousin and Sage together like that in her head.

Toeing her boots off at the edge of the water, Bryn flinched at the sight of herself mirrored on the surface. A wave of self-disgust washed over her at the sight. Her hair matted with blood and sand, her clothes splattered in reddish brown dried stains from the Rover attack.

With trembling hands, she tore off her shirt stiff with blood, pulling it over her head before throwing it aside. As if removing her shirt had triggered a sense of claustrophobia, she tore at the rest of her clothes. Her chest heaved with shallow breaths as she quickly pulled off the tan skirt she'd worn like a uniform for so very long. Then her bra and panties fell to the ground beside her shirt. She would not be putting those back on, even if they were clean. That part of her life was gone and over with.

Hands on her knees, Bryn took in deep breaths before reaching down to grab the soap she'd dropped in her anxious state, tossing the wet brown paper to the side. The pristine water rippled out from around her ankles as she stepped into the crystal-clear depths, and sunlight dappled the bottom.

The waterfall's cool, crisp water balanced the sun's warmth, creating the perfect temperature.

Wading out further into the water, Bryn dunked her head, resurfacing with a sputter spraying droplets everywhere as she pushed her wet hair from her face, unused to her body being submerged. It was unexpected bliss; the cool water enveloped her, a stark contrast to the desert's parched conditions and their meager water rations. They were lucky in Ifreann to have even an inch of rusted well water as a bath if the scorching season wasn't too bad and they'd had *some* rain to fill the tanks.

Spinning in the cool water, she ran her toes over the smooth river stones under them. Having never been around water in such abundance, she'd never learned to swim, so she knew to be careful. But for once, she wasn't focused solely on survival.

Soaping herself up, she let her mind wander, taking a moment to herself for the first time since Danu crashed into her life. To think of things other than the horrible events that had taken place in the last month, including what the Morrigan had her do without consent.

It didn't take long for her thoughts to go to the man who had yet to make an appearance in anything but his silver wolf form since the battle in Ifreann.

There were so many unanswered questions when it came to Kian. While most of their time together in Ifreann, they had been suspicious of each other; it was those last few moments when she remembered *him*. The loyal general who was always at her side.

And while the Morrigan thought of him as not much more than a tool, Bryn had seen something different. She saw the man. His witty banter, his confidence, his intelligence, and there was something else there, too. Something she couldn't put into words, but it was missing from the relationship between Kian and the Morrigan.

If only he would *speak* to her, so she could see if this was all one sided, but Danu was most likely right that he was working it out on his own.

Then there was the memory of him in his mortal form—his lean frame, piercing silver eyes, and raven-black hair—that filled her thoughts, a bittersweet ache in her chest to imagine him and know when she saw him next, it would be the wolf, not the man.

Deep down, in a place she'd been reluctant to visit, she wanted to see *more* of him, to touch him, and to feel his skin against hers. Those plush lips as they moved along her neck.

Her hand slipped over her breast as she remembered his long fingers, thinking of them moving over her stomach, between her legs ... Closing her eyes, she let her head fall back, her body dipping further into the water.

Letting her mind free to pull whatever it wanted to the surface, flashes of him from past lives ran through her mind. The image of him shirtless, leather pants, his tattoos a bright contrast to his pale skin and his raven hair shining in the sun as his muscles tensed, spinning his sword with practiced ease.

A splash nearby pulled her from the memory, and she turned to see if someone had snuck up on her. Ripples from nearby had her looking up to see a tree hanging over, something obviously having fallen.

Right. They were in an unknown place and she needed to be alert, not daydreaming.

Sudsing her hands, she ran her fingers through her long curly auburn hair, working out the tangles. Her thoughts on the welcome they'd had from the men and how quickly they had whisked Declan away. Perhaps they could stay one night but no more than that. It was obviously not their destination, and she was sure they were unwelcome. Not to mention, the Morrigan was pressing to move on, giving a sense of anxiety that would not allow Bryn's nerves to settle.

The excuse to get to Cethin before the freezing season was at its strongest was a good enough reason that no one could argue with.

"Bryn?" Declan's voice cut into her thoughts, and she let out a shriek at the interruption, stumbling back in the water. Panic flooded her veins when her feet found nothing beneath them. The water enveloped her, the shock a physical blow, as she dipped beneath the surface. Popping back up only long enough to hear Declan shout in panic, she slipped below again.

"Bryn!"

Inhaling the water from her surprise, she struggled to get back to the underwater ledge while choking, the burn of her throat and lungs unbearable. Throwing her hands out, she didn't know what to do. Terror paralyzed her; its icy fingers wrapped around her heart, stealing her thoughts.

Her vision wavered as something dark moved over her, blocking out the light beaming through the water before arms wrapped around her waist, tugging her violently to the surface until the liquid no longer touched her face and invaded her mouth.

A racking cough shook her as she pushed her hair back, her eyes catching on the silver eyes she'd just fantasized about moments before. Her mind quickly tried to take in every detail, as though he might change back to his wolf form at any second. Dark, wet strands of hair clung to his face, a face she'd missed terribly. Water dripped down his throat, over his tattoos, and back into the pool.

For the first time since Ifreann, Kian was in his human form, and she was lost to him as he moved a strand of hair out of her face.

"Bring her back, wolf," Declan ordered, his voice sharp and commanding, and Kian's eyes flashed dangerously. Bryn's thoughts were abruptly interrupted as she became aware of their proximity and her own nakedness. Not just hers, but how naked *he* was.

She found her footing on the slippery pebbles of the lake bottom as she placed her hands against Kian's tattooed pectoral muscles, his fingers burning where he held her against him. Her eyes dropped to his stomach before she stopped herself, shaking her head and chastising herself for blatantly ogling the man.

"I need to get dressed…" Bryn choked out, her voice unsteady, her throat raw. She held Declan's eyes after she spoke, knowing he would be more of a problem.

"I've seen it all before, Bryn. Just get out." Kian gave a low growl at Declan's words, his lips pulling back from his teeth, which were growing sharper. Bryn did not want him lost to the wolf again, so she needed to deescalate before Declan made things worse.

Kian cleared his throat, his voice gruff from not having spoken in over a week, his words only for her. "I apologize. I was in my wolf form nearby and heard Declan screaming, so I didn't think to clothe myself."

Placing her hand on his bicep, she squeezed when he looked away, the muscles in his jaw ticking.

"Thank you for saving me," she whispered, waiting for those silver eyes to meet hers again. When he did, it was a physical jolt to her system, and she worked hard to focus on not dragging him back to her, pushing her lips against his. Kian nodded slightly before carefully releasing her and moving through the water, while she watched shamefully as the droplets clung to his unveiled body like liquid diamonds.

Declan's sharp cough, punctuated by a sneer twisting his lips as he peered at her over Kian's shoulder, fueled her petty feelings of resentment.

It was clear he was jealous, but he needed to accept that any relationship between them was far in the past of this lifetime and others. He was the man who had laid with her before visiting her friend's brothel, who had slipped into other women's beds when they were married in previous lives, and so her emotions were no longer his to tug at.

"Bryn—"

Declan stopped when Bryn held up a hand, her stare blazing as she waited for him to turn around. With a huff, he finally did so she could leave the water and get dressed. She knew better than to expect him to leave, not with Kian somewhere nearby, Bryn having lost sight of where he went with Declan's ridiculous behavior distracting her.

Stepping onto the beach where sand met the stones, her fingers pruned from the time spent lazing about in the water, she noticed at some point Niamh had replaced her worn, torn and bloody clothes with a dark green shirt and a pair of blue jeans. A dark blue coat, white underwear and a bra, and sturdy leather boots were laid out next to the shirt and pants.

Declan was silent as she toweled off with a small, ragged towel near her clothes and got dressed.

Bryn didn't wonder for once what he was thinking. In fact, she really would rather not have a conversation with him at all. He'd abandoned them the moment they'd arrived, and she was trying to control the temper the Morrigan had so graciously bestowed upon her.

"I'm done," she said, ignoring Declan spinning around as she stood up from tying her boots. The leather was worn in, but comfortable and she was incredibly grateful to Niamh. "About your uncle—"

"Is it him?" Declan cut off her words as he moved toward her. Stepping away, Bryn danced out of reach when his hand went to grab hers.

"Him who?" she asked, not making eye contact, as she pulled on the coat that held Niamh's perfume, sending out a silent thank you to her friend for bringing her fresh clothing. A rustle of leaves nearby and a flash of silver told her Kian had honored her request but wasn't far away should she need him.

"Who?" Declan laughed. They both knew exactly who 'he,' was. "Are you serious right now? The fucking Fomorian you were eye-fu—"

"Kian." And his name sounded far too much like a whispered confession, one that Declan did not miss at all. "We have more important things—"

"Kian," Declan repeated, spitting the name out before he was standing far too close to her, grabbing her shoulders. "Maybe we were not wed in this lifetime, but I have memories of us as husband and wife. Hell, I should've been the one to save you, not him."

Yes, and drowned them both in the process since not one child of Ifreann could swim.

She pulled her shoulders back, but his hands tightened, and she narrowed her eyes. "Memories, Declan. Nothing like that has happened in *this* lifetime."

"You can't just undo centuries of a relationship." Declan pulled a hand away to rub a knuckle against her cheekbone, but she dodged his touch. "You loved me."

"I did," she couldn't deny that the Morrigan had loved him, in her own way, but it didn't feel like what she imagined love to be. "But my love for you died with her."

His hands dropped at her confession and she stepped away, moving toward the edge of the forest, shivering from both the cold and the confrontation.

"My love didn't die."

Bryn stopped, dropping her hands to her sides as she processed Declan's words. Slowly, Bryn felt the Morrigan and all her pain roll through her psyche. Silver eyes burned into her thoughts as she spoke the words she hadn't felt free to speak until that moment. "You thought you loved her ... me. Love doesn't mean you own that person, and it damn sure doesn't mean you discard them in order to find pleasure with another. Live in this life, Declan. I plan to."

Without looking back, she spoke to him over her shoulder as she started toward the tree line.

"We leave at first light tomorrow since we need to make sure we get to Cethin soon. We can stop back through—"

She turned to find Declan gone, most likely not having heard a word she said. Yes, he may think he loved her, but he didn't respect her.

Her mind went back to the look Kian had given her in the pool. A look that was more than Declan or Dagda had ever given her in the entirety of their lives together. It wasn't a look of if she or he was worthy of one another, but of understanding. Of caring, regardless of what was or wasn't happening in the world around them.

It was the first time someone had looked at her that way, as if not sizing her up at all, but already *seeing* her for what she is. The weariness of letting others dictate her value settled heavily on Bryn, and she was done with it.

Everyone, especially Declan, could accept who she was now, or they could find themselves without her in their lives.

Chapter 7

The pathway from the sad-looking shacks Bryn temporarily called home was dimly lit by flickering torches casting dancing shadows along the trees. A gentle breeze, redolent with wood smoke, pine, and the damp earth of the forest floor, stirred in the air as she made her way along the long winding path through the forest.

Once the path opened, a breathtaking sight unfolded. Treehouses, built into the ancient oaks, peeked out from the forest surrounding three large, circular buildings. Warm brown thatched roofs, homes crafted from the same dark wood, contrasted against the vibrant green canopy. Creaking wooden walkways, their timbers grayed and weathered by time, linked all the homes. Those walkways connected to large platforms with spiraling stairs made of aged, dark wood, leading the way to the forest floor.

It seemed as if they built these structures conspicuously, aiming for integration with nature. Yet, their excessive detail, with intricate carvings and spots of bright colors, clashed with the simplicity of the forest.

Beneath the trees, near the largest of the circular buildings, a lively party was in full swing, with music, laughter, and the smell of grilling food filling the air. It was unlike any gathering Bryn had been a part of in Ifreann. The experience was utterly alien, a symphony of unfamiliar sights and sounds.

Where Ifreann had music and dancing, any alcohol was under the radar and only through certain channels, also known as Declan and Niamh. No, the peaceful, candlelit celebrations of Ifreann couldn't compare to the riotous sounds and furious energy erupting before Bryn and her friends.

It was too much, and Bryn's muscles all tensed, her mind vigilant, as she slowly made her way to where the guards stood along the exterior of the village, allowing them to enter the party with a nod as they kept a lookout. Justin and Kessler stepped out from the woods, making their way to her. Sage and Jace came around from the other side where they had been waiting.

Kian was nowhere to be found since their incident at the waterfall, and perhaps that was for the best. Bryn wasn't sure how to address any of what had happened.

Bryn felt a slight heaviness as she stepped into the clearing where the tree house village stood, almost as if gravity had become slightly stronger. The Morrigan seemed to have gone quiet, so Bryn didn't think she was in immediate danger, but she knew to remain vigilant. Years of hiding and watching her back in Ifreann had taught her safety was an illusion.

"And here are our guests from the land beyond!" boomed a loud male voice before the uproar of voices drowned him out again.

Declan's uncle lumbered toward them. His barrel chest, now shirtless, was splashed with blue paint, mimicking Bryn and Kian's tattoos. Despite the growing chill of the night, the large man seemed unfazed. Bryn could see how his joyous energy would liven the surrounding party, but Bryn had her guard up, and all her instincts went on high alert when she met his eyes.

Cold and unnervingly intense, his gaze gave her a queasy feeling in the pit of her stomach. Bryn stepped in front of her friends as she lifted her chin, the hairs on the back of her neck rising, but she held his gaze as he walked toward her.

"I've been a horrible host." He waved them toward the crowd of people milling about a cauldron, dipping chalices that filled, and overflowed, with an amber liquid. "My name is Cormac, and this is my clan."

Looking over her shoulder at her friends, Bryn swallowed down her concerns and allowed Cormac to guide her them the party. The towering figure of Cormac beside her made Bryn feel like a small child, overwhelmed by his presence. He had to be well over Declan's six-foot five-inch height since obviously they made mountains in this family. Bryn had never been so happy that she was not the poor woman expected to bear children for Declan.

Several people stepped aside for Cormac as her and her group followed, clearing a path to Declan at the foot of the stairs that led up to the largest circular structure. A small group of women swarmed Declan, their hands reaching for him as they giggled and jostled. While he didn't resist their advances, she noticed his eyes were almost vacant. She found it unsettling to see him without the usual intensity burning in his gaze. With a curt nod, Declan acknowledged them, his stare cold and body tense as his uncle clapped him on the shoulder.

"I'll let you catch up with my nephew here. Please, enjoy yourselves this evening and come find me if you need anything."

Bryn did not miss the proprietary tone in Cormac's words before he walked off in the torchlight to refill his drink.

Bryn rolled her eyes and then looked at Declan. "I will leave you to your evening activities."

Turning away from the scene, she moved to the edge of the party. Bryn did not have the energy for anyone's drama. Keeping away from the center of the festivities, she watched the party unfold once again. Maybe she could control her visions to a point, but she couldn't guarantee she wouldn't have a seizure if someone touched her without Cyerra, who was spying for Bryn, there to anchor her powers of premonition.

Justin handed her a cup of spirits as he moved to stand next to her, taking in the party with narrowed eyes. Bryn moved her focus along where he was looking and noticed Declan was right in Justin's line of sight. "You know, I was enough of an idiot to think he would count himself lucky to have you that he would never even look at another woman."

Raising her glass toward Declan at her friend's words, an action Declan missed as he spoke to one of the women, she took a sip before turning back to Justin. She could almost feel his need to right what was wrong, her friend who thrived on justice and balance, but there was nothing Justin could do. "I was naïve."

"We all were. It took battle and hellfire to make us leave the place we've known since we could remember much of anything at all. Now all our eyes are open and we're not sure where to look or how to process what we see."

Bryn held his gaze. "You mean to process who we were and are supposed to be?"

Closing his eyes, he sighed. "We are still the same people, but gods, it doesn't feel like it some nights. Everything in Ifreann was black and white, good and bad." Justin held his hands up as if weighing the words with them. "Now, I feel it all on a deeper level. I feel ... a deep anger at injustice and the urge to see evil punished with such an intensity that feels..."

"Like it will consume us?"

Justin froze, holding her gaze before nodding. "If it hasn't already."

Her words detonated in the silence. It was the first time she had acknowledged her battle with the wraiths, and herself, in Ifreann. That she had spoken of it to another person who had been there.

Unable to hold Justin's stare any longer, Bryn took a long drink before she could find the words as Justin shifted next to her, shoving his hands in his pants pockets. "I made choices out there that cost lives. Including my aunt." There, the words were out in the world, but the confession did nothing to help Bryn keep the darkness back.

She had been ready to step over the line to protect her friends, to protect Kian, but she hadn't thought of or acknowledged the blood on her hands that was her aunt's. Yes, her aunt had stabbed her first during a life-or-death struggle, a blur of fear and adrenaline. Yet, Bryn had struck, ending Jace's mother's life, and she couldn't make herself talk to Jace about it, having been circling around him since they left Ifreann.

"What choice did you have, Bryn?" Following the sound of Kian's voice, Justin's gaze shifted over her shoulder, a subtle frown furrowing his brow. Bryn turned to Kian, his silver eyes searching her face. "To do nothing? To wallow and not step into the role determined before your birth? And maybe it wasn't the Morrigan, but you, who was out there fighting for the people you loved, and even those who may not have deserved it."

Hearing it said in such a way made the grief even more real, and before she could stop herself, she handed off her glass to Justin and made her way back toward the shacks. Slipping carefully through the crowd of people who had closed in behind her, she made it to the forest where the temperature dipped without the crush of bodies and heat from the torches.

Her steps grew lighter the further she got from the center of Osgar as the Morrigan stirred within her mind, frustrated, but Bryn did not have the mental bandwidth to worry about what had made the goddess agitated.

Kian's words, the ones to absolve her, punched a hole in her chest, one she didn't understand, but her inner turmoil was volatile. She didn't want to act on the feeling only to find herself full of even more regret in the morning.

Bryn knew Kian was following her since the crunch of leaves under his boots betrayed his usually silent forest prowling.

As they neared the guard shacks at the tree line, he materialized at her side, his dark hair and shadows hiding his expression. He waited until they were out of sight, then pinned her against a tree, his arms caging her in.

"Believe me, I can see the toll Ifreann is taking on you. The dark circles under your eyes, the way your shoulders slump, the haunted look when you think no one is looking ... you're crumbling from the inside out, and you're trying to hide it." His eyes held hers, his breath a whisper against her lips. Kian's presence enveloped her, and she was fully absorbed. It would be so easy to move slightly, to put her mouth to his.

Her posture went rigid as she pushed that thought away and narrowed her eyes at him. "The Morrigan wouldn't care about saving the people of Ifreann. I know, because I have all her memories."

"No," Kian shook his head. "She wouldn't."

He moved a stray curl behind her ear, and Bryn felt the weight of unspoken words, her gaze lost in the swirling silver of his eyes.

"I am the Morrigan," she breathed, her voice a fragile thing. Kian nodded curtly, his eyes lingering on her lips before he pulled his arms back, but he didn't step away.

"And yet, you are more." His eyes flicked to the path leading back to the center of the party. "It doesn't mean you will repeat the same mistakes. The Morrigan never knew what it meant to be human."

An intense blaze rolled through her blood at his words. "Be the Morrigan! Be yourself! It can't go both ways!"

Unfazed by her outburst, Kian crossed his arms, leaning back against another tree as she stomped away before turning back. "Already you are more than the Morrigan."

Snapping her attention to him, she mirrored his stance, though her crossed arms were more so armor to protect herself from this man whose opinions she actually cared about. "How so? I am just a walking body for a deity!"

Kian snorted, only helping to grow her ire. "Would an example help, perhaps?" He smiled as he straightened. "The Morrigan dealt with the same behavior when she was with the Dagda. It's like watching history repeat itself except this time you're not running back into his arms or fighting the women as if those women were anymore guilty than Dagda."

Her shoulders fell, the tension lessening as he spoke the truth. That particular pattern was one she was dedicated to breaking.

"Wow, I was a mess, huh?" She looked up at him, her gaze catching the subtle upward curve of Kian's lips as she spoke.

"Of the worst kind," Kian joked, shaking out his arms, and she knew he was about to shift. While she wanted to speak longer with him, she knew it was best not to do so when her emotions were so unstable. "Think about it, Bryn. That means not every chain is unbreakable."

A silver mist swirled around him before Kian shifted to his wolf form and ran into the dense brush lining the trails.

She wondered, in the quiet of her heart, why their bond had never transcended the battlefield into more than a friendship forged in the call of duty. Yes, he was a formidable soldier, his strength and skill were undeniable, but the Morrigan only saw him as a tool. Though she confided in Kian about some things, his and Danu's accounts made it clear—even to a casual observer—that the Morrigan was exceptionally secretive. Even Bryn was not privy to all the secrets of the goddess, no matter that she held most of her memories.

Bryn couldn't understand why the goddess kept herself so emotionally distant from those around her. People who trusted her and thought her magical because of the very things Bryn was ostracized for.

Such the opposite of Bryn's experience in this life so far.

The sharp crack of a branch snapping underfoot had Bryn pushing herself off the large tree she'd been leaning against, her heart pounding as she ducked behind its sturdy trunk. She wasn't used to the sounds of the forest yet, but she knew enough to know footsteps through dried leaves.

"...the new ones ... will they be an issue?" A male voice she didn't recognize spoke quietly as he moved through the dense underbrush, staying well off the path. Circling the large tree, Bryn anticipated their approach from the right, expecting them to emerge on her left.

"The timing is not great..." answered a deep feminine voice, their footsteps loud in the underbrush, not concerned anyone would be around. Perhaps they assumed everyone was at the party as they kept watch.

The gnawing anxiety that settled in her stomach hadn't lessened one bit since they arrived. It'd only grown, something deep in her marrow telling her they were not safe here. And her fear of the unknown, an environment so different from her own, was not the sole reason.

Declan's uncle Cormac had to be hiding something, and her power of premonition was screaming at her to be wary.

"...what can we do?"

"We hold until they leave." They were heading away from Bryn, but they stopped to look around, and she moved back behind the large tree to cover herself.

"They are staying at the edge, so they will not be privy to any information. The blacksmith said they were moving on to Cethin, so we wait them out before we move forward. The king will not hold forever."

Bryn's hands quickly went over her mouth to cover a gasp before she gave away her position.

They changed the subject to weapons practice, the rhythmic crunch of their boots on the narrow, leaf-strewn forest path a counterpoint to Bryn's racing thoughts about their altered plans and the shift in her group's dynamics. Their voices faded as they moved away, but her heart thundered in the silence they left behind.

Silver flashed in her peripheral and she knew Kian was nearby, most likely following the conversation and gathering intel.

A premonition, sharp and cold, warned her that Declan's uncle was only the tip of the iceberg. Below the surface of the still waters, something far more significant was brewing.

Chapter 8

The soft thud of footsteps on the little wooden porch outside Bryn's cabin stirred her from a light sleep where she'd been waiting on the rest of her friends to come back from the party. Bryn propped herself up on her elbow, shoving her unruly curls out of her face as a low growl and the thud of something large sounded from just beyond her flimsy wooden door.

A snap of teeth answered Declan's deep, "Fuck off, dog." Another, much louder, bang followed another thump.

The old wooden floor creaked and nearly gave way beneath her as she scrambled to her feet and made the two quick steps to the door of the tiny shack. Throwing it open, Bryn faced off with a very drunken Declan and a wolfed-out Kian snarling at him from the bottom steps of the porch.

She was never more thankful that Kian had shown up in his wolf form after his patrol, just as he did when they camped, and refused to leave the front step. It meant she would not have to deal with a drunken Declan alone.

"It's late, Declan." She folded her arms as she stared up at the man who had caused no small amount of emotional turmoil in her life.

"We need to talk," he grumbled, moving past her into the tiny cabin that shrunk in his presence.

Kian snapped at the back of Declan's pant leg in warning, his teeth just missing the denim, a low growl rumbling in his chest. Declan, without a second thought, tried to close the door on Kian, but the silver wolf slipped inside before he was shut out.

Declan crowded her, suffocating her with his size in such a small space. The scent of alcohol and medicinal herb radiated off Declan's skin, masking his natural scent.

Panic seized her, tightening her chest as she leaned against the door. With her hand hovering over the knob, she took several deep breaths before she pushed it open, falling out onto the porch. The cold air nipped at Bryn's skin as she inhaled deeply, her heart slowing with the sense of openness the porch offered, a vast improvement over the confining space within. Both men followed her out, Kian staying in his wolf form, his nails clicking on the old wood.

Bryn motioned for Declan to speak as she wrapped her arms around herself, Kian leaning against her and lending her his warmth.

Opening his mouth, Declan stumbled, grabbing hold of the porch post before shaking his head. Bryn reached out to steady him and colors twisted around him, lasting only a few seconds, if even that. But they merged until Arioch was standing before her. No, not her, she was seeing through Declan's eyes. An orb of black in Arioch's hand, a gleam in his eyes before he held the orb like a ball and slammed it into her chest. No, Declan's chest.

"I'm staying here, Bryn." Declan broke into the vision, and Bryn looked between the man and wolf, neither of them noticing she'd been in a vision. Then, Declan's words penetrated her thoughts, and she froze, her vision placed on the back burner as she worked out exactly what Declan meant. Bryn missed the silver mist lifting in her peripheral as her mouth gaped like a fish.

It seemed Kian did not suffer the same affliction. "You damn coward. You know the Tuatha Dé Danann needs to stay together if they have even half a chance at stopping the king!" Kian's eyes burned like molten silver.

Declan threw his hands up. "I know that! We also need an army." His eyes held Bryn's gaze. "We cannot do this without reinforcements, and you damn well know it."

Kian snorted and pointed to where the trees led to Osgar. "You're a fool if you believe anyone on the other side of those trees will stick their neck out for anyone but themselves."

Declan's expression turned hostile, his gaze narrowing at Kian's words. "What is that supposed to mean, dog?"

The air crackled with tension, igniting something in Bryn with Kian's next words. "It means that they are not sitting pretty in the middle of a forest because they want to see other people free. The guards freely walk around talking about working with King Bres while on patrol, so why would they help those stuck under the rule of that very king?. Why would the closest towns be annihilated by Bres, and yet Osgar remains unscathed?"

Kian was right, and though Declan fumed, Bryn knew the truth in those words from what she had overheard and her foresight that had been screaming since they first stepped foot in Osgar. These people hid away in the forest, aware enough to know there were others out there in peril, but not stepping in to do anything.

"How many people reside here?" Bryn asked, turning back to Declan. "Two hundred? Three? There were enough people to help Tanwen before it was destroyed."

Shaking his head, Declan shoved his hands in his pants pockets before looking up at her cobwebbed porch ceiling.

Swallowing, his Adam's apple bobbing, before he laughed, shaking his head again. "Nothing—" his head dropped to look at her "—and no one could have handled those wraiths outside of us."

"And yet you'd split the group up." Kian stepped up next to her, and she could feel his bare skin brush against her arm.

Not the time. Not. The. Damn. Time. Bryn.

Keeping her eyes off Kian, and his lack of clothing, she folded her arms as she addressed Declan. "We are supposed to be leaders. Both of us, Declan."

Declan threw his head back and laughed. "Oh, now she wants to be partners."

Kian growled, stepping forward, but Bryn put her hand up to stop him. "We can be co-leaders without being lovers."

"Hard to do either with that dog following you like a lost little puppy in love everywhere," Declan seethed. "I am sure he can help you lead the group just fine in my absence." Like a petulant child who did not get their way, Declan spun and stomped off, leaving Bryn and Kian to watch in silence as he disappeared down the torch lit path toward Osgar.

Looking up, the leaves were brightening, the sun already rising. "After breakfast, I'll talk with the group and we can put it to a vote. He stays and we come back to get him with an army at our backs ... or..." Bryn rubbed her hands over her face. The part of herself that warned her of change was rising to the surface, and now she knew why. Declan was walking another path entirely. "We need to agree as one. If the rest of the group feels like we need to stick together, then we stick together. We are not individuals anymore and our decisions affect other people. Hell, they affect the *world* now. We have to make them for the good of all, not just one."

Sighing, Bryn spun, moving back into the shack before she fell back on the cot. The spring squealed at her sudden weight as she threw her hands over her face.

"You could have ordered him to stay," Kian said from the doorway, not crossing the threshold.

"And what good would that do but sow animosity?" she grumbled against her palms before dropping them to her sides. Her eyes moved to Kian, forgetting for a moment he was naked until she caught the cut of his collarbones.

"And for the love of the goddess herself, get dressed Kian!"

A hearty laugh left his plush lips, hypnotizing her before she shook her thoughts loose.

"Sure, I'll get dressed, but we all know you'd rather I not." He winked before a silver mist flowed through the room, a wolf now in his place.

Bryn swallowed down her response for the sake of self-preservation.

Pulling on the oddly comforting jacket Niamh had fashioned from mismatched fabrics and a surprisingly soft fur Sage had donated, Bryn shook out her hands and emerged from the cabin. Her boots crunched on the frozen blades of grass as she stepped off the porch, her breath misting in the air with each step as she walked toward where Justin was talking to Declan.

From the fierce expression on Justin's face, Declan was sharing the good news. That thought was confirmed when Justin's piercing blue eyes slammed into her as she walked up. His fists clenched at his sides. "I suppose you ran this past Bryn as well, Declan?"

"And Kian," Bryn interrupted before Declan could answer. "It went over about as well as I assume this conversation is."

Running his hand through his unbound auburn hair, Declan let out a low, guttural growl of annoyance. "What the hell am I supposed to do? This is a family I didn't even know I had!"

Those words penetrated Bryn's chaotic whirlwind of thoughts that had been colliding with each other ever since Declan had told her.

Was she not doing the exact same thing? Searching for the family she didn't know she had? How could she begrudge Declan this, and yet how could she delay getting to her mother's people if they had a way of defeating the king?

With her eyes closed, she turned toward the trees, feeling the soft caress of a gentle breeze against her skin as she worked it out. "I understand, Declan."

"Bryn, we need to be a unit—"

Holding her hand up to stop Justin's words, she opened her eyes and turned to look into the familiar whiskey gaze she'd known for most of her life. Both in friendship and passion.

"Justin and Kian are right. Danu told us that only together can the Tuatha Dé Danann defeat the king, but we also cannot do it alone. We need to get to Cethin as soon as we can, so we have that army. I won't tell you what to do, Declan—"

"You cannot be serious," Justin interrupted, and Bryn could understand his justified anger. She'd had the same reaction to those very words.

"But—" Bryn turned to fully face Declan. "—I will be honest, I don't trust your uncle." Holding Declan's gaze, she continued. "At all. But I also won't make the decision for you when it comes to family. You need to think really hard about this and decide for yourself. You can tell the rest at breakfast and we can go from there."

A spark of fear, sharp as shattered glass, showed in Declan's eyes before he swallowed, giving a curt nod. Without another word, he left. The scent of wood smoke and smoked meat carried on the breeze from the direction he was heading, toward the heart of Osgar.

"You sure about this?" Justin asked once Declan was out of earshot. Finian jumped from the dense forest brush next to them with a rabbit in his mouth. Bryn grimaced but shook her head as she ignored the excited hound and his breakfast.

"At this point, I feel like every step I take, I'm off kilter. I'm just going with my gut on this one."

Her gut. Her intuition. Her magic gift of foresight.

Whatever it was, she hoped it wasn't leading them all to defeat.

Chapter 9

Sage, Caden, Kessler, and Jace had already made their way to the dining hall, one of the circular buildings in the center of the open area of Osgar. Windows built into the walls gave the room plenty of natural light, giving it the feel of eating outside. Dark green vines grew along the walls, blurring the line between nature and architecture.

It took a bit longer than she would have liked, but Bryn managed to gather her wits enough to face them. Once she made it to the hall, right away she noticed that Declan was absent. As frustrated as that made her, she could almost hear Justin's teeth grinding next to her. "He probably wants us to handle it for him. Just like his dad did anytime he had an issue back in Ifreann."

Bryn turned to Justin, her eyebrow cocked. "Not in Ifreann anymore, are we?"

With a subtle lift of his lips, his hand went to her lower back as he guided them to their small group, positioned as far from the boisterous Osgarians as possible. Settled at a small rectangular wooden table covered in white cloth, Sage looked up with a small smile, one that did not meet her eyes.

"Making friends?" Justin chuckled as he and Bryn seated themselves across from Sage and Jace at the table, Kessler on the end.

A small woman, her short blond hair a bright halo in the morning light, placed two plates of steaming, delicious-smelling breakfast before her and Justin, her thin limbs a whirlwind as she spun and dashed back through the door, the sound of her footsteps fading quickly.

"Nope," Kessler murmured before stabbing at a slice of meat on his plate. "That little lady was the only one to come out and interact with us at all when we first got here. Didn't say a word and kept her eyes down when she shoved the plates in front of us."

Sage pushed her eggs and beans around on her plate before she spoke up. "The feeling of us being unwanted has been with me since we've arrived. Even at the party last night, they kept their distance."

"For the best. I don't think I trust any of them," Bryn replied.

From there, silence hung heavy in the air, broken only by the clinking of silverware. Bryn really took in her friends, tension radiating from the stiff shoulders and a death grip on their utensils. They were as unsettled as she was. And it would get a lot worse when Declan hit them with his news. *If* he did.

When she looked up, Justin met her gaze, his expression somber, and offered a slight, mournful shake of his head. They both knew Declan wasn't going to show up, and it was becoming quite clear the rest of the group wanted to leave as much as Bryn did.

Sighing, Bryn placed her spoon down on the table before running her hands over her face. Leadership was never something Bryn had envisioned for herself. The effort of standing tall after a lifetime spent cowering, hiding, and passively waiting felt monumental, each step forward a battle won against ingrained habits of fear and deference.

But she had the memories of a formidable goddess who had no issue stepping up when it counted. A goddess who was a part of her, always lurking in the background even when Bryn couldn't feel her. So, when Bryn tugged at the confidence of the Morrigan and, surprisingly, found her hands empty, she remembered a phrase from one of Sage's books. Something about faking it until one made it. Bryn could do that.

"We will leave tomorrow morning at first light."

Relieved nods greeted her statement, and Bryn felt a tightness in her chest loosen just a fraction at the quick acceptance of her order.

"On foot?" Kessler asked. "I can grab my stuff and have it ready to go right after we eat."

Bryn bit her lip, working through how to explain the new predicament Declan left them in. Thankfully, Kessler gave her an opening.

Kessler made to stand up, taking his now empty plate. "I will go let Declan know while y'all figure out the details."

Damn it. Bryn felt a burning rage ignite in her chest, its heat spreading through her body like wildfire, that she would be the one to have to handle this. It surprised her the Morrigan did not feel the same since she remained quiet within Bryn.

"Wait," Bryn ordered, stopping Kessler mid-stride, and he turned to meet her eyes. Had he always been so huge? He had, she knew that. Standing, trying to be on somewhat even ground, she looked at Justin as she pushed her chair in. Justin gave her a small nod of confidence, but said nothing.

So, he would be no help. Giving Justin a sharp look she hoped instilled just a tiny bit of fear; his small smile telling her that no, she was not intimidating him at all, she faced Kessler.

"Declan came to me last night saying that he wanted to stay. I told him it was his choice and to let us know in the morning. By his absence, it seems Declan has decided to stay here."

Bryn's statement was met with disbelieving stares and a colorful curse from Kessler as he settled back into his chair.

"Each of you can ask Declan why, in fact, each of you should. One at a time, and demanding a thorough explanation, but we will move on and come back this way after we return from Cethin, and hopefully, made allies of them."

She sensed a shared, unspoken urgency in their expressions, each silently plotting their strategy to confront Declan.

"How close do you think we are to Cethin?" Sage asked as she lay her fork carefully on her plate before straightening her flowery blouse and pushed a dark curl back from her face.

Silence met her question. Bryn couldn't guess where they were relative to Cethin, since she had thought Osgar was Cethin.

"Maybe Manannán would know," Bryn said.

That would mean she would have to go across the veil, something she'd purposely avoided doing since so many souls were lost in Ifreann. It terrified her to think of who might be waiting there for her on the other side and if they were nearly as angry as Caden.

But that was where Manannán was and he was the only one who, outside of Danu, might have an idea of where to find the other places in the world after the globe fell to epic natural disasters.

Taking a deep breath, Bryn looked at the now very unappetizing food as she planned how she would cross the veil to ask the necessary questions. She could only hope there wouldn't be a welcome party of angry spirits there when she did.

"I haven't done this since Ifreann." Bryn settled on the edge of her cot, a nervous tremor running through her as her leg bounced, the rhythmic creak of the bed a soundtrack to her rising anxiety.

Kian was in his human form, leaning against the door frame, his lean figure clad in the same black slacks and a black button up he had worn in Ifreann. A single, small window in the shack cast a pale light on Kian, highlighting the stark contrast between his pale skin and the deep blue of his tattoos, his tousled black hair and clothes seeming to absorb the light. That coupled with his devilish smirk, made him look like a delicious sin, leaving her breathless and wanting more.

Choosing not to allow her hormones to take her down that road, Bryn held onto the edge of the bed, taking a deep breath. Cyerra was missing in action, and she needed an anchor, so Kian was up. It was best not to make it weird when he might be the only one who could pull her back into their world when she crossed into Faerie alone.

"It'll do no good to be in this pathetic excuse for a cabin. I can barely stand you sleeping in here, thinking it'll fall down around you. Come on," Kian held his hand out, and Bryn slowly placed hers into it. With a quick squeeze and a small, sincere smile, he pulled her out the door and into the fragrant, earthy-smelling forest.

He held branches back as they moved through an area full of wild growth, one not trodden down by mortal feet. Kian stopped at a small clearing beside a giant, old, gnarled oak tree.

"Boots off," he ordered before he lowered himself to sit leaning against the tree.

Raising her eyebrows, she did as she was told, and the moment her second boot hit the ground, his hand took hers and pulled her down between his legs. A smoky shadow that felt almost tangible spun her around, a surprise matched only by finding herself seated with her back pressed against his chest.

Shock stole her breath as his arms went around her, his hands on her bent knees. Did he not feel the same thing she did? He seemed so comfortable holding her like this when Bryn felt like she might melt down to a puddle. Even in the deepest passion with Declan, she'd never felt this overwhelming warmth, a heat spreading from the back of her neck to her core.

"Put your feet into the grass until you feel the soil against your skin."

Trying to ignore her thundering heart, she pushed her toes into the soft grass, the dew from the sun melting the frost on each blade. Her body was highly aware of each movement he made as he settled her closer to him, and she tried not to panic when he pulled her forehead back to rest her head against his chest.

"Trust me, mo ghrá," he whispered against her as his arms wrapped around her middle, clasping and closing her in as her heart thundered in her chest. Mo ghrá? Bryn tried not to over think how the words came across as a term of endearment and what he meant by it. Shifting herself as she ran the question through her mind, he tightened his hold.

"None of that. Ignore I'm here," he said as he allowed her to finish settling against him and she rolled her eyes. He had to know what he was doing, and if not, then the fact her skin was hot to the touch from both embarrassment and arousal should clue him in. Any hotter and she felt like she'd melt the buttons from his shirt. "Close your eyes and think of how you crossed the veil before."

With a huff, Bryn closed her eyes, remembering the door she envisioned in Ifreann that she could use to open the veil and walk into Faerie, but it was difficult to focus with Kian all around her. When his scent enveloped her, frost, pine, and campfire, filling her lungs with every breath she took. His legs tightened their hold around her, anchoring her, and she pushed through her body's response to his nearness. Silver ropes of light pulsed in her mind's eye, something she never seen before, but they wrapped around her arms and she could sense the veil just behind the mist accumulating in front of her. The veil thrummed with power from beyond and she let her soul be pulled across.

There was no door this time. No, when Bryn opened her eyes, she was sitting against a tree facing the cemetery from her many visits to Faerie. Senan, the black war horse that came when she called for help in Ifreann, nipped at her hair. A curious wolf pup sniffed her boot before scuttling away at Senan's stomp.

"It's becoming easier for you to slip between realms. I almost didn't realize you were here." Manannán held his hand out to her.

His silver hair fell forward as he helped her up. His black eyes crinkled to match the pleasant smile on the guardian's face. His shadow cloak shifted slightly, despite his stillness. The intricate tattoos on his neck running up to his ear glowed faintly, pulsing like a heartbeat.

"Ah." He smiled. "I can sense now you had help. Well, that works wonderfully until you master it on your own. No chance of you being lost with the silver strings."

"The what?" she asked and caught herself before she stepped on the tail of a small, curious wolf pup. Its mother moved between her and Manannán, nipping the tiny creature in reprimand. "A pup?"

"Faerie is a world all its own, Bryn, just as the mortal realm is." Turning to her, he tilted his head, reminding her of Mr. Rafferty, his alter ego in the mortal plane. "But that is not why you crossed the veil to see me, is it? I can feel your hesitation to even be here."

Taking a deep and fortifying breath, wondering if Danu were nearby to hear her, she prepared to speak on behalf of the group. She had to remember to be assertive, not back down, and gather the answers they needed in order to move forward.

"The group is splitting up—" her voice wavered as Manannán straightened to his full height, his eyes flashing monochromatic colors, and his entire body going preternaturally still.

Jaw clenched, he nodded curtly, the silence punctuated only by the frantic thumping of her heart. She continued, trepidation battling with a simmering anger, his attempt at intimidation a thin veil over the fact that she was not completely in control here.

Shoving her shoulders back, she met him on even ground, her body mimicking his.

"Declan has decided to stay with his uncle in Osgar—"

Bryn ignored Manannán's growl as she carried on, the fire deep in her soul catching oxygen as she felt herself step into the role of spokeswoman for the group, determined not to let him hold her from her mission here, even though she doubted that was his intention.

"We are planning to meet back up with him once we have traveled to Cethin." Seeing Manannán opening his mouth, feeling in her gut it was to argue, she pushed through. "We need armies, Manannán, to defeat the king. Our group cannot possibly battle the wraiths and him at the same time."

He closed his mouth and dropped his arms as he processed her words.

"You have an army, Bryn. One that is indeed in Cethin waiting for you, even if none of you know it yet. Do you really need to take the chance that something could happen to one of you should you split up? We brought you together to avoid this very thing in the first place."

"Did we ever have our power in our other lives? Or were we completely mortal when the king found us? Look around!" She waved to the worn cemetery being overtaken by the forest of Faerie and the crumbling castles in the distance. "The entirety of the Fae population depends on us. Two whole worlds do, and you know at some point, you will have to trust us to make the right decisions in this war."

With each word, her belief solidified, a comforting certainty settling over her, a shield against future doubts.

The biggest clue she was making the right decision was now that she felt the Morrigan again, the goddess was settled.

With the fragmented castles in his sights, their weathered battlements silhouetted against the fading light, Manannán sighed, a heavy sound like the wind through broken stone.

"You're right. We need to trust the Tuatha Dé Danann as we had before." Looking back at her, he gave a small nod. "I trust you in this and shall follow your lead."

A small nervous smile played on her lips as she braced herself, the weight of her next words settling upon her. Bryn probably should have led with a different question.

"Great. Do you happen to know how to get to Cethin then?"

Manannán's slowly returning smile dropped as he raised an eyebrow. Shaking his head, his long silver hair flowed over his shoulders like silk, and his laughter, a melodic sound, filled the air.

"Continue east, following the Beira Sea. As the world grows colder, you will find yourself in Cethin. You must cross the Artair Channel, but if you meet the right people along the way, that will not be a problem."

All the new people Bryn had met so far had been nothing but problems, but she kept that to herself.

She took a step back, the soft sound of her own breath filling the quiet space as she closed her eyes and released her hold on Faerie.

When her eyes fluttered open, she found herself leaning back against the tree instead of Kian. The big silver fluffy wolf butt in front of her was alarming, but not so much as the men holding crossbows aimed directly at her.

"Get up," one growled, receiving a throaty warning in reply from the wolf in front of her. As she stood, Kian backed against her, almost pushing her into the tree.

Shoving her hand into the ruff at the back of his neck, his hair standing straight up, she tried to soothe him, ignoring the men with the bows. She'd come back, unless they beheaded her, but she wasn't sure that he would.

"That wolf is not normal. Thing is too big to be real." One man held his arrow nocked and ready to be released on Kian as he spoke, his voice wavering. The other placed a shaky finger on the trigger of his crossbow.

The two men watched her intently as she stepped forward, but no one shot her. She took that as a win. Holding her hands up, she slipped in front of Kian, earning a nip at her elbow that she ignored.

"Please explain why I have arrows aimed at me while I was simply resting in the forest?"

The men laughed which was not at all a calming response. "Resting in a freezing forest with shoes off and a giant unnatural wolf wrapped around you?" said one.

They must have not seen Kian change form, which was a boon because she was sure that, had he done so in front of them, he would be full of arrows.

"I'm eccentric."

"No, you have the makings of a witch and that is something we do not take lightly in Osgar."

The rumbling growl was not from Kian this time. Red and black flashed across her vision, and she shut her eyes before the men saw the change in her. The last thing she needed was for them to catch her Morrigan side coming to the surface. Running her hands over her ears, she released a sigh of relief to feel them round and not tapered.

"I really despise when people use that word in a negative context and you will never do so again in front of me. Ever." Her anger was rising, and fast, so this needed to end now. "I need to speak to Cormac." She opened her eyes, hoping they were human again. "Now."

The men looked to each other before nodding. "Then move it." Waving his crossbow, he pointed toward where they would enter the center of the village. "Don't think of trying anything cute."

Kian huffed, his hair laying back against him. He hadn't dropped his alertness completely, but he wasn't on the edge of tearing throats out either.

"Then lead the way and let's get this over with." She waved her hands for them to take the lead, but they didn't budge.

"You first. We don't trust the likes of you."

That was when the wind picked up, and she caught the slightest scent of fear from the men. Two scared and possibly trigger-happy men at her back sounded like a recipe for disaster, but she failed to see any other choice.

Motioning Kian to go in front of her, she could see the anger in those silver eyes, but he did as she asked. She followed closely behind as they made their way through the woods, the men whispering behind her, thinking she could not hear them.

It was the standard insults she'd heard from Ifreann most of her life, but they hardly penetrated now that they could no longer find the mark in her soft underbelly.

Like she had told Manannán, strangers seemed to always lead to trouble.

Chapter 10

Sunlight streamed into the clearing as the trees opened and Bryn found herself shoved forward toward the imposing tree house that was Cormac's home, the heaviness of her surroundings weighing on her.

"Whoa, what's going on?" Justin jogged up to them, his eyes on full alert as they moved between the men and Bryn, his hand falling to the pistol at his side. Jace, Sage, and Caden were with a few of the people who prepped the meals, watching the show that was Bryn and Kian being marched across Osgar like criminals, concern plain on their faces. When Sage stepped forward, a crossbow was aimed her direction, Jace moving to stand in front of her, his arm out and brows furrowed with worry.

"I made some new friends," Bryn responded, gripping the smooth, cool wood of the railing as she climbed the wide, curved, and creaking wooden steps to the imposing building. Its larger size and central location made it clear that it was designed to reflect Cormac's natural inclination for power, overshadowing the rest of the community in both scale and significance.

"I thought we were welcome. Sure as hell doesn't look like it," Justin said to the guards, his eyebrow raised as he took in their stances and fingers oh so close to the trigger on those crossbows.

"I can't imagine what gave you the impression we're not,"—Bryn stared at the men holding their crossbows on her. — "when everyone has welcomed us with open arms since we got here."

Two guards stood impassively between her and the door, their presence a silent barrier to the room where she believed Cormac was waiting to make a show of it. Though they didn't raise their crossbows, they did have them ready to go should she make a move they didn't approve of. Bryn found herself surrounded on all sides.

"What business do you have here?" one of them asked, his voice stern and unbending.

"She demanded to see Cormac," one of the trigger-happy guys said as he motioned with his crossbow toward the door.

She was done with being pushed into corners. Her aunt, her religion, her town had all done that to her, and she was seeing now just how much Declan had put her in those situations as well. "Yeah, I need to speak to the boss." She seethed through her teeth. "At your master's leisure."

"Bryn, darlin', maybe don't make the men pointing weapons at us angrier." Justin said, but she wouldn't back down.

A silent exchange of glances passed between the men in front and those behind, before they turned to push open the heavy oak door. Kian nudged against her side, making it clear he would be going with her.

"Wolf stays outside," ordered one of the men who had been watching closely, his eyes and crossbow aimed on Kian. Bryn threw her hands up as she stepped in front of the arrow pointed directly at the wolf.

"Whoa! He won't make a problem, right?" Bryn looked down at Kian as she spoke. Their eyes met, and she saw the frustration in his gaze before he finally huffed and stepped aside.

"Then I'll be goin' with her," Justin stated with a finality that even the guards seemed to know better than to argue with. All but the one standing in the threshold.

"I will have a guard come and get you when Cormac has a moment to speak."

"Either shoot me or move," Bryn squared off with the guard, moving to stand toe to toe with him, close enough that he could not get the crossbow between them.

The sound of Cormac's hearty laugh reached Bryn's ears as she faced off with his guards.

"All in good fun!" No one else in their little standoff bothered to join Cormac in his mirth. "The guards here are great at their jobs but can be a little crass in their bedside manner. Stand down, boys."

Cormac hit her with a huge smile she could see Declan in. There were so many similarities in stature and facial expressions, coloring and features, but the moment Cormac touched her arm, every warning and alarm in her body went off.

He may be the uncle of Declan, but there was something sinister lurking just beneath the surface. That thought lingered as Cormac waved them through the giant wooden doors.

Bryn moved to take the door, letting Cormac go first, her hand going to Justin's elbow as she leaned into him. "Hold up, don't walk in front of him. We don't need the enemy at our back."

If the older male caught that, he didn't seem bothered by it.

Cormac continued on, and Justin's hands fell to his pistol, but not drawing the weapon. They both took in the building, noting more than the decor. Vines snaked between the rough-hewn logs of the undecorated walls, their green leaves a stark contrast to the bare wood. Not a lot of exit opportunities.

A young woman, barely out of her teens, came around the corner holding a stack of linens. It took Bryn a moment to recognize her as the same woman who had brought them their food at breakfast. Her blonde hair was messy, a few strands sticking to her freckled nose. Her brown eyes flicked to Bryn before she moved to the side of the wooden hall for them to pass her, keeping her eyes down. The linens clenched in her hands held to her chest as if shielding herself.

"Hello," Bryn greeted, her gaze locking with the woman's dark brown eyes, which reflected a quiet determination before she looked away from Bryn to the floor. There was something off in the woman's shy and anxious demeanor that hadn't been there at breakfast. Even as she tried to blend into the wall, there was steel in her spine.

"Girl! What are you doing standing there? Get on with those linens."

Cormac's harsh tone raised Bryn's hackles, and she found herself moving between Cormac and the girl on instinct. A shrill, accusatory tone laced with the bitter scent of resentment replaced Cormac's order in her mind. The sound of her aunt's anger, a prelude to Bryn's punishment.

Bryn felt the weight of countless lifetimes pressing down on her, each one etching lines of experience into her soul. The most recent one left the deepest scars.

"That's enough," Bryn growled, surprised it was her voice and not the Morrigan's, and even more surprised the Morrigan had dipped off again.

An almost maniacal look crossed Cormac's face before he slipped back into the easy going mask he seemed to wear so well.

Justin stepped up next to the girl, covering her other side from Cormac. "I can help with that, ma'am, if you'd tell me where you need them." Justin held out his hands to take the bundle, but the woman clutched it tighter against her chest and skirted around them.

As she moved away, the woman reached out, her fingers brushing along Bryn's elbow before words flowed through her mind like a river. It was not a vision, but something altogether different. A ripple, like dropping a stone into still water, spread through the world around Bryn as she committed the words to the deepest part of her memory. It was the original prophecy that Danu had referred to. Not the bite she'd given Bryn in Ifreann, but the whole of it, spoken into her mind by someone else. Someone familiar, but the voice was hard to place with the eeriness of the situation and the haziness of a memory.

> *Her power rises with gods and crows,*
> *a shadow army where darkness froze.*
> *The three will merge where death grows,*
> *or so the queen says the prophecy goes.*

"—doesn't speak to anyone here. Dumb as rocks some think." Cormac's voice broke Bryn out of her trance, seemingly unaware of what had just transpired, or he didn't care, as he started again toward the rooms at the back of the treehouse.

"I saw nothing but intelligence in those eyes," Justin said as he shot Bryn a look that made it clear he was aware Bryn had mentally checked out. "Sometimes silence speaks volumes about a person." Justin turned his eyes to Declan's uncle, keeping his gaze steady as they followed Cormac to a large room with a double door. Both doors showed scorched wood, with symbols crudely burned into the surface. Hands holding a half-moon, but there was something there beside the moon that had been etched out as if someone had taken a sharp instrument to remove it in a fairly violent fashion.

"Want to tell me what happened there when the woman touched you?" Justin leaned in to whisper, keeping quiet as Cormac shoved open the doors.

"Later." It was not something she was willing to bring up in the middle of a community full of unknowns.

Stopping at the door, Bryn turned to where the woman had slipped away but before she made her way down the wooden stairs, her brown eyes found Bryn. A flicker of familiarity sparked in Bryn's eyes as she recognized a kindred spirit in the woman's gaze. Steel forged in fire. There was no dismissing the pure intelligence there, along with an aura of secrets.

The gentle facade she'd presented to Cormac crumbled, revealing a woman of unexpected strength. Tilting her head, Bryn watched the woman mirror the action, a silent understanding passing between them as the woman straightened her petite shoulders, offering a subtle nod to Bryn before disappearing down the hall.

"Come on now, I don't have all day," Cormac broke her from her thoughts as Justin gave a small huff of annoyance. That huff turned into a growl of disgust as they stepped across the threshold into a room that smelled strongly of sex and alcohol. Declan's nudity, along with the presence of two naked women, left Bryn bewildered. Instead of the familiar plummeting sensation in her stomach upon catching him leaving a room in the brothel back home, she was oddly detached. Justin's grip on her elbow was firm, leaving her unsure if he was steadying her or detaining her, but it was not needed.

No, the true frustration that vibrated beneath the surface of her skin at Declan's actions was that he was wasting time on partying and trivialities.

Cormac had obviously brought her to witness this, maybe thinking she was still with Declan, and she knew for certain then that he was trying to sow dissent between them.

"Gods, Declan," Justin murmured.

"Wild night, just like his old man." Cormac's booming laughter echoed through the room, startling Declan awake. His eyes snapped open, blinking rapidly before widening into a panicked, wide-eyed stare at the sight of Bryn.

"This smells entirely of a setup." Justin pulled Bryn back toward the door.

"Now why would I do something so crass? I'll leave you to talk." Cormac winked and turned to leave, his hand on the door, and in the fleeting second Bryn saw his grin fade, the potent deranged anger etched on his face sent a chill of apprehension down her spine. He left the room, slamming the wooden door with all the grace of a drunken bull.

A bewildered Declan searched for something to cover himself. His brow furrowed deeply, a stark contrast to his usually relaxed features, showing not shame, but honest bewilderment. Finding his pants, he worked to get a foot in, tumbling to the floor.

"Brynnie!" Declan groaned, pushing himself up.

Bryn and Justin quickly turned away to give him some privacy, even though it was far too late for that. "We will step out and you can"—Bryn waved her hand to indicate him getting dressed. — "get yourself put to rights."

"Or if you'd rather they gave you more time..." a sickly sweet whisper drifted across the room, and with a curse, Justin moved to the door, taking the handle and opening it for Bryn to go first.

"No! Brynnie, wait. I'm dressed." The sound of Declan stumbling had her look back right as a woman reached for him, and he shoved her hand aside. "Stop it!" he snapped and the small, pathetic mew from the woman set Bryn's teeth on edge.

Justin clenched his jaw, his shoulders tight as he sneered, waving for Bryn to walk through the doorway. As much as she hated the awkwardness of the situation, at least Justin could see Declan for what he was capable of.

"Bryn, stop!" Declan ordered as she took careful, measured steps out of the room.

The sound of hands meeting flesh followed her movement, and Bryn turned to see Justin pushing back against Declan's naked chest to keep him from Bryn.

"Not right now. I think you've done enough talking without saying a damn word." Justin held his own against Declan which was impressive. Justin was not a short man, but he was still quite a bit smaller than Declan. "I thought better of you. Ignored rumors like an idiot thinking my friend wouldn't behave that way, but you did this in Ifreann, too, didn't you? I tried to bring her back around to you, and you pulled this crap on her over and over?" Justin shoved Declan back. "I hate to lose a friend, but I damn sure am not going to lose two." Justin's gaze moved to Bryn. "You ready to head back?"

"Justin, I'm fine," She stepped forward, placing her hand on his shoulder. "I had my closure in Ifreann."

Justin went still as stone. "And how was that, Bryn?"

Swallowing down any answers since Justin looked close to throwing a fist at Declan, she met her ex's intense, whiskey-colored gaze. Eyes that begged her to listen, but there was no need to explain the why. He was a single man and could do as he pleased. It had been the infidelity while they were together that was the problem.

"Answer me this, Declan; is this why you're splitting up the group?" Bryn tried to keep her voice steady as she spoke.

The immediate shock in his eyes belied his innocence. He was confused, but she couldn't see anything in his stare that led her to believe he was throwing them off. Yet, there was something else about him that she couldn't quite put her finger on. As surprised as he was at everything, it almost didn't seem like a drunken night of debauchery, but something more.

Declan had never been black out drunk, and she doubted with how fast their new god-like bodies burned off anything chemical—something they'd learned when they'd drugged Jace—she had a suspicion his uncle had done something to him with how he made a show of bringing them to Declan. Now, she worried about leaving Declan here by himself with his uncle.

With a sigh, she stepped back and rubbed her temples to relieve the building pressure behind her eyes. The rollercoaster of emotions she experienced in such a short time left her utterly drained, but that was the price of dealing with Declan Rafferty. The sheer intensity of the man was exhausting.

"No, Brynnie. I know how important it is to get to Cethin. No matter the issues we have personally, finding people to fight and making plans to take down the king is our priority."

With a nod, she turned. Declan's hand almost touched her arm before she jerked away, needing some space to think.

"I'm not Brynnie. I'm Bryn, and you have to earn my friendship back, so now is the time to start. Go pack your stuff. We leave tomorrow." She looked at him, daring him to argue. "All of us." With those parting words, she spun on her heel and walked away from the man she'd thought would be her future so long ago. Back when she was just another naïve lost girl he slipped neatly into his harem.

But she was okay with that and with who she was now. The new and grown-up Bryn left him standing in the doorway of his uncle's home without an ounce of guilt on her conscience.

As she and Justin neared the doors that led outside, Cormac rounded a corner, settling himself between her and the way out. His posture braced for attack, but he held still as he spoke. "He belongs here, with his family."

"Cute scene you set up back there, but Declan and I are no longer together." As she spoke, Cormac's eyes narrowed, and she knew Declan had told the man something different. Her eyes hopefully conveyed that she now knew Cormac was determined to split them up for his own nefarious game.

"He is an important part of this group and will be leaving with us tomorrow." Stepping around him, she grabbed the railing. "And no matter what schemes you dream up, Cormac, we will take what's ours."

With those words barely off her tongue, she made her way back out into the sunlight.

Chapter 11

Bryn stayed silent as she walked with Justin and Kian toward the small, dilapidated hunting shacks wishing the day was over so they could sleep and leave in the morning.

Once they hit the tree line, Kian ventured into the woods, leaving her and Justin alone. With the furious energy emanating from Justin, Bryn thought about taking off too. Justin clenched his jaw so hard his teeth ground together, his fists balled into tight knots.

"I get why I'm mad—or why I should be mad, anyway," Bryn had to admit Declan had acted and behaved just as she thought he would. She'd also expected to feel a sense of betrayal, but felt curiously untouched, as if the event lacked the emotional impact it should have. Perhaps she had gotten over him, or perhaps, she hadn't really been as invested as she thought. He was a safe place for a small fraction of her life, but now, her life was an open road with endless possibilities. He'd become an ant in the overall scale of Bryn's much larger concerns. "... but you seem a bit more livid than I thought you might be."

Justin continued walking, his boots crunching the leaves on the path, the sound growing monotonous. With a silent apology forming on her lips, she was about to shift the conversation, the weight of unnecessary guilt pressing down, when he finally broke the silence.

"We have a damn devil of a king, the dead on our tails, our town destroyed, and he is more focused on getting laid."

Justin stopped abruptly, grabbing her elbow to spin her around to face him. At the movement, Kian stepped back out of the forest, prowling along the edge of the trees.

"This is why you wouldn't say anything, and Declan acted as if you splittin' up was a mystery. That whole *damn* time, he was behaving like this?" His eyes, narrowed slits of ocean blue, and the pinched expression on his face made it clear lying was a bad idea.

Nodding, Bryn thought of when Kian had said the god that Declan was, Dagda, had treated the Morrigan much the same way. Perhaps she was more like the Morrigan than she thought before her power was returned, but she doubted the Morrigan opened up to the rest of the pantheon about her relationship woes, including the god Justin was reincarnated from, Lugh.

"Why did you not say anything? You just let us keep hasslin' you about it."

Taking his hand from her elbow, she wrapped it between her own. "You're my friend and I want to keep it that way. Making you choose sides would have caused a rift I wasn't prepared to handle. Not when I had so few people who mattered to me to begin with."

Shaking his head, he pulled her into a hug, his breath ruffling the stray curls that escaped her braid. "I will always be your friend, no matter what, but start talking to me, all right? We're about to embark on a battle that will be more than anything we've ever faced, and I need to know you'll tell me what I need to know to help you. I just want to keep you, and all our group, safe."

Bryn could imagine how hard it was on Justin not to be in the thick of things, to fix all their issues. His sense of justice was what pushed him into his calling as Sheriff of Ifreann. To make sure that not only was life as fair as he could make it, but that his people were protected. She knew he felt like he failed her, but it was her own fear and pride that had held her secrets hostage.

"I will." Bryn hugged him back, her eyes catching the silver wolf sitting at the forest edge, watching on. Always watching to make sure she was safe, and in that moment, Bryn had never felt more protected.

The flapping of wings rustled in the branches and Bryn knew Cyerra was nearby. With a small, reassuring smile, she let go of Justin, but he hesitated to leave.

"Go." Bryn shoved him playfully. "I'm perfectly fine."

Justin raised his eyebrow in a look of disbelief, making Bryn genuinely laugh for the first time in a while. "You come get me if you need anything, you got that, Bryn?"

"I got it," Bryn whispered, biting back tears at the look of concern in her friend's eyes. With a nod, Justin walked backwards before turning to finish the trek to the shacks.

Shadows stretched and writhed, coalescing until Kian stood before her, his human form emerging as the shadows retreated to the forest floor, dissolving into nothingness.

"You should head back to camp, too," he suggested, his voice tight, making it sound more like a command than a suggestion. She knew he was concerned, especially since Cormac had made his move and proved he was working against them. For what purpose, she had no idea aside from just keeping Declan in Osgar.

"He's right." A sharp voice sliced through the air from behind her, making Bryn jump. Spinning around, she saw the small blonde woman from the treehouse, her eyes blazing with defiance. Her shoulders straightened, her eyes flashed, and the woman who had seemed so meek now stood before her with an almost regal bearing. "You shouldn't be away from the rest of the group when this deep in enemy territory."

The woman's gaze held Kian's as something passed silently between them. A sense of uneasy familiarity hung in the air, a fragile peace built on a foundation of tense history. Almost as if they were two people in a ceasefire, but always ready to attack should one of them make the wrong move.

"Cormac is definitely everything you think he is, and more. I don't know what he is plotting exactly, but I know he's not on our side, and he is going to move forward with pulling Declan from you, no matter what it takes."

Bryn looked between Kian and the woman.

"And who the hell are you that you say 'our' side?" Bryn asked, confused as to why this woman of Osgar was feeding her information on their community's leader.

"I thought you'd be sharper with the Morrigan nipping at your heels, but you are apparently still far too slow." The woman held her stare on Bryn, the silence heavy with unspoken meaning as she waited for Bryn to figure it out.

With narrowed eyes, Bryn searched for an answer, but the only one that made sense to her seemed improbable. She had to be wrong and saying her theory out loud would see her laughed at.

"Does he have connections to the king?" Kian asked, his focus on the woman, but only earned an eye roll as a response.

"I would think you would know better than anyone, demon."

Bryn jolted, her eyes going wide, shocked that she'd been right after all. "No…" She stepped forward as the woman stepped back, tilting her head as if Bryn were both dense and overstepping. "How?"

"Gods, it gets old trying to make sure you're caught up on everything."

Bryn just gaped at her. "You can turn human?"

Kian snorted. "If that's what you consider human."

Cyerra narrowed her eyes at Kian. "Says the man who is made of shadows and evil and a *dog*." Cyerra turned back to Bryn. "Yes, when we were freed from the Otherworld, or as you say, Faerie, during battle, my other form joined with this one, as Kian and his hound did."

"Hound?" Kian growled.

"Furball? Flea-bitten—"

"Enough, Cyerra," Bryn muttered, pinching the bridge of her nose. "So, you took a human form to spy?"

Cyerra took a deep breath and the visage of the blonde slid away, and in its place was a taller woman with hair as black as night, threads of white flowing from her part along the left side of her face that did nothing to detract from her youthful appearance, and black as night eyes. Her skin was pale without freckles, paler than Bryn's, which would have been off-putting had her face not been so ethereal and perfect.

She wore a long black dress with flowing sleeves, almost a robe with a deep V down the front, covering her breasts, but leaving it open almost to her belly button. A pouch and crow's skull dangled from her silver belt. The silver drop earrings caught the light as she moved complementing the silver threads woven through her hair; a shimmering cascade of mercury.

"I took the form of a woman looking to escape, a docile blonde who spoke all of three words her entire life because she was stuck with a bunch of pigs in human form. She is long gone now."

"Did you…" Bryn couldn't finish the sentence.

Cyerra raised an eyebrow. "Kill her? No, but had she stayed, her father would have. My being here gives me the chance to spy, and it gives her a head start on her new life with some shiny coin. Compliments of a crow." Cyerra looked back at Kian, a small smile playing on her lips. "See? When a person has a soul, they do nice things like that for other people."

Kian rolled his eyes and crossed his arms as he leaned back against a nearby tree. "I am sure everything you do is altruistic, bird."

Bryn turned, her head swimming with the new information, needing a moment away from their probing gazes to gather her thoughts.

"So," Bryn interrupted another round of bickering. "He's up to something and wants Declan on his side, which, from what I saw earlier, he knows just how to do."

"What exactly went on in that room?" Cyerra asked, her eyebrows furrowing.

"Declan is making his way through the female population and not bothering to clean up after himself," Bryn muttered. She could almost feel the animosity from her companions thrumming through the air.

"How are you not sick of this, Bryn?" Kian seethed, his fists clenched and his eyebrows arrowed down in anger. "Him putting his needs before the good of all?"

"Calm down, Fomorian," Cyerra warned, but Bryn didn't blame him for his temper.

"I know the mistakes I made when I wasn't born of flesh and blood, but those mistakes will no longer be an issue. I will no longer put up with his behavior or let people suffer because of him." Bryn spoke, but the Morrigan appeared, threading her way through the words, a promise between both of them and to each other, as well as those who followed them.

"You remember then?" Cyerra asked, her eyes holding a spark of hope.

"I remember most of my lifetimes before I was pushed into Faerie, like I said, but there are still some blank spaces." A memory popped into Bryn's mind, and she rushed to explain to Kian and Cyerra. "Remember when I pulled the memory from Sage when we were in Tanwen? Would I be able to do that with the rest of the group?"

Kian and Cyerra looked at each other but said nothing. Bryn wondered if this was something she would have to go at alone until Cyerra spoke up.

"Yes, but they may not understand the memories until something in the physical world triggers them." Cyerra said. "But it's worth a shot. Let me know how it all turns out and try not to do any permanent damage to their minds. I have enough to deal with when it's just you." A swirling mist encompassed Cyerra before she disappeared, a crow taking to the sky.

"Be careful with that. Digging around in your friend's minds has not worked out so well in the past for you," Kian whispered, standing close enough to her that the heat of his body made her spine tingle. The attraction seemed to amplify almost every time he was near her in his mortal form.

It didn't matter though. Unlike Declan, she wouldn't put her wants or desires before her mission or her people, even if something within her knew Kian would never betray her as Declan did. She knew there was more between them than she was ready to acknowledge. That even when he had forgotten her, something kept him at her side all through Ifreann. The man who was to be her greatest enemy became her most loyal soldier, but it felt like even more than that in this lifetime.

Shaking her head, she looked to the sky where Cyerra had disappeared.

"Hopefully if I am careful, I can pull something useful to the forefront. Then I can pray it's enough to keep King Bres from resurrecting Balor and releasing him back into our world." She looked over her shoulder at Kian as he met her with a roguish smile.

"That, Bryn, I know you're capable of and have no doubt once we get back on the road, you will have a fine plan ready for us to take into action."

A knot of anxiety tightened in Bryn's stomach as she hoped his faith wasn't in vain.

Giving him a mirthful smile, she joked, "One can hope."

Chapter 12

Bryn returned to her cabin with the intention of packing her meager belongings, but froze when Caden looked up at her from where he was sitting on the front porch of her shack.

"I thought you were staying with Declan in Osgar since I haven't seen you around here," Bryn said as she walked to where Caden sat, taking a seat beside him, but giving him space.

Caden held up his arm, turning it to show her the healed scar tissue where his hand used to be.

"Healers kept an eye on me while Jace finished up using his doctor magic on it."

"It looks better." Bryn wrapped her arms around her legs, unsure where to take the conversation, letting the silence build between them before Caden broke it.

"Justin told me you blame yourself, and I took advantage of your guilt because I was fucking angry, Bryn." Caden shook his head, his long hair falling into his face, the ends drying from a recent bath. "No, that's not right." He worked his jaw side to side before he continued. "The loss of Travis had me in a blind, furious rage, Bryn. You were just..." he let out another long sigh, "...a convenient outlet for my pain."

"I get it. He was your best friend."

Caden let out a choked laugh, running his hand through his hair before looking at her. His eyes shone with tears as his gaze met hers.

Bryn felt all the words she hadn't said bubbling up in her, but the ones that spoke the loudest truth were what slipped out. One the Morrigan did not agree with, if Bryn reading the emotional equivalent of a sigh from the goddess was anything to go by.

"I could have saved him had I believed—"

Caden shook his head. "No, you couldn't have. Those wraiths were more than we were prepared for, and Travis died fighting just as he always said he would." Biting his lip, he visibly weighed telling her something.

"It wasn't appropriate according to the church, what me and Travis had together in Ifreann, so we were quiet about it."

"Oh." Bryn realized she'd never picked up on anything more than friendship between the two men.

"Yeah," Caden laughed. "We had to be *really* discreet."

"I understand. Believe me, I wasn't exactly accepted into the social circle, but Caden," Bryn took his hand in hers, "there is never anything inappropriate about love. Love is to be celebrated in all its forms, and I am happy you and Travis had each other."

As Caden blinked, tears that had welled up in his eyes rolled down his face. He squeezed her hand before dropping it to wipe at his cheeks. "Looking back, I realize now that I owe you an apology."

"What? Why?" The shock hit Bryn like a physical blow, a jarring impact that stole the breath from her lungs. This whole time, she'd been ready to fall to her knees and beg his forgiveness, and yet he felt he needed to apologize to her?

"You were the spotlight for Arioch's hate, and to be honest, as much as I hated him for it, I was relieved too. It meant no one was watching me and Travis. No one cared. We were just best friends who hung out all the time." Caden extended his hand this time, palm open, upturned and trembling. There was a silent plea in his gaze, and she gently placed her hand in his. "I am sorry I was too selfish and too weak to stand up for you. Travis was quick to do so, and I thought that was enough."

Before she could overthink it, she wrapped her arms around Caden.

"If I had known, I would have never said a word." Her voice was soft, a mere breath against his ear, and Caden tightened his arms, holding her close.

"I know. That makes what I did worse, but hopefully, from here on out, we can be friends again."

Pulling away, Bryn held his shoulders, smiling at him. "You always were my friend."

Caden's lips tilted, a small smile, but it was one Bryn had hoped to see for so long. His expression turned serious as he held her gaze, as if a knight swearing an oath to his queen. "I promise, I will help us all get to Cethin. I will be there beside you when we take King Bres down. For all of us, but especially for Travis."

"For Travis." She squeezed his shoulders before letting go. "Pack up. Tomorrow we hit the road—" Bryn was interrupted by an angry chorus of shouts. She jumped to her feet as Caden pulled himself up with his hand. Her nervous system went on high alert, the Morrigan clawing her way to the front while Bryn tried to focus on pushing her down and what was happening.

Bryn ran around the side of her shack toward the voices, entering a small grove in the trees where an enraged Cormac was at the center of their group, his face reddening and voice booming. Declan and several locals watched from the sidelines, their faces impassive, as if the argument were a pre-arranged spectacle.

"You allow a damn Fomorian among us and you dare to tell me I'm out of line?" Cormac roared into Justin's face, a sound like thunder, but the ex-sheriff remained stoic, his expression unchanging. His arms folded across his chest, a toothpick bobbing between his teeth, Justin simply watched Cormac's display as if he were not the focus of the large man's ire.

"Not this again," Kian muttered from behind her as he took her arm, keeping her from placing herself in the middle. "If I need to leave for there to be peace, I will. I won't be the source of infighting, Bryn."

Placing her hand over where he softly clutched her elbow, she squeezed his fingers. Memories from long ago swirled at the edge of her mind, ones where Kian had to prove his worth to the rest of the shadow army, those thinking he couldn't be trusted. The many challenges to fight, and Kian had bested them all, winning both their respect and loyalty. They eventually followed the man they had thought their enemy into battle over and over again until the end.

"You have fought with me many times before. It is their own delusions making them act this way."

"Look!" The yell jolted her as Cormac waved a hand toward her and Kian before stomping over. "You only keep the demon here because of his little girlfriend. A demon! It was because of a Fomorian that my brother, Declan's father, is dead and the sanctity of our home was washed with his blood!"

She felt Kian's fingers tighten before he released her all together. Bryn looked to Declan at those words, but he was looking at the ground, his arms folded. Cormac stomped his feet like a child in the middle of a tantrum, and the feral look in his eyes had Bryn stepping back before the Morrigan pushed annoyance at her.

The grin slicing across Cormac's face was unhinged as he stomped toward Bryn, her pulse kicking off as the Morrigan threaded her way along Bryn's nerves.

Cormac was playing a game that only he knew the rules to.

With a sharp cry of "Cormac!" Declan ran toward her, but not before his uncle had a hold of her, his expression manic and eyes bloodshot. His breath hit her face as he shook her before Declan grabbed his uncle's arm, spinning him away from Bryn.

His uncle's entire body went taut as a bowstring as Bryn stepped from behind Cormac. His lips pressed into a thin, angry line as if Declan had committed some terrible crime. "You'd take the side of your wife's Fomorian lover? You are fine with this when she is supposed to be yours?"

"I am no man's wife," Bryn declared, her frustration bubbling over like a cauldron, her heart pounding as the rage ignited her power, her tattoos sparking and crackling with shocking electricity.

"How do you know about the Fomori?" Justin spoke up, his voice calm, giving Bryn a moment to channel her rage before she did something she would regret. The entire group was silent as Justin dropped his hands and stepped toward where Cormac, Declan, and Bryn faced off. "I know we know about the king and his wraiths, but how do *you* know about them?"

Bryn's gaze instantly caught the subtle shift in Cormac's expression: a flicker of panic before his face went red with anger. His breath escaping his mouth in angry huffs. A subtle, rhythmic thrumming at his temple hinted at the tension within.

"Yeah." Sage looked between the men, her eyes landing on Cormac as a flash of gold rolled over her eyes. Jace and Kessler flanked her as she folded her arms across her chest and tilted her head. "How do you know this?"

Cormac looked at the faces around him, and the silence was deafening, broken only by the occasional nervous cough. "You think we all live in the dark? That being out here in the middle of the forest means we have no idea what happens in the world outside our little village?" Cormac laughed, the sound grating on Bryn's already inflamed nerves. "The battle between the gods is why us humans are in this situation in the first place!" His voice rose as he spoke, spittle flying. Throwing his hands out, he waved at everyone in the group. "No one would be without water and food had they not battled on mortal land."

A hand touched her shoulder, and her entire body stiffened as lips moved next to her ear. She hadn't noticed Declan move closer, her focus on Cormac. "You know Kian is the enemy. He was playing you—"

Bryn whirled on Declan before he could finish the sentence. "How dare you!" she snapped and shoved Declan away. She followed his retreat as he put his hands up in a placating gesture, but the tenuous hold she'd had on the Morrigan was gone. Through her eyes, the goddess advanced on Declan. "You dare tell me who is an ally and who is an enemy when I remember him jumping into a mass of wraiths to protect me on the battlefield that was our town."

Even as she continued to prowl forward, Declan stopped his retreat from Bryn and squared his shoulders.

"You know who your allies are. I shouldn't have to remind you." His words were harsh, judging. She could see another memory of a man similar to Declan, Dagda, standing before her in trees covered with snow and frost, telling her the same thing. That she was an idiot to have brought in a Fomorian as her general.

And so, she said the same words to Declan that she had spoken to the Dagda so long ago: "Those who stand with me in battle *are* my allies."

Several of the townspeople moved toward the tree line, their eyes wide, the power in the air crackling and she wondered how much they knew about the gods who stood before them now.

Declan's laugh, so patronizing, pulled her focus back to him and lit something inside her. "I thought you were smarter than that."

His words reverberated through her bones. The dormant power within her soul ignited, a searing brand that banished the Bryn of Ifreann, replaced by a raw, untamed energy humming beneath her skin. She knew what everyone saw the moment her body shifted fully from Bryn to the Morrigan. The pointed ears, black hair, black eyes with red veins, tattoos in blue ink covering her body with electricity, sending out blue arcs of power.

"I am so much more than you could ever conceive, Declan Rafferty," the Morrigan growled through her, her voice a low rumble that vibrated in the air, before unleashing a wave of raw power that slammed into him, the air crackling with black and blue energy as it threw his body against a large oak tree.

But he was quick to rise, his golden eyes blazing, muscles growing larger and bulging as he stepped toward her.

The shouts of people around them were deafening, a cacophony of fear and excitement, but Bryn and Declan only saw each other, oblivious to everything but the lover turned enemy in front of them.

"*Long time coming,*" Cyerra whispered into her mind as Bryn circled Declan, him doing the same in a preemptive battle dance. "*This will be a good way to try your power out before an actual battle.*"

"Declan!" Justin's voice broke through, but they both knew the other was too far gone. Bryn could hear Justin telling the others to get back, but his voice hardly carried over the roaring of power in her mind.

Bryn fixed her attention on Declan as he gathered a circle of bright white light, arcs of electricity shooting out from the sides, the humming a low thrum that vibrated in the air before he launched it toward her like a spear.

Golden light engulfed Bryn in the blink of an eye as Declan attempted to subdue her, the warmth searing her skin as she fought back with her power, her magic crackling.

His power felt like she was burning alive from the inside, every muscle screaming in protest, heavy and leaden as if weighted down by the desert's sands. The light, though stunning, held her captive in a breathtaking prison of color and brilliance.

A chilling darkness moved through her as she struggled, wisps of black smoke, like icy tendrils rising from her skin, leaving goosebumps in their wake. A searing pain pulsed in her temples, her thoughts a chaotic mess, but she held firm, refusing to yield to Declan. He'd attempted to control her every move, dictate her thoughts, and shape her into his ideal partner, but this last piece of herself, her soul, was one she would fiercely protect.

The sensation of ghostly hands moving over her skin alarmed her, but then there were voices rising, and Bryn could feel bones deep in the earth shifting. Death was all around them, and death was where she found her power.

Bryn embraced the darkness, her entire body humming with power yet her muscles felt taxed, like she lifted something far heavier than she should have.

The smoke grew, moving over her skin, before taking on shapes at the Morrigan's behest. Smoky birds and wolves circled her, their forms swirling and shifting, the wolves ghostly howls a chilling counterpoint to the invading light. The ball of light that was Declan's magic bulged out, fighting to stay whole as her smoke and shadows and ice pushed against it.

The Morrigan was pushing beyond what she thought her limits were. Opaque shadows moved into the light, weaving like a needle through cloth as they pierced the orb. The blue sparks and black shadows threading through his orb were now all that was holding it together.

With the last of her power, Bryn flung her arms wide, shattering the orb into countless shards of golden glass that shimmered around her like a thousand tiny suns. Her shadow creatures swirled like a vortex as she narrowed her bleeding black eyes on Declan. His own widened as his hands dropped to his sides.

"Try that again at your own peril," she whispered, the sound deep and resonant, but it might as well have been a scream with the way Declan flinched.

Who was this man? No, he hadn't been the best boyfriend, but he'd been a friend long before they had a relationship. He'd never raised a hand to her even when she punched him in the face after his betrayal at the sanctuary.

No, the man before her was not the same one who held her when she cried about losing her father or demanded justice when the town harassed or threatened her. Not even close to the man who walked the town with Justin each time they heard of a threat attached to her name.

The memory of Arioch and the black orb flashed in her mind again, but there was nothing more to tell her what happened to Declan.

"That'll do just fine," Cormac said with a smug tone to one of his men before retreating, shoulders up and with a swagger, back to the center of Osgar, the rest of his little contingent following.

Except Declan, who stood staring at his hands like they had betrayed him.

Before she could react, a wave of numbness washed over her, sending her falling to her knees where the cold, damp ground penetrated her pants and chilled her skin. Her muscles heavy and aching, and her mind exhausted, she felt the oppressive weight of darkness closing in. Jace was quick to move to her side, helping her up, but she wanted to walk away on her own two feet.

Sage focused her eyes on Declan as Bryn walked passed her, and she knew if looks could kill, Declan would be a smoldering corpse. Sage took her arm and curved it into her own in what she took as both a move of solidarity and to keep her upright. Giving one last look at Declan, Bryn turned and walked to her shack without another word. Each of the men followed Bryn and Sage, leaving Declan where he stood.

Declan could stew in his own thoughts and guilt since she was done trying to make the man see reason.

Chapter 13

Night fell over Osgar but it failed to bring sleep with it. Despite the bone-deep exhaustion from using her power, Bryn tossed and turned, her mind racing through their dwindling options, each one a bitter pill to swallow.

Declan was staying and there was no way around it. When it came to her, no matter what he said, he never chose her first. Now he was choosing a man claiming to be his uncle over years of friendship with her and their friends.

She also finally had to admit what she had been ignoring the whole time: she was the only leader the Tuatha De Danann had. All the planning and guiding she had started this journey carrying with Danu and Declan was hers alone now.

Bryn would have to step up, while fighting the Morrigan's even stronger hold, thanks to the Rover ambush, and make logical, well-executed decisions to keep them alive.

All by herself.

With an angry huff, Bryn grabbed her furs to ward against the chill of the night before slamming out of the shack, grinding her teeth.

Knowing her friends were still asleep, the world beginning to brighten as day neared, Bryn trampled the dewy grass as she made her way toward the forest to mull over what she would say. To decide what her suggestion would be on their new plan, and how to enact it quickly.

They had a general idea of where Cethin was, but that was all it was. An idea. A general, vague direction, and with the frost growing heavy as the nights had grown longer and colder, it would be an intense trip without the truck.

"Late to be out and about." Niamh's voice was smooth, not startling, the small, fractured shards of waning moonlight that made it through the trees giving Bryn a general sense of where she was. "But I understand, darling. Your wolf was kind enough to catch me up."

Bryn folded her arms to ward off the chill before moving to stand next to Niamh, ignoring her calling Kian "her wolf".

"Where have you been?" Bryn snapped as she stepped closer to Niamh, needing the comfort she had been missing for the last few days.

"Well, you kept yourself in the bloody sun and just now found a forest with enough shade for me and my girls. Perhaps you should consider how much you enjoy my presence when planning the rest of your venture." Shifting against the tree, stretching out her neck, Niamh gave Bryn one of her amused smiles. "Plus, I had to check on my girls. I cannot leave them unattended for too long or who knows what trouble they will find."

"Where are they?"

Niamh smiled at Bryn's question, her canines peeking through. "Some-where safe, I assure you." Bryn raised a skeptical eyebrow, prompting a laugh from Niamh. "I have my ways. I did manage to find my way to Ifreann with them in tow after all."

With folded arms, Bryn stared at Niamh, patiently waiting for her friend's surrender.

"Fine. Fine." Niamh waved absently. "I can move in the veil but not like you can. I cannot enter Faerie entirely, and it is very exhausting to do so, but I can rest there and continue my travels until the sun sets in this world."

That made sense since the veil was a liminal space between worlds, a pale imitation of Earth. The sun's power would be muted, its light diffused and weak.

"That's good to know, especially since it looks like I'll be leading without Declan's help."

Niamh's lips parted slightly, releasing a tiny, sibilant hiss. "Leave him here. He would be deadweight anyway. I always felt the Morrigan was more likely the one who actually ran the show."

"But it means we split, and what if there's another attack?" With a sigh, Bryn settled beside Niamh, the silence punctuated only by the rustle of leaves around them from the biting wind, as Niamh's gaze remained fixed on her.

With a light laugh, Niamh raised her eyebrow as she held Bryn's gaze. "Honestly, I thought most of your memories had returned. Isn't it obvious? You go to Faerie."

Bryn threw her hand out, grabbing Niamh's arm. If anyone else had done that, Bryn was sure Niamh would have torn through them. All Bryn earned herself was a flicker of amusement on the immortal woman's face. "We can travel through the veil, too! Ugh! That was such an obvious answer!" Bryn slapped her hands over her face.

"Don't fret, darling. You have an entire group looking to you for leadership since Danu made herself scarce with a war looming. Your mind has been quite full, what with remembering lifetimes and such. Honestly, I could wring the old biddy's neck for all she is putting you through."

Bryn looked up, her mind slowly catching up, a feeling of dawning realization spreading through her. "Caden?"

Niamh's smile dropped. "He would perish quickly in the Faerie realm."

All of Bryn's enthusiasm died. Caden was mortal and if he stayed in Faerie, he would eventually be unable to return to Earth. Bryn did remember from the hidden tales in Ifreann that mortals were not meant to be in Faerie for long spans of time. It was why the Morrigan had separated souls from bodies as the world collapsed.

Exhausted from days of worry and a battle that stole her strength, Bryn leaned into Niamh, breathing in her scent, the feeling of her nearness bringing her a sense of peace. "Goddess, I've missed you," Bryn whispered as Niamh pulled her into a hug.

"I am here, skulking around in the shadows like I did as a young vamp." Niamh pulled her arm back, pinching something off her forearm with a look of disgust before flinging it into the woods. "This is ridiculous. I need us to continue on to civilized accommodations."

A snort left Bryn that earned a raised eyebrow from Niamh before she laughed.

"Honestly, you've already become one of those questionable Osgarians. What was that horrible noise?"

Giving her friend a light shove, Bryn was happy to have her back, someone she could be her whole self with.

A twig snapped behind them and Niamh's eyes focused in on something beyond Bryn.

"I'll give you a moment with your wolf." Niamh touched Bryn's shoulder reassuringly and then silently vanished back into the dense trees, leaving only the oppressive darkness of the forest.

The world tilted on its axis as her present and a memory of the Morrigan's collided, throwing her off kilter.

Kian, positioned above her in the dark forest, stared down with wide, shocked eyes. She could feel the cold steel of the blade pressed against her throat as his hand shook, his eyes burning into her soul. With the speed and precision of a striking snake, Bryn flipped them, her own blade a silent threat to his throat now as she swiftly took charge of their fight. A sharp intake of breath followed his submissive chin lift; the unexpectedness of the action shocking her.

The memory faded as she blinked, and the present snapped back into focus as Kian stepped out from the trees, his silhouette stark against the first rays of morning light. His hesitant steps and the grim set of his jaw told her he was there to talk about what happened with Declan, and she braced herself.

"Talk to me, Kian."

His pale skin and intricate tattoos were a stark visual counterpoint to his tousled black hair and dark clothing as he emerged from the trees. "If you need me to leave—"

"No, absolutely not." Bryn's voice held a note of steel, as much an order from the Morrigan as it was her, making it clear he wasn't going anywhere. With the weight of her emotions pressing down, she realized she needed the strength he had given her over countless lifetimes as her right hand if she were to make it through this.

The realization that she relied on him so much now, when she rarely relied on anyone, was a shocking thought. It had to be more than his role as her second in command, but she was unsure what it was. The love for her friends and cousin was strong, yet a strange current had flowed between her and Kian ever since that bloody Battle of Ifreann—a silent, almost electric connection born from the moment their eyes met as the two sides of his soul merged.

A connection she hadn't felt as the Morrigan, only as Bryn.

Kian looked to the side, not making eye contact, and she wondered if the way he braced himself meant he was nervous. His words, his stance, seemed intended to bely anxiety, something she'd never seen from him before. His usual cocky swagger was gone, replaced by a hesitant gait that spoke of vulnerability, a fragility she knew she needed to handle delicately.

Bryn took a chance that, months ago, would have been a fleeting thought she'd deny herself. Stepping forward, she heard him take a deep breath before she wrapped her arms around his waist, placing her head against his chest, listening to the rapid beat of his heart.

He was so still, so tense, like a statue.

Sensing his unease, she withdrew, but his swift hands caught her and pulled her against him, their bodies flush against each other. His face nuzzled into her neck, and he inhaled deeply, breathing in the scent of her skin and hair.

"Thank you," he whispered against her neck, his breath tickling her skin.

"Why are you thanking me? Friends hug, Kian," she said back and felt him freeze before he loosened his hold. Stepping back, he ran his fingers through his already disheveled hair, the strands falling across his forehead as he turned away from her.

Hands on his hips, he looked up at the brightening sky before shaking his head. "Sorry, it's just been a long time since someone hugged me... Or I could even be hugged."

He hadn't felt any human touch in decades and Bryn could understand that.

For years, she had avoided all physical contact, fearing the visions of death they brought. But now, as the visions became manageable, a simple hug, a tender touch, felt like a sweet, life-giving nectar to her deprived soul. She could only imagine what it meant to Kian after he'd endured lifetimes without it.

Yes, that was something Bryn could very well relate to.

Kian took her in, his eyes tracing every curve of her face as if committing it to memory. Her nerves buzzed with awareness of a significant change, a subtle but undeniable shift between them.

"You better not be planning to leave and this is a goodbye," Bryn blurted, her voice trembling slightly, a cold dread gripping her stomach. "What are you thinking?"

Blinking, Kian shook his head. "Sorry. I was lost in thought. No, I won't leave you. I never would if it's my choice. I thought you knew better than that?"

"I'm sorry if I made it weird with the hug. I understand that you didn't ask for it and it was impulsive—"

Two steps, two assertive steps, and he was there. His face so close she could count his eyelashes. "Stop," he ordered, his finger to her lips, his hand at her waist, and her heart was ready to beat out of her chest. His hand moved to her chin, lifting her face. "You, and only you, are ever allowed to touch me."

They were close, their breaths mingling, the sun rising in the distance giving more light to the world around them.

Bryn was scared. Scared that she was misinterpreting his words and actions, unsure since she'd only been with one man.

Dropping his finger from her lips, his other hand went to her cheek, his forehead dropping to hers. It would take just a small tilt of her face, and her lips would brush his.

The Morrigan thundered into her emotions, her hair along the back of her neck standing up as adrenaline flooded her body.

Her world tilted as his grip tightened to pull her against him.

Not in a moment of passion, but because the ground beneath them was moving.

"What was that?" Bryn gritted out, fighting the Morrigan for control as Kian pulled her into the shadows, a tree falling right where they had been.

"Earthquake," he murmured, looking around, his eyes searching for something.

Screams tore through the early morning, over the noise of the earth shifting and breaking trees.

The Morrigan lurched against her hold as Bryn spun and ran, the forest floor crunching under her feet. Kian shifted into his wolf form in a flash, bounding ahead.

Deep down Bryn knew this was not a natural earthquake.

Chapter 14

It was after the second quake that a high-pitched, desperate wail, far more chilling than the cries of the injured, traveled through the forest.

Bryn broke through the trees, the Morrigan retreating as she ran through the high grass until she was before the platform that connected the dining hall to Cormac's home. The open field where the community of Osgar held their parties, and their dinners, was now encircled and secured by their guards.

"I warned you, boy! It's your actions that made this all happen!"

Declan stood facing his uncle, his face pale and his body trembling, ready to collapse as Cormac held a glinting knife to Caden's throat on the crowded platform. Caden sat rigidly on his knees with his hands bound behind him, his stony expression betraying nothing but a grim resolve.

"Stop! I already said I would stay!" Declan yelled, lurching forward as three guards moved in to grab his arms, holding him back from going to

Caden. The guards surrounding the platform looked frazzled, dazed, and she wondered if they were as shocked at Cormac's behavior as she was.

Declan shuffled and Justin came into view at his feet, lying far too still on the wooden surface. Finian nudged him with his wet nose, whining and laying on top of Justin. *Was he alive?*

Jace, Sage, and Kessler shot out of the woods behind her, their breathing heavy as they looked over the crowd, their eyes going wide when they took in Caden and Declan on the platform.

"What in the hell is going on?" Kessler started toward the platform, but guards quickly moved to cut him off.

"Ah, thank you for coming! I was wondering if we would have to drag you from your beds for the show!" Cormac's eyes held a wild glint as he smiled, the blade sinking into Caden's neck, a thin stream of blood tracing a path down his throat.

"Stop!" Jace yelled, shoving his way forward, only to have crossbows nocked with arrows pointed at him as he made it to the platform. It was a pivot point. Jace could continue on and be riddled with arrows until he fell and then eventually came back to life, leaving them down one in the fight. Or they kept themselves in check and potentially watched Caden die.

Damn it.

"What's the point of this?" Bryn asked as she slowly made her way around the edge of the guards with her hands up, some arrows moving from Jace to her.

"Bryn! Stay back!" Declan yelled, one of the guards cracking him in the head with the butt of his crossbow. The hit did little more than enrage Declan, and he swung on the man, yelling obscenities, another guard hitting him in the gut with a bare fist. It didn't take Declan down, but it knocked the breath out of him long enough to shut him up.

Crossbows came up from more guards as Bryn walked past where Jace was being held. A surge of dizziness overwhelmed her, causing her steps to falter and her arms to flail for balance as the world vibrated with an intense, justified anger. The quakes were growing and the steps to the platform splintered, barely holding together.

Cormac's manic eyes met hers, the man seemingly unaffected by the earth shaking. He watched her closely, and once she gathered herself, Cormac motioned one of the guards to let her through. "Bryn, darling, come on up. I'd love to have you share this moment with us."

Her head throbbed intensely on the right side with each step. Steadying herself by holding the railing of the stairs through each tremor, which were coming faster, she sluggishly ascended the stairs.

"I can't do anything!" Jace yelled from behind her, but her body felt like it was stuck in honey; the task of turning to look at Jace too much for her to bear.

"Oh, yes!" Cormac laughed, the deep joyful laugh of days ago now lost to something feral. "You cannot use your precious god magic here, so don't bother even trying," Cormac said, waving her forward again when she had stopped, trying to puzzle out what he meant.

Bryn took a deep, steadying breath, her gaze locking onto Declan. His face was a mask of rage, drawn tight with pain, as he sat with blood trickling from a head wound at the top of the stairs.

He wasn't healing like a god, but bleeding like a mortal.

"The funny thing—" Cormac lifted the knife, waving it but keeping a tight fist around the end of Caden's long brown hair. "It doesn't take much to get Declan to spill secrets, a little bit of this and that in his beer, and he has no idea who he's talking to. In fact, he thought each woman who touched him was you." Cormac's laugh was a sharp, sudden bark. "Pathetic."

Bryn shook, staring at Declan as he bowed his head before Cormac called her attention back.

"Like the fact that this guy—" Cormac wove his blade through the air as if he were orchestrating a song before the knife was back at Caden's neck. "—is human."

"Declan!" Bryn shouted, trying to force her body to move, her vision blurring as her eyes burned. "Look at me!"

Declan's only reply was a defeated slump of his head, and as the guards let go, he collapsed to his knees, his shoulders heaving with silent sobs as he clutched his head with clenched fists.

"Why are you doing this? How are you doing this?" Sage asked from somewhere behind her. Bryn was still trying to move, her legs far too heavy against an unseen force to get to Caden, her brain fogged to the point she was having trouble focusing.

Cormac rolled his eyes, the knife shifting against Caden's throat, and yet Caden's eyes cut to Bryn, a small tilt of his lips as if he had already forgiven them for this betrayal. For not making sure Cormac was who he proclaimed to be and letting Declan move around with him without question.

For her not being the leader they needed to prevent this moment.

"I'm not an idiot!" Cormac yelled, his body shaking, the knife dangerously close to cutting the vulnerable skin and shedding Caden's lifeblood out everywhere. "Girl, get up here!" Cormac yelled, pointing the knife at Bryn, spittle flying from his mouth before he ground his teeth together, his eyes searing into her.

A howl rent the air somewhere in the woods, a call and cry all wrapped into one, and Bryn knew it was Kian.

"Shoot that damn demon wolf!" Cormac ordered and Bryn's blood froze.

"No!" Bryn yelled, her voice sharp and strained as two guards, silhouetted against the murmuring crowd, plunged into the dark forest.

"*I am watching. He'll be fine,*" Cyerra whispered from somewhere nearby. "*Focus!*"

Bryn lifted her heavy foot to step onto the platform where the guards stood over a defeated Declan, and Cormac once again dug his knife into Caden's throat.

They'd been looking for help, for more people to add to their army, and they'd landed themselves in the enemy's hands.

"I'm here. What do you want in order for you to let Caden go?" Bryn's voice was steady, which surprised her since she felt like she was coming apart at the seams, her hands shaking from more than pushing against the pressure of getting to the platform.

Cormac's eyes flashed all black before returning to a human brown. "Tell me, Morrigan, what did you hear within the walls of my home?"

Bryn froze, her body swaying with the subtle shift of the wooden planks, while the deafening crack of splitting timber cut through the air from behind her.

"Come on now, I know you can see things in that little head of yours. The future, or prophecies. Declan told me all about your little group and powers." He gripped Caden's hair tighter, forcefully jerking Caden's head from side to side. "Say it!"

Her mind flashed back to the moment in the hallway with Cyerra when the prophecy had come to her. She had thought he hadn't caught it, but as with everything else so far, she was wrong.

Fear, cold and sharp, pierced her as she obeyed his command, the chilling words catching in her throat, but the image of Caden at Cormac's hands spurred her onward.

"Her power rises with gods and crows..."

"Louder! Come on, girl!" Cormac yelled, his eyes gleaming with each word she spoke.

"A shadow army where darkness froze." Her voice trembled, but she spoke louder with each word. "The three will emerge where death grows." Her eyes met his. "Or so the queen says the prophecy goes."

"So," Cormac sneered, "it is as Declan says. As *you* said, so long ago, and then you come to my camp after our world falls apart with earthquakes and flooding, your little shapeshifting demon wolf in tow." Taking a deep breath, the raw fury drained from his features, morphing into a cold, wicked grin as his gaze darted to Declan and then back to her, the ground rumbling nearby, a tree crashing down, and shrieks piercing the air with terror. "Sacrifices are made to keep Osgar safe."

Looking to the sky, he let the sun hit him in the face, as if praying to some god Bryn couldn't hear. "A promise has been kept this day as it has before! Let it not fall on deaf ears." His focus moved back to his guards as he nodded and turned his gaze back to Bryn with a frightening resolve in his eyes. One that promised terrible things. "We all have our own prophecies to fulfill."

And with that, he cut Caden's throat.

Chapter 15

Bryn was paralyzed as Cormac's gruesome act unfolded, the only sound over Bryn's pounding heart was Jace's raw, desperate scream of anguish. None of it felt real. Bryn was sure it was all a dream and she would wake up at any moment.

Cormac, his hand red with warm, viscous blood, tossed a stone into the spreading crimson stain. A stone that looked far too similar to the one that had given her back her power in Ifreann.

One of the guards jostled Bryn free of her shock as he tried to escape down the shifting stairs. Bryn shook herself, her muscles straining against the thick, clinging invisible sludge that held her captive, her own power feeling sluggish and unresponsive as she fought to reach the stone before it shattered.

"Jace!" she yelled as she took step after slow step. Bryn needed Jace to help Caden; he was the only one who could, while she made sure whatever mad scheme Cormac had thought up did not come to fruition.

Bryn's knees gave way as she pushed herself past exhaustion making it to the platform, the Morrigan no where to be found to give her strength. As she fell to the wooden planks, Bryn used her arms to drag herself, gasping, until she reached her hand out toward the smooth, shadowy black stone. As her fingers grazed it, the stone shattered into pieces, releasing a swirling vortex of dark power that filled the air with a palpable aura of evil.

"No!" Bryn clutched at the powder swirling through the air, the sandy remains of the stone slipping through her fingers.

"Nothing you can do now!" Cormac yelled. "Our village is safe once more because of your friend's sacrifice. Can you imagine how much safer we'll be if we kill those who our king hates most?"

Bryn could hear his footsteps as her eyes moved with Jace, her cousin struggling to get to Caden just as she was.

The black powder floated in front of her hazy vision as she tried to push up, something heavy holding her down.

The demonic power swirled toward and around where several guards were holding Declan. His muscles bunched and strained as he fought the guards, trying to push away from the dust full of power from the stone, but he was as weak as Bryn. A guard grabbed his head, holding him in a headlock, and the power poured into Declan's throat and nose.

"Declan!" she yelled, her voice breaking when a hand clamped down on her hair, yanking her head back so fast that her vision blurred, transitioning from the terrorizing scene before her to the harsh glare of the bright morning sky.

"Your power never worked in Osgar. Once you crossed the line into our village past the forest, you were nothing more than a mortal wasting our precious oxygen." The rasp of Cormac's breath, hot and fetid, brushed against her ear. His words were a threat, each syllable as sharp as the edge of the knife pressing against her throat, still warm with Caden's blood. "Do you feel the power of the Fomori in the air? King Bres is all powerful and we submit to only him. Not some pathetic mortals pretending to be gods."

"I used my power—" she began, but the cold steel of the knife pressing harder against her skin silenced her.

"Near the guard cabins? Yeah, that's outside of our little protective bubble. One that your friend's blood paid for, just as my brother's did, so that my people will be safe under the king's protection so long as I'm alive."

Terror, a fear so entrenched in her bones that she was all too familiar with, had her mind spinning, but one thought rose above the rest.

She was so gods-damned tired of this.

His hand tightened in her hair, the steel at her throat warm with Caden's blood before a gurgle left Cormac and his hand went slack, the knife dropping from her neck. Bryn rolled to the side as Cormac's body fell where she had just been, her eyes moving to where the blond girl who had served them breakfast, and who Cyerra had taken the place of, held a sword dripping red with Cormac's blood.

"You will never hurt another woman again," she promised as she let the sword clatter to the ground, staggering back only to gasp as a sword slid through her chest from behind. Looking up, her eyes met Bryn's, and she smiled through the blood gushing from her lips as she collapsed to the ground.

The pressure around Bryn lifted, and her movements once again became fluid and effortless. She stumbled to stand, her strength coming back, and the Morrigan pulsing with burning rage as everything around her sped up.

But the pressing danger of the guards closing in on her had her backing up toward the stairs. They'd just killed the people's leader in front of them and Bryn was sure there was no time to think, much less talk sense into the guards or the people. It looked like they would have to make a hasty retreat from Osgar.

Justin spun, a blur of motion, in his hand a sword flashing in the sunlight, the metallic clang catching the metal of a crossbow that a guard used to shield himself. With the grace of a dancer, Justin pulled the sword back and stabbed, the sound of the wet, muffled thump of the guard hitting the platform was swallowed by the roar of the growing crowd.

Bryn shoved Cormac over, grabbing the knife he'd used on Caden and threw it, the glinting projectile arcing toward a guard sneaking up on Justin.

"Justin, you grab Declan. Kessler, you grab Caden," — a small quiver broke in Bryn's voice on the last syllable of Caden's name— "and let's get out of here before we can't hold them off any longer."

Kessler already had Caden in his arms, tears flowing freely down his cheeks as Jace stepped up to press a cloth to Caden's neck. Sage took up the rear, following Jace and Kessler down the platform. Justin heaved Declan onto his shoulder, the weight nearly buckling his knees and the strain evident in his grunting breaths. Bryn covered their backs, grabbing a crossbow and the bolts near one of the fallen guards.

The sounds of battle erupted behind them, but Bryn urged them onward, bringing up the rear, her hand instinctively going to the dagger at her side that Kessler had crafted for her in his forge. The dagger, its ornate hilt cool against her skin, had been her companion since their perilous journey from Ifreann.

Breaking through the tree line, she stumbled at the onslaught of the Morrigan demanding her revenge. Catching herself on a tree, she noticed the others slowing too and pushed herself upright.

"Keep going!" Bryn yelled, a snarl following her words, her crossbow up and aimed in the direction of the noise. Kian stepped out in wolf form, his eyes focused on something behind her.

"Come on, Bryn!" Kessler yelled out, already a good distance ahead of her in the shadowy woods.

Ignoring what was following her, she ran toward Kian, grabbing him by the ruff to tug him with her, hoping he would follow her and not bother fighting an entire angry mob himself.

Several figures stepped out from the trees as she ran, and she caught a few familiar faces as they rounded on Bryn's pursuers. Each of the girls from the Sanctuary, led by Niamh, waited for their prey as they covered Bryn and her friends' escape.

"Feast, ladies! It's a long journey ahead for us!" Niamh's voice echoed through the forest as Bryn stumbled over a branch, pushing herself up and turning in time to see Niamh grab one of the guards of Osgar, her fangs tearing at his throat.

More of the women from the Sanctuary flooded the area, grabbing men and guards with their inhuman strength, tearing out throats and clawing through chests. Blood and sinew covered the ground as Bryn stumbled to catch up with the rest of the party, letting Niamh and her friends have their prey.

She stayed close to the trees in case they shot at her and she needed cover, but their pursuer's shouts of alarm and pain grew fainter. Once they made it to a clearing with a small pond, Kian and Justin were quick to establish a perimeter, Finian staying close to Justin.

Jace held Caden in his lap, cupping water into his hand as he poured it over Caden's split neck. "I can't bring him back!" Jace howled. "I can't feel his life anymore!" Yet, Jace kept trying, refusing to give up.

Bryn already knew it was far too late by how bright Caden had become, his body glowing like the sun itself. Soon, a golden aura broke away from Caden's body, bright and pulsating with energy. The intensity of it spun and grew as it neared Bryn, her hand held out as she took Caden's soul into her embrace.

"I'm so sorry, Caden." Bryn's whisper was lost to the wind as she crossed the veil, a silent bridge between worlds, her words unheard by the living.

The graveyard of Faerie came into focus around her as she held Caden's soul against her chest, silent tears falling down her face.

Biting down on her cheek, Bryn held her hand out, releasing her friend's soul for Faerie to care for.

The spinning orb illuminated the area before it burst and Caden stood before her. His dark brown eyes taking in his surroundings before he turned to her, a soft smile tilting the corners of his lips.

Bryn was sure she would split apart.

Caden stepped forward, tears in his eyes as he pulled her against him. Sobs broke the silence, both from Caden and Bryn, as they fell apart in each other's arms.

They held each other for a long moment after the tears had subsided, before Caden stepped back, lifting his sleeve to wipe his eyes. He fell silent, dropping his arm, the absence of his hand a stark, heavy presence. A mirthless laugh left his lips. "Guess we are not given back what we lost when we die."

Unable to laugh, Bryn wiped at her own eyes, wishing for a way to undo what had been done. "I'm so sorry I couldn't save you both."

Caden chuckled softly, taking her hand in his, giving it a squeeze.

"I have complete faith in you. I know the leader you were meant to be is in you, and perhaps my death will be a turning point." His eyes glistened. "Make my sacrifice worth it."

"Caden!" A voice she'd missed called out to her friend, and Caden's eyes widened in surprise before he spun around. Bryn let out a choked sob as

Travis jumped the cemetery fence, not bothering with the gate as he ran to Caden, wrapping the man up in his arms.

They tumbled to the ground, a torrent of tears and whispered declarations of love pouring from their lips between kisses. Tears pricked Bryn's eyes, blurring her vision as she stepped back, silently wishing them all the happiness, the bittersweet ache in her chest a stark contrast to their joyful reunion.

She had a way to see them again and she would. As she pulled herself from the shimmering, ethereal light of Faerie, a flash of gold, like a fleeting sunbeam, caught her eye, briefly illuminating one of the ancient, moss-covered tombstones that had been without a name in the cemetery.

Caden Fredrick Harding

Beside it was another stone she had missed the last time she had visited.

Travis William Kennelem.

Closing her eyes, she pulled herself to the mortal realm to face the onslaught of problems waiting there, but at least she could hold on to the fact that her two friends had found peace and each other.

Bryn released her hold on Faerie, the start of her returning to her body when a sharp tug in her chest yanked her back, and she found herself facing a colossal stone structure, the air heavy with the scent of ancient stone and damp earth. Gargoyles, weathered and worn but with an unsettling air of vitality about them, stood guard on either side of the arched doorway, their menacing presence a silent warning. The doors opened for her as if she'd waited just a little too long and someone inside had grown impatient.

She made her way down a long, dimly lit hallway as the world around her shimmered and blurred. The walls rippled like water, and then, as if by magic, an open door materialized where there had been only a wall moments before. The inside of the room was surprisingly opulent, with rich, dark rugs and gothic furnishings offsetting the cold, hard stone.

Tapping her ear three times, an old habit born of a lifetime of anxiety, Bryn slowly stepped past the threshold of the magical door to where Manannán stood looking for all the world like a god among men. From the time they were reborn as the Tuatha Dé Danann, he had been their hidden savior, protecting them from King Bres. His black eyes, stark against his silver hair and pale skin, no longer held the familiar warmth of the salt-and-pepper father figure who used to sit with her and Declan across the table for dinner.

"You will find this is the best course forward," he said, offering a smile that revealed unsettlingly sharp teeth, a stark reminder of his true form.

"Losing Caden? Betrayed by Declan? Sure, sounds like the best path forward." A small growl left her that was more the Morrigan than her. Bryn pushed back, the tattoos on her skin flickering with light before they went dormant once again.

With a slow tilt of his head, his black eyes like chips of obsidian, he assessed her. "You give yourself no credit still? I thought we were past this."

Bryn clenched her jaw, her molars grinding together with a low, almost inaudible sound. It was getting old hearing the same old tune from those around her. "I'm doing my best, but right when I had settled into the idea of being some ancient goddess, I suddenly become the leader—"

"You have the—"

Bryn cut him off, "—and look how well I've handled it so far!"

Manannán remained silent while Bryn lost herself to her anger. "Caden is dead!"

"You are still thinking too much like a human and not like the deity you truly are. The *queen* you are. That means not every decision will come with peace or be met with cheers, but the end result is what matters."

She couldn't help but let out a small chuckle, only to be met with a disapproving frown.

"You think I lie?" His voice held a dangerous edge.

When she closed her eyes each night, she could pull little bits and pieces of her life as the Morrigan, flashes of battle and magic. The memories surfaced for Bryn, so real she could almost smell the air from those long-ago days, hear the whispers of voices past, and feel the textures of a life lived before this one.

The memory of the shimmering, ethereal veil closing like a wound being stitched shut, obscuring her view of the wraiths battling fiercely against her people before she would split their souls. The scene was horrifying. The pull of the magic, sharp as a shard of glass, as she tore them apart, leaving half to death and endless regeneration, their cries echoing through her mind.

"I'm supposed to raise an army I betrayed as their queen." One of her biggest fears was leading a shadow army when she couldn't even hold it together with her friends. Not only that but she worried her army would reject her because of what she had put them through.

The Morrigan's rage spiked right as Manannán spoke.

"I tire of this, Bryn." His disembodied voice lifted the hair on the back of her neck as he disappeared into a swirling mass of shadows, the sudden shift in air palpable as he materialized in her personal space, his face a breath from hers.

Before she could step out of his reach, his hands grabbed the back of her neck, his grip like iron, power pulsing through him and into her. His touch was hot as molten lava and she clenched her teeth to hold back the scream threatening to erupt.

Whatever he was doing, it felt as if her soul was growing too large for her body, and she could feel the essence of the Morrigan growing stronger. Violent, unrestrained power bloomed throughout all the edges of her psyche, barely being held back by Bryn's own consciousness.

The last thread anchoring her to her mortal life snapped, and she felt the Morrigan in every cell, a oneness with the goddess of her memories and who she was now.

Power surged and twisted within, a bitter struggle for dominance and a cold, heavy pressure pushed into her bones.

Bryn felt the lives of her past selves drain away, the memories there, but no longer scattered puzzle pieces. She was the Morrigan. Strong, fierce, and determined as Bryn struggled to keep herself intact. As the Morrigan grew larger, Bryn felt herself slipping away.

"Stop!" she yelled, tearing her head away from Manannán. His eyebrows rose, his fingers closing into a fist as he stepped back, dropping his arms.

"I was only pulling the Morrigan closer to the surface—"

"You were erasing me from existence!" She slapped her chest, sweat dripping down her brow as her heart hammered against her ribs. "You may need the Morrigan, but you need me too, and I never said I was okay with giving up who I am to be only a vessel for some long-dead goddess!" Bryn was screaming, her voice breaking as her fear bled into every word.

Manannán blinked, as if trying to understand her reasons and none of them making sense to the ancient. Where was the humanity he had gathered over the many years as Mr. Rafferty? Shaking his head, a flash of light rolled through his eyes.

"I just want to be me. Free from the trauma and hurt of Ifreann, and not escaping one prison to be thrown into another." She choked out the words, sobbing gasps turning to hiccups as she wiped at her tear-stained face.

"I'm sorry, Bryn. When I have been in Faerie for too long, I start to revert to... Well, I am sorry."

Placing her hand to her chest, she willed herself to relax, focusing on calming her taxed heart.

"I've accepted that the Morrigan will always be right there in the back of my mind, but I—" She took a deep breath through the hiccup that broke her words. "—I will not accept losing myself in the process. The Morrigan is gone, and you have some weird hybrid of us both, but that is all you get."

Bryn let her hands fall to her sides, pushing her shoulders back to create a sense of bravado she did not feel. "I will get us to Cethin and I will do my best to lead whatever army I have. As me."

Manannán's gaze, ancient and knowing, pierced her very being before he gave a subtle nod and clasped his hands in front of him.

"So be it."

Chapter 16

Bryn gasped, her lungs screaming for air, as she pushed back through to the mortal world from Faerie. Kian was there, his head on her lap with silver eyes looking up at her, and she wished she had the breath to tell him thank you for being her anchor.

A monstrous roar, guttural and deep, slammed into her, as the world came into focus around her. Bryn struggled to her knees, her equilibrium off, the rough ground scraping against her palms, before she stood up fully. The movement made her stomach revolt, and she had to stop moving to keep from throwing up. Never had she had this type of reaction leaving Faerie, but she also hadn't ever had Manannán mess with her head and powers before.

When she looked for her friends, Jace and Sage were frozen, eyes wide, as Finian ran back and forth behind them, barking and growling at something behind her. Kian pushed against her side, a snarl pulling back his lips and exposing his long canines.

With a forceful swallow to hold back the rising bile, Bryn turned to find Declan charging at her before Kessler and Justin jumped in to restrain him. Declan bellowed in fury like the bulls back in Ifreann when they were in a rage.

I should have stayed in Faerie.

"You!" Declan's eyes narrowed in on her, and even with two large men holding him back, he was able to take a step in her direction, dragging Justin and Kessler with him. "You killed Cormac! You ruined everything!"

Bryn stepped back, not used to Declan going full berserker. His eyes were darker, more menacing than she could ever remember them being.

"It wasn't Bryn, Declan!" Justin held onto his arm, his heels digging into the ground as Declan dragged him.

What the hell did she miss while she was out?

"Just like you killed Jace's mother! If they don't bow down to you, you just kill them!"

Bryn blinked, trying to make sense of his words as Declan made it another step closer, Justin and Kessler struggling to hold him. Vines shot up from the ground, wrapping around Declan, and Sage's grunt behind her told Bryn the vines were having a hard time holding him as well.

Bryn felt the part of her consciousness that was the Morrigan rising to the forefront and she was unable to hold her back.

Her voice was lower than normal as she spoke. "Let him go."

"Are you crazy?" Kessler yelled, his face red and the muscles in his neck straining as Declan used more of his power to break free. "He is out of his mind! He'll kill ya before he even came back to himself!"

Kian was next to her in wolf form, but he made no move to shove her away or take his human form to argue with her.

"Release him. Now." Bryn adjusted her stance, her hands rising in front of her, the tattoos along her arms glowing.

Justin and Kessler shot each other concerned looks before they released Declan, the vines no longer able to hold him without the other men helping.

With a deafening roar, Declan charged, but stopped short as he hit the unyielding, invisible barrier she'd raised. Her hands tingled with the energy of her power as she watched Declan pace frantically outside the shimmering shield. His eyes were wild, feral and his teeth shone as breath plumed white in the frigid air.

His physical form was as it always was, but the usual sparkle in his eyes was gone, replaced by a haunting emptiness. Darkness pooled in the corners of his eyes, small black veins spider-webbing outwards, a grim sickness blooming beneath his skin.

"Declan, what did they do to you with that stone?" she asked, but Declan began frantically beating at the shield at the sound of her voice, the dull thuds echoing. A guttural growl rumbled in his chest, a primal sound that vibrated through his body, his eyes flashing with an animalistic gleam that said Declan was not at all in control.

"Everything is wrong! You ruined all my plans before and now you're back, ruining it all again!"

Bryn fumbled back a step, her shield faltering, and her ability to hold it wavering. It took a great amount of energy to summon such power in the first place, and she was running low after her jaunt into Faerie.

With nature being destroyed as it was, she empathized with Danu as the shield flickered and failed, her body feeling more and more fatigued as she tried to pull it up again. If this was how Danu felt, Bryn could understand her need to leave the mortal plane.

Declan was on her in a second, far more powerful than she remembered him being, his hands around her throat as she worked to shove him back, her magic flickering and faltering. Her tattoos grew dull, fading as she lost her foothold.

"I will end you once and for all. I will drag you across the veil and make you sit in your failure as you did me!" Declan's eyes darkened, his words like a viper's strike, slithering across Bryn's mind as she fought to break free.

What the hell happened to her friend?

A silver form collided with Declan, providing Bryn with the opportunity to roll away, clutching her throat as she fought for breath, her lungs on fire. Justin was instantly next to her, his gun trained on Declan as Kian fought him.

Kessler helped her up, both men flanking her.

"What powers did he absorb from that demon smoke?" Sage yelled out from where she stood next to Jace, both of them protecting Caden's body. Sage's hands trembled with exhaustion but she kept them outstretched, ready to call on the vines and trees to help if needed.

Declan howled in pain as Kian's sharp teeth sank into his shoulder, and he thrashed wildly, trying to shake off the snarling wolf. With a roar, he grabbed Kian by the neck and hurled the angry wolf into a tree, the sound of splintering wood echoing through her as Bryn's vision blurred with a furious red rage.

With a surge of adrenaline, she sprinted toward Declan, only to have a crow swoop down, its beak inches from her face, letting out a deafening caw. "Move, Cyerra!"

Declan turned on Bryn as she ducked beneath where Cyerra dove again at her. "This isn't over, little witch. I will be the victor next time." He slammed his hands down, the impact jarring as dark soil erupted, a gritty spray across his face as the ground swallowed him whole.

Breathing heavy, Bryn turned from where Declan disappeared and ran to Kian, who was shaking off leaves and dirt. Throwing her arms around his neck, she inhaled his scent, the smell of him filling her senses and settling her in a way no one else or anything ever had. She'd witnessed his selflessness too many times, and each time, it was agonizing.

Cyerra perched on a nearby branch. The rustling leaves a subtle counterpoint to Bryn's rising anger at Cyerra for letting Declan escape.

"He would have killed you. You used too much energy and your power was waning. I can tell."

Bryn stood, glaring at Cyerra. "You don't get to make those calls, crow."

"What the hell just happened?" Justin yelled, standing over the spot Declan disappeared. "How do we follow him when he went into the damn earth!"

"We don't." Bryn said, and every pair of eyes turned her way.

"What do you mean, we don't?" Justin asked, walking toward Bryn before waving back to where Declan disappeared. "He's our friend, Bryn. Not only that, we need him to fight Bres."

Something in her snapped. "He *was* our friend!" Bryn faced off with Justin. "A friend who showed up to fight *us* only moments after his uncle *killed* Caden! Maybe we do need all of us, but I am done trying to help him while he does *everything* in his power to screw it all up!"

Silence filled the gap between her and Justin. Steadying her breath, she met his crystal-blue eyes. "We continue to Cethin." Bryn turned to where Caden lay. "Without Declan."

"But—"

"Bryn, as our leader, has spoken." Jace met Justin's gaze, holding himself tall against the Sheriff's stare. Only when Justin looked away did Jace back down, turning to Caden before kneeling next to him, closing his eyes.

Even with the tension heavy in the air, they walked to where Jace prepared Caden, a cloth around his neck concealing the gruesome wound.

"We have to bury him here. There's no way we can travel with him." Kessler motioned to a small opening at the base of the tree. His eyes growing glassy as he spoke, his hand wiping at his cheek when a tear escaped.

"His soul has already crossed. He's with Travis now." Bryn's voice barely broke over the sounds of nature around them, but she knew they all heard.

"I will take care of him." Sage stepped up near Caden, but Jace spoke up.

"You've expended enough energy, Sage."

"It's Caden," Sage replied, kneeling next to his body. "I can do this for him. No matter how much it takes from me, he's lost far more."

A raspy "Oh, darling boy," echoed from the depths of the forest as Niamh stepped out from the deeper shadows, her painted red nails trembling against her bloodied lips. The women of the Sanctuary took up their places next to her, each reaching out a hand to steady Niamh as they stayed to the shadows, the daylight too dangerous for them to step into the open field where Bryn was.

"She's still with us? That's a relief," Kessler whispered.

Sage waited, her eyes on Niamh, not moving until finally, Niamh nodded to Sage before turning away and slipping back into the veil with the women of the Sanctuary.

Sage whispered a prayer as her hands went into the grass and soil, the words barely audible above the sighing wind, lost to Bryn's ears.

The earth trembled as roots, thick as a man's arm, inched across the ground, their rough bark scraping against Caden before wrapping around him, pulling him down into the cool, damp moss before he disappeared into the earth below.

A carpet of small wildflowers—blues, whites, and yellows—spread across the ground where Caden had been, their sweet fragrance filling the air.

Nature had taken back one of her own.

Chapter 17

As night fell, Bryn and the group set up a pathetic makeshift camp, thanks to Niamh moving through the veil to grab their gear from Osgar. Unfortunately, Niamh was now far too depleted to draw them and the Sanctuary women across the veil. Bryn could still sense the women nearby, roaming unseen through the woods around the camp.

A camp that would do little to provide them with cover, so Bryn hoped they were far enough away from Osgar to avoid unwanted visitors. With their powers depleted, none of them possessed the strength to even stir a leaf, let alone breach the veil.

Bryn sat on the rough-hewn log Kessler had pulled from the forest, the fire's crackle and snap punctuated by the pop of burning wood, its orange glow illuminating her face, her thoughts a million miles away.

Everyone had been quiet on the road from Osgar, and Bryn was sure that like her, they were working through the emotions of losing both Caden and Declan.

"I guess I'll be the one to say something. What in the fresh hells was wrong with Declan?" Kessler said as he sat beside Bryn, slapping at a bug on his arm. Seemed mosquitoes didn't mind a little god blood.

"That was not Declan, that's all I know." Justin muttered as he used a stick to push a log further into the fire. It fed in a burst of flame and floating embers.

Bryn curled in on herself, her body worn through and cold as the night stretched out in front of them. A flutter of wings brushed Bryn's ear, a sudden shift in the air heralding Cyerra's arrival as she swooped past, a burst of black energy transforming her into her mortal form beside Bryn. Everyone but Bryn and Kian froze.

"Oh, by the way, since we never had a chance to talk, this is Cyerra. She can turn into a woman." Bryn waved in Cyerra's direction with very little enthusiasm.

Kessler grunted. "Will wonders never cease?"

"He is no longer the Dagda, though he may still be in there somewhere, fighting through the evil muck, but that soul stone is one we didn't know existed." Cyerra stepped forward, making a disgusted face as mud squelched between her toes. "So much easier when I am a crow."

"Then who the hell was that?" Kessler asked, narrowing his green eyes at Cyerra.

"That," Cyerra said, holding Kessler's gaze, "was Balor."

A loud laugh burst from Bryn's mouth before she could stop herself. "Of course it was Balor! Of course!" Her words ended as tears flooded her eyes. "It just keeps getting worse."

Her friends remained quiet while Bryn felt like she was about to burst, covering her face with her hands, readying herself to escape when a heavy hand landed on her shoulder.

"You've got us, Bryn," Kessler whispered to her, squeezing her shoulder. "Not alone in this one bit."

"Really? You just threw that grenade in the room and shut the door?" Justin said, and Bryn dropped her hands, watching Justin turn on Cyerra. He'd been in a foul mood since Bryn said they weren't going after Declan and it looked like he might just aim that energy at Cyerra.

"Would you rather I sugarcoat it? Would that make it easier for you to swallow?" Cyerra cocked her head to the side.

"Balor is free, and *in our friend,* and you think you can make a joke about it?" Justin huffed as Cyerra straightened her shoulders, opening her mouth to respond before Kessler did.

"How'd you know for certain?"

"The magic radiating out of that soul stone was familiar to me. Fighting against him for so very long, I remember all too well what his magic feels like. Oily ... dark..." Cyerra shuddered.

"Gross, yes, we figured it wasn't all flowers and daisies," Niamh interrupted as she stepped out of the forest and crossed to stand at Bryn's side. "Now that he's out, which is the opposite of what we need, does that not change the whole game?"

Everyone looked to Bryn except Justin, who stared into the fire, clenching his jaw.

"No. We continue to Cethin at first light. We still need an army, maybe even more so now that Balor is free."

A whispered *"yes"* floated through Bryn's mind that sounded nothing like Cyerra. Bryn focused on it, but Niamh elbowed her and the word was lost.

"Well, then we shall carry on and find more people to drag into his battle with us. The more the merrier, eh?"

"Yeah." Bryn rubbed at her temples, her anger losing its grip as she plunged into sadness, daring the Morrigan to do anything while she felt so emotionally unmoored.

The goddess took the dare.

"Stronger. Remember..." Grinding her teeth, Bryn tried to think of anything but what the Morrigan wanted, but the goddess was relentless. *"Bring them back ... completely."*

"Fine!" Bryn yelled out, everyone around her jumping.

"Bryn?" Niamh settled a hand on her shoulder, her dark eyes filled with concern, but Bryn looked to Sage.

"Sage, remember our conversation in Tanwen? Looks like the Morrigan wants exactly that done."

Sage furrowed her brow and then her face relaxed.

"If you pull our memories, we will be able to fight him, won't we?" Sage asked.

Bryn nodded. "Or so the Morrigan thinks anyway."

"I'm sorry, what now?" Justin asked, lifting his head from where he had been staring into the fire.

Kessler settled back next to her, his arms over his chest. "We haven't had enough drama and world tumbling revelations yet, huh?"

Sage let out a small laugh before covering her mouth and composing herself. "No, but it might be helpful to have all their knowledge within arms reach instead of bits and pieces." Sage looked to Bryn. "I will go first since I know more of what to expect."

Sage disentangled from Jace on the opposite side of the fire to kneel next to where Bryn sat on the log.

"Are you sure?" Bryn asked. "I can try..."

Sage took both of Bryn's hands in her own. "I trust you."

"Don't fry her brain." Kessler muttered, making Bryn second guess herself.

Sage shot Kessler a look. "You hush." Sage nodded to Bryn and with shaking hands, Bryn moved them to Sage's face and closed her eyes.

"You wanted this, so help me," Bryn whispered to the Morrigan, a shiver tracing her skin as blue light flared behind her eyelids, a sure sign her tattoos were alight.

Instead of a memory, like in Tanwen, a spark lit up in the darkness of her mind, and Bryn reached out for it. Small threads wrapped tightly around the orb of pure light, and with a delicate touch, Bryn unwrapped it, thread by thread.

When the last thread was lost, Bryn held the orb in her hand, a feeling of warmth and comfort radiated from it before it lifted and Bryn was back in her own mind.

Blinking her eyes open, the world around her came back into focus, as did Sage's face: her eyes wide and her hand to her lips.

"I can feel her…" Sage said in awe, her hazel eyes ringed with gold.

"Who?" Jace asked, now standing behind Sage.

With a smile, Sage looked over her shoulder at Jace, laying her hand over his.

"Brigid."

Bryn lowered her hands from Justin's face, his features pinched as he adjusted to sharing his mental space with Lugh.

"Are you alright?" Bryn asked as she sat back, giving him space.

"He is very ... loud and opinionated." Justin winced as he spoke.

It seemed both Justin and Bryn had the feisty gods while the rest had settled in with their deities peacefully.

Dian Cecht and Jace seemed to settle well enough as did Sage and Brigid. Goibniu, the god of smithing, offered Kessler minimal feedback, appearing as taciturn as Kessler himself.

"Thanks," Justin ground out, pushing to his feet to walk over to the edge of the forest before disappearing beyond the trees into the dark of the night.

She would need to rectify their disagreement soon, preferably before Cethin, but as he adjusted to his new mental roommate, she would give him space.

An unexpected shiver coursed through Bryn, accompanied by a rapid mental flash of her running through a wooded landscape. Dizziness swarmed her as the vision tilted, and she was looking up at the moon, sniffing the air before tilting her head down and licking a black paw?

"Is this you?" Bryn asked the Morrigan out loud as the vision cut off and she was staring at the fire again.

"Was what me?" Niamh asked as she seated herself next to Bryn.

"Sorry," Bryn shook her head, frustrated. "I was talking to the Morrigan ... which makes me seem so crazy..."

Niamh chuckled. "Here." Niamh dropped a brown leather satchel in Bryn's lap.

Bryn lifted the bag while giving Niamh a questioning look since it was not one she remembered seeing before.

"You need new clothing. Your remaining Ifreann clothes will not suffice and you've ruined this outfit. What with all the running around and fighting and smashing your fists into rocks." Niamh patted her thigh, the pants caked in mud and blood. Wrapping the coat tighter around her,

Bryn noticed more and more how cold her legs were. As if Niamh saying something had reminded the nerves in her legs how to work.

With a glance back at Bryn, Niamh pulled an oddly shaped pack back from her. When Bryn did nothing, Niamh sighed and rolled her eyes before pulling out distressed leather items that looked incredibly soft and supple.

"A vampire is amazing at getting what is needed in the wee hours of the night. Try them on. I will see if anything else I've obtained will work for this ragtag group of misfits trudging through the forest during the freezing season."

Holding the leather clothing in her hands, Bryn tried to think of where Niamh would've gotten them from.

"Aside from the souvenirs I picked up in Osgar, more so reparations for their bad behavior now, but there is a town nearby, not far off from us," Niamh must have caught Bryn's stiffening posture as she stood from the log. "It's abandoned. The people who lived there are long gone, but they seemed to have left quickly as there were plates set out like dinner was to be served. Items molding, trinkets tarnished, nothing packed up. Burden for them, but a boon for us."

Nodding, Bryn quietly moved off into the trees, the leaves rustling softly around her as she sought a secluded spot hidden from view. Trying on the stiff leather pants, she noted the snug fit, but she welcomed the protection they offered against the biting cold, a stark contrast to the thin linen she'd worn back in Osgar. The smell of tanned leather, thick and warm, filled her nostrils, reminding her of old books and worn saddles. The boots were too big, but she could make thick socks from her remaining clothes.

The leather top reminded her of the corsets she'd seen the Ifreann girls wear for dances and weddings. The fabric slid into place, molding to her body like a second skin, its smooth texture against her breasts both secure and slightly constricting since she was a tad more endowed than whoever had worn it last. The convenient front clasp allowed easy adjustment despite the unfamiliar tightness.

Throwing her linen shirt over the outfit, she felt a little less exposed, and with the addition of a fur cloak, she was a whole new person. Or more like the Morrigan if memory served correctly, but she only received a feeling of acceptance of her clothing from the Morrigan and nothing more.

Bryn made her way back to camp, where Niamh stood with a quiver of arrows and bow in hand. The scent of leather, pine, and damp earth filled the air as something stirred in the recesses of Bryn's memory. Taking the bow and arrows seemed oddly right, a sense of purpose settling over her as she ran her hand over the smooth wood.

A familiar resonance vibrated through her as she held the bow, like an old friend. She remembered the weight of it in her hands from long ago. The feel of the pull, the flow of loosing an arrow on her enemies. A memory the Morrigan was more than eager to share with her.

Holding up the bow, Bryn mimicked the movement of shooting, the Morrigan guiding her hands and helping her to aim. It was gentle mental nudges like remembering something you learned in school long after you left the classroom.

As she secured the bow and quiver, the recognizable weight across her shoulder brought a sense of readiness and wholeness, like a missing piece was restored.

Bryn gave Niamh a quick side hug, before she stepped back to brush a stray strand of hair from her messy braid that was in her eyes, which were stinging with unshed tears at the overwhelming emotions.

"Allow me." Niamh pushed Bryn's hand away, a shiver ran along her skin as the crackling fire cast dancing shadows on the faces of her companions. The gentle touch of Niamh's fingers in Bryn's hair was calming, a soothing rhythm that had her eyelids growing heavy as she relaxed into Niamh's ministrations.

The fire was nearly out, just a few embers glowing faintly, when she opened her eyes. The warm sun shone on Bryn and her party's backs, the light dappling through the leaves.

A sudden vision of her camp through the trees from someone else's perspective had Bryn faltering before she was back in her own body again.

Bryn sat up from where she had dozed off, her eyes scanning the tree line, searching for their unseen observer. The Morrigan came forward, but not on alert, almost as if she were waiting to greet their newcomer. She pushed to stand, watching Kian to see what move he might make since the Morrigan was giving her nothing.

"...part ... of ... us..."

Or at least nothing that made a lick of sense.

A strange low growl sent a shiver down her spine, but Kian's powerful growl, close behind, gave her the strength to slowly turn toward what could be a threat. There, bathed in the dappled sunlight filtering through the trees, was Kian, his silver fur gleaming, facing a massive black wolf. The scene vibrated with primal energy, punctuated by the sharp crackle of leaves under their paws as they advanced on each other.

Bryn watched the black wolf and realized she recognized it. It was the one she'd seen in Faerie before she opened the veil in Ifreann. The same wolf who had killed Scrios Arioch when the man had been intent on ending Bryn's life.

With a low growl that vibrated through the ground, neither Kian nor the black wolf made a move to attack, their bodies going perfectly still. Bryn listened, distinguishing the wolves' guttural growls as a low murmur, a quiet exchange rather than a threatening roar.

Pushing herself up, both wolves watched as she hobbled toward them, her face contorted in pain from her numb foot waking up, a pins and needles sensation making her wince.

A blinding flash of light erupted before Bryn made it to the wolves causing her to raise her hands. When she lowered them, she saw the black wolf had shifted, revealing a young woman's form.

A very *naked* young female with bright red hair, amber eyes, her pale skin covered in freckles, and a lean body as if she spent all her days running. Being a wolf, she most likely did.

"What in the hell?" Kessler's voice carried over from where he was getting up, his eyes wide in shock, the leather satchel that Niamh had secured for him falling from his fingers.

"Oh!" the girl laughed, looking down at herself as if being naked in the center of the camp was an afterthought. "Sorry! It's been a while since I took on my human form!"

With a joyous laugh, she didn't bother shielding herself from the cold as she grabbed Bryn's hand, shaking it fiercely.

"Hi! My name is Rieka, but you can call me Rae!"

"Blessed goddess," Kessler murmured in the background before he turned away, his body stiff as he walked into the woods.

The Morrigan's laughter erupted in Bryn's mind, wispy words following Bryn barely caught on the fringes of her awareness. "*...always ... enjoyed ... antics of ... wolf pup...*"

Rae tilted her head as she watched Kessler, her eyes narrowing before a gleam lit them as if she suddenly figured out a puzzling problem that had been plaguing her.

"Hello Rae, what can we do for you?" Bryn asked. It was a baffling sight—a naked woman, seemingly impervious to the cold, standing there unfazed.

Tilting her head the other way, Rae's eyes moved to meet Bryn's. "What do you mean? Don't you mean what can I do for *you*?" Rae asked, her brows furrowed in confusion as she looked between Bryn and Kian.

"You came to our camp. . ." Bryn replied, trailing off as she worked out what was going on. Why would a naked woman show up in her camp and say such a thing?

If there was a sensation for a goddess within to roll their eyes in annoyance, Bryn was sure she just felt it.

Nodding, Rae raised an eyebrow.

"Yes, because you called."

And the smugness radiating from the Morrigan told Bryn all she needed to know about who made that call.

Chapter 18

"There is the village I spoke of, the one where I obtained some of your clothing and supplies. Perhaps we should take a detour in that direction." The dense foliage provided Niamh with enough cover to remain hidden in the shadows beside Bryn, allowing her to stay with the group.

They'd set out at mid-morning and had been walking ever since. Bryn between Kian in his mortal form and Niamh. Sage and Jace walked ahead of her, while Justin and Rae walked the perimeter with Finian. Kessler was at the back of the group, fiddling with some small metal piece, his focus more on that than walking. More than a few times Bryn had looked back to check on him right as he tripped on a rock or rogue root.

It was mostly quiet but for a simple tune Sage hummed as they traveled.

Soon the sun was at its zenith and Niamh disappeared back into the veil until the sun lessened.

"We should try traveling through the veil with Niamh," Bryn said as Niamh and the Sanctuary girls crossed the veil in the forest while Bryn and the rest of the party watched.

"The veil would be the same distance to Cethin, just without the same threats as the mortal plane. Of course, I cannot guarantee there will not be any other issues with some of the more dangerous aspects of the Fae. Regardless, you'd still have to walk since the circles are down, which means the same distance if in the veil or on the mortal plane." Cyerra pushed the explanation into her head from where she flew above them and Bryn had repeated it for the group.

"Circles?" Kessler asked, his head popping up, his focus on Bryn instead of the metal piece that had held his attention most of the walk.

Kian turned, walking backwards as he spoke to Kessler. "They used to call them Faerie circles or rings. Humans would find themselves trapped in Faerie when they played too close to one or thought they could summon a Fae. Their luck, or lack thereof, was based on which Fae was there that day and which court they hailed from."

As Kian spoke, Bryn remembered the castles, or the ruins of them, spread throughout Faerie when she'd stood upon the overlooking cliffs with Manannán. "The Tuatha Dé Danann were the only ones to move between worlds as warriors of the mother goddess without the circles, but nature was stronger back then."

Kian shoved his hands in his pockets as he turned back around, his demeanor that of a man on a leisurely walk and not someone traveling through new, unknown lands. "The Faerie circles were a waypoint between the courts and the mortal realm. After some unfortunate incidents in finding humans were not made for the food and music of Faerie, the Fae found themselves banned from coming to Earth."

His focus moved to the forest as if he'd picked up on some noise that distracted him before he continued. "The reason so many stories warn against the Fae and otherworldly beings is because encounters with them can have unforeseen, sometimes dire, consequences."

Rae must have heard the sound too and bounded away. Since Kian was still walking beside Bryn, casually kicking small rocks out of his path with his black boots, it was clear there was no immediate danger.

Bryn had to admit, Cyerra was right. At least they knew more of what they would deal with on the mortal plane, Faerie being unknown to the rest of them.

With the sun lower, a shimmer in the air announced Niamh's return. Each of the women stepped out, taking their place among the others as if they had been walking with Bryn and her friends the whole time.

Rae broke through the brush, as small, glittering lights swirled around her as she materialized in her human form, fully clothed.

"Oh good! I came with clothes this time." A huge smile stretched over Rae's face as she confidently placed a hand on her leather-clad hips. The perfect fit of the clothes on Rae sparked an idea in Bryn's mind and she wondered if she could magically alter her clothing to fit as well. That wasn't a power that came back with her memories.

"I found a town ahead, lots of bricks and dust, but no people," Rae said. "Is that where our vamp lady was talking about?"

"Vamp lady?" Niamh murmured with an eye roll before she addressed Rae. "Yes, wolf-child, that is the town I spoke of."

With a grin and a thumbs-up for Niamh, Rae shifted, her muscles bunching and fur sprouting. Kessler had moved forward while Rae spoke. His focus was no longer on the metal object but on Rae and Bryn wondered if her shy, quiet blacksmith friend had a bit of a crush on the shifter.

"We can make camp there tonight," Bryn said as she watched Kessler sneak a peek at Rae one more time before moving to the front of the group for the first time since Osgar.

"Smitten men," Niamh laughed softly and Bryn couldn't disagree. Kian made a soft hum, his eyes darting to Bryn before Justin caught up to him, pulling his attention away as they walked. Bryn had decided not to address their moment from before everything happened with Cormac. There was no time for them to do more than survive long enough to kill a king.

As the trees grew sparse, Finian's excited barking signaled they were nearing the town before Rae could tell them. Bryn almost ran into Kessler when he made an abrupt stop. "This place has to be haunted."

Ignoring Kessler's words, Bryn moved around the big guy and took in the town. As the last light faded, long shadows stretched across the mossy stones and bricks, the air thick with the musty smell of mold and decaying leaves.

Unlike Tanwen, this town was not crumbling. All the structures were in place, their stones solid and strong, yet tattered curtains danced in the breeze from jagged, broken windows. Dried brown plants, victims of neglect, were strewn amongst the gray and black stone buildings, their brittle stalks snapping underfoot.

A few buildings were Pre-Collapse architecture. The strong, if aged, brickwork hinted at a past of more resilient building. Along the road, weathered gray stone houses were interspersed between the warm red, white, and pale pink brick homes. Dangerous, uneven protrusions and missing chunks of pavement made the road nearly impassable with each step feeling unstable underfoot.

The town had seen better days.

"Doesn't matter." With grim determination etched on her face, Bryn moved forward, the broken pavement sending up dust with each crunching step. They required supplies, and there was a chance the deserted town might have some. "We'll camp here tonight and see what we can gather up for the rest of our journey."

"Can we camp outside? I'm not sure I want to stay in one of the homes." Sage shivered, her eyes scanning the road and buildings as if ghosts and monsters might appear at any moment. Jace stepped closer to Sage, wrapping his arms around her.

Bryn dropped her pack on the road between the forest and the edge of the village.

"If it'll help you sleep, yes. Keep your blades sharp and your gun next to you." Bryn took in the tree line, giving the Morrigan just enough space not to crowd her, but guide her on an action plan. "We camp here, gather supplies, and with our souls merged more firmly with our gods, work on our powers."

Without a word of complaint, each of her friends dropped their packs, Finian dropping his huge, exhausted canine body next to Justin's pack with a huff.

Kessler made his way to the center of their group where Justin was setting large stones in a circle before gathering wood. Squatting next to the wood, Kessler took out his metal object, flicking it, and a small fire started. "Nothing in it but magic, but we have ourselves a lighter." The flame jumped from the metal contraption to Kessler's hand, a ball of flame dancing as Kessler dropped it to the dry wood Rae had gathered.

"You have fire powers, as well as an affinity for metal. I must say I am impressed, darling." Niamh threw a small stick into the rapidly growing fire. Sage and Cyerra added fragrant moss, while Rae and Kian shifted to patrol the perimeter, their keen noses alert to any change in smell within the undergrowth. Finian, with his second wind, was a blur of motion, dancing between Kessler and Justin, his bark echoing as he playfully snapped at the floating embers from the fire.

"Comes in handy if I decide to continue my career as a blacksmith," Kessler said, his smile dropping at what that meant. For that, they would need a permanent place to stay, and in order to have that, they needed to win a war.

Her friends settled near the fire except for Rae and Kian, and Bryn grabbed her bow and quiver before making her way further into the forest along the road. They had walked an entire day, but Bryn had more than a few thoughts gathering in her mind that would keep her from sleeping. The Morrigan, understanding Bryn's desperate need for an outlet, sent her memories of long nights before a battle when she was in a similar state of mind.

Nocking the arrow, Bryn pulled and released, the arrow missing the target almost entirely. A strong huff of indignation within her mind had Bryn grinding her teeth.

"Yes, yes, your skill in battle is legendary, but this is all new to me, so maybe give me a break?"

Before Bryn could try again, her body was being puppeted into position.

"Stop," Bryn growled, pushing against the Morrigan, but she was stronger ever since Manannán had gotten his hands on her.

In a fluid movement Bryn had no idea her body was capable of, she aimed and hit the center of a tree several hundred yards away. The Morrigan released Bryn, and the bow clattered to the ground as Bryn gaped in stunned disbelief at the distance and accuracy. A smug sense of triumph washed over her from the goddess.

The breaking of a branch had the Morrigan on high alert and Bryn spinning to see Jace break through the tree line. As if all the energy had left his body, he plunked himself down, leaning back against a wide tree trunk as he rested his hands on his spread knees.

"Impressive," he gave her a tired, but genuine smile.

A small, amused snort escaped her lips as she settled beside Jace, and mimicked his position, the rough texture of the bark cool against her back. Both of them quietly stared out toward where the arrow had pierced the tree, letting the forest's natural symphony wash over them.

"What are we doing, Bryn?"

Bryn turned her head to really look at him, and even with the power of a god running through his veins, he looked defeated.

"We are going to Cethin—"

"I know that." Jace met her eyes. "What I mean is how in the hell do we think we can defeat some all-powerful deity that has the advantage." With a wave toward the surrounding forest, he continued. "Once the magic of whatever Cormac did runs out, so will this piece of nature. The rest of the world has to be just as bad as Ifreann, and that leaves us where? Where do we get enough power to kill a god?"

Bryn looked away, gathering thoughts that made no sense since deep down, she felt the same way.

"We've been through hell. We've lost people, back in Ifreann, and I am still wrapping my head around everything. Like my mother—"

"How do you not hate me for killing her?" Bryn asked, her words small as she folded her arms around her stomach. Even with the hum of disagreement from the Morrigan, Bryn felt like her stomach was full of stones at the memory of that pivotal moment when she murdered her aunt in cold blood.

Keeping his head against the tree, Jace rolled his head to the side to look at her. "Hate you?"

"I killed her, Jace," Bryn ground out the words again, louder this time.

Jace used the tree for leverage, pivoting to face her. "She stabbed you and was going to leave you to die. There was no other outcome than the one that happened." Shaking his head, Jace ran his hands over his face, his voice cracking. "She chose her end."

Touching her earlobe three times with her finger and thumb, Bryn gathered the courage to speak. "I am still so sorry."

Jace grabbed the hand tapping her ear, pulling her into a hug as her lungs constricted and her eyes burned.

"Don't be," he said, his voice muffled by her shirt. Loosening his hold, he sat back, tears shimmering in his pale blue eyes. "I'm glad that you made it through. After everything she did to you..."

Jace went quiet, staring off into the trees before he shook his head. "That makes me a horrible person, doesn't it? A son should be as concerned for his mother as he is his cousin, but I only felt ... I only felt relief she was gone, Bryn, and that is so wrong," he whispered. "I was relieved at the death of my own mother."

"When she chose her church, her beliefs, over you in those final moments, I no longer saw her as your mother." Bryn took Jace's face in her hands, holding his gaze as he blinked back tears. "A mother would give anything for her child, sacrifice herself for them, but she chose to sacrifice *you* instead. Mallory was dead long before she stopped breathing."

Jace started to respond, but a massive explosion had them stare at each other for a split second before jumping up and running back to camp, a plume of smoke rising to greet them. Another explosion had them skidding to a stop, holding up their hands at the intense flash of light blinding them.

Finally, the seared spots of light in her vision turned into Justin and Kessler. Justin coughed from the acrid, choking smoke as Kessler kneeled, waving his hands frantically over the roaring fire, eyes wide with what looked like a desperate plea for the flames to subside.

"Sorry, everyone!" Kessler yelled out before the fire settled and Kessler fell onto his back, throwing his arm over his eyes. Justin sagged against a nearby tree. Bryn tried to choke down a laugh at the sight of the two men coming down from their panic. "Magic got a little out of hand."

"One small fire, and it turns into an explosive blast," Jace muttered, as he walked over to check on the men.

Bryn felt that was an apt metaphor for their entire journey so far.

Chapter 19

Settled around the fire, eating from the small rations they had left, Bryn listened to her friends talk about memories they had as their other selves.

Sage and Jace both had the same memory of Niamh in a cemetery, but from alternate perspectives.

"Yes, they were the welcome party when I rose from the dead," Niamh had said. "Sage managed to concoct some herbal remedy that killed me instead of keeping me from getting pregnant." Sage flinched but relaxed when Niamh shot her a wink.

"I had a spear. I can remember the weight of it, everything, but I have no idea where it went and Lugh is mad as hell about that," Justin said as he shook his head before taking another bite of his bland ration bar.

Kessler grunted, his eyes on where Rae had slipped into the trees. "I made a functioning hand out of metal, did that magic voodoo to it so it worked like a real hand and everything. Wish I'd known about that before Caden..."

The camp went quiet after that, no one feeling up to opening that emotional land mine.

"We need to actually use these powers, not just rely on memories," Bryn said as she stood up, wiping her hands on her thighs.

"I agree." Justin stood as well, the rest of their party following. "But I'm not quite sure how to practice my so-called magic."

"You practice what you remember of combat. Each of you on several occasions used your magic to take down armies that were seen as more myth than real." Kian held his arms out to his sides as shadows and purple specs of light danced around his hands before creating daggers from shadows.

Sage threw her hand out and vines crawled across the ground toward them before peeling back. "That's about all I've figured out so far." She smiled, her cheeks darkening.

"So—" Bryn leaned down to grab her bow "—we start from what we know and if your deities are anything like the Morrigan, they will jump in immediately to correct anything you do."

They all spread out through the small village, only Kessler staying near the fire.

Bryn moved to the tree line, within range of her friends, but near enough to nature.

"You should move more into the village," Kian said from next to her as he watched Kessler holding out a chunk of metal that looked like a rusted piece of the truck they left behind.

"Why is that?"

Kian looked at her from the side with a raised eyebrow before he said one word. "Death."

"*Power ... held in ... the earth...*"

Without a word, Bryn made her way deeper into the village past her friends who were wrestling with their powers. Powers that could not be fed nearly as well as their lives before since they now pulled from a dying earth.

The shadows danced around her from the sun lowering itself in the sky as she made it to an open area, deep grooves in the road from the traffic when the village had been alive and well. Small patches of overgrown grass around the homes were bending in the gentle breeze, and Bryn settled herself in front of a home larger than the rest. The red brick was lighter than what it might have been from baking in the sun, the shutters long gone.

She closed her eyes, not stopping the Morrigan from surfacing as she tried to feel her power deep within her, the power she'd only used in dire situations so far.

Silence, even from the Morrigan met her, but a deep hum grew around her as she ran her hand over the surrounding grass.

With no idea how long she sat on the dark patch of grass away from her friends, a chill rose around her hands and ankles. Her eyes shot open, the street dark now from the sun setting long ago, and the animal part of her brain told her to run.

The Morrigan had no such thoughts and instead froze her muscles to keep her from escaping as Bryn's terror rose to the surface.

Pale imitations of the souls she took to Faerie floated around her. The cold seized her arms and legs, and there ghostly vestiges of hands breaking through the ground in front of her.

Bryn tried to scream, but her body was locked down as the souls whirled before her, becoming more humanoid in appearance, some of them grotesque, awful things having been done to them, and she knew their state was how they died.

These people hadn't left abruptly. They had been slaughtered, and from the sight of the wounds, by human hands.

Weapons such as knives and guns, the wounds too close to what Cormac had done to Caden, and Bryn understood now why the forest met this town.

Cormac used these people to feed the protection of Osgar.

Children danced, unaware of their states and Bryn sobbed inside at the innocent lives lost. Women followed, holding young babies that would never grow up. Men laughing with gaping neck wounds, their lives and deaths playing out before Bryn like a macabre play.

"Stop..." Bryn begged, barely able to get the word to loosen from her tongue.

All the ghosts of the village turned to her as the Morrigan pushed and pulled at Bryn, leaving her helpless as the ghosts took step after step closer to her. Each step bringing an onset of emotional whiplash: pain, fear, relief, deep-seated anger.

No matter how hard Bryn struggled, she was unable to tear herself from the Morrigan's grip, and though her anger at the goddess was potent, the emotions unraveling within her from these people overshadowed it all.

Whisper soft but with the power of the gods themselves, the ghostly hands touched her, and she jumped and stiffened, as if currents of electricity were fed directly into her nervous system.

A soundless scream left her as the lives of these people hit her all at once, a montage of memories from too many souls, and it was far too much.

The piercing scream that left Bryn's mouth was the only relief she felt at the onslaught, but it wasn't enough. Her body was tearing, breaking down, her mortal shell too weak for this much power.

Something jerked her back, releasing her frozen limbs, the ghosts disappearing and the hands restraining her gone, she fell.

Tattooed arms wrapped around her, pulling her into a lap as she fell apart emotionally. Her full-body sobs moving her within Kian's arms as he worked to hold on to her, whispering affirmations to calm her.

"Someone better explain what happened right the fuck now," Justin said from somewhere nearby, but Bryn couldn't say the words.

As if she could crawl into Kian for safety, she got as close as possible, her limbs not working with her as she fought for control of her body and her emotions.

"Give us a moment, please," Kian asked, and soft retreating footsteps were the only reply.

"I"—Bryn hiccuped, her sobs weakening, but not gone—"can't do this."

Kian hummed as Bryn wiped her face, the tears having drenched her, her hands shaking far too much before Kian pushed them away and wiped at her face with the edge of his shirt.

"Not tonight, and not all at once like that, but with time you will know how to control your magic, to funnel it better," he whispered into her hair, his tone turning angry as he wrapped her up in another hug. "The Morrigan knows better."

A sense of annoyance followed by a sliver of shame flowed through her at his words, before the Morrigan dipped off again.

Bryn pulled back, placing her hand against her chest and taking deep breaths to steady herself, Kian releasing his hold, but didn't let her go completely.

When she raised her head, her eyes met his silver ones, and with a quiet tenderness, Kian pushed a curl behind her ear before lowering his forehead to hers.

"We will get there, mo ghrá."

Chapter 20

Bryn stared at the stars above her, her eyes swollen and face tight from crying. Thankfully by the time she'd laid down, the others were asleep or at least faking it, so she didn't have to answer any questions about what happened.

Her brain was exhausted by the events, by what the Morrigan had put her through, and yet her body was a live wire.

The moon moved across the sky, as Kian's furry form laid next to her after he finished his patrol, falling into a peaceful slumber almost immediately. His breath a soft, rhythmic whoosh, his ears twitched slightly every so often.

With a long sigh, Bryn settled her hands on her stomach and closed her eyes, begging her body to rest. Instead of falling into a quiet oblivion, the Morrigan surfaced, jolting Bryn's already destroyed nerves.

Frustrated, Bryn pushed to sitting, causing Kian to grumble as she cursed the Morrigan inwardly right as a long, dark shadow caught her eye, revealing a shape that wasn't the familiar silhouette of a wolf.

The other members of her party each rose from their makeshift beds, instantly on alert like Bryn.

As the shadow lengthened, goosebumps rose along her skin and her spine tingled with unease as her tattoos began to glow. A cold sweat broke out on her forehead as Kian shot up, his body tense and alert, hackles raised, the sudden movement betraying his prior deep sleep.

"What is that?" Bryn whispered, her voice barely audible above the sound of ragged breathing that was growing louder as the shadow moved closer.

A shadowy, semi- opaque horse-shaped form, vast and indistinct, inched into the fire's glow, its edges wavering. There was nothing there—no body, no object—to account for the shadow.

"What in the...?" Justin asked, baffled by the shadowed creature as he armed himself with the gun he slept next to each night.

What would guns do to something that had no physical form? They could see through the horse-like creature, the houses visible and distorted through its semi-opaque body.

Kian snarled, before silver light illuminated the space and he was a man once again, cloaked in shadow, blades of shadowed starlight in his hands.

"Fae creature," Kian said, his voice deep and guttural, as if stuck in the transition between man and wolf.

Finian, who was usually up front with bared teeth, was pushing up against Justin, his tail tucked between his legs and body shaking.

Bryn's hand trembled as she felt for her dagger. A small, useless thing against something intangible, but she needed *something* to hold and feel a modicum of protection.

Her jaw tightened as the Morrigan pushed her power, then spoke through Bryn in a deep feminine voice. "A bit far from home, Puca."

"You travel far, past dead circles and dead land, and called for the Fae creatures lost. Why?" A ghostly voice, rustling like the wind through the trees, formed words in the surrounding air, its sound both terrifying and mesmerizing as it echoed through the darkness.

It stepped forward, its gait horse-like as it took in their group, its eyes a reddish orange now upon closer inspection. "But you are not merely travelers, are you?"

Kian bent his knees, ready to attack, but its question provoked the Morrigan to answer.

"No, we are the Tuatha Dé Danann, and I am the Morrigan."

With a shudder, the creature shook its head, the inky black mane swirling around it like an angry storm cloud, and a plume of dark smoke puffed from its nostrils.

"They are dead."

Now, Bryn was the one to shake her head. "We were reborn into human bodies, but our souls and powers remain. We are looking to reach Cethin—"

"To find your shadowed army." The creature cut her off. Its fiery eyes moved to Kian. "Ah, I should have paid more attention. The general returns with our saviors." It turned, the sound of multiple groans filling the air in its wake as it faced back where it had come from. "Not many travel anymore since the rift. Come."

As Kian began to walk beside Bryn, his blades, a fusion of shadow and shimmering light, vanished as they followed the Puca. "A rift?"

The rhythmic thud of footsteps behind her reassured her that her friends were following.

"The powerful ones have returned to replenish the lands once more." The wind whipped around them as the puca spoke, its lips never moving. Bryn had no idea who it was speaking to, but they were in the courtyard of the worn town surrounded by nothing but the moon and its shadows.

"They can embellish and bend their words, so keep that in mind," Kian whispered in warning. "It could either be here to bring good tidings or absolute misery."

Bryn was betting on misery. That had seemed to be a theme for, well, most of her life.

There was no response that Bryn could hear from whoever the puca was talking to, but the creature bent down, kneeling before empty air. "I will do as you say."

Bryn wanted to look at her friends, see what they thought of all this, but the Morrigan pushed her to stand tall and wait quietly. It eased her anxiety to see Niamh and the other women moving through the shadows, watching and waiting should she need them.

The creature faced them once again. "Tidings from those of us who have stowed away, crossing the veil for safety and finding none. We've waited to return home, but the most powerful of us continue to fall."

Kian moved closer to her, a purplish-blue flame with swirling shadows inside flickering in his palm as if he readied himself to call on his weapons.

"Be still. I mean you no harm." Its voice, faint and wispy, carried on the gentle breeze. "I am simply the one chosen to show myself and let you know that those of us of the Otherworld would like to leave this realm, instead of hiding in the veil. So close to home and yet unable to cross the last threshold. We ask that you find a way for us to return home."

"I've felt no rift," the Morrigan said through her, and the puca gave a very horse-like huff.

"It has long closed, goddess, when your people disappeared. But here you are, howling for the deaths of those lost, and we heard you. Perhaps the human aspect of you lacks the sensitivity to the melody of the natural world."

A thread of anger toward Bryn had her stepping back as if she could escape the Morrigan. If anyone should feel such a thing, it would be the goddess who stepped through to Faerie time and time again.

Kian was Fomorian, so he wouldn't feel such things as a rift in the mortal world.

"Stop … fighting … me."

The puca stepped away. "You will find no issue here with us, but there are those of a darker nature that roam these lands. We have no power over them, so be safe, keepers of the Fae people." With that, the shadowed creature melted away, no longer standing before them, but lost to the rest of the shadows.

Finian barked, his canine body relaxing as if he felt the oppressiveness of the situation dissolve.

"What was the purpose of that?" Justin asked, his voice piercing in the sudden silence.

Kian was the one to answer. "That was us being given safe passage by the puca as well as a warning. It will not harm us while we are here, but something else might."

"We need to find cover for the night and have more people on guard rotations," Bryn said, as herself since the Morrigan retreated, a trail of anger in her wake.

"I'm in no way sure what the hell is going on, but I guess if I have to tango with a spirit in a house for a good night's sleep, so be it," Justin muttered to the group, running a hand through his messy golden blond hair. "But no one stays alone and we have three or four on guard at all times. Not me though. I'm exhausted."

"Since I have little need for sleep, I shall keep watch." Without waiting for a response, Niamh moved toward the forest where the Sanctuary girls were roaming and vanished into the trees behind them.

"I need to change forms. Being human is making me itchy." Cyerra shuddered. "I will keep watch on the eastern side." In a flash of light, Cyerra took her crow form and flew the opposite direction from where Niamh had disappeared.

"We will stay in the larger house," Bryn said, earning a look of surprise from Sage. She knew what they thought and they were right. It was the place where she had broken down, and she wanted nothing more to do with it, but it was also big enough for everyone to stay together.

Quiet whispers moved through the group as they gathered their belongings and trudged deeper into the village where the larger house sat.

Stepping through the worn wooden front door, Kian murmured a spell from next to her, and little orbs of purple light appeared in the air, floating around the room. They weren't very bright but were enough to show the structure of the home.

Bryn raised a brow, but Kian only shrugged. "I have been playing around with my abilities, getting used to them again."

Nodding, she continued into the house, her friends following. Bryn wandered around the abandoned living room looking at photos of a family of four from long ago. As the orb moved past them, the photos showed their yellowed age from the lack of purple light. Kian meticulously inspected every room, leaving a trail of soft purple lights behind.

Without having to say anything, Jace and Sage disappeared up the stairs to one of the rooms after Kian confirmed the house was clear.

Justin followed, his shoulders bowed and his steps slow. Her friends were worn out, all of them. Worn out and traumatized. How they managed to keep going was the question of the hour.

Kian came down after Justin and Finian disappeared down the hallway at the top. "Only two rooms upstairs. We have a room down here, but that's it aside from the kitchen and living area."

"Guess me and this stud—" Rae pointed with her thumb toward Kessler. "—are on first watch," Rae said as she moved to the fireplace and settled herself, sitting against the wall.

"I, uh, I guess…" Kessler murmured as he ran his hand along the back of his neck, and Bryn could see his cheeks darken with a blush.

"We can share a space. I promise to keep all my clothing on and my paws to myself," Rae said with a wink.

Kessler gave Bryn a helpless look before settling in a chair near the window, the squeak of it under his weight a warning before it broke and he tumbled to the floor. It seemed it would be a long watch for Kessler in the night.

Rae jumped up to help, but Kessler waved her away. "I got it."

"It's us, then," Kian said from behind her, and Bryn nodded with one last look at Kessler as he swore at the chair before she followed Kian.

Stepping into the last empty room in the house, there was a padded mattress on an iron frame in shockingly better shape than the hunter shacks in Osgar.

"I can change into a wolf if you'd feel more at ease sharing space with me that way."

Bryn bit her lip before she walked to the bed, running her hand along the edge of the mattress.

"When I was the Morrigan, we never slept near each other like we do now." As the words left her mouth, Bryn fisted her hands but didn't turn to him. Nerves crawled through her at the path she was directing the conversation. She was not forward, at least she hadn't been in Ifreann, but she didn't share her mind with a strong-willed goddess then either.

"No, we had separate tents since you liked your privacy when you had … visitors." His growl on the last word made her look back at him.

"When I was with my lovers, you mean."

His jaw was tight, his eyes narrowed as he looked off to the side away from her. Bryn was scared to admit her feelings, but his reaction was enough for her to know it wasn't as one sided as she'd thought.

"So, should we…," his words drifted as he waved to the bed she was standing next to.

Bryn could feel the Morrigan, knew that she did not feel the same attraction Bryn did to her general, but she allowed Bryn to lead on without a fight. Whispered words floated through her mind. "*…must still fight … together … on field of battle. Do not … create issues … my general.*"

"*He is not yours,*" Bryn snapped, then shook her head. Both her and the Morrigan were already angry at each other from earlier and she had no desire to fight it out tonight.

Her thoughts moved from the goddess to the way Kian had held her in the forest as she crossed into the veil. Then to the moments of tenderness that she'd felt from him even before he realized he wasn't her enemy in Ifreann. "There is more to us than the Morrigan and her general this time around, isn't there?"

His silver eyes flashed and shimmered with supernatural light. The intensity in his gaze made her feel like the only one in existence. That, to him, it was only her.

"There was only our connection on the battlefield, and I was content with that."

A battle she might not win loomed, yet the thought of a life unlived echoed in her mind, a cold fear battling against her hard-won courage within herself. With bravery she didn't know she possessed, Bryn stepped up to him.

Something in her told her that if it was rejection tonight, if tomorrow was awkward, then she would still have no regrets.

Bryn Kenneally was done sticking her head in the sand.

Kian swallowed hard, his Adam's apple bobbing as their chests nearly touched. The toe of her boots met his, her face stopping a breath away, the silence heavy with tension. Her hand went to his jaw, running up it until she cupped his jaw. "And now? Are you fine with us being allies on the battlefield, and someone else sharing my bed at night while you wait outside in wolf form?"

Something feral flashed in his eyes and her heartbeat sped up to an almost concerning rate.

"The Morrigan—"

Placing her hand on Kian's chest to stop him, she rose on the tips of her toes to whisper in his pointed ear. "My name is Bryn." She dropped onto the flats of her feet and watched the storm gathering in his silver eyes.

"Be sure of this, *Bryn*. I have waited for this for far too long and once this is done, I will not share like Dagda or any of your past lovers." The room vibrated with Kian's immense aura, the wolf and the man speaking as one. "You were my ally in that life, even though I was hired to spill your blood."

A strange clarity arrived, understanding his body language and words even though the rest of her felt lost in the chaos of her attraction.

"And now?" she whispered, his sigh hitting her lips.

"Now it would be as if I spilled my own. Should another touch you, I would damn them to the abyss where the Fomori were birthed, dragging their corpse beneath the sea myself."

"Kiss me," Bryn breathed, and his hands snapped to her hips, pulling her flush against his body. There was no question of his arousal as she felt the thickness of him against her belly.

"Is that an order?" he growled, one hand going to the back of her neck, threading his fingers through her hair.

"Never."

His eyes burned into hers, the sudden brightness of the room highlighting the intensity of his feelings through his magic before his lips found hers, their tongues tangling in a heated dance. Small growls escaped Kian as he scooped her up, her legs wrapping around him, bringing their cores together.

The room whirled, a dizzying blur of sensation, their kiss never faltering. He grabbed her hands, spinning her until her back pressed against the wood of the door, his mouth ravaging hers.

Silver threads moved behind her eyelids, but Kian kept her attention as his lips moved down her neck, giving small teasing bites along the sensitive skin of her throat. Too soon, he pulled away, his gaze meeting hers.

His silver irises more wolf than man as he reach to cup her jaw, his thumb moving gently over her swollen lips. Bryn wondered if his wolf had ever been so close to the surface outside of combat.

Kian's head turned to the side, listening to something with his superior wolf hearing. He closed his eyes, the muscles of his jaw tensing, before he leaned in to give her another kiss.

A kiss that was soft, caring, and over far too soon.

With soft eyes holding a million unspoken apologies, Kian carefully let her down.

"It's too dangerous to lose ourselves." His voice was deep and rough as he spoke. "But when we find safety, we will finish this."

Kian punctuated the sentence, the statement, with one more gentle kiss before he led them to bed.

Bryn worked to get her bearings as he curled his body around her. Questions about the connection they felt gathered in her mind. It wasn't just lust, but something far more.

Her last thoughts before she lost the fight to sleep were of silver threads and what they could mean.

Chapter 21

A loud crack jolted Bryn from her sleep, and she and Kian were instantly alert. Bryn scrambled for her dagger before rushing to the door, relieved she'd kept her clothes on when she went to bed.

"It's not the Rovers," Kian said as he followed her from the bed into the living area of the home where Kessler and Rae were on alert too.

The rhythmic thunder of approaching hoof beats sent her scrambling to the window next to Rae, only for Kian to catch her and pull her swiftly to the floor, just below the windowsill.

"It's not the puca either," Kian whispered against her ear, so very quiet, knowing exactly what she had been thinking while he motioned to Rae and Kessler to get down. "We should have left after its warning. I hope the rest of the group knows to stay away from the windows."

Something hit the glass above them, and Kian put his hand over her mouth to keep her from making a noise.

The impact of another blow against the far door vibrated through the floor, making Bryn jump and stifle another squeak under Kian's hand.

"Stay quiet," Kian whispered in her ear. "If the puca was concerned enough to warn us about this creature, we need to tread carefully."

Bryn wanted to rip his hand away and look out to see what the threat was, but the hoof beats stopped right outside the front door.

The sound of someone dismounting a horse, the saddle creaking, carried to her before a huge bang on the door, raising motes of dust that shimmered in the moonlight streaming around the shadow of the horse through the nearby window. The horse shifted away, letting the moonlight flood back into the room.

An eerie whistle that felt like a harbinger of death shattered Bryn's calm. A loud knock on the door had her and Rae jumping. Kessler moved in the corner of her vision, slowly toward the door, holding something in his hand that she couldn't make out in the dark.

As a shadow fell across the window, eclipsing the moonlight, Bryn tilted her head back. There in the window was a horse, its eyes pure fire, and nothing at all like the puca. Puffs of smoke-like breath, fiery and hot enhanced its demonic appearance, more akin to hellfire than the cold night's vapor.

With each bang on the door, the whistling grew louder, and the creature's malevolent presence grew heavier in the air.

Kian pulled her further into a dark corner, his grip tightening as his shadows moved over them, obstructing the view of them from the outside, as he settled them in a place where they could keep an eye on both windows.

Rae joined Kessler by the door, not opening it, but waiting should it try to come in.

The eerie tune continued to carry through the house, echoing off the walls and reverberating through Bryn's skull, igniting her fight-or-flight instinct.

An all too familiar bark broke the silence and the whistling stopped.

"Finian!" Bryn shouted as she jumped up, Kian not moving fast enough to stop her.

"Stop!" Kian yelled, but she had her dagger in hand, shoving open the door, as she fought off Kian's shadows when they became tangible enough to restrain her.

Stumbling outside after wrenching herself free from the shadows, she ran to where Justin was shoving his hound back, both of them having been on watch when the creature came. The moon cast enough of a glow to see he only had his pistol, and not his normal rifle.

"Back inside, Bryn!" Justin yelled as the horse moved out from the open alley between the houses.

Her gaze followed the horse's outline, and as the moonlight caught it, she saw the rider had remounted. Astride the demon horse sat a figure, its body grotesquely headless, the saddle creaking under its weight.

The jaunty and eerie tune started again as the man held up something.

"What in the fresh hells…"

Bryn ignored Justin as she squinted to see what the rider was holding up and disgust filled her when a severed head came into focus. A head whistling with sharp teeth, sharper than even Rae and Kian in their wolf form. It gave her a grotesque smile after it finished its tune, its skin pale as death, its eyes sewn shut and oozing.

The mouth opened once more, a gaping maw filled with darkness, and a torrent of moths and flies erupted as it let out a long, mournful wail. That was enough to have Bryn spinning back to the door of the house where Kian was, but it slammed shut in front of her before she could make it.

Bryn watched in horrified fascination as a spine, disturbingly human-like and wet, slid back toward the creature after impacting the door with a sickening crunch.

Before she could recover, she felt the horse's breath on her neck, a soft, hot puff against her skin, its movement somehow completely silent on the rough, uneven street.

Shadows wrapped around her and then Kian was there, pulling her behind him, but she couldn't move. A wave of icy magic had washed over her, leaving her completely paralyzed.

She fell boneless to the ground, her knees hitting the hard concrete first before her body tumbled, her arms frozen and unable to break her fall. Stars danced before her eyes when her head made contact with the broken cement, and ringing filled her ears before the paralysis slowly released its grip on her.

As the world slowly righted itself, the dizziness fading, she pushed herself up and grabbed her dagger, its cold steel reassuring in her hand. Kian was in the middle of the road, moving out of range of the spinal cord, the horse's hooves stomping as it blew out fiery breath after fiery breath. The rider's focus was solely on him.

Around Kian were shadow animals. Bears and wolves, all sorts of creatures of the forest, and as Kian threw his hands out, they attacked the headless man.

Bryn had never seen his powers manifest like this before. They were similar to the shadow crows and wolves she'd called in her fight with Declan. Something that was new to her in this life, and she wondered if somehow she'd pulled, or borrowed, those powers from him.

The moon disappeared behind the clouds and an unnatural darkness fell on them, making Bryn lose sight of the creature. Stumbling in the dark, Bryn tried to narrow her focus, her eyes taking in as much as she could with so little light. The Morrigan settled along her skin, readying to take over even as Bryn pushed her back.

When the clouds parted and the moon shone through again, the headless man was right in front of her and Kian was nowhere in sight.

"Kian!" she screamed, as the rider stretched out skeletal fingers, the last bits of decaying flesh clinging to them, toward her. Before it reached her, the rider was seized from behind and thrown to the ground.

Niamh stood over him, her blood-red eyes blazing, serrated teeth bared in a terrifying snarl, long canines glinting in the dim light. Her nails had transformed into sharp, curved claws as she flexed her fingers.

"Hello again, husband."

A shadowy Kian coalesced next to Bryn, not fully formed, but undeniably there, the air shimmering slightly around him.

Niamh circled the creature on the ground, her face contorted with malice before she raised her head, her eyes burning a deep, blood-red. "Bryn! Darling, let me introduce you!" Niamh gave a throaty, threatening laugh before grabbing the rotten head from the man's hand. "This is my first husband!"

"Yes, that very one, friends!" she yelled out as Justin stepped out into the moonlight, Kessler and Rae following. Jace stood in the doorway of the house they'd slept in, at least his shadow, a lamp lit behind him where Sage was trying to see what was happening.

"He killed me and now he rots away, running around in the middle of the night, torturing people because he didn't get enough sick satisfaction doing so in life." Niamh threw her husband's head, its mouth open in a silent scream. A loud grotesque thud sounded in the night as it hit one of the brick walls of a nearby house.

The body of her husband launched itself toward Niamh, but she was too fast, especially since it was off-kilter in its movements. It spun, narrowly missing Niamh, then lunged again, and this time her hand slammed into its chest, spraying blood all over Niamh as it fell to its knees.

Releasing the lifeless weight of his body, Niamh gently cupped his heart in her hands. The slow, steady, and dying beat a stark contrast to the surrounding stillness. The darkness that had cloaked the town lessening until it fell completely away.

"I finally have your heart." Niamh smiled with a mouth full of sharp teeth, squeezing it, her wicked claws tearing into the flesh. "Wretched thing."

With a determined glint in her eye, Niamh spun and walked off with it into the darkness of the forest, the object clutched tightly in her hand.

The weight of Niamh's unspoken intentions pressed down on Bryn, making her unsure if she dared to follow. Soon there was a flash of fire, the roar of the flames lighting up the trees of the forest. The satisfaction of revenge was Niamh's, but Bryn thought it a hollow victory after her friend had lost so much.

"I am not sure how much more I want to learn about this group," Justin whispered, and Bryn couldn't say she disagreed.

The demonic horse nickered, letting out a huff that sounded more like a sigh than anything as Niamh came back out into the road, wiping her hands off on her dress. She walked toward the horse, stepping over her husband's body like it was nothing more than a discarded piece of trash.

Niamh reached up toward the horse, and Bryn was about to step in and stop her before the horse rubbed its nose against Niamh's face and neck. "You poor thing. You spent so much of your time on earth as nothing more than that wretched man's tool.

"He never saw us as anything more than objects. We were never living creatures to that wicked demon of a man." Niamh's voice cracked on the last word, a sob escaping her lips as the horse nuzzled her shoulder, offering a comforting equine hug. "Bryn? Darling?"

Stepping forward, Bryn carefully skirted the restless horse as Niamh turned to her, her eyes like polished obsidian.

"Will you help my friend here pass to Faerie? He doesn't deserve what was done to him."

After a slight hesitation, Bryn nodded, unsure if it was any different from moving a human soul over. She'd never worked with animals before, but she would try for Niamh, and for the innocent animal that Niamh seemed to have a connection with.

"Rest now, my dear," Niamh whispered, kissing the horse on the forehead before stepping away, her eyes glassy.

Bryn took her place and put her hand out, calling on its soul and the horse's body shivered as it broke down, flesh to bone to dust.

Well, that was new, but the horse was already technically dead, and so Bryn pressed on.

An orb, the horse's soul, shone brighter than any human soul Bryn had ever seen. It hovered, waiting for Bryn, and as her fingers reached out for it, she felt so much all at once. An innocent animal, mistreated, held out hope that one day Niamh, the only human who had ever shown him love, would return. Looking for her night after night, never forgetting her. That Niamh would free him and give him those delicious cubes that she always snuck him when she came into the barn at night while the mean man slept.

Closing her eyes, Bryn held the soul tenderly against her chest as she crossed the veil. It was far easier than it was when she was moving a human, slipping seamlessly through to Faerie, where Bryn found Senan waiting.

"Senan?"

The horse moved forward, pushing at the soul with her nose. "*He is safe now. The others will care for him. Thank you, Bryn.*"

The soul shimmered and grew until a horse of light appeared and shook itself next to Senan, rubbing its head along the underside of her giant warhorse's neck before taking off into a run, truly free for what was most likely the first time in its existence.

With a small dip of her head, Senan turned and walked after the horse, and with that last beautiful vision of an innocent free from the pain of mortal life, Bryn pulled herself back to the mortal realm.

Blinking her eyes as the world came back into focus, Kian was there, pulling her into a hug as he let out a long sigh of relief, his heartbeat thundering against her ear.

"Was Niamh not from another continent? How did that ... thing get here?" Sage asked, as she and Jace walked up.

"A place called Ireland," Niamh said as she started to wander, her gaze intently fixed on something on the ground. "A long way from here across a huge ocean."

"That could only mean one thing." Kian said as the Morrigan whispered the words at the same time through her mind. "There is a functioning faerie circle somewhere,"

Bryn pulled back from Kian, working through what that meant as Justin came over, yelling out to Niamh. "What are you looking for, Niamh?"

"A souvenir. You know, he never brought me anything from his travels in life, but he did in death. Perhaps some men are capable of change."

The group all turned to see Niamh as she held up the spinal cord her husband had used as a whip.

"Look! I found his little cowardly lover's spine!"

Chapter 22

Bryn spun out from Justin's blade as it landed against the tree instead of where her head had been. The Morrigan pushed at her, but Bryn wanted to train as Bryn, not with the goddess controlling her.

It seemed safer that way. At least for her since she felt like giving the Morrigan too much time gave her more power, and one day, Bryn might not come back at all.

She was sure that was the reason she'd felt so unsettled since they'd moved to the clearing to practice battling with weapons instead of power. The Morrigan probably wanted to take over while Bryn kept a firm hold, or as much as she could with how powerful the goddess had grown.

"Who knew Justin was so damn good with a sword?" Kessler said from his makeshift fire where he was heating and manipulating metal they had found in the abandoned town more than a week ago.

Thankfully Niamh had grabbed Declan's bag, one that could hold unlimited amounts of goods, when she snuck back into Osgar. That gave Kessler a way to grab enough metal to make weapons.

Before she could have the normal guilt and worry over Declan that had been following her, Justin sliced near her ear and she pushed away at the last minute, a small nick on her shoulder welling with blood before closing just as fast.

"Bryn! Pay attention!" Justin yelled dropping his sword, his eyes narrowed as Kian stomped out from where he was watching them.

Justin held up a hand, "I didn't mean to."

Kian stopped, his eyes molten as he snarled at Justin before looking Bryn over.

"I wasn't paying attention." Bryn shoved her dagger into the strap on her thigh.

"Alright, my turn to play," Kessler said as he walked up with a huge ax. "Couldn't make it pretty without my forge, but it'll get done what needs to be done."

Justin laughed and raised his blade. "Well come on then!"

"Then I will take a break," Bryn said as she stepped out of the open area where they had been sparring, Kian coming up next to her and taking her elbow. "I'll talk with Kian. Find out what he found on patrol."

Both men snorted, Justin rolling his eyes. "Sure. That's what they'll do with their mouths hidden away in the forest together."

Kessler let out a loud bark of laughter as Kian pulled her past the tree line. Her face was flaming in embarrassment, especially since the entire week of travel, she'd only managed to sneak a kiss once more, and of all times, Justin had walked up right then.

It was what they'd bring up at every opportunity just to watch her burn with embarrassment.

Once out of sight, Kian grabbed her by the waist, spinning her to a tree where he leaned into her, his mouth crushing down on hers with a feverish intensity. He leaned over her as she pulled back, his arm bracing himself against the tree above her head.

"Been waiting to do that for a while," he whispered as he ran his thumb over her bottom lip.

"Without an audience?" Bryn replied, her voice breathless, eyes moving between his as she spoke.

Kian smiled. "For once."

She knew it would go no further since the one time they did manage to sneak off, they had been busted since Kian was more focused on her than he was their surroundings.

"I need you to pay better attention when you fight, Bryn. If Justin hadn't pulled himself back at the last minute…"

"I know!" Twisting out from beneath his arm, she paced away, feeling like something was itching beneath her skin at his words. "I just can't seem to focus. I don't know why."

Bryn rubbed her arms, walking further out when she felt the Morrigan push, telling her without words to keep walking.

"Where are you…" Kian followed her. "Wait … is that?"

Kian took off in front of her, running and Bryn followed, trying to keep pace with him.

"It's a Faerie circle!" he laughed as Bryn circled a tree to where he stood, walking around an open area encircled with mushrooms and moss. It pulsed with power the closer Bryn got to it, and the Morrigan settled within her, but there was a feeling of relief from the goddess.

"Do we know where it goes?" she asked, unsure of how close she wanted to get to it. Even if the Morrigan was comfortable with it, and apparently Kian as he kneeled next to it, she was wary.

He looked up at her. "Only one way to find out."

Bryn folded her arms across her chest. "And then find ourselves lost? That sounds like a wonderful plan."

Kian stood back up again and walked to her. Putting his hands on her shoulders, he pulled her attention to him and away from the circle.

"This is where I need you to trust your instinct and listen to the Morrigan. We can use it and she can help us know where we end up. If I remember correctly, she was well versed in where they led and how to use them."

The circle pulsed again, a ring of unseen power moving out from it and tapping Bryn's magic as it went over her before fading out behind her. This was what had kept her notice while she had been trying to practice with Justin. It called to her.

No, to the Morrigan and the goddess wanted her to use it.

"Then let's get the rest of the group and see what they think."

Kian let her go, raising an eyebrow and she knew exactly what he was thinking.

"And then I can make the final decision after I..." Bryn waved her hand. "Converse with the Morrigan."

Every day her life grew more and more strange.

Chapter 23

Freezing wind went straight through all of Bryn's clothing as the temperature plummeted to levels Bryn had never felt before. It was far colder than even Ifreann's harshest freezing season.

Bryn dug through her pack for her furs from Ifreann, throwing them around her shoulders as the rest of her party did the same. She exhaled warm breath onto her cold hands, cursing herself for not finding gloves as she looked around the new environment. It had only been a day since they'd found and used the Faerie circle in the hopes to cut down on their travel. By the frigid temps they'd stepped out of the circle into, Bryn assumed they were close to their destination.

Niamh appeared at her side, as did the rest of the Sanctuary women since the thick cloud cover diffused the sun enough they could safely leave the veil.

Each frigid blast froze the tips of Bryn's hair and whipped painfully around her face as she took in a vast glittering sheet of ice that stretched out before them. Something told her this was the Artair Channel, frozen over. It met the impossibly distant, snow-capped mountains that loomed large and daunting, their peaks piercing the sky.

"This must be the channel that Manannán told me about in Faerie." Bryn said aloud and the immediate surge of excitement from the Morrigan confirmed they were closer to Cethin than she thought.

"...feel ... the shadow ... army ... closer."

As much as she hated the Morrigan talking to her, to hear that was a huge relief. For once she didn't immediately push the Morrigan back down but stayed on guard in case the goddess took advantage.

Small flakes of ice and snow filled the wind as they moved, snow stinging their exposed skin. If she hadn't been a newly made immortal, she was sure she would have perished relatively early on their journey. Shivering violently, she wondered aloud if her godlike powers were the only thing keeping her from succumbing to the biting cold.

Niamh laughed when Bryn brought it up. "Twice over. Be thankful for that little rock back in Ifreann."

What had possessed her family to live in a frozen tundra? Perhaps now she would have those answers, ones she'd waited a lifetime to know.

The wind and snow picked up even more, and Bryn could have cried if she wasn't worried the tears would freeze her eyelids shut.

"I found a cave where you can dwell in for the night." Cyerra projected a vivid image of the cave into her mind, and a wave of relief washed over Bryn. She wasn't sure how they would fare at night in such elements without trees to shield them from the biting wind. A fire would have been impossible out in the open.

"There is a cave up ahead!" Bryn yelled out to the party, the wind howling so loudly that the ones at the front had to be tapped on the shoulder and pulled in to hear.

They stepped onto spots of ice, their boots slipping as they walked. Each person took slow, steady steps, holding on to one another when hitting an ice patch for balance.

Using Cyerra's mental map, Bryn tried to focus on where she was going in the white abyss, slipping on the ice more than a few times in her struggle to find the cave she'd seen in the mental image. As they neared a giant white monstrosity that was one of the snow-covered mountains, the ground crunching as ice turned to frozen earth, Bryn could vaguely make out the darkness of a cave.

Bryn picked up her speed again, her frozen toes numb as she stumbled and then pushed back up, running in a weird loping manner before she broke through to the entrance to the cave, the wind immediately dropping off. Her friends were not far behind, coming in quickly behind her. Kian and Rae shook off the snow before starting the shift to their human forms.

Kessler pulled his gloves off with his teeth, holding his hands out and calling fire, cupping it in his palms. The others in their group settled in while Justin created a more permanent structure to contain the fire, and Kessler pushed the flame onto the dry sticks Justin had found in the back, shaking his hands out as the fire caught.

Kessler's eyes darted to the side, the flames reflecting in their depths, before snapping back to the fire, ensuring the embers glowed steadily. Bryn didn't miss the quick look to where Rae was mid-shift. The feisty female was standing over them before she lost the last of her fur, holding her hands out to warm them. "I've got more body heat than most, but it's bloody cold out there!"

"*Try being a crow,*" Cyerra pushed into their minds as she flew in, settling on Bryn's shoulder and cleaning her feathers.

"You're clothed this time," Bryn smiled as she settled against the cave wall. "I need to learn how to magic some clothes for myself."

Rae's laughter, loud and unrestrained, erupted. "Yeah, you used to embrace nudity a lot, so I imagine that wasn't in your arsenal of spells." Rae's hand brushed against Bryn's as she settled next to her.

An image fluttered into Bryn's mind, a memory from long ago as the Morrigan. The room in the vision was small, all wood like a tiny hunting cabin, a hole between the slates letting in a frosty wind that refused to be held at bay as it rattled the wood and windows with its fury. Along the walls were plenty of items to skin animals from their hunts with.

It was on the dirt packed floor that a small girl lay, her wrists bloodied from ropes and trying to free herself to no avail.

"I hate being bound," Rae whispered to Bryn, pulling her out of the memory, and Bryn realized she had summoned it from Rae's mind by accident. Rae pulled her knees into her chest, her wildly curly, long red hair falling over her face as she lost all the light playfulness of moments ago.

"Did..." Bryn was unsure what she should say, or even if she had the right to ask.

Rae looked up at her, her eyes watery, studying Bryn's expression. "You found me tied up when I was younger. Hunters ... I was playing in the woods with my friends, and they killed them. Tied me up..." She swallowed. "... they hurt me." Rae looked away, her eyes distant. "Did as they pleased to a weak little girl, but you found me and brought me home. You saved me."

Another memory, compliments of the Morrigan, flowed across Bryn's mind. Rae had been the child of one of her shadow clan members, and they had been searching for the girl as soon as her mother noticed she had disappeared while the rest of the clan had gone for a run. Rae was born to a female shifter and a human, and her human side dominated, which meant the little one couldn't shift and escape to heal herself.

While what Rae remembered was Bryn saving her, Rae didn't know she was already dead by the time help had arrived. Bryn had seen the soul, bright as the sun, when she'd entered the tent near the hunting cabin and ended the lives of the men who had taken her. Then she'd called on the wild hunt to handle them so she could see to the innocent soul.

The Morrigan had crossed into Faerie holding the soul of the little one, when the female alpha of the wolf kin had greeted her, having felt the pain of the small girl's last moments. The alpha had lost her life to hunters, as well as her pack, and she refused to allow more harm to happen to innocents.

So, the magic of the Morrigan allowed the alpha wolf to take her place in Rae, and when the child came alive once again, she had the ability to shift.

Memories piled onto Bryn of both shifters near her.

Cyerra lying in the woods, dying from an arrow to the chest, her eyes wide, but her expression fierce with determination to survive. To make it back to her coven with the medicine for a baby born weak, its mother dying. The Morrigan's crow familiar in Faerie had crossed over, just as the alpha wolf had, to be merged with the dying woman in the woods.

No, the shifters had some of Bryn's magic, but Rae and Cyerra *were* her magic.

They were each a small piece of the goddess themselves that Bryn had given when she'd stepped into Faerie that final time. All three of them together made up the entirety of the magic that was the Morrigan.

"You've been by my side ever since. Until..." Bryn trailed off, but Rae nodded, knowing what she meant.

"I was. I grew up learning to fight alongside your army, slipped into my role fairly easily with the wolf part of me." Rae settled against the wall next to Bryn, Cyerra hopping onto where Bryn had pulled her knee. "I was fighting alongside you that day when you had to split our souls to save us

... again." Her eyes were intense as she spoke, and Bryn couldn't imagine what she was thinking as she sat next to the goddess who had kept her soul from crossing into Faerie. "And when you did, I found out the wolf in me is your magic, not something I was born with that just took too long to show up. I am forever attached to you."

Bryn let out a long sigh, knowing she should say something, an apology, perhaps. She wasn't sure.

"Thank you."

That was not what Bryn expected Rae to say at all and found herself at a loss for words as Rae gave her a beaming smile brighter than the sun. A smile that would etch itself in Bryn's memory forever. A smile that reminded Bryn that her power was to be revered and not feared.

"I am honored to be your chosen and to work alongside you to rid the world of the magic that is the Fomori."

"Rae, I'm really glad you found us," Bryn said, and Rae tilted her head back, all her wild curls falling back as she laughed.

"Me, too, Goddess. Me, too."

"Touching moment as this is, tomorrow we will reach Cethin. Any thoughts on how to address our potential new allies?" Cyerra spoke, but her words were softer, a stark contrast to her usual biting wit.

Bryn sighed and looked over the rest of the group who were readying themselves for a night of sleep within the cave. Kian stood by the door, looking out, his focus on something in the distance.

"We ask for an audience with whoever is in charge and tell them what we have seen and been through. After that, we ask for their help in standing up to the king." Bryn laughed. "It's ridiculous I haven't thought that far and tomorrow I am supposed to ask them to die for us."

"The Morrigan would have stood on their doorstep with an order on her lips and murder in her eyes."

A hum of agreement rippled through Bryn from the Morrigan at Cyerra's words.

"Yeah, that can be plan B," Bryn said, letting her head thump back against the stone. "Now I just have to stay up all night working on plan A."

Rae snorted. "Such a human thing to say."

Bryn rolled her head to look at Rae as the shifter scooted over to lay down. "You have humanity in your eyes now. It's nice. I don't feel like you're going to cut my throat in my sleep if I displease you."

Ouch. Bryn winced at the words, unsure if Rae was joking.

"I like this version of you best." Rae said with a wink before closing her eyes.

Chapter 24

Sleep was quick and then altogether elusive as Bryn's thoughts twisted and turned until her group slowly woke up. Her nerves had her hands shaking as they readied themselves for another day of travel in the freezing environment. The moment they put the fire out, the frost quickly crept back in.

All too soon, with her few furs from Ifreann covering her exposed skin and her pack on her back, Bryn stepped out of the shelter of their cave and faced the land of her birth. Their brief solace in the cave was lost as hard-driven snow stung their faces, and a lashing wind howled like a banshee. The bitter cold seeping into their very bones.

Leading the group in their shifted forms, Rae and Kian's sharper senses were on high alert. Meanwhile, Cyerra dove and landed on Bryn's shoulder, body shaking with the cold as she fluffed up her feathers, doubling her size.

What felt like hours passed by, the frost accumulating on their clothing and furs. Bryn focused on keeping herself moving, imagining warmer days as they worked to steady themselves on ice. It was a sad day when she missed Ifreann's scorching desert heat.

When they were no longer sliding on ice patches, finally leaving the frozen channel, Bryn could have jumped for joy if her muscles weren't frozen.

Bryn flinched as her ears popped, and the wind abruptly ceased around them, leaving an eerie silence.

"What in the hell just happened?" Kessler stopped suddenly, and Bryn ran into his back before looking around him. A thick, stagnant fog blanketed the world in front of them.

Backing up, Bryn's ears popped again as she crossed back into the howling wind. Kian was suddenly there, his hand clutching her arm and pulling her back across whatever invisible boundary there was. This time, Bryn readied herself for the change in pressure by opening her jaw wide.

"We have to stay together," Kian muttered, holding her tightly against his side as he pulled her back toward the group, the fog growing denser with each step. "This fog isn't natural, but I don't think it's dangerous."

The others huddled tightly together while Rae, who had been leading the group, shifted back to her human form, shaking her head as she rubbed her eyes.

It was her people they were trying to reach, so Bryn took the initiative, her heart pounding, and strode to the front of the group.

"Keep a hold of each other," Bryn ordered before turning back to the fog and starting her trek. Kian took the hand she held out at her side, as each member grabbed another's hand or belt, creeping through the mist as it grew more and more oppressive.

Bryn held out her other hand, the one not being held by Kian, in front of her, but the crushing fog swallowed it whole as they moved further in. The cloud was heavy and thick, a suffocating blanket clinging to her skin and making each pull of air into her lungs a struggle.

Her thoughts went immediately to Jace, who, as a young child, always had issues with his breathing, and though he was much healthier now and a god, she still worried about him breathing in the soupy wet air.

Kian had said it wasn't dangerous, but it was difficult to remind herself of that as it cut her off from the world around her. Only Kian's hand anchored her, reminding her she was not alone.

The temperature quickly rose, and the heavy furs along her shoulders began to stifle Bryn, making her sweat profusely, but the damp air felt as if it were turning solid in her lungs. Her chest burned, her eyes watered.

In a panic, she dropped Kian's hand to grab at her throat, but Kian was quick to pull her back in, tugging her against him as he pulled her forward.

She stumbled and swayed as she fought her growing weakness to keep up with him, but her vision dimmed at the edges, blackness encroaching as her head swam from lack of oxygen.

Hands pushed at her, someone running past turning up the foggy cloud. She knew they were all as panicked as she was, but each thought unraveled just as quickly as it came.

Kian pulled her into his arms, carrying her against his chest as she choked, begging her lungs to work, to get the oxygen she needed as her fingers pushed into the skin at her throat like she could manually make herself breathe.

And then, the fog vanished, leaving Bryn gasping for breath as Kian's weakened knees buckled, losing his grip on her as they both fell. Landing on her side, she rolled onto her stomach, coughing violently with each inhale. Each breath was a desperate struggle as her vision slowly came back into focus.

Slowly, Bryn turned her head away from the churned earth to look for her friends and found them scattered, drawing in deep breaths as she had been. Reaching for Kian, her fingers finding his pant leg as his firm hands pulled her to stand, giving her a sense of stability amidst the chaos. Unsteady on her feet, he wrapped an arm around her waist as she gazed at the sea of golden wheat rippling in the breeze, the rich scent of soil completely unexpected after so much snow and ice.

Children and adults alike emerged from the rows of ripening wheat, their baskets swaying as they stopped to observe her and her friends. A small boy close to where Bryn stood scrambled away, taking refuge behind a lean, weather-beaten man. The child's little face could be seen peeking carefully out from behind the man's legs.

Two large, menacing figures, each wielding a scythe, stepped between her and the people watching, their posture tense as they sized up her group.

"Where are we?" Bryn asked, finally managing to stand on her own two feet as the dizziness faded.

Sage pushed past Bryn, her hand flexing as she looked out at the fields of plants. A glint of gold crossed Sage's eyes when she looked back at Bryn and then back to the fields, her friend humming with energy and power that Bryn had only seen a small glimpse of in Osgar.

Beyond the fields, nature surrounded them, a riot of color unlike the familiar trees of Osgar. There were vibrant greens, rich browns, fiery oranges and deep reds in the flowers, all of it nature. It was a breathtaking spectacle that reminded Bryn of Faerie.

Bryn turned to speak to her friends, but shock stole her words as Niamh and the women from the Sanctuary stood before her in direct sunlight without turning to ash.

"What magic is this?" Niamh let out a low growl as she looked down at her hands, her chest heaving with unneeded breath. Niamh looked up, past Bryn, her eyes blood-red, her rage palpable and sharp in the air. "Is this some kind of sick joke?"

The onlookers, their initial curiosity now replaced with stark terror, stumbled backward from the furious vampire. Several more men came out from the fields, scythes up and ready to be brandished as weapons.

"You will put your fangs away, Niamh Gwyer."

Niamh hissed as she turned toward the voice of the newcomer, but she froze before her hand mindlessly clutched the red stone pendant hanging at her throat.

"No ... Cae?"

Bryn looked between the two women, unsure what was going on, but neither said another word.

The woman confronting Niamh had hair like iridescent pearls, styled in two long braids that flowed over her shoulders. She wore beige linen pants and a green flowing top, wooden beads adorning the trim, and a necklace made of rocks in colors Bryn had only ever seen in Faerie.

But it was when the woman looked at her with familiar greenish-blue eyes that Bryn forgot all about Niamh's odd reaction. The woman had *her* eyes. The eyes she saw in the mirror every morning in Ifreann and had stared back from rivers they'd passed on the journey to Cethin.

"Are you ..." The remaining words caught in Bryn's throat, thick and unyielding, as she approached the woman.

"You were dead. I laid on your grave," Niamh whispered, her voice breaking on the last word. Bryn felt her stomach knot at the realization that this woman had been Niamh's true love that she'd lost to the violence of her husband.

The woman stood tall, seemingly unmoved by Niamh's emotions. "Once you're done with your fit, we can have tea and speak like civilized people." When neither continued to speak nor move, she nodded. "Come, let's get you all settled and I can explain some things." The woman turned her back on Niamh, and the lost look on the vampire's face almost broke Bryn's heart.

"First off, where are we?" Justin asked, Finian following closely at his side.

The woman looked over her shoulder and smiled, dazzling white teeth shining in the sun as she moved with an air of quiet authority, reminding Bryn of Callum's serene demeanor. Bryn wondered if she was a druid, too.

"Why, Cethin. That was where you had planned to come, correct?" The woman waved them forward. "Come, let's get you all settled."

They followed the woman through the rustling crops that opened to a village of long, narrow log homes perched on stilts. Smoke curled lazily from the large cook fire in the center of the village, the smell of sizzling meat making Bryn's stomach rumble. They'd been low on food and hunting options for a while on the last leg of the journey.

"Would you prefer to eat lunch before I show you your rooms?" the woman asked, hearing the growl emanating from Bryn's stomach.

"You knew we were coming?" Justin asked, suspicion plain on his pinched brow and narrowed eyes.

"Oh yes, I knew one day soon you would all return. We all knew." She waved her hand toward the people milling about the quaint village.

"Ominous bullshit," Rae muttered as they walked up the wooden stairs before squeezing through the door to the largest longhouse, and Bryn couldn't disagree with Rae's assessment.

Even inside the building was full of life, vines creeping along the walls and small lines of white and silver threading through the grain of the wooden floors and ceilings. The hallway opened into a large circular room, the polished dark oak of the tables and chairs gleaming under the dim light, a smaller circle of seating within the larger one, sparsely occupied. A few women and several men walked into the room with trays full of food in their hands, placing them on the tables for people to fill their plates in a less than formal manner.

Bryn followed as she watched the woman, the way she greeted people and how they greeted her. Bryn wanted to yank her back and make her answer every question she'd ever begged to know, but the woman spun toward them as she waved for them to have a seat at one of the tables.

"As I've said before, this is Cethin, and my name is Callie." Her eyes were on Niamh as she introduced herself, but she quickly looked away. "I know it is not easy to travel through the fog since it wears on the soul as much as it does the body, so please have your fill and then you can rest."

The moment Bryn's butt hit the chair, a mountain of food was placed before her, the aroma of roasted meat and freshly baked bread filling the air. Alongside it were round green vegetables, corn on the cob, and a mound of soft, white food she'd never seen, all glistening with the same delicious sauce. She was quick to fill her plate, her stomach growling as fiercely as any shifter.

This was a king's feast compared to anything they had in Ifreann and Osgar.

The people of Ifreann usually dried vegetables into bars, and because of travel limitations, very little fresh produce remained for the town through-out the season. It was the same rotation of meats, breads, and beans.

"Um, maybe we could get some more information before we eat the nice stranger's food?" Kessler asked, eyeing the plate in front of him with an intense look of hunger, but keeping his hands below the table. Bryn put her fork back down, her cheeks burning with embarrassment that she'd acted like a ravenous animal in filling her plate.

Each member of their group turned to look at Niamh since it was obvious she knew the woman.

Niamh's fangs gleamed as she spoke, her eyes never leaving Callie. "She will not poison you. Maybe me, but none of you."

Bryn didn't miss the fact that Callie said nothing to the bold statement, but the rest of her group each picked up a fork, slowly taking bites until it was obvious the food was safe.

The group ate in silence, their stomachs too empty to focus on much more than filling them.

As soon as the last bite of food vanished, Justin's face settled into his official sheriff's expression, jaw clenched, eyes narrowed, as he looked at Callie.

"Now, you can explain everything," Justin ordered, and Bryn sat up straight as Callie held her gaze as she took a seat across from her.

"Yes, darling, some explanations if you would, please?" Niamh tilted her head toward the woman, and Callie's eyes narrowed before she shook her head and faced Bryn.

"You look almost exactly like my daughter, Aine."

The words were gone from Bryn's lips before she could hold them back. "You're my grandmother?"

Callie nodded, and Niamh sprang to her feet, a pained expression clouding her eyes before she fled the room.

Bryn jumped up to follow Niamh, but Callie stood. "Wait."

With a final, worried glance toward where Niamh had escaped, Bryn shifted her attention to Callie as she approached her from the other side of the table.

"I did not agree with the plan that took you from me, but I am so very glad it brought you back." Without another word, Callie pulled Bryn into a tight hug, and Bryn froze before slowly lifting her arms to hug her back.

Her mind was full of questions about her mother, her grandmother, and the village she should have known, but one question loomed largest: where was the shadow army?

However, the shock of everything was wearing her down when she was already so exhausted from their trek.

"Rest," her grandmother whispered against her hair, letting go of her to step back. Kian moved in to take Bryn's elbow as Callie shot him a thin-lipped narrow-eyed look. Grandmotherly softness quickly replaced it as she spoke to Bryn before she could question the behavior. "I will be here in the morning. Organize your questions, and we will discuss them at length when the sun rises." Callie reached for Bryn's hand, giving it a squeeze before releasing it. "There is plenty of time."

Too tired to argue, Bryn nodded like a sleepy child before realizing she didn't know where to go. With a soft laugh at her confused look, Callie took her shoulders and aimed her toward the doorway where a man waited with her group.

The man paused at each room as they trailed behind him, and the group dwindled until only Kian and Bryn remained.

"Here is your room, now sir, if you would follow me—"

"No need," Kian said as he picked Bryn up, opening the door and giving the man, who was now looking a bit scandalized, a wink before closing it behind them.

Bryn wanted to protest that she could take care of herself, but her eyes were drooping as he laid her on the bed. He tugged her boots off her feet and dropped them onto the floor with a soft thud.

"You could magic away my clothes instead of undressing me," Bryn muttered, working to roll over, but Kian stilled her with his hands on her thighs, warming her through the leathers.

"Yes, but it's the act that means more when done with care, and I mean to take care of you."

Her whole body warmed as he stripped her pants and leather corset, leaving the linen shirt. Her arousal was there, but she was far too tired to act on it. Kian did nothing more than fold her leathers, putting it and the boots away, before peeling back the covers and laying her down between the sheets.

The last thing she remembered was the warmth of his body, his arms wrapped around her tightly as they drifted off.

Chapter 25

Bryn settled at a table in the communal dining room the next morning as a lean older man with a fatherly smile placed a plate heaping with eggs, bacon, and toast in front of her.

With a nod of thanks, Bryn grabbed her fork, ready to dive in. She only managed one bite of her eggs before Rae sat across from her and Cyerra next to her.

"Late start this morning?" Rae asked, eyeing Bryn's food.

Nodding, Bryn moved her plate of toast toward Rae who immediately started to devour it.

"Did you not just have a large breakfast, wolf?" Cyerra asked as she took a sip of tea from a white porcelain teacup similar to the cups Niamh used to have at the Sanctuary.

"I did, but shifting burns a lot of calories, bird." Rae smirked before stealing a piece of bacon.

"Has anyone seen Niamh this morning?" Bryn asked. She had been worried about Niamh all morning.

Both women shook their head.

"I think she is with the Sanctuary women. When I went for a run this morning, they were all along the edges of the village." Rae took another slice of bacon as she finished, the older gentleman bringing Bryn more and settling a heaping plate of meat in front of Rae.

"I like this place!" Rae said before digging into her carnivore only meal.

A small chuckle left Bryn's lips before she could stop it. Rae was animated and full of energy. It was difficult to be down around such a personality for long.

"Anything interesting on your run aside from seeing Niamh and the women from the Sanctuary?" Bryn asked as she grabbed a slice of her replenished bacon.

"If you're asking about the shadow army and where they might be, neither of us found any clues." Cyerra sipped her tea as Rae nodded, swallowing down her mouthful of meat before speaking.

"The rest of the village then?" Bryn asked, frustrated that nothing had been found about the shadow army, but still curious about the village her grandmother had welcomed her into.

"It's a pretty decent size village with lots of wolves running around the perimeter. I think they are in charge of protection."

"I ascertained the same. They had very coordinated movements and rotations. They stay at a camp on the north edge of the village."

"Not in the village?" Bryn asked, thinking it odd that citizens would hold themselves apart from the rest of the community.

"It's not so weird. Shifter packs stay close to their pack mates. If a town is already established, we tend to stay on the outskirts." Rae shrugged. "Hey—" Rae waved a piece of bacon at Bryn. "—we need to work on those dagger skills. I was busy playing guard on the road, but now I can help, and good goddess do you need the help!"

Memories of the wolf shifter in battle threaded through Bryn's thoughts as she nodded to the woman shoveling eggs in her face.

"Rae was your strongest, bravest, most reckless soldier, so your gift in battle is with her." Cyerra gently placed her teacup on the table. "She would be the best in renewing your rusted skillset."

Rae smiled, a small bit of egg in her teeth, and Bryn huffed out a laugh. The girl was silly, but when she'd torn Arioch's throat out to protect Bryn from the religious leader and monster of Ifreann, there was no question she was equally dangerous.

And now that she thought about it, it was when Rae had crossed the veil as a wolf that the art of combat had returned to Bryn. When she'd become the Morrigan of old, slaying all the wraiths.

"So, yes, we know what we're in for because we hold a part of you within us. Your power is ours, and we need each other for this battle." Folding her hands on the table, Cyerra tilted her head to Bryn.

"My visions in Ifreann changed when you came to me as the crow..." Bryn was working through the timeline and it was all syncing up.

"Your visions are easier to deal with when I am around because that's part of the power you bestowed on me. Without me, and you being mortal, it was like a live wire, unpredictable and hard to control. Rae is war, and I am fate."

Bryn sat back in her chair, taking in what Cyerra was saying. That her two friends were made again with aspects of her power. How central they were to Bryn's own control, the missing pieces to her being whole herself as the Morrigan.

"Gotta go." Rae jumped up, the fork falling to the table as she darted out the door, where Bryn caught a flash of Kessler's back as he walked past.

"Brave in combat, flighty in the day-to-day. Rae was always there for a joke in a bad situation, a blade in the throat of an enemy, and to disappear when something shiny was near." Cyerra's eyes met Bryn's. "Given how they orbit each other, I would be genuinely surprised if they weren't mates."

"Mates?"

Cyerra nodded, a small tilt of her thin lips. "Yes, wolf shifters generally have mates that the goddess Danu predetermines."

Bryn's mind twisted around to Kian. Was his mate out there somewhere waiting for him? If she were his mate, surely over the past several lifetimes there would have been some clue, right?

"Good morning, granddaughter!" Callie broke into Bryn's tumultuous thoughts, placing her hands on the table and leaning forward. "Once you've finished breaking your fast, I can show you around Cethin and answer all the questions I can."

"I'm ready." Bryn pushed her plate away, eagerly standing to follow Callie as they walked to the front of the longhouse, everyone nodding to them as they passed. Some asked questions about the day's activities or farming as they left, which reinforced that Callie was in charge here.

Sage, Kessler, Jace, and Justin were standing outside, turning to face them once the door opened.

"Right on time! If you will follow me..." Callie moved to the front, Bryn following as Sage stepped into place next to her, the guys behind them.

Finian ran to Justin, almost barreling the man over as the hound bounced playfully to a stop, then took his place at Justin's side.

All around the open area where the longhouses stood were a variety of lush trees in varying shades of green. Small cottages painted white, yellow, and blue were nestled among the trees, with green vines winding around them and draping over the roofs like the cottages were a part of nature itself.

A garden overflowing with herbs perfumed the air to the left of the cottages, and small cobblestone walkways ran up and between each home. Like a quaint little neighborhood untouched by the harshness of the world outside of Cethin.

The Morrigan vibrated within her, the natural elements around them thrumming with life.

Turning to them, Callie smile failed before she caught herself and held her arms out wide. When Bryn looked back, she knew why as Niamh and Kian walked up, Niamh's eyes solely on Callie. Both of them came to stand with Bryn and Sage, but Niamh was not mentally there with them in that moment.

Callie watched them closely before clearing her throat to speak. "These are the homes of the Shattered Moon coven. The people within these trees can cure any ailment, make or break any spell, and fulfill any need, their skills honed by the ancient forest itself." Letting her hands fall back to her sides, Callie wore a proud smile. "They work with nature, like the ones known as the green witches, and help us to grow our food in what was once an inhospitable environment."

"Yeah," Justin said from the front of their small group. "About that. A plentiful garden and semi-warm city in the middle of that inhospitable environment? A sun that doesn't hurt our friend here?" Justin waved to Niamh, who stood next to Bryn with her arms folded, keeping silent as he spoke.

"We have our own powers, thanks to the ancestors and Tuatha Dé Danann." Callie held her palm facing up and a ball of water swirled above her hand before turning to ice with a whisper of cold.

Faster and faster it spun before launching into the air, exploding in a shower of glittering ice crystals that settled around them like a gentle snowfall. "I can keep the weather back while the witches under my care preserve our way of life. The fog you pushed through was no natural fog."

Kian snorted. "That was obvious. Fog usually doesn't try to smother people."

Callie gave a sharp smile. "We must protect ourselves."

"And the sun?" Niamh asked.

"There is magic all around us, protecting us from the storms outside, which means all elements are kept out. The sun we have here grows our food but does not burn the fair skin of our people. Isn't magic wonderful?"

"If … could I speak to the witches here?" Sage asked, having moved closer to the cottages while everyone was distracted.

Callie's heartfelt smile was so infectious that it brought a small smile to Bryn's face too. "Of course! They would love to speak to the goddess from whom they derive their power."

"Now, while she spends time with the coven." Callie took Bryn's arm, holding her elbow and turning her toward the small herb garden. "I can show you—"

"What's over there?" Kian asked, pointing to a foggy area to the right of the witches' neighborhood. It was hard to see clearly through the trees and a light mist, nothing like what they had walked through getting to Cethin, but it distorted the visual. Bryn narrowed her eyes to see the skeletal remains of dead trees and large canvas tents, flapping gently in the breeze and haphazardly scattered across the barren landscape.

"The mountain range is that way, but also the wolf shifters chose to make that area their home to protect us from the more beastly type threats that come from the north."

Callie turned away to start again, guiding them back toward where she wanted them to focus, but Kian wasn't quite finished.

"Who is the alpha?"

Now Callie turned back to him with a neutral expression. "I'm certain he will introduce himself at the welcome feast tonight." As if remembering she hadn't said anything about it to them, she nodded before she spoke. "Please, at dinner time, join us in the communal area and we will welcome you all in the Cethin way."

While it was an invitation, Callie's demeanor had chilled from Kian's questions. Without another word, Callie turned and walked back toward the long houses that made up the center of Cethin.

Each of Bryn's party looked at each other, aside from Sage who was wandering around the cottages, before they all followed Callie quietly back to the center of the village.

Chapter 26

Bryn held a cup of spirits in her hand as the people of Cethin gathered around the large bonfire in front of the communal house. The welcome party had been a whole other level of tame compared to Osgar, but a lot more enjoyable than anything in Ifreann.

Jace and Sage sat with the witches of the Shattered Moon coven, while near the crackling fire, Kessler and Rae chatted with some locals. Nearby, Justin was engrossed in a lengthy conversation, with Finian resting completely relaxed at his side.

She had yet to see Cyerra or Niamh, but after Niamh took her arm and gave her a squeeze of comfort as they walked back from their tour, she had hope that it would all work out.

"Bryn, right?" One of the young men who had been working the wheat field when she had crossed from the fog into Cethin smiled at her. "Sorry we were a little less than welcoming when you first showed up."

The Morrigan perked up in interest at the male with a gorgeous smile and beautiful green eyes. He ran a hand along the side of his head, his black hair shaved on the sides and long on top in a nervous gesture that was somewhat endearing to Bryn.

"I can understand why. Strangers coming out of the fog looking half dead?" Bryn laughed as she took another sip of the wine the witches had been plying everyone with all evening. Thankfully they had fed them all well with enough meat and bread that would have lasted her good week back in Ifreann so she wasn't as tipsy as she could have been. Something that normally wouldn't be a problem for their godlike metabolisms, but the wine had enough magic in it to inebriate anyone with power,. It made sense since everyone Bryn had run into in Cethin had some kind of magic.

"Jim." He held out the hand not holding wine and Bryn shook it.

"Nice to meet you." She smiled and wondered when had she felt so relaxed in the presence of others? Especially allowing herself something as simple as a handshake.

"...if you're interested?" Jim had a hopeful smile on his face, and Bryn wondered what she had missed as she zoned out thinking about her new ability to allow touch without repercussions.

"I'm—"

"Not interested," a deep voice came from behind her, the words lengthened by an almost threatening growl.

Bryn spun to where Kian was walking up to her, his arm going around her waist and pulling her into his side.

"Kian—"

Jim's hands went up so fast, his wine spilled over. "I'm so sorry, I was unaware she was with you. I'll just..." Jim pointed behind him before he spun and took off toward the large group by the fire.

"Well, that was rude," Bryn said before taking another sip of wine, the cup being claimed by Kian immediately after.

"He was offering you more than friendship for the night and I was not going to be pleasant about that." Kian's eyes darkened as he took a sip of her wine, handing her an almost empty cup back.

"Also rude." Bryn tilted the almost empty cup toward him before she finished the wine, and Kian gave her a taunting smirk. His behavior reminded her of how he was in Ifreann, before the battle, when his playfulness was always on the edge of something bigger than Bryn could fathom.

His body caged hers against the side of the long house, his hand cupping her jaw. "If you're interested, you can probably talk him back into it." There was a warning in his tone.

"Maybe I'm not interested in Jim."

The Morrigan began to stir more, becoming increasingly difficult to ignore as she pushed Bryn to step away from Kian.

"...*play ... fire ...*"

Ignoring the goddess, Bryn pushed onto her toes, grabbing the back of Kian's neck and crushing her lips against his.

She felt the warmth of his smile against her lips as he deepened the kiss, reigniting the passion lost to her since their last encounter.

Kian lifted her, her legs going around his waist as the kiss turned savage and demanding between them. She could feel every part of him against her, his hardness at her center making her lose all sense of the world around them.

Silver flashed in her mind's eyes, and with a gasp, she opened her eyes to see the silver strings slowly dip between and around her and Kian.

"Bryn?" Kian asked, pulling back to look at her, but not letting her go.

Her eyes were following where the strings had been, her hand reaching out to them as they dissipated completely. "I keep seeing these silver ropes or strings when we kiss." Bryn looked back at Kian as he swallowed before returning to a neutral look.

"Oh yeah?"

"Kian? What are they?" Bryn pushed back, Kian holding her a moment longer before letting her go. "If it has to do with my power, then I should know."

A defeated look moved across his face as he turned away to run his hand through his hair. "So, you see them too?" he asked, still looking away from her.

Bryn moved in front of him, his eyes staying over her shoulder as she stepped into his space, her hand going to his clenched jaw to force him to look at her. "Tell me."

Even the Morrigan was staying quiet on what was happening, and that concerned Bryn. Shouldn't she be made aware of anything regarding their power?

"Kian!" Bryn grabbed his shoulders, shaking them since he was still looking away. "What are you keeping from me?"

"It's not on purpose!" he yelled back, before giving a frustrated laugh. "It's not the time. Trust me, it's just not ... time yet."

"Oh!" Bryn pushed away from him. "Well that's sates my curiosity. Thanks!"

"Bryn..." Kian reached out, but she dodged his hand.

"No. Declan lied to me all the time by omission and now what you're doing is not any better! I never thought you would do this, Kian!"

She turned to walk away, but Kian grabbed her arm.

"I swear to you it is nothing bad. I will tell you, but not right now," Kian was intense, almost as if he were trying to say something aloud that couldn't be said.

"Is it a geas, like what happened with Niamh?" Perhaps that she could forgive since there would be no choice.

The look of pleading distress on his face told her the answer to that.

"Then you have no excuse." Her voice went cold as she pulled her arm away from him. "You are choosing to keep something from me."

"Please, Bryn," his voice was ragged, emotional in a way she never imagined he could be.

"Hey you two! Quit making out and get out here!" Justin yelled out as he turned the corner to where Kian and Bryn were, his body immediately tightening up as he took in the tension between them. "You okay, Bryn?"

Quick to step toward Justin before Kian could say anything else, she nodded. "Just fine. Let's go finish this party up."

Without a backward glance, she left Kian in the shadows where she felt he belonged.

Bryn tried, but she couldn't stay with the party, not in her mood. A mood made substantially worse by the Morrigan giving her an almost smug sense.

Quick to excuse herself, her grandmother nodding with a concerned look but saying nothing, Bryn walked through Cethin before making it to the cottages.

Lanterns lit the small cobblestone walkways, the light casting an almost ethereal glow that reminded Bryn of the fairy tales she'd read from Niamh's collection in Ifreann.

Fairy tales she almost believed in until Kian started with the secrets. She hadn't realized how much she had come to trust Kian in such a short period of time, and how much such a betrayal would cost her. Especially since she had been with Declan longer and even that hadn't bothered her as much as Kian keeping secrets from her.

Idiot. Only an idiot would trust someone so quickly in such a short period of time. Someone who had been sent to kill her in a past life. Yet, hadn't and became a trusted general instead.

Bryn grabbed her hair and growled, tugging at the roots.

It was more than that and everyone including her damn well knew it.

A pulse of power rippled out from her, running along the ground, and something thudded back at her in response.

"Shadow..."

She ignored the Morrigan and followed where the responding pulse came from, moving past trees and the cottages, further from the center of Cethin, past the tents where the wolves stayed.

To a place where dead trees spread out, meeting the wall of fog surrounding Cethin. In the center of the lost trees was a huge one, bent at an angle, high enough to look as if it reached the sky.

Bryn walked toward the large tree, drawn to it in a way she couldn't understand nor explain, but the Morrigan was buzzing beneath her skin, saying something about shadows over and over. It felt like the Morrigan was more right then, not pushing against Bryn to escape, but at peace in a way, and working along with Bryn.

It was as if they both were reaching forward, placing a palm against the dark rough gnarled bark of the tree. The hum of distant voices grew as she connected to the tree, the Morrigan felt less a presence inside her own head and instead all around her and inside of her at once.

At the same time, there was darkness filling the gap between her and the tree, the voices calling out, but the void quickly took their voices. It was almost as if even with both her and the Morrigan, whatever was going on here was above their ability to understand.

She pulled her hand away, blinking up at the tree that stood a silent sentinel among a forest of the lost.

There was power here. Untapped, and begging for someone to release it, but Bryn was unable.

Even if she did, was it a power that should be released, or something that could make it all worse for those around her?

It was not something she wanted to take on herself.

A branch snapped nearby and Bryn swung around, the foggy air not much for hiding behind the skeletal trees, and yet she saw nothing.

Only the feeling of now being watched followed her as she returned to Cethin with more questions than she had when she arrived.

Chapter 27

Bryn woke up to the sun lower in the sky than usual and groaned at all she had to deal with.

They'd had their party, now it was time to settle down and get some answers and hopefully a new army pledging to help them rid the world of King Bres.

"Time to..." Bryn trailed off at the empty space on the bed next to her. Kian was usually always there, human or wolf form, but he'd not shown up when she'd gone to bed, nor now when she woke up.

Sadness filled her chest, that after so much time and intimacy, he wouldn't even try to explain it to her after the party. With Declan, he'd have been banging on her door all night to explain.

This was yet another reason why Bryn should ignore men until the war was over. There was no time to be wandering about, trying to reason who did what wrong.

The Morrigan sent a sound agreement to her statement. The woman and the goddess had finally both aligned on something.

Too bad it was over men and relationships instead of how to deal with the battle ahead.

Bryn dressed quickly before moving through the long house in search of Callie, finally finding her in a small room with a desk and two chairs, a large window letting in the false midday sun.

"Bryn!" Callie stood and walked around the desk to hug her before pulling back. "Time to talk, I suppose?" With a grandmotherly smile, Callie pulled Bryn's arm through hers before they began walking. "Come, we need to break our fast as much as we need to talk. No one should be milling about in the dining hall so late in the morning."

As they settled at a small table with only two chairs facing each other, Callie patiently waited for Bryn to be served some eggs and sausage, and settled with her tea before a word was said.

"You've come a long way, on a journey I knew would happen eventually. So, ask what you've been needing to know for so very long." Callie placed her hands on the table, her teacup giving off wisps of steam, as Bryn fought down the fear of the truth that had been her constant companion since she understood the necessity of this meeting. Of the journey as a whole.

"I..." Bryn trailed off as she placed her fork next to her plate, unsure of what to do with her hands, feeling incredibly self-conscious. "Should I not wait for the others to do this?" She felt ridiculous for asking out loud, even more so when Callie raised a brow.

"Should you?"

"We ... us..." Bryn swallowed as Callie patiently waited for her to get it together. "Where is my mother?" Bryn blurted out instead of what she meant, knew, she should ask.

"Ah." Callie reached for her tea before taking a sip. "Here I thought you came for help."

"We did, I do…" Bryn wondered if she should just tape her mouth shut and get Justin for this, but she was supposed to be the leader.

"Aine, your mother, was always such a force of nature. Even as a child. Before I came here, I was a part of a coven that was a bit more … sexually driven with their magic." Callie maintained eye contact as she spoke and Bryn wondered if grandmothers normally spoke like this to their grandchildren. Callie gave a little laugh at her obvious discomfort before moving on.

"I'll not go into detail, but she was conceived between me and another witch during a ritual. As I'm sure you know, I'm not attracted to men, so that was probably the only way I could become a mother after the world was destroyed."

Bryn didn't bring up Niamh, but she wondered if Callie had spoken to her friend. Niamh and the women from the Sanctuary had given the village plenty of space, to the point where Bryn missed her friend, but understood she was working through the mind bender it must be to find your lost love alive and very angry.

"She came of age while I was working to make Cethin a safe place for witches and the like against Bres. I wasn't as vigilant as I should have been. I should have noticed her running off to the wolf camp more and more, and then one day, she tells me she is pregnant. Having a wolf cub of all things."

"A wolf?" Bryn had never shifted, nor felt anything like it, but how would she even know since she'd not been around shifters until Kian. Her father had never shifted either … then it hit her what all Callie was saying.

Callie nodded before taking a slow deep breath and then continued.

"I wasn't happy, but I wasn't going to stop her from seeing the father. The damage, so to speak, was already done." Callie rolled her jaw back and forth before her gaze met Bryn's again. "I didn't expect her to fight with me and your father before running away."

"She's gone?"

Callie gave Bryn a slow nod. "Even with all the witches of this place, she is long gone to who knows where. Even your father couldn't find her, and after I accused him of hiding her... well, we've not been on the best terms."

"Who is he?" Bryn dared to ask, unsure if she wanted to know more or less, but committed all the same.

Her grandmother reached across the table, taking her hands. "He is the alpha of the wolf clan here in Cethin."

"The tents..." Callie nodded at Bryn's words.

Her father was here. Her real father was not the man who had raised her in Ifreann. Bryn tried to pull her hands back, but Callie kept them a moment more.

"You are my grandchild. You came here for help in a war that none of us want at our doorstep, and had someone else come in your place, it would have been an immediate no."

Callie wrapped Bryn's hands, folding her own over them in the center of the table. "I understand why you're here, and I will give you this. An audience with our council and my support, but you must state your reasoning. It is time for you to be the one to stand up and ask for what you want, my dear."

Bryn could barely hear anything in her surroundings with the roaring in her ears as she walked through the forest toward the wolf encampment. Several times she had stumbled over a root or rock, not paying attention, and forcing her numb body to continue.

She could meet her father.

Her real father. Who was not the man who raised her in Ifreann unless somehow he had made a miraculous recovery from death and came here.

Another root caught her foot, and she fell to her knees in the soft, wet grass. The cold of it seeping into her clothes as she gave up trying to stand. Hands over her face, she let the tears fall, her father's death hurting all over again.

The fact he wasn't truly her blood relative didn't undo the grief and void that his death had left.

Now she was finding out there was another man out there who actually sired her, and who knew if he would want anything to do with her.

Arms wrapped around Bryn, pulling her close to a warm firm body and her muscles relaxed as she shed years worth of tears.

He said nothing, just holding her while she fell apart in the middle of a strange forest.

"My father ... he wasn't—" Bryn hiccuped, trying to pull herself together. "—my real father is the alpha here. He has been here this whole *damn* time."

Kian readjusted them to where she was sitting in his lap as he laid against a tree. Bryn shoved her face into his neck, clutching his shirt in her hands as he rubbed her back and tried to soothe her. She knew her and Kian had their own issues to deal with, but the fact he put that aside to help her, not push her to speak, she appreciated.

It was sad how low the bar was because of her time with Declan, and how it took her this long, and distance, to realize that. They would still save him, he was still her friend, but there would never be anything romantic between them again.

"Have you spoken to him?" Kian broke into her thoughts, his body holding her firmly against his. Asking nothing more than to let him be her anchor right then.

Bryn shook her head, pulling back to wipe her face. "I just found out. Callie told me when I was supposed to be asking for an army ... and I couldn't. I asked about my mom instead." She gave a bitter laugh. "I'm a selfish leader."

Kian took her face in his hands. "No. This whole time you have been leading the group against the odds stacked against you. You've been dealt a blow, and with that, a leader would figure it out and get back to the front lines." Pushing her hair from her face, he pressed his forehead to hers. "Speak to your father and then go from there."

Bryn grabbed his wrists, looking up at him as she swallowed down her pride.

"I know everything is weird between us right now, and I still have questions for you, but will you go with me to talk to him?"

The seriousness in his eyes, the look of pure emotion, was gone as fast as it appeared. Bryn had no idea what it all meant, but Kian nodded before standing, holding his hand out for her to grab.

"I will always stand next to you, no matter what is happening between us personally."

Bryn took his hand, letting him pull her up. Before she could second guess herself, she wrapped her arms around his waist, hugging him as tightly as she could. Kian wrapped her in his arms, and Bryn felt a safety she'd only ever felt with him nearby.

Without a word, they released each other and walked hand in hand toward the camp where the wolves were loitering about.

The camp buzzed with the sounds of waking shifters—the rustle of furs, the clanging of cooking pots, and the thud of running feet—but Bryn's eyes caught more than she expected as they moved around camp, several still nude after a shift.

Bryn guessed the magical clothing wasn't a power she'd bestowed upon all of them, just Cyerra and Rae.

As Kian and Bryn stepped into the center of camp, all the wolves froze, watching her closely, some sniffing the air and narrowing their eyes.

Two of the older wolves stepped out a tent, their eyes wandering over the camp before catching on Bryn and Kian.

"Gods above and below," one of the two men said, his hand going out to take the other man's shoulder. "It can't be..."

Bryn stepped forward, Kian keeping close behind her as she walked toward the stunned man.

"It's not," the other man said as she stopped several feet from them, unsure of how welcome she was. His eyes watched her every move until the other man dropped his hand, and Bryn could see he was shaking as he tried to compose himself before walking toward her.

"You look just like her," he said as he looked her over just as she did him. Although not as huge as Cormac, he was a large man, his build solid and powerful. His light brown hair tumbled over a face where amber eyes, like polished stones, held her gaze. He was lithe and graceful as he prowled toward her.

"Aine? She was ... is my mother," Bryn's words felt so small before this larger-than-life male, but they were enough to knock him a step backwards.

"Aine." With that one word, he fell to his knees, his body fighting the shift as the other wolves moved out, making themselves scarce. The other man moved closer to him, but kept his distance as he shuffled, cutting around him to where he was between Bryn and him.

A long hair standing howl ripped from the man on his knees before he fell forward, punching the ground.

As the dust settled around him, he looked up at her, his eyes the gold of his predator. Kian moved next to her, both men now blocking her from the man that had to be her father.

"Move," her father growled as he stood up, and the other man that had come over tilted his head before he moved out of the way, but Kian held strong. "Move!" her father roared, but Kian didn't budge, even as the alpha sent out a pulse of power aimed at Kian's wolf.

"Not until I know you will not harm her," Kian said, his voice steady and strong.

Her father looked away, taking in ragged deep breaths before he looked back at them, his eyes amber once again. He nodded to Kian, and Kian stepped aside as her father stepped closer with a hesitance she wouldn't have thought him capable of after that display.

With shaking fingers, he reached out toward her, waiting until she chose how much she would allow. Bryn bit her lip and closed the distance between them as her father wrapped his hand around the back of her neck and pulled her against his wide chest.

A deep breath followed his sigh as he wrapped her up in his arms, his heart pounding against her ear.

"My cub," he whispered in a voice full of love, shock, and heartbreak. "You've returned to me when I thought you dead."

At his words, Bryn closed her eyes and let her tears fall once again.

Chapter 28

It was obvious at first glance that Bryn had her father's nose and chin. There were far too many similarities between her and this alpha to deny his parentage, but then who was the man who claimed to be her father in Ifreann? Why had he taken her?

"My name is Torin," her father said as he waved between himself and the other man who had walked out with him. "This is my brother and second, Leif."

With a wave, her father signaled her and Kian into his tent, where Leif held the canvas open for them before following them in. Bryn hadn't even made it to the chair before Leif was there, pulling it out for her.

"You're fine—"

"I insist, please," he said, pulling out the chair with a soft scrape against the ground. Bryn, too flustered to refuse, took the seat. The smooth wood pressing against her back as he pushed her in. Kian took a seat next to her, taking her hand under the table and giving it a gentle squeeze, anchoring her to the present.

The tent was much larger inside than she had anticipated as Torin sat across from her, and Leif stood behind him. They gave her a minute to take in the tent: the pile of furs and pillows in the corner that served as a bed, a simple wooden table in the center worn smooth by time, a few mismatched chairs and, off to the side, surprisingly, an antique wardrobe.

"You haven't lived in tents this whole time, have you?" she asked, staring at the ornately carved wardrobe that was so out of place in the canvas structure.

Torin's gaze moved over the tent, as if trying to see it through her eyes. "We had homes here well before this became Cethin. My ancestors worked alongside humans in our daily jobs, no one knowing we were any different, until the world fell apart taking our city with it. My great grandfather worked on things called computers that had the ability to perform tasks we have to do ourselves now."

Settling back in his chair, he nodded to Leif, who took the seat across from Kian.

"There were a few battles between the wolves and the witches in the beginning, but by the time Cethin existed, we had a peaceful, but temporary, agreement in place. The witches would keep the land stable and the wolves would protect it, but we never meant to stay permanently. We had planned to start our own village for our pack, but the king changed all our plans."

"Are there any non-magical mortals here?" Bryn asked.

Torin shook his head. "There was at the beginning, but slowly more and more left to the wilds beyond the fog after we let in a group traveling from Osgar."

Kian and Bryn gave each other a look, one that was not missed by Torin.

"I see you've run into some people from Osgar on your travels?"

Bryn looked at her father. "They took people from towns for sacrifices to keep their people safe and the forest thriving."

A small growl left Leif as Torin crossed his arms, his jaw clenched.

"Took our humans for that?" Leif snarled.

"Because the witches would've known and fought back." Torin turned back to Bryn. "Did they hurt you at all?"

Bryn shook her head, biting her lip before she spoke.

"My mother ... do you know what happened to her?" Bryn's question hung in the air while Torin looked meaningfully at Leif. Something passed between the two before Torin answered her.

"No one knows for sure. When we found out she was pregnant, Callie was less than happy, and they had an argument. Aine came to live with us after that, and then one night ... she never came home."

Bryn leaned forward in her chair, her hands covering her face, her eyes burning, as Kian rubbed her back.

"We searched all of Cethin, and miles and miles around, but never found a trace of her," Leif added, his voice solemn. Before anything else could be said, Leif cleared his throat, and Bryn dropped her hands to look at him. Something passed between her father and uncle before Torin nodded. Leif sighed and continued.

"Before she left, she spent a lot of time in the dead forest. That is where her smell was the strongest when she disappeared."

Kian's eyes spun with silver as he looked toward Bryn before addressing Torin. "I ran through there this morning. Those woods unsettled my wolf more than any battle."

Bryn leaned forward toward her father and uncle. "Show me."

Torin guided them through the tightly packed tents, the shifters watching them and their eyes grew solemn as they noticed the direction they were heading. A heavy sadness followed them, thick as a death shroud.

A penetrating chill seeped into Bryn's bones, making her shiver as they entered what her father called the dead forest. The smell of decaying vegetation and damp earth greeted them as a swirling fog obscured the black, skeletal trees.

There in the middle was the ancient, gnarled tree that had called to her, its roots clawing at the earth.

It felt consuming in its need for her to come back, to lay her hand upon the bark as she had the other day.

Kian anchored her as the air grew suffocating, the trees emitting auras the same as humans near death did before their souls left their bodies. But that wasn't the most shocking part for her though: she knew them and they knew her.

"How?" she whispered, unsure if she were speaking to Torin or herself. "Are they…" Bryn couldn't manage the words. The souls were tightly wound together, but the Morrigan was pulling them apart faster than Bryn's mind could comprehend. She found herself lost in their emotional turmoil as she felt the pulse of anxiety and pleading whispers thrumming through the forest, carried on the wind and through the roots of the trees.

Bryn went back to the large tree overlooking the others in the forest, and touched it just as she had before, but with a different result. The screams and images of battle were too much, and she jerked her hand back from the freezing cold sensation burning her skin everywhere it made contact.

She turned to Torin and Kian, shaking out her hand. "They've been here this whole time?"

Torin walked to a smaller tree behind the one she'd just felt, laying his hand on it and grimacing, but he refused to pull away.

"In the beginning, the witches and wolves had their area set up here, their natural gifts in nature allowing them to grow and harvest what they needed." Torin wandered near the large tree where she stood but didn't touch it. "No matter what they tried, this area never grew anything. Then outsiders began attacking and stealing what they could, using this area to set up their little ambushes. Callie created the fog, but she refused to cover this area. I never could understand why until the voices started when us wolves moved our camp here."

Torin folded his arms across his broad chest. "I lost myself to grief, and challenged Callie in my anger, thinking she did something to Aine for being with me. She refused, which surprised me as angry as she was and dealing with her own grief. I'd understand if she wanted to freeze my bones and be done with me, but instead, we made a non-verbal agreement to stay away from each other. From there, my sole focus became my pack and securing the borders."

He went quiet and stared off into the trees, all of them lost souls. "I still remember the first time I saw your mother. I knew she was my mate immediately but had to bide my time since only wolves know when they've met their mate."

Kian shifted closer to her but didn't touch her. His closeness enough to help her through this conversation.

"Some days I wish Callie had killed me so I wouldn't have to live without Aine. I thought she was punishing me by keeping me alive, and I made sure she knew every day how much I hated her for it." Torin turned his wolfish amber eyes on her. "Now I can never repay her for saying no."

Bryn bit down on her cheek as Torin put his hands on her shoulders, his eyes reflecting a storm of emotions—fear, uncertainty, and a flicker of hope. Even without the obvious physical features they shared, there was something in her soul that recognized this man as her own blood. There was no question that she was his child.

"I thought I had lost you as well as her."

She stepped forward, the crisp frost crunching under her boots, and wrapped her arms around her father's waist in a hug. He was quick to respond, holding her tightly in his arms. The strong alpha wolf shifter who was her father cried as he held her. His daughter.

A connection between her and her true father sparked to life, and she finally felt like she was somewhere she belonged for the first time.

Chapter 29

Bryn made her way through the woods by herself, taking in all the new truths laid bare of her past and what it meant for her future. As much as she wanted to talk more with her father, to speak with Kian about the truth of what was between them, she needed time to process before she could have a coherent conversation.

A small stream ran parallel to her path, and she stepped toward where the water flowed over brown and beige pebbles. Her reflection stared back at her, her features a tad sharper now, her ears more tapered than they had been. Small changes from her merging with the Morrigan.

At some point, she would have to accept that her fear of the Morrigan taking her over completely would be a hindrance in their battle against the king.

It was time to address it, even if she feared losing her identity.

Bryn closed her eyes, and for the first time without a battle or dangerous situation at play, she tapped into her magic. It unfurled like a flower in bloom, opening within her chest, its warmth spreading through her limbs. A pleasant coolness rippled through her body from her head to her toes, and the familiar tingle of magic swept through the blue Celtic tattoos on her arms.

Breathing into it, Bryn tore down the wall she kept up between herself and the potential within her soul, letting herself feel every part of her physical body and mental self. It was terrifying and yet exhilarating at the same time.

"Embrace our power." The Morrigan's voice was stronger than it had ever been, but Bryn didn't feel like she was losing control for once.

"Don't make me regret this," Bryn whispered and did as the goddess asked. She embraced all of who she was. Of whom she could be.

In her mind's eye, she walked through a bleak, monochrome desert. The withered, gray trees cast long, skeletal shadows that stretched across the cracked earth, and the strong, howling wind whipped around her, mirroring the turmoil within. Words and wind passed over and through her.

When wolf and witch merge as one,
The ancient war has just begun.
The old will rise, the threads will tear,
And claim a world laid cold and bare.

The world around her seemed to sync with her heartbeat as she walked, the rhythm quickening as she approached a small opening in the sand. A sinkhole opened enough for her to see what the desert had caught in its trap.

From beneath the sand, a more youthful version of herself looked up, her dry and cracked lips mouthing a plea for help as she tried, and failed, to raise her small arms. Weak and starving, Bryn panicked at the sight of her younger self so neglected.

Looking around, she ran and broke off one of the withered branches of a nearby tree, making her way back to the hole. Lowering it down for the girl, the adolescent version of herself tried to grab hold, but was far too weak to pull herself up, to even hold on to the branch at all.

The sun moved across the sky as Bryn begged her younger self to try again, to just hold on. Time was moving faster than Bryn could comprehend, and soon, the girl wasn't moving at all.

"Bryn!" she screamed, the sound sharp and desperate as the wind pulled her words away from her, yet the girl didn't react, her chest motionless. Falling to her knees next to the dark, gaping pit, Bryn cried out, her anger a hot, throbbing pulse in her chest.

"You are still not using your magic. You still fight it even as you claim to embrace it. Only you can own our power and be who you were truly born to be, not what they made you."

As the sun dipped below the horizon, painting the sky in fiery hues, the moon quietly took its place, bathing the world in silvery light before the sun rose again. Time was meaningless, but Bryn stood, her knees stiff, and shook off the criticism, fear, and pain she'd endured, a tangible weight lifting from her shoulders as she did what she never thought possible.

The anger she'd felt—a burning resentment stoked by others' judgments—finally lifted, revealing the true self she'd hidden behind her reclusive nature, and later, behind the formidable power of the Morrigan. Bryn allowed herself to become the person she might have become had she not left Cethin. Had she never been around her Aunt Mallory or Ifreann and its population of religious zealots.

"Never to bow. Never to break. Fierce as a wolf, cunning as a crow."

In her, there was a leader. One who would do all she could to protect her people. She'd always possessed an inner resilience, yet the overwhelming pain and turmoil had blinded her to it.

"Now you understand, Bryn Kenneally."

Feeling the soft, yielding sand between her fingers, she sculpted steps, the damp earth clung to her skin as she carefully scooped up the child, the girl's light weight a comfort in her arms.

Stepping out from the hole, Bryn called on the rain, the wind whipping around her as she pulled in heavy, gray clouds. The first fat drops splattered on her skin before a torrent fell, reviving her inner child.

The question, "Mama?" hung in the air, but the shake of Bryn's head was a heavy blow, crushing the little girl's hopeful spirits. "She is gone forever."

"But we are here, and we hold the line. Never to bow."

"Never to break," Bryn whispered as she opened her eyes once again to her reflection, her gaze cutting.

"I will get you the answers you need, little Bryn."

Bryn stepped out of the long house into the harsh glare of the artificial sun. Instinctively, she reached up to push back her wild curls, only to remember the tight braids she'd painstakingly woven in the mirror when she'd returned after her moment in the woods. The very same braids she had worn when she was the Morrigan.

It was a nod to her acceptance of who she was, who she could become, and for once, the Morrigan stood with her instead of being something she had to fight against.

Bryn would bow to no one, and for damn sure not the false king.

"Now you understand. It's a shame it took so very long."

With an eye roll, Bryn strode through Cethin in her worn leathers, the now familiar coolness of her magic humming beneath her skin. The grass yielding beneath her boots with each step, much like those who opposed her would soon bend.

Few people were up and about, but none of them were Callie. Her friends were either still asleep or grabbing breakfast. Kian was again running through the trees as he did every morning, but this time he ran with her father's pack.

Eyes followed her every move as she walked through the camp, taking in her new stride, and she was sure since she was among witches, her new confidence in finally accepting her power.

"They will learn to fear you."

Bryn opened her mouth to reply that she didn't want to be feared when Callie strode up to her.

"Good morning, granddaughter! Looking for me?" Callie pulled a glove from her hand, a basket full of gardening supplies and seeds hanging from her wrist.

The woman's shrewd eyes looked over what Bryn knew to be the grim set of her jaw, and catching the difference from the Bryn of yesterday, she was sure.

Callie took in a deep breath, and nodded, "A serious chat I assume."

Bryn nodded. "I appreciate your hospitality in hosting us, but we need to move forward with our plans of ridding the world of Bres, and now Balor."

"Balor?" Callie's gaze sharpened. "He's back on this plane?"

Bryn answered with a curt nod. "The leader of Osgar used his nephew, my good friend, as a host. If you know who I am, then you should know that the friend in question was the reincarnation of the Dagda."

"No," Callie's jaw dropped and she stumbled back a step. "He wouldn't."

Callie turned away from Bryn and took deep breaths, her shoulders rising and falling.

"How much do you know of the battle ahead?" Bryn asked as she moved around to face Callie. The blue-green eyes so much like her own met hers.

"We need every one of you to end this." Callie's words were mere whispers. "I have waited for lifetimes, did as I was asked, and yet, this time ... it could be all for nothing! Everything we've been given and all we have sacrificed." Her eyes watered. "Everything that Niamh and I..."

Her grandmother spun away, her gaze searching. "Niamh!" she shouted, her voice ripe with emotion.

A silver blur of wolf darted into the village from the trees, shifting mid-way to her, and then there was Kian, walking at a clipped pace toward her. "Bryn, we need to talk." His tone grave as he spoke.

Callie spun on Kian. "Is this because of you? Did you change the dynamic?"

Kian squared his shoulders. "And how would I do that?"

"You were the general and nothing more! The Morrigan was always meant to be with the Dagda."

Kian narrowed his gaze on Callie. "Yes, the Morrigan, but not Bryn."

"They are one and the same!" Callie yelled, turning bright red.

Everyone remained silent while Callie, her panicked eyes surveying her surroundings, appeared to be coming back to herself.

She apologized with a shake of her head, a fleeting look of frustration appearing before she deliberately closed off all emotion, her facial muscles tensing. "I apologize. This news has my emotions close to the surface."

Callie cleared her throat and pulled her shoulders back. "Yes, we need to discuss our next steps. Obviously, Cethin is with you."

"And the shadow army?"

Callie gave Bryn a sad smile. "I wish I knew how to help you with that, but the shadow army was gone long before I found my way here. I've never seen them and have no idea where they truly are."

Before Bryn could say more, Callie walked off toward the forest, and she wondered if that was where Niamh was. Ever since they'd first arrived, Niamh had made herself scarce.

"If you want to chime in at any time on where our wonderful shadow army is, feel free," Bryn growled, but the Morrigan didn't respond right away.

"I have ... thoughts."

"I don't know where they are, but there is something deeper going on, and I have a feeling the shifters can help us unearth it." Kian took her arm, and she didn't correct him in that she was talking to the Morrigan and not him.

Bryn really looked at where her father lived as Kian guided her, taking more of it in than she had when she came by before. The closer they were to the shifters, the less there was of nature. Such a proud group, so intimately tied to the rhythms of the earth and moon, their lives governed by the lunar cycle and the turning of the seasons, wouldn't normally live in an area bereft of the very needs of their kind.

But then everything shifted as the Morrigan woke up and took notice within her, her body following Kian without really seeing.

A shudder ran through her as the air changed, and an iridescent layer shimmered around her disappearing as quickly as it came. A memory.

This was where she had stepped through the veil for the last time.

Where she had split the souls of those the Morrigan had thought of as her own.

The last time she had seen her shadow army.

Chapter 30

“**B**ryn?” Kian waved his hand in front of her face as she shook her head.

“Here. Right here!” she yelled, turning in a circle to take in where she was. To the left of her were the wolf tents, and to the right, the large tree that towered over Cethin and its dead forest.

“Here, what? Are you okay?” Kian asked, trying to grab her shoulders, but missing as she darted away, letting herself feel the magic, her magic and its echo from long ago.

“I tore open the veil here. I can still feel some of the Morrigan’s residual magic.”

Kian looked around, his eyebrows lifting. “I felt...” He stepped back as if taking everything in. “I knew something was familiar here, but I only felt the change by the tree. I thought maybe something happened there and was wondering if you noticed.”

Bryn made her way to the tree, Kian now following her, and the immediate pulse of power was a jolt to both her and the Morrigan.

She placed her hand on the tree and lifetimes of memories flooded her, all ending in a collective image of wraiths coming toward her. The feel of being split apart, as if their hearts were being ripped from their chests, before the world spun in a vortex and it all went dark.

"I remember. They would stay in this state until I came again."

"Like Kian?" Bryn growled the words, anger at the goddess's choice. "Was this supposed to save them? The pain, the darkness?" Her words ended on a shout.

Kian grabbed her arm before she could walk off. "Bryn, what's wrong?"

"The Morrigan split everyone's souls, painfully, without even knowing what would happen!" Fire burned through her veins as the anger from both herself and the goddess built up.

"It was to save them. Would you rather have them shredded by the claws of the wraiths? Lost and set to become the soulless sluagh for all eternity?"

At the calm, almost cold tone of the Morrigan, Bryn grabbed her hair, tugging at the roots. "Would that be worse than having your soul ripped from your body and being lost to darkness for eternity? Will they even be sane?" Bryn dropped her hands and turned, Kian's face having lost all its color. "Kian, I'm sorry—"

"Did she really not know or was it that she didn't care?" he asked, his voice barely above a whisper.

"I..." Bryn waited for the Morrigan to say something, but the goddess's silence was damning. *Say something!* Bryn yelled into her own mind.

"I do not expect you to understand, only know that it was what had to be done."

Kian nodded, seeming to understand without her saying a word.

"I followed you for years. I turned my back on my people to lead your armies and you repaid us with this?" Bryn shivered at the anger in his expression and the coldness of his voice. "We trusted you and you betrayed us."

"I did nothing of the sort, Wolf!"

Bryn did not repeat the words for Kian, it was all too clear he knew where this was going.

"I don't need to hear you say it, and while I know Bryn is not you, I know you live within her." His eyes softened before he shook away the emotion. "How can I ever trust you will have our best interest at heart when you've already betrayed us? How can I—" He swallowed before looking away. "I need time. I don't know how to move past this ... how to see just Bryn anymore and know that she won't do the same."

Bryn clenched her jaw, refusing to promise him anything. She knew in her heart that she would never do such a thing to him, but what if the Morrigan did something without her say so? What if she took control when Bryn was weak and unable to fight back?

With a huff and a nod, Kian turned, hands on hips.

"You could promise me, Bryn."

Biting her lip, she closed her eyes, begging the burning to stop.

How could she promise something she might break since she could hardly control the Morrigan?

"We work together now."

Until when? When will you choose to start making decisions without me like you did in Ifreann.

"That was for your survival—"

And next time? Will you take the time to discuss it before jumping right in?

"I am a goddess! I do not need to get approval from some mortal girl who chose to live and potentially die at the hands of pathetic Balor worshippers!"

Exactly.

Bryn opened her eyes, and Kian was gone, only the dead forest around her.

With her heart in her stomach, Bryn turned back to the trees as she fell to her knees. Her mind torn between Kian and the very people she had betrayed.

Somehow, her people, her army, were trapped there. The Morrigan had split their souls, but from what Bryn had gathered, she hadn't thought of where they would end up when she went across the veil.

"There was a myth long ago about a tree of life," Torin said as he sat next to her on the grass. "I always wondered if that was something real."

She bit her cheek, trying to move past her frustration and anger to speak to her father.

They both sat in silence, surrounded by skeletal limbs and a chilled breeze.

"Did they care for you?" he asked, his voice gruff and she knew exactly who "they" were. It was also a question she didn't want to answer.

Bryn kept her gaze on the cold dirt beneath her feet as she spoke. "The man I thought was my father was kind, but he took me to a place where they were not, and then he ... died."

"This place, Ifreann, what happened there?" It was a question, but also a demand, coated in the power of his alpha status. It didn't work on her since she was the reason he had the power to shift, but she understood his desire to know was strong just from the effort.

"They were religious, and I had no idea that they worshiped Balor when I was young. I didn't even know who Balor was until Danu came ... and yet, they called me *evil*. Called me a witch."

Her father shifted, the muscles in his forearms tightening as he clenched his fists over his knees next to her.

"Why do you say witch with such sadness? Your mother is a witch." Bryn didn't miss how her father spoke of her mother as if she were still with them. "Such power is a blessing from Brigid herself."

Bryn gave a small huff before she leaned back on her elbows, looking up at the top of the dead tree that should have bloomed, full of life.

"Witches were considered evil in Ifreann. To be a witch meant you were evil incarnate."

Torin surprised her by laughing. "And yet, they bowed to the greatest of evils."

Bryn couldn't deny that.

"The man I called father had a sister who was quick to immerse herself in the culture and religion there. She was sure I was evil and made sure I, and everyone else, knew it."

A deep, menacing growl vibrated through her father. "I'll kill her."

Bryn lifted her chin. "I already did." And for once, Bryn didn't flinch at the words. Jace was the only reason she felt an ounce of guilt, otherwise it was a huge relief that the woman would no longer darken her doorway.

"Good. That's the wolf in you," Torin said in a proud voice. "But there is no reason my daughter should have felt an ounce of pain when you were meant to live with me. To be raised by me and your mother."

Bryn could not count the years she had wished for that, but now she understood. She hated it, but she understood.

"As much as I wish that had happened, I wouldn't have been with the Tuatha Dé Danann. I wouldn't have seen the evil at work through Balor and known what he is capable of. Goddess, how I wished for someone to be there for me, but I understand now why I had to go through this."

Torin wrapped an arm around her shoulders. "Well, now that I've sunk my teeth into you, I'm never letting you go, kid."

Bryn couldn't fight the warmth curling in her chest, as much as the anger pushed at her, his words were a balm to her tattered nerves.

"But the man who raised you ... he was good to you?" Torin asked with a soft tone and concern shining in his amber eyes.

She nodded, feeling guilty that she still thought of him as a father with her birth father right next to her.

His knuckle ran over her cheek. "You grieve him, and that is fine, my child. He was a father to you when I could not be, and for that, I thank him."

"How can you not be angry at him for raising me when you didn't?" Bryn shocked herself with her outburst but reined it back in when Torin stood, pulling her up before he put his hands on her shoulders.

"He found you and cared for you until his last breath. That's all I could hope for."

Bryn swallowed down the lump in her throat, before turning back toward the forest, her father dropping his hands.

The dead trees creaked in the wind, a mournful sound that mirrored her feelings as she took a deep, ragged breath.

"You'll figure out how to reach your army," Torin said, reaching up and squeezing her shoulder as a wolf trotted over to him. Without a word, Torin nodded to Bryn and took off after the wolf.

Bryn sat cross-legged on the packed earth between her father's tent city and the skeletal remains of forest. The sun moved across the sky, Bryn meditating on everything, coming to no conclusion on how and where to access the army. Or how to speak to Kian after what had transpired.

"Nothing can ever be easy, can it?" she whispered to herself.

"Not even if you lived many, many lifetimes."

Bryn shot to her feet and turned to face her grandmother. Yet this wasn't the woman who had greeted them when they first came to Cethin. Something about her was younger, almost ethereal. Though she wore the same clothing, the same hair plaits, her hair was a sunny golden blonde instead of white.

Looking around, Bryn wondered if Niamh was okay, not having known the outcome of their discussion.

"Niamh—"

"She still needs time." Callie took a deep breath. "When she is ready, I'm sure she will cross the veil to speak." Callie didn't quite look like she believed that. "But the most important thing is that our guardians are ready for what is to come."

"I know—"

"Then we move forward and work together, if you know." Straightening her shoulders, her chin up, Callie gave her a serious expression "My past hurts created a narrow worldview, leading to the mistakes I made. To see the choices of those around me, the path I was put on, as a sacrifice, not something for the greater good." Callie dropped to her knees at Bryn's feet. "You have my magic and you have my fealty as both your grandmother and as Cailleach."

Bryn worked through her grandmother's words as ice, glittering like a thousand tiny diamonds, flowed over Callie's body, forming a protective armor. Frosted pauldrons, etched with hands delicately holding a crescent moon, adorned the pure ice knight standing before her.

Callie extended her hands, and a shimmering sword of ice materialized, its surface cold and smooth to the touch, before she sheathed it in its icy scabbard.

"I will avenge the deaths at the hand of the Fomorians who killed my world, my people, my coven. The witches are with you and will come when you call for us."

The frosted armor slid away in a wash of water, leaving Callie before her as she was, dry as bone. The ground beneath Bryn warmed, and turning, she watched the frost recede from the north side of Cethin, the trees slowly straightening as the snow melted, the fog lifting to reveal a landscape bathed in sunlight.

"I've lived in anger at the loss of Niamh, at how my life changed, the magic Brigid gave me when I woke up from death in my grave besides my husband's. All the trauma took hold of me in a way I should have fought against." Stepping closer to Bryn, Callie held a look of genuine apology in her eyes. "Even so, I'm thankful that if I could not have Niamh, she was there to guide you. To love you, as my own daughter would have."

A branch broke, and there was Niamh, her eyes watering as Callie and Bryn turned to face her.

Silence punctuated the intensity between them before Callie ran to Niamh, falling into her arms, both women lost in each other after so long apart.

Bryn quietly left them, allowing them their private moment to reconnect, as she retreated to Cethin.

If only Kian would forgive her as well.

Chapter 31

Bryn nodded to several of the witches sitting with Sage and Jace at lunch, Sage waving her over.

"How have you been?" Jace asked as Sage gave Bryn a wide smile.

"I've ... been better," Bryn whispered, and Jace stood to sit next to her. Sage's eyes were full of questions until she saw Bryn's expression and disengaged politely from the witches to focus on her.

She must look as much of a mess on the outside as she was on the inside.

"What happened, sweetie?" Sage asked, taking one of Bryn's hands from across the table as Jace nudged her with his shoulder.

Bryn gave a half-hearted laugh. "Where do I even start?"

"From the beginning," Sage said, her eyes full of concern.

"My father ... he is not my actual father. The alpha here, Torin, is my birth father," Bryn started, and, unable to look at her friends, all her feelings and revelations spilled out, ending with Kian's anger toward her. By the time she looked up, Justin, Kessler, Rae, and Cyerra had joined her.

Jace rubbed his face but said nothing to the revelation that she was not his actual cousin.

"Wow." Justin leaned back in his seat. "That's a lot ... even for us."

"Helpful," Jace murmured before poking Bryn in the arm, waiting for her to look at him. "We're still family, blood or not."

Bryn's eyes watered as she tried to stave off the tears from hearing the words she so desperately needed to hear. Jace pulled her into a side hug, keeping his arm around her in an act of comfort that unleashed a few tears she was quick to wipe away.

"Not just Jace, all of us here," Kessler said, and the rest of the group nodded.

"Maybe others are not as keen on trust right now," Justin interrupted, earning a narrowed look from Sage before waving her off, "but we trust you. The Morrigan or not."

"If anything, you can keep her more human," Rae said, hopping in her seat a bit. "Maybe Kian can't see it through his anger, but you've humanized her. So many times I've expected her to lash out at me through you, but it seems like she is more ... settled?" Rae looked at Cyerra, who gave a slight nod.

"You worry she will overpower you, but she wouldn't be able to. That's something she would never allow you to know, but the power is yours now. The power of a goddess, a wolf, and witch all in one person. You are more than the goddess was all contained in the mind of a mortal. Honestly, I'm surprised none of the rest of you have broken to the sheer power of the gods within you."

"Reassuring." Kessler rolled his eyes, folding his arms over his chest.

"A simple truth, blacksmith."

They went quiet, Bryn contemplating what they all said in the silence.

"If I bring them back, somehow, will they hate me like Kian does?" Bryn whispered, and all eyes were on her. "Will they be angry enough to choose not to follow us?"

"When has life held any guarantees?" Cyerra responded. "Yet, we still try. What would be the point to come all this way and not do everything we can to create an army worthy of the Tuatha Dé Danann?"

Bryn gave a watery laugh. "Yeah, now we just need to figure out the *how* of getting them back here. I have no idea where to even begin."

"Well, what have you tried?" Rae asked as she leaned forward on the table. "Aside from staring at the tree."

Cyerra rolled her eyes but waited on Bryn to respond.

"I've felt them in there, but I guess I hoped that the Morrigan would step in and help." The Morrigan hadn't bothered to be involved much since the falling out with Kian, so both her connections to the past were unhelpful.

"Come on then," Cyerra stood, waving for Rae and Bryn to stand as well. "Let's see what we can do about this. There must be some clues the three of us can dig up together."

Bryn stood with Cyerra and Rae flanking her as they faced the tree. The two parts of her magic cleaved from her own, the weight of her divided power heavy in the air, a silent tension humming between them.

The Morrigan slid closer to the front, still not saying much, and Bryn was sure the goddess had her ego bruised or was irritated that Bryn bothered to question the Morrigan at all. How silly it was that a mere mortal questioned a goddess of prophecy, war, and death.

"I am not so easily bothered by the trivialities of your kind."

"Then why have you been so quiet? I assumed you were licking your wounds."

A burst of irritation flooded her, leaving as quick as it came.

"Naturally I am displeased by both you and my general questioning me, but what displeases me more is that my army is stuck in a tree."

"Fair enough."

Bryn dropped to her knees next to the large tree, placing her hands against the roots, feeling for the souls. When she'd touched the bark, she'd been flooded with memories, but now it was nothing but an echo of what she'd seen before, the memories rippling like water along the surface of her consciousness.

"You all right?" Rae asked, putting her hand on Bryn's shoulder and immediately, Bryn connected to someone. Not just the echo of memories, but a touch to the soul of another, one that the soul took notice of. When Rae removed her hand, Bryn yelled out for her to stop, to put her hand back. Rae quickly did so, and Bryn caught another soul. Not the same, but the thread of it led her to a woman.

The soul pulsed with power, sending it down the thread Bryn had a hold of. There were no audible words, but the sense of familiarity was enough that the Morrigan held tight to the front of Bryn's consciousness, watching through her eyes.

"Focus on the lines."

Bryn did as the Morrigan asked, trying to widen her awareness to bring in more threads. They were gold, some brighter than others, some frayed with no soul attached to the end at all.

"We've lost some. Perhaps the madness of the darkness." The Morrigan went quiet, contemplative before Bryn nudged her. *"You were right, mortal. Both you and my general were right. I chose poorly."*

She said nothing as she continued to search, but as much as she was finding, she couldn't quite connect with them.

"Cyerra," Bryn said without opening her eyes. "I need your power too. It's a theory, but—" Before Bryn could finish the words, Cyerra's hand was on her other shoulder and everything, every soul and tether, lit up around her like the sun mid-day in Ifreann.

Overwhelmed, Bryn began to pull back, but the Morrigan stayed her.

"Center, look where the threads are tethered. Not to us, to the tree."

A wave of dizziness coursed through her, but the Morrigan pushed her to focus.

"It's too strong. I did not realize how much magic I left with it. It is my lifeblood that had sealed them in, and my power that guards the door."

Her legs grew numb, her body shaking, yet the Morrigan cursed her weak mortal shell and pulsed more power through her body.

Bones buried beneath the surface vacillated, their power responded to the Morrigan's rage-filled search for an answer.

The bones sent the vibrations out, but only in one direction down the soul tethers. The tremor led to a mass of roots, all writhing together, deep beneath the plagued forest. The roots were alive and healthy, vibrant, and could be strummed as easily as guitar strings.

Bryn visualized them in her hands, touching one root that led into the mass of tangles. In her mind she could see a man laughing as he twirled his bride before kissing her.

Another root showed a young woman receiving her first sword.

Each root held a story of the person they were, Bryn pulling the strongest memory from their souls.

It was the ninth root she touched that had Bryn's lungs constricting.

Her father kneeled before a woman, one with Bryn's coloring, and kissed her rounded stomach. Bryn held onto it with all her might, not wanting the visual to fade away. Her father looked so much younger, happier, with a smile of pure delight on his lips.

Bryn's mother laid her hands over where he embraced her stomach.

The vision faded, but something lingered within Bryn. A spark of power, a small flicker of light within the bundle of roots.

Bryn moved deeper into the thorny ball, the prickling sensation throughout her soul growing more intense as she felt the beating pulse of energy from so many other souls held within. The light grew brighter the closer she got, until it overtook the entire world around her, planting a seed within her.

She couldn't move, her body freezing, the soul tethers wrapping around her arms and legs, trapping her. Her tattoos pulsed, the power igniting from her and the Morrigan lighting them up, only to drain away as the bonds grew even tighter around her.

"Wake up! Now!"

Another wave of power moved over her, not her own, but something darker, more chaotic. The Morrigan snarled at the onslaught before she recognized it and pulled back. Waves of dark blues and purples wove around her as she struggled to break free, her mind wearing down.

The power tore at the bonds, shaking with frantic energy before she was able to open her eyes, back in her own world and no longer pulled into the tree holding the shadow army.

Bryn couldn't feel anything, the world blurred, and she could only see Kian above her. As he shifted her body moved, so he must have held her as he yelled at someone. "She used too much!"

"Grab them and get them to the healers!"

"How could you let this happen?"

Voices warred over Bryn's own thoughts. Kian stood, holding her and carrying her as her head fell limply to the side. Kessler was holding Rae, her eyes, ears, and nose bleeding, her body far too pale and still.

Had she killed her friends?

With a small moan, she tried to shift in Kian's grip, but his hold on her was pure steel.

Kessler ran his hand along Rae's cheekbone, and while Bryn's mind was hardly stable, she could see the concern in her friend's eyes. Concern that went above and beyond friendship, and she wondered how she missed that connection as they disappeared from view.

"She'll be fine. They just overloaded themselves. Power has consequences if too much is used. It's not limitless." Bryn could hear the hesitation and fear in Kian's voice. She knew him far better than she did anyone else, and even he wasn't sure they would be fine.

"Cyerra?" Bryn managed to mumble, choking as liquid spilled over her own lips.

"Already with the healers, which is where we're going right now," Kian said, as he walked with her curled against his chest. The tightness of his jaw told her not to bother arguing, he was mad before, but now he was beyond pissed.

She let her eyes close, not having the energy for a fight, and let the darkness take her.

Chapter 32

Bryn woke up to a room overflowing with vibrant green plants, the air humid and thick with the scent of petrichor from the wet earth and damp leaves. She was lying on a surprisingly soft bed with the familiar weight of a wolf shifter, thick fur keeping her warm and toasty.

She met Kian's silver eyes, and he did not look happy. When she tried to sit up, he lifted his head and let out a low, rumbling growl.

"Okay, relax," she grumbled, lying back on the bed, which was probably for the best, since the slightest movement sent her head spinning. Her entire body felt bruised and leaden.

Sage popped her head into the room, checking she was awake before coming in and standing at the side of her bed.

"Oh, thank the goddess you're awake. Here, drink this." Sage helped her to sit up, and put a cup to her lips. "A new herb the witches worked with to help those of us who burn through modern human medicine quicker. It will set you to rights."

Bryn took a sip, grimacing but finishing the cup as Kian watched her intently until she handed the empty cup back to Sage. It tasted bitter with the grainy consistency of sand, but Bryn already began to feel a little less stiff.

Kian's head lifted before Jace walked in, nodded to the wolf in her bed before coming around to the side where Sage was.

"Not a great day when your cousin is lying on the ground bleeding out," he chided, as he lifted his old doctor's bag from Ifreann. Bryn swallowed the lump of emotion that settled in her throat, hearing him speak to her as if nothing at all had changed. Yet, his old bag was a reminder of how much had altered their world in such a short period of time.

"Not my finest hour," she managed, her throat raw. "Cyerra? Rae? Are they all right?"

Jace huffed out a laugh. "Rae is fine, trying to leave, but now Kessler is like a barnacle at her side, driving her nuts with his refusal to let her do anything but rest. I think she may have even bitten him a few times."

At Jace's words, she looked at Kian, who continued watching with narrowed eyes even as he laid his head on his paws. "I can understand that feeling," she said, earning another growl from Kian that she ignored. "What about Cyerra?"

Jace waved her toward him, running his thumbs along the front of her throat before making her open her mouth wide. "She took off the moment she woke up. Against medical advice, mind you." Bryn squinted as Jace shone a bright light in her eyes before clicking it off and placing it back in his bag. "Hard to get a crow to stay still. Once she shifted, I gave up."

"Thankfully," Jace looked at Kian before shutting his bag. "I think you're well enough that Kian can quit guarding you so obnoxiously."

A small laugh left Bryn as Sage shot her a wink, and both she and Jace stepped out of the room, closing the door quietly behind them.

Kian closed his eyes as Bryn settled back against the pillows, watching him.

Say you're sorry, Bryn said to the Morrigan in her mind. *We don't need animosity between us and our general. Isn't that the very reason you were so worried about my feelings for him?*

"The animosity I worried about was a scorned lover, which we both know all too well how that goes. Also, what would I apologize for? Saving them from an eternity as a wraith?"

For not preparing them or at least letting them have a choice on how they waited for your return.

"Mortals have such a narrow view on how many choices they actually have in this pathetic timeline."

I can work with you, or you can put us at a crossroads again. Choose, goddess.

Bryn was met with silence before the Morrigan pushed her way forward, Bryn stepping back for once instead of fighting her. The Morrigan took over, sitting up higher, and Kian's eyes opened, narrowing again as he seemed to realize who he was facing and that it was not Bryn.

"General, I seem to have made a grave mistake in which I must apologize. I did not think of what would happen to you when I split your soul, instead, I acted rashly. Bryn informs me this is the hubris of my godhood, and I must atone for what I've done in the past to harm you and the rest of our army."

Kian watched her, not moving, and Bryn started to feel her nerves growing stronger than the magic of the goddess. She was about to take back over to try her best to smooth it out before silver lit the room and Kian was standing next to the bed.

"I would come around to forgiving you for what you did to me, but what you did to Bryn out there was unforgivable."

Bryn's mind went blank at his words, but the Morrigan grew in her ire.

"You mean working with her to bring back our army?"

"Cut the crap," Kian growled.

"You dare!" The Morrigan pushed Bryn up further, almost moving her to stand before Kian was there pushing her back.

"I do! You knew what it meant to push her power like that! Do you have any idea what I thought when I saw her, lying motionless against the tree, blood coming from her mouth, eyes and ears?" Kian shoved his hands in his hair before moving them to the back of his neck. "I thought she was dead." His words were choked, his eyes misty.

"She survived. Perhaps you should have more faith in your goddess."

Kian's head snapped up, his eyes going cold.

"In my goddess? Oh, I have faith you can crush and destroy to your heart's content, but you will not use my—" Kian snarled. "—Bryn for your power plays! If she dies, I will never again stand at your side. The next vessel you use can burn for all I care."

The Morrigan was silent, not even speaking to Bryn. She waited for either one of them to say something, for the Morrigan to lash out, or for Kian to back down, but it was obvious he would not budge.

"I see," she said through Bryn.

"Do you?" he taunted, but his eyes were serious.

Bryn felt a subtle, insistent pressure from the Morrigan, urging her to nod. "It seems even a goddess isn't aware of everything. I will be more careful and look to your council in the future."

"Bryn's council as well, but ... thank you." Kian turned and left the room, his shoulders tense, his body stiff as he slipped through the door.

She had no idea what happened between them, and when she felt the Morrigan slip back from her consciousness, she knew any answers would have to wait.

Chapter 33

It wasn't until later that afternoon that Bryn was up and around again. The moment she stepped outside, there was Cyerra, staring at her as if she'd been inconvenienced with Bryn's convalesce. As if the crow wasn't also suffering from the effects of their power merging.

"I have received word from some of my crow friends. They say that Osgar is gone."

Bryn halted in her tracks. "Osgar is gone? How? Why?"

"It appears Balor returned and razed the village to the ground. His wraiths tore the entirety of the village and people apart."

"Balor." Bryn folded her arms. "Wearing Declan's face, I assume."

Cyerra's eyes softened as she nodded. "It happened right after we escaped. The crows in the area just made it to Cethin to inform me."

"Gods above," Bryn whispered, thinking of all the people who had lived there. Not all of them were guilty of Cormac's crimes, but even the ones who were ... she had seen what the wraiths were capable of, and no one deserved that.

Well, in the darker part of Bryn she felt Cormac deserved it and was sad he hadn't been there to see that all go down. Not that she would say that aloud.

"I would."

Perhaps, Bryn thought, *we are more alike than I thought.*

The Morrigan gave a gentle hum of agreement as Bryn focused back on Cyerra. "Did the crows inform you of what direction they were heading?"

Cyerra looked up, gentle caws called out from the trees above. "No, now that Balor is free, he is powerful enough to use the dying earth to move himself through it. Much like you can the Faerie circles."

"Thank them for me," Bryn said as she turned to find her friends, needing to divulge what she had just been informed of. To warn Callie that Balor was capable of moving through the earth and hoping she had a way to stop him should he try for Cethin.

"Bryn!" Callie called out from behind, and she turned, her grandmother and Niamh walking together toward her. Only once they were closer did they see the look on her face. "What happened?"

As Bryn caught them up on Cyerra's update, Justin joined them, Finian walking behind him, sniffing everything and getting pets from all the witches walking by.

"Hey," Justin laid his hand on her elbow, and the moment his skin touched hers, a searing white light filled her vision, pulling her into a swirling vortex of words, their shapes shifting like a restless wind.

The words she spoke out loud resonated through her bones, but not her mind. Each syllable added depth and meaning to the sentences she couldn't catch on the wind. As the final words formed a new prophecy, energy crackled and visibly vibrated around her, a tangible hum in the air.

The blinding white vanished, and Bryn was thankful she was still upright, slowly realizing arms were banded around her middle, her back against a strong body. At least the vision hadn't rendered her immobile and seizing on the floor, but the rest of the world had halted as the people who had been working, laughing, training, and going about their daily chores had all stopped to stare at her.

"Did I do anything embarrassing?" Bryn whispered, and it was Kian's voice that spoke next to her ear, not Justin's.

"Your eyes went white, and you spoke a prophecy. But nothing more than that. Let's head inside."

Bryn pulled away. "I'm not an invalid." Her words were less than believable as she tripped over her own foot, but the vulnerability she felt made her cranky. Not to mention it was Kian here, who had just walked out of a serious conversation like Bryn wasn't there to still talk to after the goddess finished her apology.

Holding his hands up, Kian's eyes widened in surprise. "I never said that, Bryn, this just usually takes a lot out of you."

Bryn rubbed her eyes, giving a small nod. She didn't feel the need to apologize for her feelings, which were was a first, but the prophecy that had been shoved into her mind was more important. "Did you hear it all?" She asked Callie and Niamh as the villagers returned to their work, whispering and looking over their shoulders at her.

Callie, Niamh, and Cyerra quickly gathered around her to keep her out of sight of the others, as Justin and Kian led the way to somewhere Bryn assumed they could talk.

"Yes, but some made very little sense to me."

"What did I say?"

"The dark king's doom is sealed by kin, One of his blood, the light within. With a radiant glow to pierce the night, He'll end the reign with truth and light,"

Justin said as he held open a door to one of the long houses, his eyebrows furrowed as he spoke.

Bryn sighed. "That is now three prophecies, if they're that, since we left Ifreann."

With that, she stepped into the long house with another prophecy to deconstruct and frustration bubbling beneath the surface of her skin.

"I'm sure we can understand most of the first one, even breaking it down," Justin said, running his hand over his scruff as they went over the three prophecies in Bryn and Kian's room. Jace, Sage, Kessler, and Rae joined them. "Her power rises with gods and crows, a shadow army where darkness grows. I'd say that has been pretty straight forward."

Bryn paced, biting her nails, an unfortunate new habit she had picked up on their travels. It was much less harmful to tap her ears over and over, but it seemed as her power evolved, so did her nervous tics.

"The first one tells us of the Tuatha Dé Danann coming back, then I am assuming the part about the villain's soul in one they trust is Declan having to carry around Balor, and I hate to say greed and lust when he is not here to defend himself..." Sage trailed off at that thought.

"So, we meet our fates, and a new king comes in? The world unbound?" Kessler rubbed the back of his neck, Rae sitting close to him, his other hand along the back of her chair. Bryn was guessing Kessler never let her stray far these days.

"Yeah, if we get rid of Bres and Balor, is there another waiting in the wings to take over?" Jace asked, his eyes flickering to Kian.

"Well, it's not Kian, I can assure you that." Bryn's voice was gravelly, a growled warning thrumming through her vocal cords that surprised even her. She no longer wanted his Fomorian heritage held against him. He'd shown himself to be trustworthy over and over again, and it was time they accepted him.

"No one is saying that, Bryn," Justin was quick to play peacemaker. "Though the next one really confuses me. Saying his kin of the light will kill him? Radiant glow and piercing light in the night? Truth? From what I've gathered, the Fomori are unlikely to hold those descriptions at the best of times. No offense." Justin said to Kian, who gave a small nod back.

"So, we need to find the person who can end him, who also has magic in the realm of light. Is there a possibility he had children with a mortal? Or, even more of a stretch, a Fae, before they met their demise?" Sage asked, crossing her arms, her face clouding over in thought.

"He had a daughter," Cyerra broke in from where she had been quietly mulling the conversation over in the corner of the room next to Niamh.

Niamh narrowed her eyes at Cyerra. "I do not remember a daughter."

"No one would. He locked her away in some castle or tower long before the veil failed."

"Again, information I could have used before now," Bryn said to Cyerra, her voice tight with frustration.

"Yes, well I did not realize when you came back to us, I would need to go over the entire Fomorian royal line. My job was to keep an eye on possible threats, and since she wasn't a threat locked away, I didn't bother with thinking anymore about it."

Bryn groaned, shoving her face into her hands before she looked back at Cyerra. This information unsettled the Morrigan, but Bryn could feel her acceptance of what Cyerra had said, since the daughter had never become a threat. "Any other information on the daughter?"

Cyerra shook her head. "Only what I've spoken here."

With a sharp nod, Bryn knew their next action, a silent plan forming in her mind.

"Then we have to find the daughter."

Chapter 34

As Bryn and her friends gathered with Callie and her advisers, one of the witches nudged a map forward, its crinkled paper a stark contrast to the smooth wooden tabletop.

"Could have used that," Justin murmured from next to her.

"It is not current, but it shows where the Faerie rings were before the Collapse." Callie stepped up, pointing to the map. "Here is Cethin, the ring where you came from Osgar is here." She moved her finger along the map until it met another star on the other side of Cethin. "This ring used to work to move between the realm and where Dover is now."

Cyerra nodded. "Dover is our best bet. From the rumors, his daughter tried to drown herself while imprisoned and Dover is the only standing coastal city on one of the magic lines the Fae used to move about the realm."

Callie nodded as she sat back in the chair across from Bryn in the dining hall before taking a sip of her tea. Niamh settled closer to Callie, the two having obviously made up if the gentle touches and closeness of their bodies were anything to go by.

"Magic lines?" Bryn had never heard of that.

"Oh, right, yes. They called them Fae Lines or Ley Lines in folklore, but they can be a sort of magical highway between realms. Faerie circles were used as checkpoints, but they moved parallel to the mortal and Fae realm. I'm unsure how strong they are now, but from what I gathered over my substantial years, the cities that survived the Collapse had all settled on the checkpoints."

Kian shook his head. "How did I not know that?"

"Even if you were the most trusted general in the world, your Fomorian background would have kept even the Morrigan from giving you the secrets of the Fae," Cyerra replied, but there was no malice in her tone.

"It is true, but things have changed now," The Morrigan said to Bryn, and she agreed. Which was why Kian would be in all the meetings that Bryn was in.

"So, can we try to use these lines to get to Dover?" Bryn asked, hoping they wouldn't have to walk. The trek there could take just as long as the trek to Cethin, and they were running out of time. Who knew how long Declan could hold out before Balor took over completely? If he hadn't already...

As hard as it was to admit it, Bryn was almost glad it was Declan and not one of the others. If anyone could hold out, keeping Balor from breaking free and taking over the world, it would be Declan. The man was stubborn and had serious tenacity.

"It hasn't been done in ages, but I kept the ring hidden ... just in case." Callie waved at them to follow, walking from the dining hall, greeting several people along the way before they found themselves in front of the witches' cabins. "We can only hope the ring in Dover wasn't destroyed. I worry it might have been since it was so close to the coast, but as Fae yourselves, you would simply return here, or to the Otherworld, if it's closed. Mortals would find themselves trapped in the veil until a Fae grabbed them."

"Ah, I remember the old stories of the Fae taking off with mortals," Niamh laughed, and Bryn could imagine Niamh using those stories to her benefit long ago.

"Not stories," Callie corrected as she held a branch back to let them pass by. "They were all too true. I, for one, was not the best version of myself during my darker years. Once I woke from my long sleep, blessed with my power as the new Cailleach and a guardian of the realm by Brigid, I found myself with far too much power and far too much loneliness. I played with mortals just as the Fae did."

A silence moved over the two women, and Callie looked worried that Niamh might have an opinion on that.

Niamh reached over and squeezed Callie's hand before they moved into an open space in the trees. Mushrooms grew along with the rest of the flora, but what stood out was the ring of them with nothing in the middle. As if the red and white mushrooms refused to grow in the tiny section.

"There is the Faerie ring to Dover. I'd suggest only one go through at a time since I'm unsure how stable it all is."

Kian stepped forward, but not into the circle. Holding out a hand toward the ring, he twisted his wrist over it a few times as Bryn wondered what he was up to. He nodded as he dropped his arm and moved to stand next to Bryn. "Definitely still magic moving through it."

"Then we pack and leave tomorrow. We have to find Balor's daughter before he does something we can't undo." Bryn looked at Callie. "Before he finds Cethin."

Callie took Bryn's shoulders before pulling her into a hug. "Be safe, my darling granddaughter." Callie pulled back, holding Bryn's face in her hands. "And thank you for coming home."

Bryn gently wrapped her arms around Callie, letting herself have this moment of peace between her and her family member. To remind herself that she was not alone in the world. She had friends and now her family.

"I'll come back," Bryn promised, patting her on the back lightly before Callie pulled away.

"I know you will, and with you, hopefully, the solution to our little king problem." Callie let Niamh take her hand with a squeeze. "I will see you off tomorrow."

Her party watched as Callie disappeared into the shadows before Niamh turned to Bryn.

"I feel like I should come with you, but..." Bryn shook her head at Niamh's words and took her in her arms. She knew Niamh's heart was here where she could walk in the sunlight, no longer bound to the shadows. The woman she loved and thought lost was alive, and now they had time to make up while Bryn went out to make sure they never lost each other again.

This was what was best for Niamh.

"Well." Niamh pulled away, running a finger under her eye. "Enough of that. We have all the time for goodbyes tomorrow between us since unlike my love, I am all about a good show." With a wink and another swipe at a rogue tear, Niamh followed Callie.

Bryn nodded, her and the Morrigan agreeing it was the right choice before she started back toward Cethin. Kian grabbed her hand, holding her back, and the look he gave her told her it was time for the talk. She waved her friends on before turning to Kian.

"Can we talk tonight?"

There was nothing in his expression to indicate this would be their own goodbye, but there was still anger between them. That needed to be resolved before they stepped onto the battlefield.

Bryn nodded before she walked off, not saying anything more, knowing she needed time to work out what she would do if her general said he was no longer working with the Morrigan.

Chapter 35

The moment dinner ended, Kian took Bryn's hand and led her through the lively, chattering village, the shadowy, whispering forest, and finally past the still, dark trees where her shadow army slept.

"Where are we going?" Bryn asked, genuinely confused.

"Somewhere you haven't been in centuries," he said, his shaky voice not helping her nerves about their upcoming talk at all.

Bryn followed him past the last of the dead trees and gazed at the distant, imposing rock, its gray surface etched with the passage of time. Healthy green trees sprouted up, encircling the rock as if sentinels before the fog met its borders. She moved slowly to stand beside him. Looking up, she saw it wasn't natural rock—the precise angles and smooth surfaces hinted at deliberate construction.

It looked like an old rock building ... or a temple.

One that the Morrigan knew well. Where she had planned battles and celebrated victories alongside the shadow army.

"It was built for you, but you used it as more of a war room between victory feasts," he said, remembering it just as the Morrigan had.

Bryn hiked up the rocks broken by time and weather before pushing herself up the hill to navigate the uneven path. Ancient stone benches, slick with moss, still stood before the arched opening. It felt like a sacred space, unlike the hateful church of Baleros.

People would leave offerings while she stood over battlefields. When she returned and settled her army, and herself, she read through the prayers. The ones from the female soldiers she answered first, anger at how the world grew, and yet allowed very little in the way of choices for their womenfolk.

The old, weathered stone was cold and damp beneath her hand. Its surface slick with moisture, and the chill penetrated her skin. Then she saw it as it was: a canvas of candlelight, the air filled with the sounds of laughter and the quiet stillness of those lost in thought. Soft blankets, steaming bowls of hearty stew, and mugs of hot cider were scattered throughout the temple, creating a cozy scene. A large wooden throne, its surface inlaid with intricate leaf carvings, supported her as she sat, radiating power as the Morrigan. A large avian skull, its empty sockets seeming to stare ahead, adorned the back.

She had been every bit the goddess of death and war when she had sat upon the throne long lost to the elements.

"I remember," she whispered, and there was Kian from the past, standing beside her. His leather armor creaking softly with each movement, his long hair tied back with a leather cord. He was everything she had imagined: a deadly assassin with the sharp eyes and lethal grace of a predator, but also a general who led armies, his bearing commanding respect.

"I did a damn fine job leading your troops too after my life as an assassin. I was very skilled, but grossly underpaid."

Snorting, Bryn gave him a light shove, and with those quick assassin-like reflexes, he hauled her into his chest, wrapping her within his arms as they swayed side to side.

"I don't want us at odds, Bryn." His face was completely serious now as he pinned her to his chest. "Whatever issue I've had with the Morrigan is separate from who you are."

She looked into his eyes, seeing the truth there. "How? When we are the same person?"

Kian gently placed his forehead to hers as she swayed, a light dance to music only he could hear. "You're not her. You haven't been since I was looking at you across that battlefield in Ifreann. When I saw you, truly saw you, for the first time."

Bryn shook her head. "What do you mean?"

His eyes and lips softened as he stopped swaying, his hands moving to cup her jaw.

"You asked about the strings? The silver ones?" He waited until she nodded to continue. "I didn't want to say anything until we won. I worried it would distract us, or you ... no." Kian shook his head. "That was my excuse. I was scared. Scared of telling you and how you would respond."

"What are they Kian?" Her heart pounded against her ribs, a frantic rhythm she was certain he could hear.

His thumbs moved under her eyes, running along her cheekbones. "To a wolf shifter, the strings connect us to our life mates."

Bryn waited for him to say more, but he only held her gaze as if he too were waiting.

"Life mates?"

He nodded. "Or soul mates. That's a term used, or was before I was split, among the wolf shifters. I've never seen the strings before and thought maybe the Fomorian part of me kept me from having one." His hands moved to the back of her neck. "Then my soul merged and I looked across the battlefield to a beautiful woman, auburn hair, freckles, bluish green eyes … and the strings attached her to me."

A soft laugh escaped him. "The irony that I might die when I had finally found you."

Bryn's hands moved to his wrists. "You knew then?"

"I did."

Bryn closed her eyes, unsure what to say, realizing that she had felt the pull to him all along. There was a part of her that already knew this. Without opening her eyes, her lips found his; the kiss soft and vulnerable.

"Please don't hate me," he whispered against her lips between kisses.

"Never." Her hands went to his hair as she pulled him closer, the kiss deepening.

Then her hands went to his chest, pushing against him. His eyebrows rose, his face a mask of confusion.

There was a wildness thrumming through her veins as she took in her mate.

Some long ago instinct, one driven by the power of the goddess and the genetics of a wolf shifter, pushed at her, and Bryn spun away, sprinting into the trees.

A howl rent the air, but not one of emotion, one of challenge, and the feral part inside her rose to the surface.

She didn't dare look behind her, knowing Kian was fast and had many more advantages being a wolf shifter.

At the edge of the trees, she turned back, making her way toward the temple, taking long and lazy routes instead of a direct path.

With the circuitous route, she managed some lead time; she pushed herself hard in the last sprint, seeing the stone structure ahead and knowing she had gained ground.

Something collided into her side, and then Kian shifted back to a man, holding her head in his hand as they rolled together in the grass, his shadows keeping them from hitting anything that could cause damage to themselves or the forest.

Before they stopped completely, his lips were on hers, both of them on fire from the thrill of the chase. Two predators, two lost souls, finding themselves in each other.

Bryn ripped Kian's black shirt, not even thinking of using her magic to disrobe him, but he was just as lost as he formed a claw and cut her shirt off, their lips never leaving each other.

Shoving down her pants, it felt like a dangerous coupling, but the thrill of it had Bryn lost. Her soul was leaning hard into her to consummate this relationship and reinforce what both their souls knew.

To claim him as her mate in all ways and bond them together for eternity.

Her hands pushed at his pants, and he quickly shucked them off before moving back to her. Their kiss deepened, his lips gliding over hers, the softness and yearning more than just the lust between them.

The ties between their souls glowed over them, the silver lines reaching out for purchase in the waning sunlight. Bryn bit her lip, closing her eyes as she lost herself to Kian.

Her hands moved over his back, but the urge to challenge him was far more powerful, and Bryn rolled out from beneath him, ignoring how her naked flesh pebbled against the frosty air. Backing up, Kian stood too, and she could see the wolf in him fighting for control with the man from the primal expression on his face.

Before she could do much more, he was on her, pushing her back against a tree, his hand taking both of hers and pinning them above her against the smooth bark. His other hand lifted her leg around his hips, his erection at her core, his lips moving along her neck, his teeth scraping along the skin.

He released her hands, his eyes pure silver, as something in them asked for permission. She nodded and then suddenly his teeth sank into the skin between her neck and shoulder just as he pushed himself into her.

The pain of the bite, his thrusting deep into her, aroused her nervous system enough that stars lit up behind her eyelids, Bryn unaware she'd closed them again.

It was raw and primal and *perfect*.

Something in her screamed to take over. To take control.

He kissed the bite mark, and then she pushed him to the ground, his body glistening and his tattoos radiant as he smiled with lips stained with her blood.

Her primal self was a live wire as she lowered herself and crawled over him, taking him in hand before guiding him back into her body.

Throwing his head back from the sensation of her moving up and down his length, he exposed his neck, and Bryn took her turn, biting down in the same spot on him that he'd bitten her. Blood. Something she feared deep in the marrow of her bones flooded her mouth, but this was not scary. Nothing about this triggered any of her previous fears.

Instead, she was filled, body and soul, with the very essence of Kian.

The most shocking thing of it all was, as she pulled away, her lips leaving his throat, she could feel the very love that triggered the moment he had looked into her eyes across the battlefield.

Kian let her take the lead, his hands moving over her body, his whispered words letting the depths of his emotions ring true in her psyche, leaving no room for doubt. Silver spun around them, the threads connecting, and jolts of pleasure shot through Bryn with each thread finding its mate, until at last their souls were irrevocably intertwined.

Her body tensed and the world around her had an array of bright lights as she lost herself. Kian flipped her over onto her back, growling, thrusting erratically as he followed her over the edge.

Panting, he fell to his elbows, nuzzling her neck before he moved out of her and fell beside her. Not giving her a chance to escape, Kian pulled her to him, resting her head on his chest and pulling her leg up over his thighs.

Something inside her settled. Bryn, as both herself and the Morrigan, felt whole for the first time in the entirety of her existence.

Chapter 36

B ryn blinked awake, not sure what had woken her as she pushed away from Kian, the sun breaking in the sky for a new day.

The smell, a sulfurous odor, hit her mere seconds later.

Before she could ask Kian, he had shifted, his hackles up as his eyes darted around the woods, looking for a threat.

Bryn worked to find her clothes, pulling together the shredded linen shirt she wore around Cethin, as she searched for her pants, finding them hanging from a tree branch. Her underwear was nowhere in sight.

A loud ripping noise had her covering her ears before eerily similar howls rent the air.

"What the hell is that?" she gasped, running toward the village, but Kian's jaws closed around her wrist, pulling her back.

Screams drowned out any curiosity, and before Kian could let go, she'd ripped her hand away, throwing herself into a full sprint toward the village.

Skidding to a stop at the edge of the forest next to the witches' cottages, Bryn could see the entire village engulfed in darkness.

"You have to go now!" Callie was yelling as she ran toward her, meeting her at the edge of the woods as she tore off her linen shirt and shoved it at Bryn, leaving Callie in a thin undershirt.

"What's happening?" she asked as she dressed, but the all too familiar ghostly wails from her recent past began, sending shards of ice down her spine.

"Get to the Faerie ring!" Callie was pulling her, but Bryn's mind was back in Ifreann, wraiths tearing through her town, blood and ash covering the sandy road.

Travis.

"Bryn!" Kessler and Justin were running with weapons, while Sage and Jace followed without anything, but they were lethal enough in their powers.

Cyerra was moving through the skies, and Rae was nowhere to be seen.

As soon as they made it to Bryn, she and Kessler asked the same question at the same time. "Where is Rae?"

Neither of them knew, which was not good.

In her crow form, Cyerra could hear Bryn, so Rae had to have the same ability.

"*Rae?*" Her skull pounded with the intensity of the silence before Rae's voice broke it.

"*The wolves are holding off the wraiths! Go!*"

The wolves ... her father.

"Get to the Faerie ring, now! Cross to Dover and I will meet you there," Bryn ordered her people, turning toward where she could feel her connection to the wolves pulling her. Kian, in his human form, stepped in her way.

"And what will you be doing?" Kian asked, Kessler behind him as Justin, Sage, and Jace corralled people toward the Faerie ring.

She sensed his fear and trepidation not just by observing him, but also by feeling an echo of it within their bond. "I have to keep my father safe. I will not lose another one."

"Rae..." Kessler kept his eyes scanning over the area as Bryn worked to push him and Kian toward the circle. Both men were statues, like rock, completely immovable and Bryn gave up with a huff.

"She is with the wolves up front," Bryn said to Kessler before turning back to Kian. "You have to go too, Kian."

"Absolutely not. If you fight, I fight," Kian growled.

Bryn wanted to strangle the man, but instead she took his face in her hands. "If you die this time, I cannot guarantee you would come back like the rest of the Tuatha Dé Danann. I won't risk you."

A loud, piercing screech erupted behind them, and Bryn didn't need to have lived in Cethin long to know that the wraiths were breaching the edges of the village.

"But I can risk you and that's all right?" Kian asked, grabbing her elbows to keep her facing him.

She winced as a sharp crack echoed, followed by a deep rumble that shook the ground beneath her.

"Not now, Kian! I have to go!" Bryn whirled away, but Kian caught her arm.

"Not without me—"

"That's an order, general!" she snapped, and the moment the words left her mouth, she knew it was a mistake, but she wouldn't, couldn't, watch him die. Not again.

He released her, and she could see and feel the anger and betrayal swirling inside of him, an angry vortex of fire, all-consuming and moving through their bond. He pulled away from her, his jaw tightening, and spun around, the air crackling with his cold fury.

She would allow herself to feel guilty later, once this was over and people were safe. Kian was safe. Bryn sucked in a deep breath before turning. Emotions had to be put aside while lives were on the line. She knew this, even as much as she hated it.

Bryn ran to where the snow was breaching Cethin. The sunny day built from her grandmother's power flickered out like a light. The overcast, violent skies from outside the protection of Cethin's walls perpetuated the fog rolling in.

The swirling, undulating mass of the wraiths pushed against a tear in the veil over Cethin. Beneath the horrific view, witches and wolves were at the front, holding the line.

Bryn could see their magic working in the air, the witches trying to form a shield, but the Morrigan knew it wouldn't be enough.

"Time to test a theory," Bryn whispered to herself as she took in a deep, shaky breath, walking toward the darkness in the frozen landscape outside the village.

"Go back and shield the center of town," Bryn ordered the witches. "Protect the rest of the villagers and find out if they can travel through the Faerie circle with the Tuatha Dé Danann." Her command was answered with a unified howl, and the wolves and witches instantly retreated, leaving Bryn to confront the wraiths alone.

All but three wolves, a crow, and a blacksmith.

It seemed Kian, Cyerra, Torin, Kessler, and Rae were choosing to only obey orders when they felt like it.

"*What is your plan?*" Cyerra spoke into her mind as she landed on Bryn's shoulder.

Bryn knew that Rae and Kian had heard Cyerra, able to feel the connection between all four of them now that the power and magic of her mate was a part of her.

"It is an interesting idea our girl here has, Crow. It seems human minds are more adaptable than I thought." The Morrigan sounded almost proud of Bryn.

"Something that will probably end in all our deaths since you've decided to ignore my order to retreat."

"You always said I was never great at listening," Rae responded.

Kian stayed quiet. She could feel the rage emanating from her wolf mate, but that was a problem for another day, should they both live to see it.

Focusing on the souls around her, Bryn closed her eyes and watched as auras lit up behind and beside her.

But she needed to see the ones in front of her, the ones the wraiths had consumed.

Rae nudged up against Bryn, and she fell into a deeper focus, connecting to the other threads of power she'd bestowed on the wolf and the crow. Kian's aura moved to stand in front of them, and she hated that they'd said such sharp words to each other. Especially since there was no way he would be able to protect them from what was coming, and she knew he would die trying. If they died, all she had was knowing they would die together, and could finish their argument in Faerie when their souls cemented there after death.

Something flickered to life in front of her. Not the golden souls of the gods and shifters, but something inky and black, small sparks coming off them like two rocks striking.

"Now would be the time to hurry, they're almost here..." It was the first time Bryn had heard panic in Cyerra's voice.

Bryn worked to connect with the souls trapped in the wraiths, to take control, to undo what King Bres had done to them. Finally, she felt resistance and called on her power to strengthen her hold.

Opening her eyes, Bryn lost her grip on them for a second before she managed to get them back under control.

They were right on her. There was nowhere to run, nowhere to hide, and the trapped souls were tethered to her *and* the wraiths.

"Do something now! We are about to die!" Cyerra yelled, her voice echoing in Bryn's mind as she worked to focus.

The wail of the wraiths grew closer, and she widened her feet to anchor herself, the Morrigan pushing her power until her tattoos were so bright she was a beacon in the darkness.

It was a split-second decision, a risk she would look back on and chastise herself for taking.

Bryn tore open the veil with her power and tightened her hold on the wraiths before she tore the souls from them, letting the wraiths hit the wall that was the protection of the veil.

The souls moved through to Faerie while the wraiths exploded into ash on contact without souls to guide their passage.

Once the last wraith was nothing more than dust, Bryn snapped the veil closed with her power.

Falling to her knees, Bryn knew she had used too much, even with the help of Cyerra and Rae. Even with Kian's power fueling her, she was the only one who fell, her body sinking into the deep, powdery snow, the cold seeping into her bones. Her eyes drifted shut as the world around her went to a pinpoint before everything disappeared.

But before she was lost completely, beyond the icy grass and torn protection of Cethin, stood a man wearing a cloak and Declan's face. A smile full of promise that they would meet again soon.

Chapter 37

Bryn jolted awake, her eyes darting around, absorbing the unfamiliar surroundings.

Kian's warm hand cupped her face. "Hey, you're safe."

She nodded, gathering her wits as she took in where they were. The rock walls shimmered with an iridescent glow, like a field of multifaceted crystals catching the light. The absence of streamlined corners was striking. Soft edges dominated, creating a sense of gentle curves and relaxed forms.

"Where are we?" she asked, pushing herself up into a sitting position.

"We made it. I carried you through the Faerie ring and Jace was standing by, ready to help the moment my foot stepped into Dover."

Bryn released a long breath, and relief suffused her as she fell limp back onto the bed, her hand still in Kian's as he intertwined their fingers.

"How mad are you?" she asked, rolling her head to the side to look at him. He was clearly worn out; his eyes heavy with exhaustion. Yet, he was still the most attractive man she'd ever met.

"I was furious when I brought you here, but after a day, I just felt…" He wrinkled his brow in thought as his thumb moved across the back of her hand. "Unsteady is far too weak of a word, yet it was mix of that and sadness."

"Because I told you what to do out there?" she asked, her gaze lost in the swirling silver depths of his eyes as he shook his head.

"That you would look death in the eyes without me by your side. That you would be fine with letting me watch you fall and not allow me to intervene."

"You can die, Kian. If I do, I come back."

He raised an eyebrow. "Are you sure about that? Can you guarantee that a wraith or enemy will not deal a critical blow that even Jace cannot fix?"

Bryn bit into the side of her cheek until she tasted copper. "No."

He dropped his head onto their joined hands, pressing his forehead against her fingers before he lifted his face and leaned forward. His lips were a caress against hers, one that she wanted more of. Her hand slipped behind his head as she deepened the kiss, a small groan leaving him as he met her halfway.

The kiss slowed, and he pressed a small, chaste kiss against her lips before he pulled away, sitting on the edge of the bed as he pulled her into his embrace.

"We're equals now. The moment we took each other's bite, we became partners. Can you deal with that and work on not shutting me out? I'm your general, but now I am also your mate, too. We should fight side by side on equal footing."

"I promise to work on that." She laid her head on his chest. "I can't promise the Morrigan will remember that in the heat of battle—"

A small chuckle vibrated through his chest. "I will handle the Morrigan. I'm used to dealing with her. It's having a mate that is completely new to me."

A sense of resigned frustration could be felt from the goddess, but she said nothing in response, which was fine by Bryn.

"Rest," Kian ordered as he ran his fingers through her curls before placing a kiss on her head. "Tomorrow will be here soon enough and then we have to figure out how to get Dover on our side."

Exhaustion came in a strong wave at his words, as if she, or the Morrigan, had been holding it back until they were sure they were safe. Bryn closed her eyes, safe in Kian's arms with a goddess protecting them both.

Sleep claimed her far faster than she could ever remember.

Escorted by Kian, Bryn entered a chamber right outside the room she had been in, where water cascaded down the walls, the sound a soothing hush. Trays of iridescent shells along counters in the hall held alien instruments, their surfaces gleaming under the soft light filtering through the watery walls. The curved doorway opened into a vast hall, its smooth, cave-like walls stretching in multiple directions.

As Bryn passed an alcove, she heard the faint murmur of voices, recognizing them as Kessler and Rae in hushed conversation. Though she knew better than to eavesdrop, the weight of her worry pushed her closer, hoping that they hadn't been injured in the battle.

"Well, finally admitting that you, the big strong blacksmith man, might need little ol' wolf me?"

"I'm saying that as mates, if you decide to throw yourself in front of a wall of death, you give me enough of a heads-up that I can be with you. You're not alone in this, Rae, and I'm not going to watch you die."

Rae was quiet, and Bryn bit her lip.

"So, what you're saying is you love me and cannot imagine a life without me?"

A groan from Kessler made Bryn smile.

"You will be the death of me, wolf."

Bryn knew all too well that feeling, and Kian seemed to agree with a squeeze of her hand. When the sounds moved from whispered confessions to kissing, Bryn moved on with a lightness in her step that her friends were not only safe, but had found what she had.

She followed Kian, her fingers still laced through his as she marveled at the vibrant rainbow of aquatic animals swimming in the holes dug into the walls, their scales shimmering under the light. Deeper into the structure, they discovered a room; the wooden beams, like a boat's skeleton, held up the walls, creating a unique, almost nautical atmosphere. From the wood, strings of pearls dangled, interspersed with sea glass, creating a cascade of color against the iridescent walls, which shimmered like the pearls. The sharp, briny scent of the ocean mingled with the fragrant, unfamiliar spices of exotic foods. The chatter of people as they ate, unbothered by the events happening outside of their cave.

A throne of swirling, pearly shells, radiating a soft light was positioned at the far end of the room, away from where Bryn had entered. The air buzzed with laughter and conversation as people gathered around the smooth beech wood tables.

Justin, Jace, and Sage looked up from where they sat at one, waving her and Kian over.

"Where are Finian and Cyerra?" Bryn said as she sat down, Kian taking the seat next to her.

"Cyerra refused to come below ground and Fin is in my room. He is not ... meshing well with the Merrow people," Justin said.

Bryn wanted to ask more questions, but one of the women stood up from a table close to the shell throne and made her way toward them. As she did so, her form flickered, and Bryn realized they were glamored.

The woman's glamor vanished when she made it to Bryn, revealing a lean female with shimmering, fishlike scales, gills that pulsed faintly along her torso and neck, and hair resembling swaying seaweed. As her ears elongated into delicate, fin-like shapes, a membrane stretched between her fingers, creating a webbed effect. Bryn could see nothing overtly female along her body except for the two small mounds that used to be her breasts in her mortal form.

"Welcome to Dover, Great Queen. My name is Cadhla, but you may call me Ada."

Bryn nodded at her greeting, though the title was something to get used to.

"Thank you, Ada, for taking my people in." Bryn's gaze swept the room, eventually settling back on Ada as the Morrigan pushed words out of Bryn. "Please, there is no need for glamor on our account."

One by one, at her words, each person in the room released their glamor to reveal varying shades of blue, yellow, and aqua skin.

"It is uncomfortable to wear such glamor for long. This should gain us some favor with the Merrow people." The Morrigan said into her mind as Ada gave her a smile of thanks.

"We never know how humans will react to us, but I suppose you are not truly human, are you?" Bryn gave a small snort that had the Morrigan mentally rolling her eyes and Ada giving a tinkling laugh. "Please eat. My father, the king, will come once he is done speaking with his advisers and we can speak about what happened to you and your party."

Ada waved a lithe azure female Merrow over, who placed a large plate of food in front of Bryn. Bryn gave a small, yet confused smile at the offering as she tried to make sense of what was on the plate.

A pale pink, oddly textured sponge of some kind, glistening with red sauce and bits of seaweed, stared up at her from a silver plate.

Kessler and Rae appeared, settling themselves at the table while the Merrow woman placed plates in front of them from a pearlescent tray.

Rae skewered a piece of food off Kessler's plate with her fork, earning a snort from Kessler as she sampled the cuisine. "It's not half bad."

As she chewed, her eyes moved over Bryn, and a smirk crossed the wolf shifter's face at Bryn's neck. Her hand went to the spot Rae was staring at, and her fingers caressed the raised mark where Kian had bitten her, sending a little jolt of pleasure through her that she quickly covered with a cough. Rae snorted a laugh and dug into her food with more enthusiasm than Bryn thought the offering deserved.

"What happened in Cethin after the wraiths were gone?" Bryn whispered, unsure how well the Merrow people could hear. The people in the room had begun their chatter again once the princess took her seat, but Bryn was paranoid after Osgar.

"The wraiths exploded in thin air and you hit the deck." Kessler shoved some of the food into his mouth without flinching, so Bryn braved a forkful herself. It tasted like wet grass and had the consistency of chewing on a sponge. "We made it to the circle that Niamh and Callie held open for us, and now here we are."

"Cyerra was last to go through," Rae finished. "She said that Callie begged that we get the Merrow's on our side as soon as possible."

"How have they managed to stay out from under the king's thumb?" Sage asked, moving her food around on her plate without taking a bite.

Bryn couldn't blame her.

"We're underground. This is an island. A channel separates it from the mainland. The Faerie ring led us to right outside the cave entrance to this place. Had a Merrow not been on guard, we'd have thought the cave was shallow and uninhabited. These people know magic." Everyone stared at Rae as she finished. "What? I like to snoop."

All the Merrow in the room stood up at once at the sound of a deep bellowing horn that echoed through the cavern. Bryn and her friends followed their lead as they kept an eye on the front of the room.

The Merrow bowed as a man, shorter than most of the Merrow people, entered. His skin was an iridescent violet that stood out from the others; some blighted scaling around his gills revealed his age.

It seemed the king of the Merrow people had arrived.

Chapter 38

The king said nothing as he settled on his throne of shells, and his eyes immediately focused on the table full of newcomers. With a slight nod to his entourage, one of the smaller males who entered with him quickly made his way to Bryn's table as his king watched on.

The Merrow stopped at the end of the table with his hands folded together and nodded in greeting. "Once you have finished your meal, King Murdock would like you to join him for a drink to discuss the current situation."

"We would be honored," Bryn responded, and with another nod, the Merrow returned to the king's side to settle near his feet.

With his message delivered, the king motioned for them all to sit, so Bryn did.

All but Justin, whose gaze remained narrowed at the king, his expression pinched, as he sat slowly, long after the others.

"You okay, Justin?" Kessler asked before Bryn could say anything.

Justin shook his head. "Something felt ... familiar to Lugh. Something about this place... these people."

"Well, Lugh can ask him all the questions he wants to after we secure the alliance with the Merrow," Bryn said, trying not to make it sound like an order when in fact it very much was. They needed the king on their side and interrogating him would likely not end with them going into battle side by side.

They sat in silence, Bryn thinking of how she might word their plea for assistance to a king. Her grandmother was one thing, but a king she didn't know meant a lot of unknown variables.

Now would be a fantastic time for some political knowledge on how to sway a king to our cause.

"I hardly negotiated deals and treaties. I am not sure what kind of goddess you thought I was, but it was more of the action over words kind."

Bryn, lost in her thoughts and conversation with the Morrigan, came back to reality when her fork clinked against her now empty plate.

Rae threw her napkin over her plate. "I'm done. Let's do this."

Kessler shook his head. "She never slows. She just goes until she literally drops."

"You weren't complaining about it last—" Kessler threw his hand over her mouth, and Rae playfully bit it.

"Children," Sage admonished with a tilt of her lips as each member of their group stood, letting Bryn and Kian take the lead.

A Merrow quickly cut them off before clearing their throat. "Your hound is ... loose again."

"Damn it, Finian." Justin waved them on. "I'll catch up once I get Finian to quit terrorizing the Merrow. Damn dog..."

Bryn watched Justin leave, the Merrow following quickly behind him before she turned back to the king, bracing herself. She was unsure of how to start, and Bryn let out a long internal sigh of relief when the king took the initiative. With a regal nod, he signaled his attendants to lead her group to an adjacent area from the throne room.

It was a vast, echoing chamber with three walls of enormous windows, revealing a breathtaking underwater panorama. Sunlight streamed through the water, illuminating schools of vibrant fish.

"That glass is sturdy, right? It won't break and flood the room?" Rae asked, standing near the doorway, her eyes wide.

The king tilted his head, watching Rae before turning and walking to the glass. He gave Rae a small smile, then moved to the glass and struck it forcefully twice with his fists. Rae jumped, giving a small growl before she caught herself.

"It is sturdy. No wolves will drown this day." The king laughed before waving for everyone to take a seat on several velvet couches of the deepest blue.

Bryn stepped further into the room, taking a seat on one of the couches and seeing that the fourth wall was a terrifying display of weaponry. Crude clubs rested beside gleaming swords, telling Bryn the Merrow were far from peaceful people.

Two Merrow males arrived with bright purple drinks on a tray, handing them out to each of their group and the king. With a lift of his glass in toast, the king took a sip before placing it on a small driftwood table next to his couch, waiting for them rest of them to indulge as well.

"My people were surprised when you appeared out of thin air in that circle of fungi." King Murdock said as he settled back on the couch, his ankle crossed over his knee and arms thrown out. He took up more space than he needed.

"A lot is changing now. I'm sure you've heard of Cethin?" Bryn asked, taking a sip of the purple liquid and grimacing at the taste. It was pure alcohol.

"I have, and that you brought the wraiths to their doorstep. Just as you did Osgar." King Murdock's laissez-faire attitude disappeared. "Only that we are beneath ground do I allow you entrance into my domain."

"We brought nothing. If we did, it is because Bres sees us as a threat." Bryn leaned forward, letting the Morrigan show through her eyes. "He knows the end is at hand."

"Then I'll ask the obvious. What does this have to do with my people and why have you brought this war to our doorstep?" King Murdock leaned forward, mirroring her position. "We have stayed out of the way of the king all these years." His jaw tensed before he spoke again. "And I'm sure you've just shone a spotlight right on us."

Bryn held his penetrating gaze. "The king will not leave you alone in the end. He will come for you once he's done with the rest of what is left of the world. Now you can choose what side you will fight with, because remaining neutral stopped being an option the moment Ifreann fell."

Sage cleared her throat, breaking into Bryn and King Murdock's posturing. "It is something to think on, your majesty. As for why we are here, there are two reasons."

Bryn turned to Sage, the Morrigan furious that their discussion was interrupted, but in Sage's eyes was the gold of Brigid, and of all her divine siblings, the Morrigan trusted her the most.

"In time, you will see that aligning with the Tuatha Dé Danann is the best option, but in the meantime, perhaps you can help us find Balor's daughter?"

The king waited, looking between the two women before he downed the rest of his drink and slammed it on the driftwood in front of him. "You're out of luck. She is long dead."

Bryn felt the oxygen leave the room with his statement.

"The prophecy..." Sage turned to look at Bryn.

"Maybe it was wrong, maybe..." But even Jace seemed unsure and the Morrigan bristled at the implication that anything she prophesied would be considered wrong.

Not the time for ego.

"How did she die?" Kian asked, leaning forward from where he sat next to Bryn.

"I don't have the slightest clue. It was before I became king, but rumor has it, she drowned herself after Balor drowned her babes." Sadness flickered in his expression before he was handed another drink. "I'm sorry you wasted your time in coming here, but I have no answers for you, and I won't put my people in danger with a war." He took another drink, his eyes lost.

Bryn heard the king's dismissal all too clearly.

"You will lose people whether you choose to join or not. When he comes, and he will, you will wish you had allied with us." Bryn stood, as did the rest of the group, but a pulse of jagged, angry power came from behind her. Everyone in the room turned to Justin in the doorway, his chest heaving, his eyes blazing like the sun with untamed magic.

Justin prowled into the room, focused only on King Murdock. "Where did that come from?" Justin demanded in a low, threatening tone, pointing to a weapon on the wall. A long spear. "*Where. Did. You. Get. That?*"

The king followed his gesture. "My father had it from his father and so on." He waved his hand in the air before turning back to the group.

"Give me the spear," Justin demanded as he moved toward the king, the Merrow near him moving into position to fight Justin, their spears aimed at him.

"Justin, what are you doing?" Bryn asked, but Justin wasn't listening.

"You'd be wise to step back, human," the king seethed, before his eyes moved to Bryn. "Every one of you will leave this place *now.*"

"Not until you give me back what is mine!" Justin roared, his fragile control shattering as he lunged at the king, a spear lodging in his shoulder failed to halt his charge. Only the shadows from Kian wrapping around him slowed his attack. Justin seemed to grow larger as his muscles bunched, all his power flooding his body, lighting him up as bright as the midday sun. The light burned her eyes as smoke rose at the points where light and darkness touched.

While Kian struggled to hold Justin back, the pressure in the room rose, her ears popping painfully. Justin's light only grew brighter while Kian's shadows fought for control.

The sound of cracking glass reverberated through the room, preceding a loud screech that ripped Bryn's battered eardrums open.

"What the hell was that?" Kessler yelled, his voice barely audible over the damage to Bryn's ears. A high pitch shattering noise echoed through the throne room as water flooded in, breaking more of the glass away.

"Oh, hell no," Rae growled, grabbing Bryn's arm and yanking her back.

"Get to the tunnels!" the king yelled, and the Merrow swarmed.

Bryn stumbled, looking for Kian in the chaos, Merrow taking their king as she worked her way through the now waist deep water.

Kian was suddenly there, tugging her behind him as he tried to push through the bottleneck leaving the throne room. Bryn fought the water surging around her, but it slowed them significantly, and panicked people jammed the hallways.

The cracking along the cave walls and rocks falling into the water as the structure gave in on itself caused the panic to increase. Bryn tried to hold on to Kian while looking to make sure her friends were evacuating too.

A massive boulder tumbled down, but Kian swiftly pulled her out of the way, though their escape was now blocked.

"Damn it," Bryn said through her teeth as she opened the veil, a struggle when her focus was split. "Go!" she yelled, feeling the strength she had just gotten back from her restful slumber draining.

The Merrow shook, their eyes moving between the tear in the veil next to Bryn and the blocked escape route. The light shining through the emptiness, the hesitance to jump into a possible new danger clear on their faces. Bryn wasn't even sure it would work, but she would not let these people die.

"You either go through or die here. Choose!" Bryn looked to King Murdock, who was just as hesitant.

"This better not be a trap," he ground out before he stepped into the veil, his people following him as the rocks continue to fall and the tunnels collapsed.

Bryn gritted her teeth, the rip wavering and trying to reseal, but she held out, sweat dripping into her eyes until Kian grabbed her hand and pulled her through, the entire cave ceiling falling as the veil sealed back up.

She fell onto her back in the liminal space, taking in huge gulps of air. Kian was next to her, helping her to sit up, his breathing just as labored as hers, his hands shaking as he held her.

"Everyone ... made ... it?" she asked between breaths.

Kian nodded, his gaze focused on the king as he closed in on her.

"Are we in the Otherworld?" he asked, and Bryn shook her head.

"No, the veil. It's between the mortal world and Faerie ... the Other-world," she corrected as she leaned against Kian, his arm wrapping around her waist to steady her.

"You truly are the queen of the Tuatha Dé Danann."

Bryn looked up at the king, frustration and exhaustion making her feel less than charitable now that she realized he had assumed she was lying.

"Yes." She stood to look the king in the eye and straightened her shoulders. "We are the Tuatha Dé Danann. Just as I told you before."

"Except him." Rae pointed to Kian and then herself. "Or me, but I guess we kind of are in a way?"

Bryn said nothing as she stood, turning her attention from the king to the problem at hand. They were alive but stuck in the blank slate that was the veil. She was worried about moving too close to the surface of the veil where it connected to the mortal realm, but she knew they needed to make their way back to the surface and out of the tunnels.

"Use the ley line. It should be stronger here in the veil," the Morrigan said, and Bryn felt her connect them to the power running beneath the earth. It crackled and sparked, like a loose connection, but it gave her a direction.

It was their best shot and the only way she wouldn't lose them all here.

"Follow me," she ordered and pulled them all closer to the surface of the veil with her magic. People yelled, thinking the rocks falling were going to hurt them, not realizing nothing could touch them while in the space between. Thankfully, they followed Bryn through the tunnels to the outside, near where the Faerie ring was.

As the last of the Merrow left the tunnels, Bryn pulled them all through to the mortal plane with the help of the ley lines.

The sun met Bryn as she stepped out of the veil, closing it behind her with the last of the group ahead of her. It was more of a struggle now that she was exhausted, but at least no one had been lost.

Bryn checked on her friends. Sage and Jace were checking people over, finding mostly only bruises and anxious parents. Kessler, his arm around Rae's shoulders, stood next to Justin as Finian pushed against his leg with small whines. Kian was next to her, her shadow and her equal as she walked to where King Murdock looked back at the broken rocks she assumed had been the cave entrance.

"You may be gods—" King Murdock said as he looked out over the destruction, water lapping at his feet. "—but you will get no help from the Merrow."

"You're angry—"

Murdock spun on her, his fists clenched and gills flaring.

"Angry? You came into my home and destroyed it over some lost spear." He stepped closer to her, ignoring Kian's warning growl. "And brought a war to my doorstep I never asked for!"

Bryn met him, toe-to-toe. "No one asked for war, your majesty, but wait until it actually makes its way to your people. Wait until you are facing an army of wraiths with no gods at your back." She gave a mirthless laugh. "In fact, why don't you ask Tanwen, Ifreann, and Osgar how that would go. Oh wait ... you can't!"

Kian rubbed her arm, trying to calm her, but Bryn was far too angry to pull back now. Even the Morrigan was giving her this moment to unleash without interfering.

Murdock shoved his face into hers, his breath hot on her skin. "Using the loss of lives for your cause?"

Bryn could only see red as she ripped her arm out of Kian's grip, shoving Murdock away from her and ignoring the gasps and warnings of those around them.

"We have lost so many people, friends, along this path and we're only looking to build an army big enough to stop all the death and destruction. Nothing more, and nothing less. To stop the wraiths, to eventually stop the king, and to finally give humanity and Fae the chance to live a life without fear."

King Murdock turned to his people. "Hear that? She promises if we fight, we can live in peace." He swung back around on Bryn. "Which we were doing perfectly fine until you showed up. Imagine that!"

Bryn bit into her cheek, working to calm her rage, before she spoke to his people just as much as she did him. "We have an unchecked tyrant burning through the lands, and yes, you can remain safely hidden away, head in the sand, but not forever. He won't stop at the border of Dover and turn around. He will break down every barrier until he controls everything and everyone." Bryn tried to gauge their reactions to her words, but most whispered between themselves, others staring at the ground.

"That's enough. Take your people and leave. Now," King Murdock said as several of the Merrow guard began to encircle her and Kian.

Bryn ground her teeth together and nodded. "Fine. I grieve the deaths of your people because you're too callous to see anything beyond your own front door."

Murdock folded his arms, and even though she caught a flicker of doubt, he did not budge.

There was no winning here, and so Bryn walked toward where her friends waited for her. Several watched Murdock, reproach in their eyes before they turned to walk with her.

"Time to go," Bryn said as she walked to the Faerie ring. The stares of the Merrow burned into her back as they left and only dissipated when they made it over a small hill not far from the beach and were out of sight.

The mushrooms glowed, small lights dancing as they got close. Bryn assumed they had activated it with their magic until it lit up and a humanoid form, curled in on itself, appeared within.

Jace dropped to his knees as the light dimmed and one of the Cethin witches Bryn had seen in passing before they left looked up at them, blood crusting around his nose and mouth. A gasp escaped him, and though his voice was weak, he finally managed to utter one word.

"Help."

Chapter 39

Bryn and her friends stepped out of the Faerie ring and straight into chaos.

"Gods above," Sage whispered from beside Bryn, breaking her out of her shock, and Bryn ran toward the center of Cethin. Her heart raced as she ran past the burning homes of the village witches, the trees black and broken around them. The fake sun flickering overhead, the dome of power keeping the winter weather out was fading in and out, frost forming on everything.

Her feet faltered as she made it to the village center where the long houses were, or had been. Now there were burnt husks, recently put out as witches and wolves walked through with lost expressions. Her father's head snapped up, his eyes focusing in on her before he made his way to her, pulling her into a fierce embrace.

"You're alive," he whispered against her hair, his hold tight as if she might disappear.

"What happened?" Kian asked from somewhere behind her, and her father released his grip, but kept his arm over her shoulder.

Torin ran his other hand across his mouth, his expression pinched with pain. "A second wave came through after you left. We did the best we could, but we had to eventually fall back and ... we lost a lot of people." His voice cracked. "A lot of wolves."

Bryn gasped, her hands flying to her mouth as tears welled in her eyes, overwhelmed by the sheer magnitude of the loss. If she had stayed—

"None of that." Torin lifted her face with his knuckle. "I don't have to read your mind, but I can see the guilt in your eyes. It is more important you rally the Merrow to our cause, especially now that we've..." He shook his head, blinking to hold his own tears back.

"The Merrow refused to join us." Bryn's words were hollow, soft, but heavy with regret.

She let the silence hang in the air until Torin growled. "Then we find a way to fight then with what we have."

"Not to be crass, but how are any of you alive?" Justin asked, Bryn and Torin turning to him as he spoke. All her friends were there, all with looks of sorrow and defeat on their faces that made Bryn want to scream. To yell that it wasn't over, they could fix this!

And yet, there was no real idea of how to do so. Cethin was going to be the army at their backs, and it was cut down while she argued with a king who had no intention of helping them.

"Callie," Torin responded, his voice taking on a reverent tone. "She burned herself out to pull the protection ward back into place and destroy the wraiths in one large blast of power."

Bryn spun to her father. "Is she alive? No, she has to be! The protection wards are still in place!"

There could be no more loss. Bryn had lived through so much, and just finding her grandmother, only to lose her, no… She refused to accept that.

Torin nodded to a large makeshift tent off to the left of where the long houses were. "They won't let anyone in, but maybe they will you."

Bryn was running to the tent the moment he finished his sentence, steps following behind her, but her focus was on getting to Callie.

Two witches stood on either side of the tent flap, but Bryn didn't bother asking for permission to go in, and when they closed in to stop her, the Morrigan hit them with a zap of power. As they shook their hands out, she pushed into the tent, Jace coming in from right beside her, shoving off someone trying to grab his elbow.

"Leave them be," Niamh ordered from where she sat at Callie's side, her hands wrapped around Callie's frail one.

Hesitant, Bryn stepped further into the tent, the flap falling and darkening the room, only a lamp giving any light to see with. Never had Bryn seen her grandmother look so frail. Her hair was thinner, her bones more prominent, as if by using such a huge burst of magic, it ate away at her physical form.

"Will she…" Bryn swallowed the words, fear of saying them aloud and making them come true holding her back.

"I don't know." Niamh looked down at Callie. "I don't bloody know, darling."

Bryn could hear the pain in Niamh's voice and moved to her, wrapping her in her arms, letting her tears fall as she embraced the only mother she had ever truly known.

"I just got her back, Bryn," Niamh's voice was rough with emotion, and arms like steel banded around Bryn. She pulled back, cupping Niamh's face and holding her gaze just as Torin had done with her.

"She is still here, and we will find a way to help her." It was both a promise and an oath.

"Niamh, is it alright with you if I examine her?" Jace asked, standing by the tent flap still, keeping his eyes on Callie.

With a nod, Niamh wiped at her face. "If anyone can fix her, it is you, Jace. Please."

Jace stepped past them, giving both Bryn and Niamh's shoulders a squeeze as he settled into the chair Niamh had left when Bryn pulled her into a hug.

They both watched him work, Bryn holding Niamh as her strong, vampiric friend trembled.

"Can you call Sage in" Jace asked, not looking away from Callie.

"Move," Bryn heard Sage from outside before either of them had to chance to look for her. Sage immediately went to the opposite side of Callie, placing her hand on her grandmother's forehead and closing her eyes.

"Sage?" Jace asked and was immediately shushed by her.

"It was us, Jace. We were the ones to bring Callie and Niamh back with our power. We should be able to save her."

Niamh let out a sob at Sage's words, turning her face into Bryn's shoulder.

Bryn watched as Jace and Sage both placed their hands on Callie's shoulders, closing their eyes and their expressions going blank as they focused. A subtle golden glow moved over Callie's body from where Sage and Jace touched her.

"The power of life was never one I held, but I feel honor every time I see my brother and sister perform such feats of magic."

Bryn agreed.

"Our magic is in the bones of the earth and the souls of Faerie. Our godly blood connecting them."

The Morrigan's words triggered a memory, one that even the Morrigan forgot. *"How could I forget such a pivotal moment?"*

It couldn't be that easy ...could it?

"We'd be foolish not to attempt it, wouldn't we, little goddess?"

She had no idea how long Jace and Sage worked, but when they pulled away from Callie, Niamh and Bryn held their breath.

"She will recover," Jace started, but his eyes went to Sage's, a sad look passing between them.

"What?" Niamh demanded, stepping forward and out of Bryn's grasp.

"Her magic was depleted to dangerously low levels." Sage sighed before she continued. "If she does this again, pulls more than her body can take, she will become mortal."

Chapter 40

Bryn checked on Callie once more that evening, but her grandmother had yet to wake up. Thankfully, she knew her grandmother was in good hands as Niamh watched over her.

She said nothing about her plan to her friends after dinner, but with the idea fresh in her mind, she walked to the dead forest. The wolf tents had been moved to the center of Cethin since there were so few people left, and it made sense not to be spread out any longer. However, the lack of activity made the forest all the more eerie.

As she made her way to the larger tree, she pulled the dagger out of the sheath along her thigh.

This had to work.

The memory of the Morrigan's blood quenching the earth as she tore souls in two and moved across the veil was clear as day in her mind now.

"I guess we will find out if our blood truly connects both worlds."

She settled down before the tree along its far-reaching roots before placing her hand to the bark, letting the feel of the souls within ground her.

Though she didn't recognize any of them, flickers of familiarity from the Morrigan would occasionally spark in her mind as the memories of the souls floated through her.

Without opening her eyes, Bryn held the blade in one hand before running it across her palm, the sting of it making her hiss before she placed her bloodied palm on the tree trunk.

Small flits of light ignited, but died down to nothing, leaving Bryn and the Morrigan in complete silence.

"I don't understand," Bryn whispered as she opened her eyes and pulled her palm away. "The only difference was the blood, right? We opened the veil before, do we need to open it now?"

"Perhaps, but that is dangerous with Callie unable to use much more magic. The wards weaken since she is no longer feeding them."

Bryn scrubbed at her face, forgetting the blood on her hands since her godly magic had already healed the wound.

"Would it not be worth it—"

"Bryn!" Justin yelled from somewhere nearby. Finian's bark a subsequent demand of her attention.

"To be continued." Bryn pushed up, turning to where Justin was running toward her, Finian and a silver wolf flanking him. A look of panic was so strong in his expression that Bryn's heart dropped as she ran to meet him. She barely managed to stop before she crashed into him, her hands on his shoulders steadying her as Kian shifted next to them.

"What's wrong? Is it Callie?" Please, please let her grandmother be alive.

"No, not Callie," Justin said as Kian took her by the waist, pulling her into his side.

"What then?" she looked between the two men, her relief that it wasn't Callie lost as the anxiety built up again.

"Balor is near Dover…" Justin shook his head. "Not sure if he followed us there or—"

"His wraiths attacked the Merrow?" she gasped, looking to Kian, but Kian only shook his head.

"No, but it was a Merrow messenger who used the Faerie ring to tell us." Kian turned her to face him, his face as grave as she'd ever seen it. "Bres opened the gate beneath the sea where the Fomori live and Earth. He brought an army of Formorians over."

The howl of rage that left the Morrigan deafened Bryn as she fell back a step and her legs gave out altogether. Her knees hit the dirt, Kian grabbing her arms to settle her back, but she was numb. Her mind unable to comprehend what that actually meant.

"He has a larger army…"

Kian nodded as Justin settled himself nearby, Finian immediately in his face for loving, as Justin pushed his head down and petted along the dog's back. Finian settled his head in Justin's lap, his big puppy eyes staring at Bryn in concern.

"We've lost half of Cethin and the Merrow won't even consider working with us." Her gaze moved from Kian to Justin. "We have no hope, do we? With Declan gone and Balor using him as a puppet…"

Bryn shoved her face into her hands, biting down hard on her cheek until her mouth filled with the taste of iron. She could feel Kian run his hand along her back, but it was a ghostly sensation, unable to break through the pain and fear bleeding into her from the news.

Shaken, Bryn tried to reach out to the Morrigan, hoping the goddess might have some clue on what they could do, but she had gone silent.

Even the goddess was abandoning her now.

This was their last chance to bring the world back, to undo all the Fomori had done to humanity and the earth. To end the king who held no love for his subjects, only his greed.

A soft whine sounded as Finian nudged her, attempting to move her hands from her face for a comforting lick, but she turned, burying her tear-streaked face into his rough fur. Finian did nothing more than hold still, letting her fall apart while he stood for them both.

The whole of Cethin was darkening into night before Bryn had gathered her wits about her and made her way back to the center of the village. Justin, Finian, and Kian had left when she asked for some time alone, but she knew they would have stayed if she had asked.

Every moment, every action, was a testament to how strong the ties were between her and her friends. Even before Ifreann fell, her friends had been there, quietly supporting her, lending her strength for years.

Once again, she would be calling upon that strength, and for the first time in her life, she knew someone would be there. That they would answer that call.

It was hard to walk past the charred remains of the village, but the people of Cethin were already at work, making meals and finding ways to rebuild what was lost. It would be a long road, but she could see this community would endure.

She only wished the war wasn't still knocking at the door, ready to finish what it had started here.

"We are doing guard rotations, two wolves and two witches, until Callie is back to full health," Justin said as he walked up to her from where he had been working with some of the citizens on creating something from wood. "The ward is weak, but it is holding with the witches focused on it while the wolves provide protection."

Bryn nodded, standing in the middle of Cethin, before the long house that they had been staying in. It was nothing more than blackened wood and rubble.

"We have been making tents for everyone to use. There are not enough, but the wolves have provided canvas from their own tents to make smaller ones." Bryn barely heard Justin as she walked around the remains of the long house.

"Who is on guard right now?" she asked, running her fingers along a metal tub that was charred, but overall relatively undamaged.

"Sage and another witch she has been working with. For the wolves, Leif and Kian."

Bryn nodded, still saying nothing, but her eyes moved over the horizon. "Where?"

Justin knew what she meant and pointed to an area behind the new tent community they had created. Bryn walked toward them, she could hear Justin sigh behind her, but he didn't follow as she made her way to where the witches were working to protect their city, and the wolves protecting them.

As she broke through the last line of tents, Sage stood in the dying sunlight, her skin like shining copper, her curls a wild halo around her head. She looked every inch the goddess she was. Another witch stood next to her, their eyes closed and hands clasped together as they worked their magic.

Kian was settled on the ground a few feet away in his wolf form, lifting to stand as she walked near them, but she shook her head. No, she wanted to observe, quietly, and contemplate what they could do in such an impossible situation.

Lief, her uncle, caught her attention as he walked toward her, having not shifted yet, he waved and settled to the ground next to her, patting the dirt.

Bryn sat, Kian watching them both as he laid back down, and she let wrapped her arms around her legs as the witches worked to strengthen the ward.

"It was a shock when you showed up on our doorstep."

Looking up at Leif, her father's brother and second, he smiled down at her before turning back to the witches, his voice quiet. "I never thought I'd meet my niece. We all believed you were gone, though Torin clung to the idea that you were still alive."

With a gentle exhale, he shifted, his knees drawn up and his hands resting loosely over them.

"You were to be named Corvina, so I have always thought of you as Corvina in my head. To hear you called Bryn is disorienting." He smiled, and she saw how his lips tilted to the side so much like her father's. Like her own. His gaze moved over her face before he looked away.

"You were hurt, I can see that without a word needing to be said," Leif growled, a protective instinct she thought only her father would have for her, but she felt it from Lief too. "We all have our own stories, our own scars. Torin doesn't even know all of mine. He was the perfect alpha child, and my father had no use for me aside from following orders."

He held his hand out, the sleeve of his shirt inching up and revealing cruel scars around his wrist.

"Sometimes, when people hurt us, we feel so beneath others that our entire identity relies on their approval. Then one day, you look at those scars and you think, 'Wait a minute, why do they get to judge my worth when they didn't earn it? I was the one who survived the trials, so I should be the one to say what my worth is.'"

Bryn's eyes stung at his words as she met his gaze. A kindred soul looked back at her, a look of understanding for something she'd never been able to put into words herself. He bent his neck to make sure she was looking at him, never reaching out to touch her, and she knew it was not a lack of love, but that she hadn't given permission.

"No one, not a parent, not a friend, a sibling, or a lover, has that power unless you give it to them. You get me, Bryn?"

Bryn nodded, tears hot on her cheeks as she squeezed her eyes shut, fighting back the sobs. "I get you," she whispered.

He held his hand out again, and she knew this time, he was asking. Without hesitation, she grabbed it and pulled her uncle into a hug. The large wolf gave a small 'oomph' but held her just as tightly as she did him.

When they broke apart, he smiled at her.

"When you live in the fire, you become it, so rise and burn this fucking world to the ground. It's time to start over."

With a wink, her uncle stood and left her alone with her thoughts as he shifted nearby, coming back as a large beige wolf. The entire conversation with him felt like it had been a mere second, and yet the longest of days.

But his words had loosened something in her, as if she had been waiting for permission to allow her full self to surface. Not the Morrigan, but who Bryn was before the abuse, before the fear of death for being herself.

Leif was right.

It was time to burn the world down and start over.

Chapter 41

Bryn had settled into a trance, thinking over what her uncle had said, and when Kian finished his watch, he had taken her by the hand to lead her to a small canvas tent.

Everyone else in Cethin was asleep, only the two wolves taking over had been there when they left, her father one of them, but he said nothing as Kian walked off with her.

Probably because he was in his wolf form, but she didn't bother looking too hard at his expression.

Kian motioned her to a leather and fur bedroll, only the moonlight illuminating their small tent.

The exhaustion hit her hard and fast, her eyes raw from crying, her soul broken as she laid there. Kian laid across from her, pushing her hair out of her face before he pulled her into him.

"Rest," he whispered against her hair, and her eyes closed as if she were too weak to ignore the order.

When she opened her eyes, snow was falling around her, soft and peaceful unlike the storms that had greeted them outside the ward of Cethin.

The sun shone through the dormant trees, reflecting off the snow making the world seem so much brighter than she had ever seen it. Small animals with bushy tails and long ears she'd only read about scurried through the powder. An arrow struck one, the red of its blood leaking out into the snow around it.

And then there was Kian. Not the man she knew in this lifetime, but the man who had lived many lifetimes before.

With long hair past his chin, clothing made of furs, and a sturdy wooden bow, he walked past Bryn to the animal, pulling his arrow from its neck and cleaning the arrowhead off in the snow before returning it to the quiver at his back.

"A memory of who he was before," The Morrigan was giving her this memory. *"He has been waiting so long for you. Perhaps I forgave his attempt to kill me because somewhere I knew he was needed down the line."*

He kneeled next to his kill, and as he did, a woman appeared behind him. Her gaze completely focused on Bryn before Kian stood back up with the animal, its legs tied together.

Kian hefted his prey onto his shoulder and walked forward, moving through Bryn like a ghost.

She felt nothing as he passed through her, then there was a flash of silver and he was gone.

That only left the woman, who stood still among the dormant trees, her serious eyes on Bryn and Bryn alone.

Her long black hair flowed around her, a stark contrast to the simple cotton gown she wore—wholly inappropriate for the chilly air.

There was fear in the tremble of the woman's lips but resolve in her steady approach to Bryn.

"Who is she?" Bryn asked aloud, but the woman said nothing.

"Fomorian..." The Morrigan growled. *"Familiar, but not one I've faced before."*

When she was in front of Bryn, only slightly shorter, she lifted her chin. Her aura was radiant and Bryn wondered if some Fomorians were not dark and bent on the destruction of their world. Perhaps there was good among them just as there were bad among Bryn's kind.

Brazenly, making the Morrigan growl, the woman grabbed Bryn's hands. There was nothing threatening about the woman, nothing to make Bryn or the Morrigan consider her a threat.

"Please, I beg of you, keep my sons safe. I did all that I could, and it wasn't enough."

Both Bryn and the Morrigan realized at the same time who this woman was. They'd found Balor's daughter.

"Where are you? If you're alive, we can help you!"

The woman shook her head. "My time is long past, mine and my loves, but our sons, they still live and my father would see them dead."

"I will do my best, but who are your sons? Where can I find them?"

The woman opened her mouth to respond, but her eyes widened in fear before she took Bryn by the shoulders. "My father is here! You must go! Now!"

And with impressive strength, the tiny woman shoved Bryn out of the dream, leaving her gasping, awake in the frigid air of her tent.

Chapter 42

When Bryn pushed out of her tent, needing air, she was met with an eerie silence. No one in Cethin was awake, Kian was still in their tent, fast asleep. It was her and the quiet of the world.

The dream had her imagining she would wake to Balor standing over her. Thankfully that wasn't the case, but the chill in the air was concerning.

Above her, the stars were not as bright, and she wondered if the ward was failing again.

Two more people came out of their tents, their breath frosting in the cold early morning air.

"Bad dream?" one of them asked Bryn. "Or this frigid air wake you up like it did me?"

"A little of both," she murmured, remembering the woman, Balor's daughter, in the vision warning her that her father was here.

"Has anyone checked on the watch?" Bryn asked, the two witches look-ing at each other before shaking their heads. Bryn was already walking their direction when Justin popped out of his tent.

"Cold as—" Bryn walked past him as he rubbed at his arms. "Where ya going, Bryn?"

"Watch," she yelled back over her shoulder and ran the rest of the way. When she made it to the opening behind the tents, there was no one there. No witches or wolves, and the sky above was filling with clouds.

"Where are they?" Bryn spun, looking around to see if maybe they had moved, but there was no one but Justin and the two witches who had followed her from the camp. "Who was on watch?"

"Uh," one witch looked to the other, "not too sure. I wasn't scheduled until tomorrow, so I really didn't bother paying attention."

Bryn's eyes found Justin's, and before she spoke, he was already saying he was on it and moving.

"Wake everyone up. Every witch and wolf." Bryn marched back to camp, leaving the two witches stumbling in her wake.

Her hand went to the tent flap as Kian threw it open, shoving his arms into a leather jacket one of the wolves had given him. "What's going on? What happened?"

She didn't bother asking how he knew. Being mates had certain advan-tages that went a long way to helping in situations like these.

"Our guards are gone."

Kian looked at her before moving to check out the site himself, several other wolves joining him, including her father.

Bryn made to follow, but Niamh stopped her. "The women from the Sanctuary have been doing their own rotations out of sight. Yes, I know." Niamh waved her hand. "I have tried to get them to come into town, but I won't force them. Anyway, they just informed me that the ward has failed in several areas."

Which left them wide open.

"Callie it still so weak, but should I have her try to bring it back up?" Niamh asked, but Bryn shook her head.

"No, we need to find the witches who were working the ward and disappeared. Are there any that Callie would say are the strongest? Ones capable of getting the ward back up?"

"Already on it," Sage said as she walked past Bryn, three other witches following her. Jace and Kessler followed behind as well but stopped by Bryn.

"Rae is working with some wolves to look, but they are stationing a few by Sage and the others. Any idea what's going on?" Kessler asked.

Bryn bit her lip, if she had learned anything from Ifreann, it was that she needed to keep communication open between her and her friends. Even with the risk of feeling foolish if mistaken.

"I woke up from a dream where Balor's daughter told me to look out for her sons. Before the dream was over and she could tell me who and where they were, she told me her father was here and shoved me out."

Her friends looked at each other and she wondered if she had made herself look foolish. It was just a dream after all.

"Could Balor have managed to get across and grab our people?" Jace asked. He was taking her seriously, and by the looks of Niamh and Kessler, so were they.

Bryn was finally getting it through her thick skull that she wasn't alone anymore.

"Niamh, have the Sanctuary girls keep vigilant and maybe check for entry points." Niamh nodded at the orders and disappeared into the veil.

"Jace, I need you with Callie and since she is in the largest tent, that can be a triage point should we find our people injured."

Jace nodded and took off as Kessler turned to her.

"Kess, have you got any idea the kind of weapons they have around here?"

A small smile lifted Kessler's lips. "I sure do."

"Great. Can you round them up and find wolves who are not shifted to hand them out to and see which of the coven knows how to fight?"

"With pleasure."

She watched Kessler walk away with urgency before she turned around to find the wolves and see what they knew.

A loud crack echoed through the village, and people ducked, covering their heads before looking around.

Bryn took off at a run, almost slamming into Kian as he stepped in front of her, grabbing her arms.

"Tell me you found them," she begged, but his face was too serious for any good news.

"We found their blood. Too much of it."

The hair along her arms lifted as if lightning were about to strike. She grabbed Kian's forearms, her stomach twisting.

"Oh gods, Kian. He's here isn't he?"

"Who?" Kian demanded and listened as she explained her dream.

"I know it was just a dream and not a vision—"

"Your visions came in dreams, too, Bryn."

She closed her eyes, taking steadying breaths as she reconciled that truth, and then went into explaining the orders she had given out.

"Good," Kian responded, pulling her into a hug as she took in a deep breath that was leather and forest, all Kian.

The Morrigan pushed so hard against Bryn that her body spasmed, Kian leaning back to see what happened, but Bryn took in a huge ragged breath.

"Get the rest of the Tuatha De Danann, now!"

Bryn tried to respond out loud so Kian would know and would stop looking at her with worry, but she couldn't get any words out.

"Get everyone inside the ward!" That time it was not the voice of the Morrigan, but Cyerra. *"Balor is here!"*

Chapter 43

The Morrigan had released Bryn long enough for her to get out the words, though staggered and labored, that Balor was here.

Kian went into action immediately once she was able to unlock herself. She tried not to feel embarrassed; it was her own power surging through her that had frozen her muscles, but still it was shameful.

Bryn now stood in the center of Cethin, barking out orders alongside Kian. She told them where to go and Kian told them how best to defend the position.

They worked seamlessly together since the Morrigan already knew his mind, and Bryn could sense his presence and emotions.

Callie limped out of her tent, her arm in Niamh's keeping her steady.

"I can help," she said as she worked to straighten her back, but it was obvious Callie still needed time to heal.

"Then help me by gathering the witches and working with them on ways to defend our village."

Bryn hadn't realized until she had said it that it was her village too, but Callie's smile was radiant as she nodded, not even arguing with Bryn that she could do more. Niamh winked at Bryn and turned them toward where the witches were gathering.

Kian's head snapped up, bringing Bryn's attention to something going on behind her. Several wolves had stopped patrolling, but their hackles were up as four figures in the distance stumbled toward the center of Cethin.

"Who is that?" Bryn asked, but Kian was already walking toward the wolves growling, Bryn at his heels.

"Smells familiar ... but wrong," Kian said as the figures moved closer.

It was the witches and wolves who had disappeared, but they had an odd gait and were shaking their heads. When they were within earshot, she could hear the moans.

"Everyone take the defensive! Sluaghs!" At Bryn's words, the four creatures that used to be part of their community shrieked, throwing their eyeless heads back, their split, jagged mouths open wide before they began to run at the wolves nearest to them.

The wolves went in for the kill, the sluaghs not having completely become wraiths yet, but the victory was easy.

Bryn knew better.

And she was right.

A dark cloud she'd not seen broke through a weak point of the ward, and the ward around Cethin went down completely. Snow and ice and fog made the terrain almost too hostile for the battle, the wolves and witches unable to see the threat until it was too late.

Bryn bit down on her lip as she palmed her dagger, hearing the screams of people she had grow to care for in the winter oblivion.

"You were so kind as to gather my grandsons all in one place so I can finish off the threat to my power," a voice whispered near Bryn, Declan's voice, but there was no one around her. As the fog grew more and more dense, she feared anyone could sneak up on her.

"Show yourself!" Bryn yelled, only to be met with a chuckle.

"Are you sure about that? Do you truly want to see what remains of your past lover?"

Bryn's palms were sweating, her grip on her dagger slippery as she tried to figure out where the voice was coming from.

A dark shape moved toward her, and the Morrigan took hold of her body, ready to defend them both. The fog slowly dissipated from the shape, and there stood someone in a long black cloak that she recognized even before he pushed his hood back.

"Oh gods, Declan," she sobbed as she took in her friend. His eyes were pure black, with dark veins running down the sides of his face that was a map of raw scrapes and purple bruises. His teeth glinted like tiny daggers as a smile stretched across Declan's lips.

"Not so much Declan anymore, though he put up a delicious fight for so very long before he ceased to be."

Bryn lost herself to both guilt and horror, the Morrigan stepping in for her.

"Balor, you're not welcome here among these innocent people. Leave before I make you."

"Ah, there you are. The Morrigan. One of the last to grace this land before you ran with your tail between your legs across the veil."

Before Bryn could stop her, the Morrigan threw the dagger with pinpoint accuracy at Declan's chest, but Balor caught it midair.

"It has been so long since I had a worthy opponent. This should be a delightful battle," Balor said before he tossed the dagger off to the side and stalked toward Bryn before freezing, the fog around them swirling and the screams of the dying going silent. Balor turned to see Callie with her arms up, her entire body shaking, as the fog and snow melted away, leaving the battlefield open.

With a snarl, Balor ran at Callie, but Bryn got there first, jumping in front of her grandmother and shoving Balor back. Balor launched himself back up, but vines grabbed at his feet, and his entire body locked up. Jace and Sage came around opposite sides, holding him in place while Kessler walked over with the biggest axe Bryn had ever seen.

Balor opened his mouth, and streams of smoke left him, creating another army of wraiths. Niamh was there with her bow and arrows, and Bryn immediately shot arrow after arrow at the wraiths swirling while Niamh covered Callie.

Justin ran through the mass of chaos, almost falling to his knees at the sight of Declan.

"It's not him!" Bryn yelled, slamming her bow into a wraith that got too close. "It's Balor still."

Kian in his wolf form bit through a wraith's neck on his way to Bryn's side.

Bryn ran out of arrows, and backed up to find her dagger, where it settled against the trunk of the tree where the shadow clan resided. She hadn't realized how far she'd gone into the fog, that she'd made it to the dead forest.

Silence had her grabbing her dagger and spinning to the fight, where everyone was frozen. Not from magic, but fear, and she soon saw why.

There, before Balor, were Justin and Kian, on their knees, the wraith's claws far too close to their necks.

"What are you doing?" Bryn asked, wanting to move but scared Balor would order the wraiths to attack.

If Justin was beheaded ... even with Jace's magic, there was no coming back from that.

"Doing what should have been done years ago." Balor stepped up to Justin and Kian. "My grandsons and my downfall, but not anymore."

"No!" Bryn and the Morrigan screamed at the same time, the scream coming from the depths of both their souls, the power of the banshee echoing through all of Cethin.

Only three people remained unaffected. A woman, a wolf, and a crow.

Cyerra dove at Balor as Rae ran through the wraiths, pulling their attention away as Bryn broke from her cry and grabbed Kian and Justin, pulling them out of the way.

"You bitch!" Balor yelled, launching himself at Bryn, black smoke swirling around him as he slammed into her. It felt like thousands of knives shredding her skin as the smoke was somehow sharp enough to cut.

Silver slammed into Balor, giving Bryn time to get back up; her wounds healing.

When she looked back up, Balor held a snarling Kian with a long-clawed finger aimed at Kian's heart.

"Tell me, Brynnie," Balor used the nickname Declan had given her. "Who will you save? End me and get Declan back but I kill the pup? Let me go, and you keep your lover for us to meet another day."

Her eyes moved over their group, the wraiths being temporarily held back by Balor, but once they descended, she was sure it was over for everyone.

"I will take my wraiths with me, Brynnie. Make your choice."

"We need Declan," Justin whispered, sadness in his eyes. "I'm sorry, Bryn, but we do."

Bryn shook her head. They would hate her, but her choice was made. "Give me Kian."

"Bryn, no!"

"You want him?" Balor smiled. "Here ya go." Balor ripped Kian's side open with his clawed hand. The howl of her mate tore through her before he tossed Kian at her. Unable to see through the tears, she crawled to Kian, her mate's labored breathing reminiscent of the battle of Ifreann.

Jace made it to Kian as Bryn stood, her dagger in hand, her body trembling.

"Balor!" she yelled, and the beast possessing Declan narrowed his eyes at her as she brought the tip of her blade to her chest, right over her pounding heart.

"See you in hell." Bryn thrust her dagger home before tearing it out and stabbing it into the tree. The Morrigan tore open the veil, and a surge of shadowy souls, wailing like a dying wind, rushed past her, hurtling towards Balor and his wraiths.

Chapter 44

The shadow army tore through the wraiths, while some split off and became human to fight Balor while Bryn fell to her knees.

Jace was suddenly over her, his face pinched with anger, his eyes wet from tears.

"Not again, damn you," he whispered as he poured water over her wound.

"You know..." Bryn hissed through her teeth at the pain. "I'll ... come back."

Kian was suddenly there, his black hair falling into his face as he picked up her head and laid it in his lap. Someone shouted his name, but he only looked up, nodded before he looked back down and wiped the tears from her eyes.

"You're ... alive..."

"I am," Kian whispered back, leaning down to kiss her forehead. "Why did you have to aim for your heart, mo ghrá?"

"Life blood ... more potent. Jace!" She snarled as her cousin messed with her wound, but Jace only shoved her back into Kian's lap with a hand to her forehead. "Mo ghrá? You keep ... calling me that..."

"My love. It means my love."

Bryn met Kian's silver eyes, tears falling, and reached up to wipe them away before she realized how bloody her hand was and tried to pull back. Kian grabbed it, cradling it against his cheek before kissing her palm.

"Like I said, Bryn, I've known we belonged to each other for a while."

It hurt. So much, and whatever Jace was doing was making it so much more painful, but the pain suddenly abated, Jace sitting back to view his work.

"You're lucky I know more of my magic now so it won't take you weeks to heal," Jace eyed her as he spoke. "Next battle, you better not be the one bleeding to death on the ground. Understood?"

Bryn nodded, but Jace only side eyed her as he packed up his bag.

"He's gone." Justin looked at Bryn but spoke to Jace, his rifle in hand, his eyes narrowed. "She'll live?"

"She will." Jace said and walked to where some witches were working on healing several of the wolves.

Justin watched him leave before looking back at her, then to Kian, his eyes cold, before shaking his head and turning away.

The dismissal stung, but she could somewhat understand. He wanted her to save Declan, but he also just found out he'd had a brother all along, one who he might have even considered an enemy at one point. She was sure Justin was torn up emotionally right now, so she tried not to take it personally.

Kian helped her stand up, and as soon as she was steady, her mouth was on his. She needed to know he was alive and whole. He deepened the kiss before pulling back, then crushing her in an embrace. "Never again, mo ghrá."

Bryn shoved her face into the place between his shoulder and neck, loving him calling her that, and taking the small moment they had to just feel each other.

All too soon, the world came back into focus when she pulled back and looked around to check on her friends. Callie, though frail after her second magic surge, appeared unharmed as Niamh sat before her, and Sage continued to assess her while Jace provided medical aid to others. She knew Justin was okay, but unsure of where he'd gone off too, especially since Finian was with Kessler, and not him.

But Cethin had been torn apart, even worse than before. The tents all shredded, blood and body parts littering the ground, but that wasn't what held Bryn's notice.

It was the people, all in clothes that were made of leather and fur, weapons from long ago, standing in the center of it all.

The remaining witches and wolves were off to the side, unsure of the newcomers. Kessler and Rae were there, almost as a liaison between the groups.

Bryn straightened her shoulders and walked toward them. Each member watched her closely, with narrowed eyes and curious looks.

"I think you should take it from here," Bryn whispered and the Morrigan acknowledged her by pushing to the surface. "Welcome home, Army of the Shadows."

They shifted their feet before one of the women, long red hair and brown eyes, moved to the front of the crowd. "Goddess?"

Bryn nodded. Kian stepped up next to her as their eyes went wide in recognition of their goddess and her general. One by one, they placed their fists over their hearts and bowed before them.

Her army was finally free.

Chapter 45

Bryn led the army toward Drystan, the youth staying back in Cethin with some of the witches and a healer.

It was not the army of her past, but they were all she had. She knew they were still too small, not as powerful as Balor, and it worried her enough to make it next to impossible to sleep. Kian was there to wear her out, which led to some shuteye, but it was never enough.

She watched them laugh and move between the groups in camp, but her fears consumed her at the thought of how many of them she might lose in battle. The Morrigan understood losses, but these people were becoming friends. Her family.

Bryn couldn't lose them.

They'd made camp three times since they left, and the first night they stayed within their own groups. By the third night, they were moving in between clans, taking turns hunting and providing for the whole of the army. Plenty worked with other clans, showing different forms of combat from their cultures.

It would be at least two months before they made it to Drystan, the king's territory. Bryn had been unable to find a Faerie ring with enough juice to move an entire army, but the time spent traveling gave them more time to work on their strategies and combat.

It was a lot, it was inspiring, but they all knew it wasn't enough.

They needed more, but there were no other places to find anyone else. The land across the great oceans was lost to them, and humanity was scarce, far too few compared to the droves of Fomori that had come from beneath the ocean. She knew her number was too small, but they would do their best. They would put every ounce of blood and sweat into this battle and fight as hard as possible, even to the bitter end.

"You cannot stay up worrying," Kian came up behind her and rubbed her shoulders. "They need their leader rested and ready to make the hard decisions."

"We are not enough to defeat him. I cannot sleep thinking that once we arrive, once the battle begins, we will lose so many."

Kian's arms moved from her shoulders, wrapping around her stomach, and pulling her back against him as he placed a kiss on her neck.

Bryn turned in his embrace, opening her mouth to say something, when she froze. Her eyes stuck on the shimmer in the darkness behind Kian before a tear ripped through the trees before her, opening to Faerie on the other side.

Everyone around them stopped, Kian turning and moving next to Bryn, eyes wide, as Fae spilled out of the tear, armor like she'd never seen before reflecting the light of the fire. In their hands were unique weapons of all shapes and sizes that glowed.

They lined up outside of the tear in formation, spreading outward to create two long lines. Two people, their silhouettes backlit by the sun in Faerie making it hard to see their features, walked toward Bryn.

Her hand flew to her mouth to stop the sob from breaking free, and then Kian was the only thing holding her up.

"You said you needed an army, so I brought you one."

The words, the voice.

Bryn trembled as she stepped forward, unable to stop the tears as she fell into Caden's arms, Travis coming around to pull them into a group hug.

She was dreaming. She had to be.

"We're here, and we can help," Travis whispered in her ear, his strong arms holding her and Caden tight.

Suddenly, Kessler, Sage, Jace, and Justin were there, pulling each man into a hug. Finian barked and danced around their group, his tail a blur.

Once they were released from the group hug, Niamh stepped forward, the women of the Sanctuary behind her before she rushed in and pulled Caden into a tight embrace. The other women joining her as they hugged both Caden and Travis, the men laughing as the vampires fretted over them.

Bryn looked over at the massive group of Fae standing straight and not moving. Walking toward them, they bent and took a knee as she passed by. Caden came up behind her, placing his hand on her elbow.

"This is your goddess," he called out to the Fae, "and we will fight alongside her and her people."

A cheer rose from her army, but the Fae gave small nods.

"Yeah, not the life of the party, but they can fight," Travis said, quietly. "They are some of the last of the Fae left, and they want their home back. The other courts are ready to march on your orders."

"And you both? Are you truly here?" she asked, turning to her friends she had thought lost.

Caden and Travis looked at each other. "For as long as we can be. We do not have the power of the gods, but we can move between realms for small amounts of time." Caden took a deep breath. "I am a liaison of sorts between this world and theirs—"

"Manannán made him the human king of Faerie," Travis interrupted, "and they are working to reestablish the courts. So, we had to make sure you had an army at your back." Caden smiled at him, and Bryn saw the love between them then. How had she ever missed it?

For the first time, Bryn felt the stirrings of true hope beneath her breastbone. Bres had limited time on this earth.

The Tuatha Dé Danann and their army would make sure of it.

@LUNAR

Also by

Want to be the first to know about new releases, giveaways, etc.? Sign up for my newsletter!

Also By C.D. Britt:

<u>Reign of Goddesses Series</u>

Shadows and Vines (Reign of Goddesses #1)

Sirens and Leviathans (Reign of Goddesses #2)

Storms and Embers (Reign of Goddesses #3)

<u>Blood of Saviors Series (spin off of Reign of Goddesses)</u>

Reaper of Chaos (Blood of Saviors #1, Reign of Goddesses #4)

<u>Clan of Shadows Series</u>

Prophecy of Gods and Crows (#1)

Blood Debts (#1.5)

Omens of Wolves and Witches (#2)

To see content before anyone else and be a part of our community, join my Street Team on Facebook!

C.D. Britt's Legends of Halcyon

About the Author

C.D. Britt has been obsessed with mythology since elementary school. The obsession has only grown, so she started writing mythic fantasy with significantly happier endings than the original lore. She currently resides in Texas where she has yet to adapt to the heat. Her husband thrives in it, so unfortunately, they will not be relocating to colder climates anytime soon.

Their two young children would honestly complain either way.

When she is not in her writing cave (hiding from the sun), she enjoys ignoring the world as much as her children will allow with a good book, music, and vast amounts of coffee (until it's time for wine).

C.D. Britt is the author of the *Reign of Goddesses* and the *Clan of Shadows* series.

Stay Connected!

www. authorcdbritt.com

https://linktr.ee/Cdbritt

Acknowledgements

This year has been one challenge after another, and I wasn't sure this book would make it out into the world.

But here we are.

This is a love letter to those who stood by me while I figured both myself and my life as an author out.

Thank you to my editors, Enchanted Author Co., Katie Bucklein, and Nikki Fixtion. With huge evolutions and massive rewrites, we somehow made it through to the end. Now, book three is up to bat!

Thank you so much to my Alpha and Beta team! C.S., Kenneth, and Lynda, thank you so much for going the extra mile. I could never have made it through the final stretch without you!

To my ARC/Street team, thank you for the support through this all. Your positive words and encouragement were a balm to my burned-out soul.

To my friends Jennifer, Katie, and Alyssa (who inspired Niamh, Sage, and Cyerra) thank you for helping me push through on the exceptionally hard days.

To my husband, I cannot express how much I appreciate you. The long days of writing, being my biggest cheerleader when I was ready to drop, going to my events and standing with me. I love you.

My children, my blessings, thank you for loving me even when I failed to love myself.